Han Suyin was born in Peking. Her mother was half Dutch, half Flemish and her father was Chinese. She attended university in Peking and later went to Europe. In 1938 she returned to China with her husband and lived during the Sino-Japanese war in the interior. Her novel . . . *and the Rain My Drink* is about Malaya during the Emergency 1952–56. It is a brilliant story of the struggle of people of all kinds during that time of terrorism and tension.

D0211754

Also by Han Suyin in Panther Books

Destination Chungking
A Many-Splendoured Thing
Cast But One Shadow
The Four Faces
The Mountain Is Young

The Crippled Tree
A Mortal Flower
Birdless Summer
The Morning Deluge vol I
The Morning Deluge vol II

Han Suyin

... and the Rain my Drink

I will go to the forest for justice
The wind for my garment I wear
... and the rain my drink.
(Old Chinese Ballad)

Panther

Granada Publishing Limited
Published in 1973 by Panther Books Ltd
Frogmore, St Albans, Herts AL2 2 NF
Reprinted 1976

First published in Great Britain by
Jonathan Cape Ltd 1956
Made and printed in Great Britain by
Richard Clay (The Chaucer Press) Ltd
Bungay, Suffolk
Set in Linotype Plantin

This book is sold subject to the condition that it
shall not, by way of trade or otherwise, be lent,
re-sold, hired out or otherwise circulated without
the publisher's prior consent in any form of binding
or cover other than that in which it is published
and without a similar condition including this
condition being imposed on the subsequent
purchaser.
This book is published at a net price and is
supplied subject to the Publishers Association
Standard Conditions of Sale registered under the
Restrictive Trade Practices Act, 1956.

Contents

This book is fiction. Any resemblance of the characters to anyone alive or dead is purely coincidence. Exception is made for the author, who insists on occasionally appearing in the chapters.

*

The poem by A. E. Housman on page 206 is quoted by permission of the Society of Authors.

List of Characters

LAM TECK	Chinese businessman and occasional police informer, friend of Luke Davis.
LUKE DAVIS	British Police Officer in Malaya.
CHE AHMAD	Malay Police Officer, friend of Luke Davis.
AH MEI	Captured terrorist, turned police informer.
BETCHINE	Euro-Indian woman doctor.
DORÉMY	Tamil (South Indian) staff nurse at the hospital.
AH KAM	Chinese amah employed at the hospital.
ROSIE YIP	Chinese Policewoman.
FONG KIAP	Chinese rubber tapper.
DR. ENG	Chinese doctor at the hospital.
NEO	Chinese rubber tapper.
NEO SAW	His wife, rubber tapper.
SON AND DAUGHTER	Neo's son and daughter.
BIG DOG TSOU	Chinese rubber tapper.
MENG	Chinese, weigher of latex, executed for attempting to inform the Police.
CHAN AH PAK	Chinese, jungle guerilla soldier of the 10th Independent Regiment of the Malayan Races Liberation Army. Bodyguard to:
SEN	Chinese member of the Politbureau of the Malayan Communist Party.
AH KEI AH LOW AH LAM AH MAO	Members of the communist organization inside the jungle.
SMALL CLOUD	Member of the communist organization inside the jungle, in love with Sen.
MAXINE GERRARD	British confidential secretary, engaged to Luke Davis.
QUO BOON	Chinese multi-millionaire, head of the Clan of Quo.
SIR MOKSA BAKRAR	Politician, leader of the Progressively Independent Party (PIP); married to:
FRAGRANT ORCHID	Chinese, daughter of Quo Boon, also known as Alice and Moonface.
INTELLECTUAL ORCHID	Chinese, also known as 'The Abacus' and Betty; daughter of Quo Boon, business woman, married to:
JOHNNY TAM	Chinese millionaire and banker.
GOLDEN ORCHID	Also known as Pearl, Chinese girl student. Sixth daughter of Quo Boon.
BOB STEWART	British Police Officer.

8

List of Characters

MR. CLERKWELL	British Official of the Malayan Civil Service.
MR. STALLART	British Chief Police Officer.
ENCHE ISMAIL	Malay official, friend of Quo Boon.
CHA AZAMAH	Malay, second wife of Enche Ismail, and politician.
MR. POH CHO-YEE	Chinese millionaire.
HINCHCLIFFE	British Commandant of a detention camp.
MRS. HINCHCLIFFE	His wife.
MUI SET	Chinese girl of 14, rubber tapper, daughter of Ah Kei the terrorist.
OLD GRANDMOTHER	Mui Set's grandmother, an inmate of the detention camp.
MISS LEE	Chinese, surrendered terrorist, turned Police informer.
EVANGELINE	Chinese, twelve years old, captured in a jungle camp.
FATHER DESTIER	French, Catholic priest of Todak New Village.
TOMMY UXBRIDGE	British Resettlement Officer of Todak New Village.
OLIVER DALEY	British, ex-missionary, later Resettlement Officer, Todak New Village.
CRUFTS	British Police Officer in charge of Todak New Village.
ABDULLAH	Malay Police Officer in charge of Todak New Village.
AH KIM AND GEORGIE	Father and son, Chinese contractors, Todak New Village.
PANG	Chinese detective.
MR. BEE	Chinese Committee man, a 'baba' Chinese.
MOTHER WU	Chinese, a detainee and a witch.
MR. TAY	Chinese Interpreter, a 'baba' Chinese.
MAHUDIN	Ex-student of the University of Malaya, detained under the Emergency Regulations.
PEARL	Sixth daughter of Quo Boon. (See Golden Orchid.)
JOHN SYMONDS	British Police Officer, friend of Luke Davis.
FANETTE ARCHWAY	British business woman, mistress of Johnny Tam and friend of Intellectual Orchid, his wife.
MABEL	Chinese, amateur weight lifter, nurse; adopted daughter of Intellectual Orchid.
JIMMY LO	Chinese, employed by the British Government as Propaganda Officer.
AND OTHERS.	

9

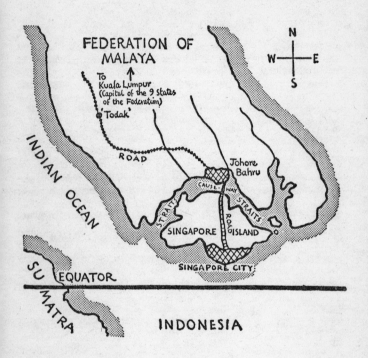

Peacocks as comets catapult across the tarmac road in a tail-flurry of blue-green and gilded palm-frond feathers, to drop staggering, clutching, swinging their meek sharp heads upon the wire fences which ring the Sultan's Zoo. Tulips, poppy red, grow in clusters forty feet up towards the sun-bleached sky, on the round-leaved glossy tulip trees. In the Sultan's gardens the verdigris statue of an arrow-spending cherub springs from the centre of a water-lily pond where stagnate black-scaled timorous fish. Two ponies rough-maned and gentle, amble from the gardens, with discerning hooves high-lifted among the bayonet-serried grass, to graze the cropped lawn of the Judge's house, where a white board props up the English word PRIVATE, and a doorless yellow structure, privy-narrow, exhibits the open visitors' book. The Judge himself walks the road towards the Zoo, a cane on his arm and a purposeful missionary look upon him, the emotional garment with which the whites invest even their laziest leisures. In his white shorts' pocket reposes an egg for the sad and furious Indian mongoose in his cell. Everyone but the judge has forgotten the narrow sinuous animal with the muted war-song in his throat, for there are three tiger cubs, caged golden sunsets, lolloping in an enclosure with their two dog mothers (wet-nurses, their own mother died), whose bellies are pink and milkful; faithful thin and dark wet-nurses barking fondly at their monstrous golden pups. All around the low enclosure the children climb the fence, and Leica-dangling men aim and aim again at the lovely burning-bright felines rippling in the harsh mid-morning glare of sun over Malaya.

So many other things are Malaya: the mosque, triple-domed, Victorian, always embellished on photographs by the appropriate distance and fake moonshine (a special red filter produces the milk-soft whiteness of moon-washed walls). From its high cupola the protuberant black trumpets of a four-mouthed loudspeaker lament five times throughout Friday; the muezzin at the microphone, praising and blessing the Lord Allah. On their bicycles the soft-moving, quicksilver Malays slither and whirr, silver-soft, down the road towards the entrance pillars of the mosque, which carry no gates and no bars. They are all male, going to the mosque, wearing black velvet round caps called *songkoks*, and sometimes a white stitched *Haji* cap for holiness,

11

badge of a pilgrimage to Mecca. Their breeze-swollen, loose shirts about them are pastel turquoise, cinnamon and apple green; their sarongs are woven with large squares of pink, blue, mauve, gold, purple, cinnabar and orange; their white trousers fall to the naked ankle, and the nude feet are clad in shoes of black and brown leather, plum and grey suede.

Little boys, hands linked like flowers in chains, laughing, go towards the mosque, sinuous cohorts of pink and yellow and pale green satin shirts advancing up the road. In the hollow by the bridge which spans a rank, weed-overgrown canal, pullulant with miniature silver minnows flashing coral dots along their flanks, lies the sonorous prison, whose glistening wall tops are embedded with glass chips. It gives out jazz music all day: 'Oh how I love you, Rose Rose I love you.' A tune started in a Shanghai cabaret, sung by a sweet-throated actress of eighteen, and now heard in Spanish in Manila, in Japanese in Tokyo and in six languages in Malaya.

The road again, the blue-grey, heat-hazy tarmac, and on either side the jungle kept at arm's length by a battalion of Tamil women. They have faces of polished rosewood, encrusted with mother-of-pearl and ebony eyes. They stand and behead the rough long grass, precursor of that other kingdom of the living, the vegetable universe. Over their heads and down, at the end of dark arms bared by movement, they whirl their angled scythes and softly the stalked grass flies upwards and falls scattering like cut hair.

Hieratic as sunset-straddling cattle I see them, the women, swathed in scarlet, azure, ochre and emerald, cheap cloth so soon faded in the Malayan sun. Their ear lobes are yawning holes circled by a string of flesh hanging to the shoulder and supporting knobs and cubes of gold, their savings through the years, weighing the elastic flesh into a loop of skin which sways and swings as the women wheel their scythes.

Watchful, enormous trees, too high and too wide, bearing foliage too thick, leaves too many, too large – thick, succulent, grey-green – stand to massive attention right and left of the road. Lanky coconut palms poise their bomb-loads of fruit. Years later I shall not have lost my first discomfort towards the dreary oppression of unchanged, round-the-year green, the manifestly eternial voracity which sprouts, fungates, ferments, germinates, blurs and befogs every sharpness of the red sandstone land, smothers hill and rock with leguminous bulk. The heart of a Malayan city, with bare streets and pink-roofed bungalows, white walls and tamed trees strung to fit the road, is always a small clearing wrested from the jungle and, too easily, turns jungle again.

This is the enemy, Brobdingnag, second empire of the living, growing its sheer preoccupation with survival and reproduction into every joint of thought and emotion; wrapping effort in a miasma of numberless repetitious leaves, the extravagant monotony of unceasing verdure; spawning, cradled in its own decay, the foam and surge of new plant life; never to be stripped by winter, never to be relieved in the starkness of death; never to know the resurrection of the spring. Gone the pendulum of the four seasons, poising in harmony the searching mind, providing in each bud's fruition contrast and comparison, effecting through human senses a sting to alert perception, renewing things well known into magic strangeness, breeding young dreams and visions.

By the ever-recurrent downward-sweeping rain of the roots of a banyan tree lounges a tethered sick elephant, owned by the Happy Chung Circus, touring South East Asia with Japanese and Filipino amazons, ringworm-encrusted lions, seals and a cruel young man with a long whip which swirls and snatches at lamentable tigers. The elephant, moving bony haunches, tramples a bunch of large golden bananas (tasteless the larger, and less savoury, as women, say the men of Malaya) which a curly-haired Bengali boy, sandy loin-cloth about him, hooks away with a bamboo stick, then squats by the elephant's fragrant molehill of dung to eat.

'I am sending my eldest boy to tour with the circus; it is an education, a valuable education,' says Lam Teck, a Chinese *towkay*, businessman, in the front seat of the car next to the white police officer driving the Wyvern. The windows of the car are down, and the grey torrid metal carapace would insulate us from the softly pulsating life streaming past on the road, but that Lam is with us, and Lam is Malaya, with his nylon transparent shirt, worn outside trousers, through the breast-pocket of which can be seen an envelope with brush-neat characters, some rolled dollar bills, and the red folded jacket of his identity card.

Lam has plastic teeth, a fact to mention first because he is so proud of it. He owns four sets, one so good, so expensive, so American, that he wears it only for funerals. He has a face unlined and smooth, as his son's; dark shining hair waved and polished with Yardley lavender oil; only one lung. One lung saves him when two years later he is imprisoned for dealing in gold and opium, and trying to bribe the Harbour Police during six long months; one lung is enough to spare him rigorous, hard labour. Lam is a friend, alive, cheerful, informative, and sending his young son with the Happy Chung Circus, out of Malaya into the world, Indonesia, Siam, Burma, perhaps the Philippines, the world of South East Asia.

'Because,' says Lam, 'as you know, Suyin, what is there for a young Chinese in Malaya but the jungle, the hellish green mouth of the jungle.' He moves his arms, which immediately become tree tendrils, twisted and contorted. Poetic he becomes when his anger is with him, the growling repressed pent fury inside the voice, never above it, always smothered with a denying smile. His hands narrowly miss the face of the driver, the white man who makes fun of himself, calling himself 'red-haired devil' (because here in Malaya in the mouths of the people every white man is a red-haired devil or a white ant). The driver, impassive, listens, looks at me in the rear mirror, and winks.

The car now climbs the road in front of it; climbs a hill like a shoulder, upon which lean, melting the horizon line, the clouds crowding to the daily rain storm over Malaya. The entire sky heaves and sags with clumsy, paunched bodies of cloud, a ponderous elbow-jostling assembly. The season is dry, hence only a noon-storm, curt and soon over, every day.

Lam says: 'I want my son to know life, I want him to have an opportunity. Two years in a circus will be wonderful. He might even become an artist, make a lot of money,' The magic word 'money' provokes Lam to prolonged computations.

The car rolls past the Straits, the sequined ever-changing water. Sea comes inland to lap the roots of the rain-trees along the shore. 'The rain-tree,' says Lam, 'is Malaya; in this country of no seasons, the breathing symbol of growth gone mad.' The trunks are shagged and prurient with one hundred and twenty-seven epiphytes and parasites, tendrils and trailers clinging, tenacious root feet clawing into fleshy bark, until there is not space to put a finger between. Above its devoured trunk the rain-tree raises a delicate-leaved canopy against the sky, its flowers sunwards not seen from the ground. In the water-green light under the green boughs children stand sucking lollypops; Malay Government clerks snore on marble benches, intent Chinese hawkers shake noodles, sliver meat and chicken, spread pepper and ginger and chilli on hot rice cupped on sliced banana leaves; Indian snake-charmers sadly flute their round baskets where invisible snakes sleep. Across the dappled floor of water lies the island of Singapore.

The car stops. We walk to the stone edge curbing the impotent drifting sea at mid-tide. Lam's outflung hand sweeps across the Straits to reach and point at Singapore.

'The big city!' he exclaims softly. 'You know, that is the way the Japanese must have looked at it, gazed with longing eating up their faces after the long jungle paths, coming down south to *Shonan*[1] the beautiful. And look! Look! Here is the monument, now a pile of stones, of no character, which they put up at this spot. This is where they crossed the water to capture Singapore, from the back.'

From where we stand, Singapore is a shore fringed with coconut palms, and further a grey haze out of which emerge a few factory chimneys, tall and spare and spouting smoke. Lam suddenly looks clever.

'This water, it is so convenient for smugglers, isn't it?'

With his eyes he turns to Luke Davis, the white man, as if nudging him in the ribs, sharing with him the secret of the communist smuggling which goes on. It is a well-known joke that in this fifth year of the Emergency, daily and nightly, bullets and hand grenades, towels, rubber sheets, shoes, paper, printing ink and cigarettes are smuggled to the jungles of Malaya from Singapore. But to us, standing across half a mile of water, it is a grey-green haze, ringed by opalescent water.

We turn and re-enter the car, while Lam speaks of the smuggling, and follow the road past the Sultan's gardens with the tall red and yellow canna lilies, sentinel flags leading to the modest bungalow called the palace.

'The old palace!' says Lam, who has appropriated the landscape and doles it out to me. 'What is your impression?' He continues: 'Not very modern; no air conditioning. Bathrooms not very many.'

And here we are. On the left the pink-washed buildings, the fence, a strong well-built fence jutting outwards at the top. The *mata-matas*, police constables in khaki lean on their rifles, the tranquil vegetable placidity of their brown gaze upon us. A large, bearded and turbaned Sikh police sergeant lurks like a suspicious bear behind their palm-like tranquillity. The bear, officious, peers, then straightens to salute the white man with a clash of boots, and we crunch up the gravel road, down which armoured cars packed with policemen clutching sub-machine

[1] *Shonan*: Japanese name for Singapore.

guns whirr with rough and dreadful importance in this war-not-war in Malaya.

'Police Headquarters,' says Lam unnecessarily to me, and smiles with beatific humour, 'where my friend works,' he adds, 'my dear friend.' And looks at Luke, tender, affectionate, as if he would put his arms around him, but does not; says 'works' as if it were highly comical, but also a pity; and there is compassion in Lam's face as he jeers at the white man who works hard and long at the war of the jungle.

Police Headquarters lies sweltering in the pre-storm mid-morning heat, upon its own little elevation, the cloud-shouldering upslope of a hill. The sky is now all white-grey patched, and the dark Nissen huts crouch under it with an air of surly resentful expectancy. The strident ticker-tape of crickets in the stubbly grass around the wire fences, the faint whirr of fans from the offices, and the spasmodic rattle of typewriters from the registry secretaries drag their certain noise through the ominous silence of heat. So it will be, a mounting sullenness, until that first startled rattle and clap of the coconut trees across the road as they strike and rub their fronds against each other, clapping heralds of the storm-bringing wind.

Our driver, our guide, Luke Davis, the white man with the grey shirt stuck to his back with sweat (for sweat comes readily off him in spite of his years in Malaya and his repeated assertion that the climate suits him), leads us to his office on the second floor, and immediately changes, metamorphoses himself into a uniformed figure of military bearing with a granite face; takes upon him as a garment the gestures of authority, presses a bell for lemonade, motions us to two straight-backed chairs, and shifts the papers on his desk. Lam enjoys all this, looks with black fond lively eyes that pat the shoulder at this display of power, and feels that he, Lam, must have power too, to be the friend of such a mighty person as a white police officer in Malaya in 1952. For, besides his business interests, never certain, his transitory opium dealings, his cautious and friendly procuring, his gambling and his three wives, in three cities, to manage his affairs, Lam is also a police informer, an agent of the British Government in Malaya.

Enters Che Ahmad, the Malay, who belongs to the silver people of the mosque, and brings with him under the clicking fan the spiritual posture, the cool repose of Islam, suffusing even the chair on which he now proceeds to sit, with knees outspread and feet tucked under him as upon a mat. He wears a pale pink shirt and lavender rayon tie, fawn corduroy trousers baggy round the hip and tapering to a tightness round both ankles as is the fashion. He looks a prince disguising greatness, and his large brown eyes rest on the white man with tolerant amusement, while on the floor stand his grey suede shoes, removed of course. He thinks best in bare feet.

'Good morning, sir,' says he.

'Good morning and congratulations, Che Ahmad,' says Luke, smiling. 'I hear you have another son, the seventh, is it not?'

Che Ahmad bows his head to hide a smile of ineffable sweet triumph. He is a man of seven sons and six daughters, two wives, and he is thirty-two. 'I have too many children,' he says, deprecating his prowess, and glowing with his last achievement. 'I just came in to say hello, sir. I've brought you the file about Lee Kok, sir. It's complete now.' Che Ahmad turns to business, though it would give him great pleasure to speak of the son of his body. 'The captured female prisoner Ah Mei is waiting to see you. I don't think it is important. A personal request, I think.'

'Again?' says Luke Davis. 'What does she want now, I wonder? Come in!' He shouts unnecessarily, for the girl has already slipped into the room.

'Morning,' says Ah Mei in English, grinning widely with all her face. 'Morning,' she repeats, and stands grinning there, contemplating us, obviously lost in delight at seeing us, as if her morning's purpose were achieved, to walk into this office room and say 'Good morning'.

Behind her in the door's embrasure the Malay mata-mata who has brought her, stands with a shuffled click of boots, salutes, and then withdraws.

Ah Mei is Captured Enemy Personnel No. 234, comrade taken in jungle combat, and in the dingy office, suffocating in spite of the fan, she stands, a patch of brightness, her white trousers and fitting coat with small collar joyful with pink chrysanthemums. Her hair is straight and soft and falls to the shoulders, held back from her face by two small pink plastic clips. It is not curled, for Ah Mei is out of the jungle and a puritan therefore, and 'permanents' are an Imperialist invention, as everyone knows. The day will come when Ah Mei will buy herself a 'permanent' and look like every other girl, rubber-tapper, baby-amah, factory worker, every other Asian girl in Malaya. But that day there will be symbolic meaning in the gesture, for that day, perhaps, she will no longer believe.

There is something extremely charming about Ah Mei's face, so softly round, so smooth, that none will note beauty at first glance. Only later shall I see the wide brow, the chin, the up-curving cheekbone and the large black eyes. Today I only remember the childish short upper lip giving her face an abiding air of enchanted wonder. Lam also looks at her, a connoisseur, and notes the faintly golden skin, the hands and feet very small, the diminutive toes perfect like a baby's in her open rubber slippers.

'You may ask her questions,' says Luke Davis. 'She says she is now twenty and was two years in the jungle before capture a year ago.' He adds that her sentence is ten years under the Emergency Regulations, for she was caught with a grenade in her hand. 'But she has been such a help to us that we are trying to do something about it.'

'Well now,' says he to the girl, in a stiff, official voice, 'what did you want to say to me?'

'It's my arms,' replies Ah Mei. 'I want to go to the Hospital again. The last medicine was no good.' She holds up her arms, and round the elbows they are faintly dotted with black and mulberry marks. She says, because Lam and I are strangers: 'They are leech and mosquito bites when I was cooking for the People Inside.'

Luke turned to me: 'Somehow I don't understand what the word "Communist" means to people like her. I wonder whether she really believes in anything? I wonder what was the real reason for her going Inside?'

'Especially,' puts in Lam, with a wilfully clever look at Ah Mei's face, 'especially after she has been so co-operative and sincere with you.' All Lam's words are triple-edged, sheathed in demulcent adjectives. All have hidden meanings. It is obvious that he thinks Luke Davis should have taken liberties with Ah Mei ... and if not, what a slow-witted fool he is.

'You mean such a good stool-pigeon,' replies Luke, 'what do you think, Che Ahmad?'

And Che Ahmad says without moving: 'Don't think there are no crocodiles because the water is calm.'

Luke turns to Ah Mei. 'I'll have you taken to the Hospital later. This lady,' he points to me, 'is a doctor, just come to Malaya. Perhaps she will have a look at your arms?'

I straighten up after a look. 'These are just insect-bite marks. They'll go. Does she really need to go to hospital for that?'

Luke looks at Che Ahmad, who significantly puts up his

thumb. 'Number One's orders. You know what he's like. Never displease valuable informers.'

'Okay,' says Luke resignedly, 'let her go and waste the hospital doctor's time, then.'

Ah Mei and I look at each other. After a while I pull my mouth together again, guilty of so much secret mirth, and she turns her head but goes on smiling, gazing away and towards the window at the now gathered storm outside. The sudden wind has three times clapped its hands among the coconut fronds, and now springs up the hill and into the room to blow her hair, and behind it large tepid drops of rain spatter in. Ah Mei smiles, happily, for of all the treats which come to her because she is such an excellent informer on her previous comrades, going about in a comfortable police car is her chief pleasure.

'You'll get used to it,' said Betchine. 'You'll get used to Malaya, my dearr girrl.' Her R's rolled in the fashion of the Scots University town where she had studied. Dr. Betchine was tall, Euro-Indian, draped pastel georgette sarees on her body and a stethoscope round her neck. Her large brown eyes, long lashes, aristocratic features, would look well on the cover of *Life* magazine, sub-titled: Woman of Modern Asia.

It was my first week as Lady Medical Officer in the women and children's clinic of the Hospital, taking over from Betchine now to be transferred to Kuala Lumpur. In one week, I had become a witch's cauldron of seething irritation, boiling resentment, and hissing rage. Betchine assured me, unsoothingly, that it was Malaya.

'They're all like you, when they start,' she repeated. 'They' referred to doctors like myself, newly recruited into the Service. 'After a few months, they calm down. This is Malaya. Everything takes a long, a very long time, in Malaya. Things get done, occasionally, but more often they don't and the more in a hurry you are, the quicker you break down. I got a breakdown in Kuala Lumpur, in those barracks they pretend is a hospital. Now I'm posted back to it.' She laughed, good-natured, hearty, high-pitched laughter, and twirled the end of her stethoscope round and round. Her laughter mocked herself and the confusion, the inadequacy, the overcrowded room around her. Thus had she laughed when, on my first day, I exclaimed that half the wards of the Hospital were closed down. 'Shortage of nurses,' said Betchine.

'Look at this waiting-room, my dearr girrl. Wouldn't you think that a building as imposing as this one, costing millions of dollars, with corridors eighty yards long and five yards wide, would have a decent waiting-room for women and children patients? But of course not. Women still don't count much in this country. They give us this fourteen-feet-by-twelve cubicle where each day one hundred and ten patients cram themselves to be seen by me, and after today, by you.

'That's why I call this place the whited sepulchre,' she concluded with her habitual mirth. 'Actually there are worse places. It isn't the doctors ... many of us are hardworking enough, but we get tired of fighting the creeping paralysis called administration. We are frustrated at every turn, and finally give up. It's the Emergency which is to blame. There isn't enough money, and things don't get done without money.'

'I'm tired hearing the Emergency blamed for everything that is not done in Malaya,' I replied. 'Because of the Emergency, many things which otherwise would not have been tackled at all, have now been done. The trouble with this country is not only the Emergency. I know a town up north where it takes nine months and many thousands of dollars' bribes to get a licence to run a truck. I visited a hospital where the attendants wait three to five months to get their first month's salaries paid to them. Meanwhile they borrow from money-lenders to live. I hear that in a certain State hospital the nurses have not had their increments paid to them for the last two years. You can't blame this sort of thing on the Emergency. It's red tape and the cancer of corruption, not the terror of the jungle.'

'We have a word for it here,' said Betchine. ' "Tidapathy" is the name. It's the most important word in the Malayan vocabulary, and the sooner you learn it, the quicker you'll feel at home in Malaya. *Tidapah*. It means never mind. It's compounded of *je m'en fiche* and *mañana*. It's also the Will of God. Tidapah. The less you do, the less you show up your colleagues' "tidapathy", and the sooner you'll get promoted. Do nothing, and you can't do wrong. I used to row with people, wear myself out with work and worry, until the Medical Superintendent warned me. "You are an over-zealous young lady," he said. Now I say tidapah with the best.'

But I knew that Betchine went on pitting herself against sloth, against tidapathy; lashing out with her tongue, tearing off the masks of make-believe; crashing through the strangling criss-cross of pull, influence and family connections, so important in securing service, or position, in some government department; rising at two in the morning to check the babies' feeds ... Betchine was a good doctor. I wondered how long it would take before she broke down again.

'Tidapah, doctor,' said Staff Nurse Doremy, she of the immense and doleful eyes. Doremy was Tamil. She had mothered dozens of medical officers, English, Chinese, Indian, Eurasian and an occasional Malay, serving their turn of duty in Outpatients. Her years in government service numbered twenty-three. Because of the lack of nursing staff, she had been called from retirement to serve again. During the Japanese occupation she had planted tapioca, dug for yams, walked miles for a little black market rice, sewn jute bags, cut grass as a labourer. She had eight children of her own, and four adopted ones. She dealt with one hundred screaming patients with complete calm, but became an incoherent, stuttering incapable in front of the English Sister-in-charge, who strode briskly into Outpatients at ten o'clock, scolded Doremy, glared at the doctor, counted the syringes, ordered the amah to sweep the floor under the patients' feet, then, with a look at the round wall clock (always fast), departed to her other charges, the Senior Officers' special doctor, the Male Outpatients, the Antenatal Clinic ... there were not enough Sisters to go round the mammoth Hospital.

'Tidapah, doctor,' said Staff Nurse Doremy, and the word on her lips was sonorous consolation. 'Doctor must not excite herself, lah. Will get all heaty in this weather. Anger is weakening to the body. We should have a big waiting-room, like the men. But what to do? Many doctors must write many, many letters to the Department before can get, lah. But patients are quite happy, doctor. They are happy so long they see woman doctor. Man doctor they don't like. Before you we had poor Dr. Sandrishan. He good man doctor, but patients never let him examine them. So what can he do? He has to guess every time.

'Dr. Sandrishan attempted one day to examine a Malay girl suffering from what he thought might be heart disease, and got sued for outrage to modesty,' said Betchine to me.

'Anyway, doctors must have some coffee now,' ordered Doremy, looking at the clock. 'After ward round, coffee, then Outpatients. Otherwise cannot stand it. This place not healthy,' she told me. Doremy was a genius at stating the obvious in such a way that one felt like exclaiming: 'How true!'

'Diphtherias sitting with whooping coughs, and t.b. old ladies spitting on the floor, and little babies being sick at both ends at the same time. I always tell the amah, Ah Kam, to put more lysol in the water to wash the floor, but Ah Kam is lazy, too, and sometimes forgets. Ah Kam, Ah Kam!' she shouted suddenly in Malay, 'make some coffee for doctors.'

At that moment the thickset policewoman in khaki with black and silver badges on her shoulders and a beret smartly pulled on her curled hair, pushed her way through the crowd sitting, standing, squatting, or lying on the waiting-room floor among the pulped banana skins, the half-eaten oranges, the crumbled soda biscuits, the melting chocolate slabs, the vomits and the urine; offal to be swept up at the end of the morning with a flourish of lysol in water by Ah Kam, the amah, who had tuberculosis, five dead babies, and was assigned to Outpatients, where work as an attendant (asserted the Regulations) was light.

Robustly, elbows outstretched, the policewoman advanced, disregarding the backwash of indignant mutters behind her. Authority meant priority. Close at her back came Ah Mei and Fong Kiap carrying her three-month-old baby born in the detention camp. Once in our small examination room, the policewoman clicked her heels and saluted. Doremy would have pushed out anyone else, but this was Police; she closed the door and wedged herself against it so that pressure from the waiting crowd would not send it flying open again.

'This prisoner complains her arms are bad,' said the policewoman in English, pushing Ah Mei forward.

'There's nothing wrong with her arms,' said Betchine. 'I've seen this girl before. I've told her so. These are only bite marks, leeches, mosquitoes, or what have you that bite in the jungle.'

I looked at Ah Mei and thought again: 'How charming she is, such gentleness in her smile.'

Dr. Betchine said to Ah Mei in rather bad Malay: 'I'll give you some more ointment to rub on your arms.'

'The ointment smells bad, it makes my head giddy,' Ah Mei said to the policewoman in Hokkien. The policewoman, whose name was Rosie Yip, and who spoke six Chinese dialects, Malay and Malayan English, translated this into the latter language: 'She says ointment makes her smell no-good, doctor.'

'I suppose she'd like something special, with perfume,' said Betchine, sarcastically. 'Really, that girrl's the limit.'

Doremy now took matters in hand by translating this briefly into Malay to Ah Mei: 'Doctor says no can do, don't be such a *sombong* (stuck-up) girl.'

Ah Mei, who knew Malay quite well, but scorned to show it, smiled.

'There is also this babee, if doctor would see,' said Rosie, pulling Ah Mei back by the arm and shoving Fong Kiap forward.

'*Sakit.*'[1] Fong Kiap smiled broadly, her round pointing stomach, ill-covered by her short flowered top, shook with repressed laughter. She politely bared her teeth to the gums at us. The four top teeth were edged with gilded brass. The original enamel peered from heart-shaped windows cut out of the glittering metal framework. Hearts and diamonds were the commonest shapes found in Chinese mouths in Malaya, and I had

[1] *Sakit*: ill or sick in Malay.

discerned a stray spade in the top row of a Malay special constable.

'Sakit, very sick,' repeated Fong Kiap, gurgling with pure misery. The baby had a shrunken, wizened face, a glaze drawn tight over its open eyes.

'Haha,' laughed Rosie Yip, whose round Chinese face and boot-button eyes, neat as her uniform, made her the Asian counterpart of a typical London bobby, 'Fong Kiap said "sakit, sakit" yesterday to the red-haired devil newspaperman who came to the detention camp to write about it. "Sakit, sakit," said Fong Kiap. The red-haired devil thought she was telling her name. "That's a pretty name, Sakit," he told her.' Rosie Yip slapped her thighs at the story, and laughed again.

Ah Kam guffawed and translated into Malay to Doremy. Rosie, surmising that Betchine would object to the term red-haired devil, the current name for Europeans, had switched to the Cantonese dialect for this story.

'Laugh, laugh,' said Betchine, who had been examining the baby and was not happy about it, 'you Chinese always laugh. It's nearly unnatural vice with you. We Indians' (Betchine was one of those post-war Eurasians who would rather be all Asian) 'cry. We weep and wail. It's more realistic. Come, hold your baby, while I write the admission form.'

Fong Kiap took over baby, and started putting on baby's clothes, the belly band, the little wool cap, the wool socks and the small quiltwork blanket. Baby began to shrink. He suddenly looked tiny bundled against Fong Kiap's large breasts. Round baby's neck hung a small cross, present from the Catholic priest; a tiger's claw, silver mounted; a wisp of feathers and a silver lock; talismans and safeguards of another tradition. On baby's left wrist was tied a yellow thread. How many devious small bribes, how many whispered supplications had been accomplished by Fong Kiap, through how many wardresses and attendants at the camp had these charms been relayed to reach, at last, the baby; to ward disease and death from baby. But here he was, very sakit, very ill.

'Laugh, laugh,' Betchine repeated, holding the telephone receiver in one hand, for she had started the laborious process of ringing the children's ward to announce baby's arrival, otherwise Ward Sister might send it down again with the crisp note 'No cot'. 'My fiancé (he's in the C.I.D.) was prosecuting some bandit helpers last week. They were the usual rubber tappers, going in a lorry to the rubber trees. It had rained, the road was slippery and round a bend the lorry swerved too sharply. The tappers standing in it were thrown off balance as it skidded. WHOOSH WHOOSH, out came the rice, out from the cloth on their heads, from their pockets, their shirts, their belts, their blouses. They were plug full of rice for the jungle people. "You never saw anything so funny," my fiancé said, "as these tappers scrambling to their feet laughing, laughing their heads off, pretending they couldn't see the rice on the floor of the lorry, they didn't know where it had all come from."

'My fiancé was in court, prosecuting the case. One of the girls in the dock, the usual People's Movement worker of about seventeen, could not stop laughing. The Judge became very angry, banged the table, shouted at her: "What's so funny? You've committed a crime, now you are being insolent. Will you tell the court what you're laughing at?" The interpreter was frightened because the Judge looked so angry; he said: "Quick, tell why you laugh, or it will go hard for you." So the girl said, still giggling: "Because he has such a funny, big nose," pointing to the Judge. He wasn't hard on her though, she got three years' rigorous, same as the others.'

'He is a kind-hearted man, lah, Judge Banks,' interposed Doremy piously. 'He knows what young girls are like. Got some growing daughters himself.'

The abandoned door (Doremy had left it to collect our coffee cups) now sprang open and into the examination room, wholly naked, on hands and knees, crawled a Tamil labourer woman, grey-haired, lips excoriated with burns from chewing betel with too much lime and letting the saliva trickle down the corners to her chin, purple with old thick scars. Garlic oil and cow dung had been smeared over her body. She advanced uttering screams. Doremy and Ah Kam sprang at her, pushed her out and shut the door.

'Mental, that one,' said Doremy, chattingly. Already I was under her care. Taken in hand. She had charming, dark hands with pale pink glossy nails, the beautiful South Indian skin, soft, finely wrinkled like parachute silk.

'Don't tell me there isn't a cot,' Betchine shouted into the telephone. 'This baby is coming in ... well, put that girl on the floor on a mattress ... I don't care if it *is* the British Adviser's head gardener's niece. ...'

Fong Kiap suddenly understood that baby was going into hospital. The held-back weeping gushed out in one long wail. All laughter gone, she clung to baby. He would die of fright without the comfort of her arms. She must be admitted with baby. Or let doctor give an injection, and she would nurse baby in the detention camp. Rosie told her in Hokkien, Teochew, Cantonese and Malay not to be silly. (Rosie was obviously showing off.) Fong Kiap shook her head, tears rolled down her cheeks, and she appealed suddenly to her husband's ghost. 'He is dead and since then people have been harming me. They have falsely accused me and now I have been in prison for many months . . . I have never done anything wrong.'

'Nothing wrong!' shouted Rosie, boisterous but not unkind. 'Then where did this baby come from, tell me that.'

'We are between fire and water, we the people,' wailed Fong Kiap. 'We are caught between two terrors, the Police, and the People Inside. I do not want to live any more.'

'Quiet,' said Rosie Yip the policewoman. 'Don't bring shame on your ancestors with your big talk. Do you really want us to believe you were clever enough to get another male to do the work of your Old Man of the Jungle?' She used an obscene, good-natured workaday word. 'Consorting with bandits, that's what you are in for, even if it is your husband.'

Ah Kam, the amah, guffawed at this, and translated in Malay to Doremy who looked suddenly tragic, as was her way with mirth. Fong Kiap grinned through her tears, and gazing fondly, passionately at baby, son of her man in the jungle, followed Doremy out of the room and to the ward. Adjusting her uniform belt after one last, sharp, rattling salute, Rosie went with them, completely forgetting Ah Mei, her other prisoner, who was thus left guarded by me.

While Betchine, with Ah Kam's help, began sorting the patients, wading into the crowd and picking the obviously ill ones from those who came to acquire medicine for nothing, or to obtain sick leave, Ah Mei, in a corner, talked to me in standard Chinese. Like all Chinese in Malaya, Ah Mei knew at least three dialects, but she also spoke standard Chinese because she had been to a Chinese school for two years, and then in the jungle.

'I am acquainted with Fong Kiap,' she said, her face of childish innocence lifted to mine. 'The baby is really her husband's child, and he is of the People Inside. She let the People sleep at her hut . . . she gave them food, and on their way up north, the couriers stopped there to rest. Fong Kiap does not admit that the child is the son of the man in the jungle. She is afraid that the red-haired devils will hunt him through her, force her to write to him and thus trap him. So she has told the red-hairs that the child was by a travelling salesman. Of course, everyone knows it is a lie, except the red-hairs. They were not sure until they asked me.'

'Why do you tell me this?' I asked.

Ah Mei did not reply. She appeared not to have heard. I did not want her to fear me, and so did not repeat my question. Rosie Yip returned with Fong Kiap, and all three left in a black police car driven by a Tamil chauffeur.

Unpremeditated, night falls. Here is no long-drawn parting of the worlds, light and dark. Night's black doors close suddenly upon a sunset universe of strident colour, an orange and purple conflagration tangled in swamps of opal water, stretches of pink sky rimmed by deep blue hills. At once the splendour goes behind shutters, is lost to sight, sunk in the thickness of night without the respite of evening and the slow-paced arrival of early stars. Later the stars will shine, the moon appear; but at first it is only plain, immense night over Malaya.

At night, the Hospital, already vast by day, becomes enormous, a fantasy of disproportion. All the public buildings are of prodigious size, as if giants had planned to work in them. From one end of the tiled corridors to the other end, my footsteps snap at me, dead, flat, devoid of echo, for in this gargantuan heap of stone, brick and cement, reverberation is choked and smothered. Walking the corridor at night I am filled with panic, that I shall never reach its end. While pacing thus I have felt unreal, as if life had lost meaning, as if, at the bottom, living was only that, the walking of one long night-filled corridor, the treading of an endless, shallow, dark ravine.

Perhaps it is Malaya, as Betchine says. Everything seems to me out of gear, awry, disproportioned, tedious and grotesque and therefore unreal. I must not try to make a meaning and a shape out of this. Like my footsteps in this corridor, at the moment there is no resonance to any event, no significance to any gesture, no illumination to any explanation. There is only repetitious exuberance, the raw undiluted essence of growth, a violence in all that I apprehend, in which I must not instil insignificance, for at the moment it dispenses none. This is Malaya. And there is no pattern as yet. Only confusion.

At the end of the corridors are the wards. Here unrelenting darkness clusters, sombrely untouched by a few electric bulbs spaced along the two arms of the T-shaped ward. Each arm is eighty yards long and ten yards wide. Along both sides, the sheeted grey beds need the sting of flashlight to reveal their huddled contents or their disarrayed emptiness. Where the ward arms intersect is the massive platform on which the night nurse sits, and the single bright stab of a reading lamp bent over the table at which she writes, interminably writes, the endless night's report.

Night nurse in charge of the ward is overworked, as all the nurses are; she watches one hundred and twenty beds, goes up and down, ministering. When busy in one of the arms, she can have no inkling of what goes on in the other arm. It is out of sight, out of hearing. It would take a strong man's shout, a healthy man's din, to bring her running on the slippery tiles in the half gloom. When an injection is due, she rushes twenty yards to the room where the trolleys are kept, hurries back with the rattling trolley to the patient's bed, returns to the platform. I see her lift light-dazzled eyes to interrogate the dark-filled three tunnels which radiate from where she sits; she cannot distinguish me, nor has heard my steps, till I stand two yards away from her. Suddenly I see her, uniform and all, elongated by some monstrous, invisible power, pulled abominably in the shape of the cross she rules over, her feet stretched to reach one end, her finger tips touching the doors at the other two ends. Her head remains under the bright bent bulb. She peers and smiles, for at last she has seen me. 'Good evening, doctor,' she says, with the pleasant Malayan English insistence on the second syllable of bi-syllabic words. 'What can I do for you?' Her sweetness brushes away the nightmare woven round her, like a spider web, but not its repetition every time I walk the wards.

The Hospital is garrulous by night. Within the four dense walls of darkness, flat, without echo, rises the formless muttering, soft clamour of the sick, who talk and shout, laugh and sigh, weep and whistle and sing. Inside the precincts of night these various utterances, even the startled screaming of children, blend into one, coagulate into phraseless modulation without meaning, which seeps and floats, up and down the building, a flat tide lapping at sandy shores, unseen.

Those who lie here are Asians forced in the cleft between two magics, the new and the old. Western medicine may be potent necromancy by day, to be invoked desperately when older, time-potentiated charms have failed, but the same audacity holds not at night. Then the old beliefs wax strong; then the invulnerable root and the blood-stained claw make mock of the new mystery, day's syringe. Then conjuration with thorns and the spell of enchanted names will fend the witch that drinks blood by moonlight. *Polongs* and *shaitans*, daemons and ghosts appeased by the magic formulae scribbled in daylight by white-coated magicians wielding that new enchanter's wand, the stethoscope, wax strong and wrathful with darkness. The patients walk about, since the irksome command of repose prevails only by day; they eat forbidden and highly spiced food smuggled by relatives; they gamble; they transact business; they anoint themselves with ointments and swallow remedies from the herbalist, the witch doctor, or the Chinese medicine man. I came upon two large Sikhs doing some forbidden deed, and felt a spy, unclothed of authority. They turned on me their bearded faces, and the glance of their night-sure, other-world eyes, made me continue walking, past them, and out.

From ward to ward, up and down the stone stairs, the sinusoid of sound pursued me. Words, words, words, all adding up to this soft cacophony, this unending flat unquietness. Words in all the dialects and languages which are spoken in Malaya. Is not so much of what happens in this country a reciprocal confusion, rooted in ignorance of each other's language and customs, producing blindness, intolerant inhumanity? I begin to feel, uneasily, that Malayan episodes are a comedy of errors due to this division between the ruler and the ruled; not one in a hundred of the rulers can boast to speak well the language of the ruled. A few speak it so badly, and on such a low scale, that thereby only another source of error is created.

Malay, Chinese, Indians, English (count the latter I must, though they persist in not belonging, and place their loyalty not in this land); Chinese, Malay, Indians, three words, three sweeping generalizations out of which it has been planned to forge a new nation, to create a country called Malaya, a single people to be called Malayans (always to be confused abroad with Malays, one of the three ingredient races).

The word Malay means Javanese, Sumatrans, Indonesians, people from Minangkabau and many another East Indies island, Arabs and Arab-educated Mahomedans, as well as Malays proper from Malaya itself; Chinese include half a dozen subgroups from the southern provinces of China, by feature and emotion Chinese, but divided by dialect into Teochews, Hokkiens, Hakkas, Cantonese, Hainanese and smaller groups. Indians include Tamils, Punjabis, Sikhs, Pathans, Bengalis and many others. In each ward of the hospital at least three kinds of food must be served. In each ward the nurses must act as translators as well as nurse, and where they fail, an orderly, or an amah, must be found to interpret, with all the inaccuracy and the florid inventiveness of the illiterate Asian. Among the doctors few can speak to all the patients, for in Malaya a university education, by its very insistence upon excellence in English, hampers a doctor from acquiring the vernacular languages of this country.

And thus at night, when the patients confide in the darkness and in their own tongue what they have withheld from physician and nurse, I begin to understand the terror, the confusion, the essential need to prevaricate of those who are always at someone else's mercy, because they cannot communicate with those who decide their fate, except through an interpreter.

In the process, how many deviations, changes, sifting, warpings and twistings; how many opportunities for blackmail and corruption, before, transformed, sometimes unrecognizable, the stories of the poor who do not speak English reach their rulers, who are hand-picked, among their own peoples, on the basis of their knowledge of English.

Pacing the corridors, night dark, of the hospital, I heard the poor talk, Malays, Indians, Chinese, and asked myself whether out of this babel reassembled, a pattern would emerge.

In the hospital prison ward the young terrorist was dying. The hospital attendant in charge, a handsome Malay with the tranquil refinement of voice and feature which endears the race to so many, said: 'He is going, doctor. Soon *mampus*, lah.' Mampus is a word for death which is used for animals only.

I had seen the terrorist arrive, brought in strapped to a stretcher. The armoured car with the regimental badges painted on the back, with the soldiers leaping out so briskly, had stopped at the back gate of the hospital. The young English sergeant, his green jungle uniform rank with sweat, his pink face thick and bloated with tiredness, still carried a gun in his hand and waved it, as if he had just used it. 'Steady, mates, steady, don't knock them about too much,' he called, as the stretchers were lowered. On one was an older man, with sharp sallow face and fiery eyes, and a leg enveloped in bandages through which the slowly seeping blood spread, a widening blot. On the other the young boy groaning, half unconscious, with bullets in the belly.

'They got them near Todak,' explained Dr. Eng the anaesthetist, watching with me. He was a Chinese from Penang, and had done underground anti-Japanese work during the Occupation. 'Todak is now a resettlement camp, with barbed wire round it. It is known as a Bad Spot.'

Of course, it was always places which had done the most fighting against the Japanese in the last war, places once famous for their heroism, which had become notorious bad spots in the present trouble. Thus it was that Tanjong Malim, mentioned in Chapman's book (Dr. Eng was very enthusiastic about the book), and Kulai, and Labis, and Yong Peng, and Todak, were now bad spots. He knew a village which had been twice razed to the ground. Once by the Japanese, and last year by the British. The first time the people had been warned by the jungle guerrillas, and many had fled Inside. Those that could not escape, the Japanese had massacred. The second time the British had come at dawn, and surrounded the village. In six hours the whole population had been carted away in trucks, the pigs slaughtered, the crops mashed, and the whole area destroyed by fire. 'Collective punishment,' giggled Dr. Eng, spreading sudden glee over his face, as Chinese will do to hide other emotions. Laughter is the open fan of the well-bred person masking the yawn of boredom, the twisted lip of pain, the clenched jaws of hatred.

While we were talking the theatre called for Dr. Eng. The young terrorist would be operated on, to try to save his life. 'So they can hang him afterwards. What a waste of time,' was Betchine's comment.

The boy was now dying. The older one was a hard case, as the attendant put it. 'He won't even take an injection for the pain, doctor.' He lay with his head propped on a pillow as we passed his cell with its wide bars and its Malay policeman standing guard. His eyes followed us, contempt evident.

We stood by the young man's bed; at his head also was a Malay mata-mata on guard, just as young as the terrorist. The glucose-saline transfusion set had stopped. Unnecessarily, I felt his swift small pulse. He had a smooth face, regular features, black hair growing in a point on the forehead. He looked like hundreds of other young Chinese, slim, neat of feature, spareness different from the beauty of the Malays, who, lacking the sharp, tense quality of the Chinese youth, make up for it by a more suave and sensual charm.

While we were looking at him, listening to his very shallow

breathing he opened his eyes and saw me.

'Doctor,' he said.

'Yes, what is it?'

Although his intonation was Cantonese, he now spoke standard Chinese, both because I had done so, and because it is the language which the People Inside will use, whatever dialect group they may come from.

'I am glad to see a Chinese doctor. The one who came this morning was a *Kling* devil, an Indian.'

'It is all the same.'

'I wanted to be a doctor, but my family was killed by the Japanese devils. I was saved by an uncle who took me to the jungle. I was Inside for four years.'

'Why did you go back to the jungle this time?'

His voice was very weak, interrupted by sighs as his breathing became more shallow.

'The Japanese went, the British came. I could not get any schooling. They said I was too old. I could never be anything but a coolie, all my life. My friends were all Inside. Those that had come out were going back. There was no way out for them. There was no other way for me. I went back Inside.'

I could not answer him. He was only repeating what many of the young had already said: that there was no door to the future for them, save through the green mouth of the jungle.

'Once we have thrown the British out, we can be free, I can be a doctor,' he said.

'But it is wrong to kill and murder, don't you see?'

He did not reply. When he spoke again, he had wandered to something else.

'We were four comrades the day we went Inside again. We took a taxi from Singapore. We came to Johore Bahru in the taxi. We sang songs all the way. The driver was one of our People.

'I remember how we arrived too early at our meeting place. The man we were to meet wasn't there. So we went to the zoo for an hour.

'Monkeys, tigers, lions, elephants, parrots and peacocks and crocodiles. All in cages. Only man could be free. I felt as if I too had been behind wire, like an animal, but now I stood on the edge of freedom. When we liberate Johore Bahru, I thought, I will go to the zoo again and open all the cages.'

'When you were Inside, old brother,' I said, 'what then? Did you get the freedom you wanted? Did you come nearer to being a doctor?'

There was no answer. His eyes widened suddenly, yet he appeared to go to sleep. After a while he stopped breathing. 'Mampus,' said the attendant, and the policeman on guard assented with a flickering smile.

We left the dead young terrorist and passed the hardened case on our way out. He stared at us again, the fixed contempt on his face unchanged.

Neo turned with care and lifted his body on an outstretched right hand. His daughter and son slept between him and his wife on the mat-covered wood planking, the family bed. Through cracks in the plywood walls of the hut a lighter darkness seeped.

In the cloth hammock suspended from the roof beam the larger baby gurgled and scuffled hands and feet. Neo Saw slept, mouth half open, the smaller baby at her breast.

Neo bent across his children and shook his wife's arm. She groaned and sat up, eyes still closed. The smaller baby rolled off her breast and wailed. She crooned 'Oh *sayang*[1] *sayang*' sleepily; mechanically put him back, holding him perched upon her right hip with one crooked arm. The smaller baby curled its legs round her waist, grasped her pendulous wrinkled right breast with both hands, and sucked at the large dark nipple, pulling strongly.

Neo Saw shuffled outside the hut through the small kitchen to the privy, narrow as a sentry box, five feet from the hut. It was so dark she could not see, but she smelt the smoke from the stoves of Fong Kiap and Big Dog Tsou, her neighbours to left and to right, a sharp tang within her nostrils which woke her up. She returned, seized the face towel inscribed 'Good morning' hanging on a nail in the wall, dipped it into a basin of water, and wiped the smaller baby's face around his busily sucking mouth. Then she washed her own. She swilled water in her mouth, rinsing and gargling, and expectorating in the tangle of tapioca, which grew its sprays of leaves on man-tall thin stems between the privy and the hut.

Neo lit the small kerosene lamp, and the black and gold shadows of flame danced upon wall and faces. Daughter, padding barefooted, lifted the larger baby from its hammock and took it to the privy with her, whistling enticingly. When she returned she took the tin of condensed milk out of the food cupboard, with its wire net doors and its legs dipping in cigarette tins full of water, and measured two teaspoonfuls of gluey yellow liquid into a glass. The rubber twigs in the earth stove were burning and the water was hot in the aluminium kettle. Neo Saw poured some water into the glass, and Daughter

[1] *Sayang*: darling, beloved.

stirred the mixture, dribbled it into a feeding bottle, capped it with a rubber teat, and pushed the teat into the larger baby's mouth. He drank eagerly, choking over the air sucked in with the warm milk.

The family swallowed their morning rice, shovelling it with chopsticks into their mouths. Neo Saw fed the babies spoonfuls of rice, and later spoonfuls of muddy black coffee streaked with condensed milk. Neo put on his black tapper clothes, stiff with spilt latex. Neo Saw, baby hanging fast to her, knotted her sweat cloth round her head. They took their tapping knives, wheeled their bicycles out of the hut, walked them down the dirt road of the wired-in labour village to the police post guarding the gate. The smaller baby, ten months old, sat astride Neo Saw's left hip, supported by a piece of cloth which went round his buttocks and over his mother's shoulder. Daughter, aged eight years, carried the larger baby, aged two years. Son, aged thirteen, came behind, stumbling sleepily, his thin arms wrapped round a bottle of water, the only food or drink allowed out of the perimeter wire fence which surrounded the village.

In the cool, iron-grey softening of dawn, the stars were small, remote and high. Shafts of pallor surged and ebbed in irregular waves above the trees to the east, and Son remembered a grey-blue balloon he had burst. Wrinkled and small, dark and crumpled as night in a hut, it had lain in his hand. He had blown into it, and it had grown, had swollen and thinned into a translucent sphere, shimmering with silver streaks, as now shimmered, with pale light spurting above the trees in gusts, the orb of a rapidly thinning sky.

In front of Neo walked other tappers, among them Fong Kiap in her dark clothes, wheeling her bicycle. Its chain whirred, a soft, hasty tick and prick of the stillness. Fong Kiap had a large, calm face; she was sturdy and big with child, and from her waddle every tapper knew that she had food hidden between her thighs.

Neo slowed his steps, not wishing to be near Fong Kiap, should the Malay mata-mata at the police post find her out. His thought, of few words, dull and slow, duller now because of the constant fear that was upon him, as upon them all, informed him that it had been thus during the years of the Japanese devils, and that it was natural and wrong that it should be thus again.

Neo and Fong Kiap's husband had run away together to the jungle to escape being massacred by the Japanese. That was ten years ago. Neo Saw had smuggled food to Neo her husband then. Fong Kiap was now smuggling food to her husband, who had gone back Inside. He had become one of the People Inside, and Neo was now afraid of him, nearly as frightened of his old friend as he was of the Police.

As Neo slowed down, Big Dog Tsou glided past on noiseless feline feet, walking softly, treading a jungle path always, a quiet and dangerous smiling man who collected money and food for the People Inside.

At the police post the tappers handed in their identity cards; the Malay mata-matas kept them till their return from tapping on the estate. The mata-matas searched the tappers, ran their hands over them, undid their belts, looking for rice, meat, beancurd, cake, tinned food, ammunition, matches, cigarettes, tobacco, a watch, a pen, a pencil, paper of any kind, money, jewellery, an extra garment or towel, a small rubber sheet, string, a fishing hook, a penknife, a piece of soap, medicine pills. They tasted the water in the bottles to make sure it was not sweetened. They shone their torches on the tappers' shoes to see if they were new. They poked the bicycle saddles, squeezed the tires. Sometimes they ran their hands through the women's hair. Neo's mind, geared to evasion, refused to remember how his wife in Japanese times had smuggled tobacco under a piece of sticking plaster on her belly, and money in her private parts.

A young mata-mata put his hand on Fong Kiap's belly and she tittered, a chuckling coy sound. The boy grinned, withdrew his hand and waved her on. Rubber estate mata-matas were usually slow, indolent boys, hastily recruited from the Malay kampongs, cruel only by fits and starts, when their religious or racial feelings were inflamed. Most days they found it too strenuous to search, and waved the tappers on but they sometimes searched the women, for their pleasure.

It was Neo Saw's turn, and Neo, pretending indifference, looked blankly away, feeling the tightening in his heart, the coiled rankling fury which dwelt within him at the sight of another man's hands upon his woman; rage unbetrayed by tremor or word, endured, as so many things were endured in these days between two terrors, that of the Police, and that of the People Inside.

They passed the police post and the wire gates, and were outside the village and on the road to the estate. A man grinned, a woman jeered. That dawn Fong Kiap had carried out a *kati* of pork between her thighs, Big Dog Tsou three messages on thin cigarette paper in his mouth, Old Heng's son an extra pair of drawers, and his mother, who had two other sons with the People Inside, six bullets from a revolver bought from a rapacious mata-mata on estate patrol fifteen days ago.

Neo and his wife, each with a baby tied to the body, with Son and Daughter astraddle the saddle carriers, rode the mile and a half to Division 1 of the Langtry rubber estate where they tapped, bumping and dipping on the uneven road, and came to their portion of trees to tap.

There was always a feeling of dissolution, a languid and inescapable stupor, a pause which fell upon the tapper when he walked under the trees arched so regularly overhead, in endlessly repeated criss-crossing alleyways. Perhaps it was the overwhelming uniformity of hundreds, thousands, tens of thousands of trees, equidistant from each other, all the same height and size, thousands of acres of rubber, millions of rubber trees. Not a breath of air moved under their identical foliage. At seven in the morning already the coolness was going. An insidious, moist heat oozed between the rows, clinging to the tappers' clothes, to their sweat-covered faces, their damp hands, and the knife handles. It was light enough to see the straight boles dappled with patches of silver and rust, girded with sloping broad belts of shorn bark. Along their lower rim the grey-white congealed latex of the night ended in a glazed runnel into the collecting cup, fastened with wire round each tree. Tree after tree after tree, through which the earth's damp rose, sucked upwards in the trunks, lifted drop by drop, to vanish, insubstantial vapour in the pale empty sky. Tree after tree after tree, quietly bleeding its white, smooth seeping blood, latex, into cups.

Daughter and Son ran ahead, stripping the greyish hardened latex along the cut, scrap rubber, to be handed in to the estate. Husband and wife followed quickly, sprinting from trunk to trunk, bending over the cuts like black parasites gorging, their tapping knives gouging thin, precise strips of bark. Too deep a nick, a careless slash, and the tree, wounded, would bleed to death. And now so many trees in rows were slashed at night, by the People Inside.

The sky, now blue, was peopling itself with the white, full-bellied muster of rotund morning clouds. Leaden-footed, the heat trod in the orderly man-made jungle of rubber. Mosquitoes sing-songed round the tappers' heads, then dropped to the damp hollows in the clefts of boughs. A stray bulbul began to state its beauty-haunted tune, but lost the thread, faltered and stopped. A muted lowing echoed distantly from the cattle of the Tamil rubber tappers who tapped Division 2 and 3 of the estate.

At this time of the morning, all over Malaya's gigantic monotony of rubber trees, tappers were tapping, as Neo and his wife, gouging the bark, stripping, and sprinting to another tree; a performance repeated hour by hour, tree after tree after tree. Cut, strip, sprint; cut, strip, sprint. All over Malaya, rich and creamy, languorously drop by drop, the white latex dripped into the cups.

Ten o'clock. Neo had finished five hundred trees and his wife three hundred. They stopped, trembling with weariness, unable to wipe the sweat off their faces, licking their dry lips with dry tongues, tasting the salt on their skin. Son and Daughter lay on the ground. Silently, they all shared the water from the bottle. Aching cramps in their muscles, aching bellies. Sweat and hunger. But they would have no food, and nothing else till two in the afternoon when they returned. For such now was the harsh law: No food out of the fence; to starve the People Inside. Now they would collect the latex from the cups, pour it in pails, carry the pails to the collecting shed for weighing, watch it immersed in the coagulating tank, hand in the scrap rubber. They would chalk up with the head of the labour lines their daily wage, paid to them once a month, within the fence, by the estate manager.

It was this afternoon, Neo remembered, that he was getting paid. The babies cried, and Neo Saw gave each a breast to ease them. Two o'clock in the afternoon before they would be back inside the fence, and hastily finish the remnants of the morning meal. Then Son would go to the schoolmaster whom the tappers paid to teach their children, Daughter would clean the house, Neo Saw would wash the clothes, go to the shop to buy food, and cook the evening meal. Two meals a day. Neo Saw found it hard taking the small ones with her to tap. But there was no one to look after them without money. And if she did not tap, there would not be enough money for food.

It was then they heard the screams. The first was the worst of all, a long, terrifying ululation, rising and rising and suddenly bent off in the middle, then two short screams, then moans, and silence.

Daughter and Son, still unguarded, looked up, grey-faced with fear and exhaustion, and Son said: 'What is it?'

'Hush,' said Neo Saw roughly. 'We have not heard. We never listen. We do not know.'

Neo turned to curse his daughter, meaning the words for his son. 'Busying yourself with what is not your concern. Come and help me collect the latex, quick.'

They rose and started emptying the cups into the pails, keeping their eyes fixed on the latex which ran, smooth as milk, into the pails. Soon the pails were full with the first load, and, staggering a little, panting as they carried, their hearts beating against their chest walls with fear and weariness, they clenched their jaws, and set off at a quick, swinging trot towards the weighing shed.

On his second collecting trip Big Dog Tsou was waiting for Neo, squatting at ease beneath a rubber tree, and with him was a girl whom Neo had seen once before collecting subscriptions for the People Inside. And then Neo remembered, pay day this afternoon, subscriptions tonight and tomorrow. Neo remembered the girl. She was dressed as a rubber tapper and had a black handkerchief round her head and tied under her chin, as his wife had, framing her smile.

'Meeting, comrades,' said Big Dog Tsou, smiling.

And now out of the vaporous heat between the rubber trees they came, the tappers from the four corners of the estate, greeting Big Dog Tsou carefully.

'Tell your mother to carry the pails without me,' Neo told his son and, speaking of himself as of another person, 'tell her he will be back in half an hour.' And he followed Fong Kiap, waddling in front of him, again, as in a repetitious dream.

As he walked he found himself noticing, through the floating membranes of exhaustion, everything else alive, small things, like small silver fish going through an ever-spread net ... the bark of trees, scurfed with ridges, and the millimetre amplitudes of their cuts through which the pitiless white drip fell into the cups. In this part of the estate the lallang grass grew thick up to a man's thigh. This was the part of Division 1 abandoned to the People Inside by the mata-matas and the weeders, and the Estate Manager had not come round since the last shooting. The mark of the people Inside was over all, with slashed and dying trees.

'Truly,' thought Neo, words going through his mind as if spoken in his ear, 'truly the People Inside are strong and it is dangerous to go against them.' He passed a tree with a great dark gash, pith congealed. 'Fire and water,' he thought, 'we stand between fire and water, between the Police, and the People Inside.' And then they were at the old smoke house, with the derelict rubber press like a misshapen instrument of torture gone dead in the middle, for the wooden parts had burnt down and the rusty iron alone was left. About thirty tappers were there. Among them, dressed as tappers, the People of the Movement, eager and talking, going from one to the other, happy and excited.

Neo joined them, and saw the covering tarpaulin in the centre of the standing circle, a circumference of feet. And then the girl approached, smiling, with Big Dog Tsou, and removed the sheet, and Neo looked, and knew: 'This is Meng, who weighed the latex. That is why he was not weighing today.'

'Comrades,' said Big Dog Tsou, 'this was a traitor and we have punished him.'

There is knowledge that is not knowledge, not in words and yet inhabits the mind, informs it with facts and events. And although no one told the story, yet this is what Neo grew to know, without once acknowledging that he knew.

How Meng went to the Estate Assistant Manager one day, ostensibly because he was ill but really because he wanted to inform on the People Inside, for Meng was greedy for money, and the People Inside had a price on their heads, each one of them.

But the Estate Manager was away, and so Meng, in his impatient lust for money made of selling man to man, took the estate bus to town twenty miles away. And there, bold and daring (for as a weigher he had had some authority), he went to the police building.

When he came to the wire fence, secure and solid and always fresh round the large yellow building with black-painted rain-pipes running down its walls, he looked fearfully round, afraid of a watcher, and seeing no one pay heed, gleaned foolish courage from his ignorance and greed, and went in and asked to see the European officer, the white man. He could not trust one of his own race, not knowing whether they might be of the Movement, and anyway he did not want to pay blackmail money for ever after, to a Malay or Chinese detective.

The police post was open day and night. Informers were promised the strictest secrecy, but there is no secrecy in Asia, not for anything, and least of all in the Police, which is for ever buying and selling information and then writing it all down in many copies for anyone to read. If one is an Asian, no European officer will be there to go straight to and whisper, and then go out again by another door. In front of everyone in the waiting hall, one walks up to two Malay constables, and asks to see the white man, and there are always loiterers about the station, and in the entrance room.

But Meng was foolish. He sidled up to the mata-matas in charge and grinned and put his hand to his forehead in the recognized salutation, *tabek, tabek*, and asked in Malay: '*Tuan, orang puteh*, the white man?'

'He is out,' said one Malay, surly and suspicious because Meng was Chinese. 'What do you want?'

Meng wanted to go away. He backed, smiling, slapping his hand against his forehead again and again, but the Malay did not let him go. He rose from behind the desk, and with his companion advanced on Meng. 'Come, come,' he said, and Meng, resisting, was half-dragged, half-pushed inside the building. There was another Malay sitting behind a table, who said: 'Speak or I will put you in prison.'

Meng was terribly frightened, and he stuttered: '*Saya suka chakap orang jahat*,' which he intended to mean, 'I like to come here to speak of bandits,' but really what he said was, 'I like to speak of bad people.' Badness means communism in Malaya.

A smile widened on the face of the officer behind the desk. Tenderly he bent forward and said softly to Meng: 'Are you then a communist?'

'Yes, yes,' said Meng, a reflex action, because he always said 'yes' to a uniform, a stranger, in answer to a question not understood.

'Come, then, with me,' said the Malay, and two of them pulled him into another room, and then along a corridor, and suddenly he was pushed in a cell, the barred doors clanged behind him, locking him in.

'*Salah, salah!* A mistake, a mistake!' he cried and shook the bars, but the Malays laughed gently, and walked away. They were taking no chances. He might be an informer, he might be a surrendered bandit, he might be anything. They had him safe behind bars until the white man came back. The tuan would decide.

It was after curfew, which was at seven at night, when the tuan rang up to say he was back, and was there anything new?

'A surrendered bandit, tuan,' they told him.

'Good God,' said the police lieutenant, 'surrendered? I'll be there right away,' and jumped in his Morris and was soon at the station.

Meng was brought out of his cell in front of him, a Meng terrified, terrorized, wordless with fear. When he saw the police officer, he wanted to kneel down to him, but was prevented.

'Has he brought his gun?'

'No.'

'Oh!' The white man looked disappointed. 'What's his name?'

Meng sobbed, wrung his hands, gestured, screamed. It took an hour to make him talk, to say that he was a poor man weighing latex, come to the police station to ask for the address of a doctor. Meng had now decided to say nothing at all about the People Inside.

'You are sure you didn't speak about communists?'

No, no, all he said was he didn't know anything about communists. The white man shrugged his shoulders. He was very tired. It had been a long hot day.

'Oh hell,' he said, 'I can't understand half of what he says, his Malay is even worse than mine and nobody here can speak Chinese, anyway. Obviously this is just a poor guy frightened out of his wits. Let him go.'

And now it was night, dark swallower of the jungle, the huts, the roads and the barbed-wire fences, and too late for Meng to go home. He would have to wait in town till the curfew lifted. He wandered on the five-foot way and squatted with his back against a damp, fungus-eaten wall, and waited for dawn and the first bus drawling along the roads not yet flayed by the sun.

But Big Dog Tsou, back in the small wired-in village, had come in the previous afternoon to Meng's house, for Meng paid a larger subscription, being a weigher, and Big Dog Tsou wanted him to buy some medicines the next day, for the People Inside. 'He has already gone to town, to see a doctor,' his wife told Big Dog Tsou. And Big Dog Tsou wondered, knowing Meng healthy and avaricious.

At night Meng was not back. Big Dog Tsou, from the coffee shop of the village, rang a coffee shop in the town. Coffee shops are useful places: they relay telephone messages, they are accommodation addresses, they are underground post offices, and every small town, every village, has at least one, if not two, three or four coffee shops.

A young waiter, with sleek, brilliantined hair, in which he wore a large clip, and slippers on his feet, ambled out of the coffee shop in the town, and went strolling round the police station, and leaned against the fence, hands in pockets, enjoying the cool night. The prostitutes who waited for the Malay policemen to come out, passed and re-passed in front of him, plunging deep glances in his eyes, giggling and nudging each other. But he went on chewing gum indifferently, and it was he who saw Meng stagger out of the station, look fearfully round him, and sidle away to crouch in the five-foot way, to wait for the dawn bus back to his wired-in village.

4: The People Inside

Being the diary of communist terrorist (C.T.) CHAN AH PAK, *Wanted List No. 0789, member of the 10th Independent Regiment of the Malayan Races Liberation Army, in operation in the jungles of the State of Johore, Federation of Malaya.*

January 13 Comrade Sen addressed us for twenty minutes. We had eaten breakfast, and Ah Kei made burping noises for he suffers from stomach ulcers. Comrade Ah Low was publicly reprimanded for muddling the accounts of the Protection Corps and the Sabotage Squad. We held a minute's silence for Comrade Chong of the People's Movement who has been hanged by the criminal government. His age was twenty-one and he had been to school for four years. He was eager to educate himself further, and in his spare time, when he was not slashing rubber trees, collecting food, distributing pamphlets or otherwise working, he would read and study and attend meetings. He was caught by the pig-faced soldiers passing ammunition procured from a police post. Be peaceful, Comrade! You sacrificed your life gloriously for the Revolution! Thousands of young men will rise to take your place in the fight for freedom!

Ten new recruits are coming Inside for training. Some of them from Singapore.

January 31 Comrade Sen has left to report to the Central Executive Committee on the situation in our area. There are rumours of changes in tactics this year. We have had much success; food and money have flowed in from the people, and we have done a great deal of work. The comrades were speaking of Sen. We are impressed with his bearing, and want to make him our model. He has been longer Inside than many.

In our self-criticism meeting this evening Ah Mao made us laugh. He was criticizing himself, and considered his chief fault to be secrecy. We roared with laughter. Ah Mao is a gossipy duck. News pours through his mouth as water through a leaky pot. I was criticized for being aggressive in bearing towards the workers, and too critical of new helpers.

February 17 Our Corps Commander announced that a new teacher would soon arrive.

February 24 Weather clear. Cut a thousand yards of wire (seven comrades). Went to Langtry Estate and warned the Tamil weeders to stop weeding. The head contractor promised to obey us. Ah Low again made a mistake in collecting subscriptions from the workers. His cousin, Big Dog Tsou, invited us to his house after work. We changed into our rubber tapper clothes and went. We ate meat dumplings and drank coffee. Big Dog Tsou then took us behind the rubber smoke-house to collect our rice and meat, and also gave us two katis of smoked ham, sausages and some messages.

March 2 At today's meeting our Corps Commander informed us that we were blamed in our Red Star newspaper for not fulfilling our working plan last year. We were some thousands of trees behind plan, and our quota of executed traitors, estate managers and running dogs, fell short of the target. The Flag of Merit has gone to the Segamat Unit in North Johore. We are said to be idle, afraid of rain and bad weather, and so on.

We protested this was unfair. Ah Kei pointed out that the Segamat Regiment had only red-haired troops opposing them. Whereas here we were fighting the Gurkhas!

Now red-haired devils are clumsy, make loud noises, suffer from the heat and the leeches; but the Gurkhas are ferocious and noiseless as the Japanese whom they resemble. They come upon us suddenly with their knives, they are fond of cutting off heads to take back, and sometimes hands. This frightens the new comrades, who are afraid of becoming headless ghosts in death, wandering for ever in the jungle without escape.

March 14 General distribution of towels, cigarettes, a pen for me to keep accounts and copy books. An 'Uncle'[1] has arrived with some messages; he is new to this region, transferred from his courier route up north when the bandit Imperialists raided one of his junction posts.

March 29 Slashed two hundred and forty-seven trees (three comrades). Ah Low now collects food, and Ah Kei helps me with subscriptions. Yesterday collected three hundred dollars from Langtry estate, and also many small voluntary gifts from the people.

Ah Kei's wife, a food supplier, came Inside today. She fled just in time. A traitor had informed on our people there and the

[1] 'Uncle' is the jungle term for courier.

45

red-haired soldiers raided the estate. The soldiers captured her sister and her four children; Ah Kei's old mother hobbled after them (she has bound feet) screaming: 'Take me too, take me too.' She was afraid of starving if left behind, so they also took her away in a truck with many other workers. Ah Kei's wife wept as she told us this. Her daughter Mui Set is among those taken.

April 1 Burnt two buses of the reactionary Nam Fatt Bus Company, whose manager is a running-dog traitor. He co-operates with the British and refuses to subscribe to Party funds. But he will give us money now, as he cannot stand the loss of more buses.

April 4 Came to an agreement with the police constables on Langtry rubber estate. When we arrive they hand over one or two weapons and some ammunition, then fire in the air and pretend to have been attacked. We guarantee their safety. They will also forget to patrol the labour line fences in a certain area, and let the *lallang*[1] grass there grow high, so that our food suppliers slip through easily at night.

April 7 Two comrades have arrived from other camps to join us. One is my old friend Ah Lam. When we were children, our houses stood next to each other in Segamat town. Ah Lam left the town when the Japanese murderers arrived, and came Inside. At sixteen he joined the Organization, and fought in the Malayan People's Anti-Japanese Army, which is now our glorious Revolutionary Force in the jungle, the Malayan Races Liberation Army.

When the Japanese surrendered, Ah Lam marched in the Victory Parade in Singapore, and the British who re-occupied our country gave him a medal and three hundred dollars for his gun. But when they began to arrest our comrades here and there, Ah Lam returned Inside.

His soul is steeped in bitterness, for his father and mother have been killed by the Japanese, and his only sister and her three small children were killed by the Malays in a massacre of our people during the re-occupation by the British after the war.

The other comrade is a female, shifted from an estate near Labis, where she had organized the women workers and col-

[1] *Lallang*: long grass.

lected subscriptions. Her Party name is Small Cloud.

April 10 The new teacher has arrived. He is thin and suffers from tuberculosis and is always swallowing medicines. He has a shrill, high voice and can be heard very clearly.

Went out with ambush party. Burnt an estate lorry and lectured the workers. Reprimanded two recruits for complaining about the leeches. It is most important not to notice the jungle we live in. To live in it, we must be unaware of it, and walk as if it were the wide streets of a city. That is why the red-haired devils suffer much when they enter it; they notice every patch of swamp, every thorn and leaf, they are frightened of the tangled leaves, the caged-in heat, the caterpillars like moss, and the moss that comes alive under one's hand. Once we begin to notice the jungle, it is not possible to go on living in it very long.

April 28 It will soon be our tremendous anniversary, Workers' Day, and food is coming in to us from the people outside for a feast. The new recruits are thinking of their homes and telling about what they do at home, what they eat, and so on. Stopped them as it is bad for morale.

Stayed the night in Fong Kiap's house with members of Sabotage Squad in Langtry estate. In the morning set off to transport foodstuffs. We separated and warned all food collectors on two or three estates. After that had nothing to do but read all afternoon. After our meal at five, got ready. Walked back in the direction of Langtry Estate, but warned of an ambush. Meeting place was changed. Met our food suppliers and began our work. Everybody was very happy and there was so much to carry, some of us set off to get help. Finally there were about twenty of us. The young workers of the Movement were so happy carrying the foodstuffs that they were about to come in a group and join us. Things were so plentiful, that we had to make the journey twice. Half way, comrades of the Sabotage Squad came to help us. Small Cloud cooked the food for us, with Ah Kei's wife helping her. Small Cloud is a good comrade, always cheerful. In the evening sang songs and told stories of our childhood days.

May 15 Executed a traitor named Meng on Langtry Estate by tying him to a rubber tree and hacking him with a *changkol*.[1]

[1] *Changkol*: a sharp spade.

Big Dog Tsou then showed him to the tappers, so that they would understand his treachery, and our might.

May 30 Comrade Sen returned. New directives: To become more selective in our targets; to avoid antagonizing the people or frightening them; wherever possible to lecture them. To pick out only estate managers who are hated by the workers, and spare the others. To be friendly to Malays and show respect and consideration for their religion.

Comrade Sen interrogated the recruits and spoke with Ah Lam and Small Cloud. It is Ah Lam's birthday, he is twenty-four and has now been eight years in the Organization. Except for one year outside, all this time he has been Inside. I gave him some cigarettes and a new diary book. In the evening cleaned and oiled our weapons and talked of the old days under the Japanese devil oppressors.

June 5 Small Cloud brought us some nipah palm, coconuts, pork and two chickens. She has been to Langtry estate and had bad news. After the punishment of Meng the traitor, Big Dog Tsou, Fong Kiap and some other rubber tappers have been taken away by the police. Like a net, the police catch all kinds of fish, useful and worthless!

But this is nothing. The Organization works everywhere. In detention camps such men as Big Dog Tsou will know how to continue working for the Revolution.

June 10 Very rainy weather. The new teacher is ill and spits blood. His face is flushed with fever.

Ah Mao whispers that ex-Comrade Loke at Segamat has been executed by the Organization for deviationism and treachery. He was spreading defeatism through the units, that our tactics were wrong, that people in the Resettlement Camps were getting frightened of us, nearly as frightened as they are of the British and Malay Police. Sen is here and Ah Kei wonders whether he is looking for deviationists. Certainly he will find none in our camp!

July 1 Last night we launched a mass attack on Ulu Cheli Resettlement Camp.

The people of Ulu Cheli hate and fear the oppressors. They were farmers living on jungle clearings. All through the Japanese war they supplied our troops with food. When times changed, they did not, but went on helping us, in spite of threats. One day the British imperialist soldiers came and took them all away in trucks, burning down their huts and their crops, and slaughtering their pigs. That was six months ago. For two days the people were in trucks. The sun beat upon them and they had no food or drink. Then they were brought to Ulu Cheli and put in a camp with a wire fence round them, to stop them passing food to us. When the British had decided on this camp they had seen the land in the dry season, but when they brought the people it was mud in the monsoon. They ringed the camp with wire, and ordered them to start their huts and lives again.

How could the people build huts on this flooded land? Water came up to their ankles, and many children became sick. The red-haired devils came, and looked, and went; more came, and shook their heads. And they told the people to be patient, and brought some stones and sand and laid it on the mud. Now the people have found work rubber-tapping on the estates round them, and have put up their huts. They cannot grow much food, and they hate the British with a great silence.

So this morning when the sky was still darker than the belly of a fish, we launched our attack on Ulu Cheli.

We waited in the lallang grass outside the barbed wire fence stretching round the camp. Inside the fence, huddled near the closed gates, we could see the women waiting with their latex pails, their tapping knives and their children. The bolder women were grumbling because already it was getting light in the east, yet the mata-mata had not opened the gates. And that meant going out later in the heat of the day collecting the latex, and neither they nor their children would eat or drink for the next eight or nine hours, until afternoon, when they stop tapping and return home.

At last someone went and rapped on the closed door of the police post; the Malay came out, sleepy, dressed in a torn sarong and holding a shotgun. He did not search the women for food hidden on their bodies, he was too sleepy. He opened the gates. At that moment we sprang at him out of the darkness and the tall grass, and gagged him and took him away before he could shout. The women and children were frightened but before they could cry out, Ah Kei said quickly and clearly, pointing to the star on his cap: 'Don't worry, it is us, the People Inside.' They knew us at once, and walked out quietly looking straight in front of them as if we were so much mist and nothing to be seen.

We then rushed the post. There were four more policemen. We sprang on them before they could rise. One of them, Ah Lam recognized as having been a torturer of our people, an informer in Japanese times, who led parties of Japanese devil-soldiers in Segamat looking for Chinese girls to rape. So we hacked him to pieces with his own *parang*.[1]

The others begged us to let them go. We made them say they hated their masters, the British, who treated them like lapdogs; that they only did this work for food; and so on. We made them apologize and promise to help us. They gave us food and ammunition, eighty rounds and three rifles and a pistol. We burnt the police post and went back to the jungle. Thus we avenged the wrongs of our people.

Tonight the red-haired troops have arrived and are searching the district. No one in Ulu Cheli is allowed out of huts, even to go to the latrines outside. The soldiers are searching each house and each person. But the news of our justice has spread, and the rubber estates will know about it.

July 15 The people of Ulu Cheli have been taken away in trucks to a detention camp. Yesterday an officer holding a stick came with an interpreter, and shouted at them, calling them wicked and bandit-helpers. The women muttered to each other: 'You have burnt our homes and killed our pigs and wasted our crops. You have put us in this mud hole where our children die. Heaven has eyes. We appeal to Heaven.'

But one or two said: 'If the People Inside had not attacked the police, we would not suffer thus.' They did not understand the tactical necessity of our action.

July 20 Troops are searching this area, and prices are offered for our capture. We crossed the swamp to the north and after a day's march arrived at another of our camps. I said to Ah Kei that it was like in the old days, fighting the Japanese. Old comrades like ourselves who had a taste for the jungle do not find it difficult. We are tough and trained. But recruits are too enthusiastic at the beginning, get disheartened, and then are tempted back to the prison outside. Some of them have come Inside through spite, or temper, and have no proper thought-training or knowledge of revolutionary principles. Many are

[1] *Parang*: a heavy-bladed short sword.

50

now coming Inside because of the government Manpower Regulations. They are frightened of being forced by the British into the Police or Army. But these young men and girls are often soft and subjective. Some will surrender and turn traitor if hardships come.

Comrade Small Cloud said that when she was tapping near Labis town she and her girl friends often incited the young men to come Inside. Her girl friends teased the young men that unless they had connection with the Organization they would never marry them. 'Do you want to be one of our People Inside, or do you want to become a pig-faced soldier?', they would ask the young men. My respect and admiration for Small Cloud grows daily.

August 24 Our new teacher is very stingy with his medicines. He is always sending messages through our couriers, asking for drugs. Our new 'Uncle' puts these slips in a hole in his tooth. Today I had a headache and asked him to give me some Tiger Balm. He replied that he did not have any. He is popular with the new recruits because he will compose songs, teach wrestling, sing scraps of opera. But he is unable to find his way in the jungle and never dares leave camp at all.

August 28 Comrade Sen is here again. There is a rumour of two people executed at the next camp for deviationism. Comrade Sen reviewed our achievements. Out of forty-six thousand trees slashed last month, thirty-four thousand were slashed in our State. The night train has been derailed twelve times in the past two months by people of our Unit. The imperialists go in fear of their lives, rushing about in armoured cars, forcibly recruiting thousands of ignorant Malays in their Police and Army Forces. They are bringing more red-haired troops from Overseas, they say it costs them half a million dollars a day to fight us. They confess they have a hundred and fifty thousand soldiers and police against us. They also say that we are a mere handful of five thousand 'bandits'. Yet they have kidnapped in their prisons and in their detention camps thirty-five thousand people, and put half a million more behind barbed wire in resettlement camps!

At the end of our meeting we were filled with hope and strength, and clapped hands and shouted slogans.

September 1 Small Cloud told me that her mother had been

detained six months ago, together with her small brother. She is able to pass news to her mother in detention camp because another woman there, who is friendly with her mother, has a cousin married to a Malay mata-mata in the camp. He costs very little. There is also a girl police informer who sleeps with one of the white police officers; she is willing to help if she is paid. I was astonished by the amount of information that Small Cloud is able to pick up about everyone and everything. I said I hoped she had reported all this to our Corps Commander. She said Comrade Sen knew about it.

September 5 Comrade Ah Mao is dribbling stories again. He says that Sen and Small Cloud are having a love affair and have asked the Party to approve their union.

I reprimanded Ah Mao for his gossip. Time and again Ah Mao makes up stories about comrades. He was a travelling salesman for bicycle spare parts, and did much work for us turning grenade casings on a lathe in a garage in Singapore, before the police raided it and he came Inside. In spite of his subjective attitude, everyone puts up with him; he is very capable with weapons.

September 10 Suffering from headache. Our Corps Commander gave me malaria pills. One of our new recruits has brought a Brownie camera with him and took a picture of me while I was sleeping. The new comrades like to take group pictures of themselves in full kit. Some are quite foolish, although old in years; the youngest is already eighteen. When I look at them, I feel as if I were an old man of forty, and can scarcely remember that I am not quite twenty-two.

September 26 Execution in our camp.

Small Cloud and I were computing food expenses for the Sabotage Squad. Suddenly we were called to a meeting. The traitor was kneeling, hands tied behind his back. I did not know him. Ah Kei said he used to leave rice bags for some of our units, but informed the police on us, and it had been decided to punish him.

Ah Mao stepped forward and told how they had captured the traitor. Four comrades had gone to the shop where he was staying, next to the smoke-house where the workers bring the rubber to the presses. They waited for him, but he did not come. They went to his house, and saw him walking up the road. He did not suspect anything. Ah Mao told him to come for a walk in the jungle, as there was something important that the Corps Commander wanted to say to him. Then the traitor said he was too busy, he would come tomorrow. So Ah Kei suddenly told him to put his hands up and not to move. He tried to run away, but one comrade tripped him up. They tied him with rope and led him through the rubber to our camp.

Our Corps Commander, head of Sabotage Squad, and the teacher were the judges. The traitor was asked why he passed information to our oppressors. He said he had not passed true information, only pretended to do so, because the detective was suspicious of him, and always coming suddenly to his house, asking him questions, and threatening him. Once, he said, he had got into great trouble for stopping his rice lorry in a side road. He was just going to dump some rice for us, but six of the police suddenly came upon him. They took him to the Station and questioned him for hours, but all the information he gave them was made up, and without value.

But Ah Mao then shouted that it was his information which had led to the capture of two of our food suppliers by the Gurkhas. The traitor denied this, but the evidence was against him; he had received two hundred dollars for his betrayal. He began to weep, and said he had to give a little information to save himself, but he had been faithful and loyal to us, and often supplied us with food. But our temper was up, so he was sentenced to death and we chopped his head off with an axe, after making him dig his own grave.

After supper we were still talking about the judgment, and how the traitor was questioned, how he was caught, and how he died.

October 5 It is now official that the Party has been asked to approve the union between Comrade Sen and Comrade Small Cloud.

October 6 I met Small Cloud alone washing vegetables on the river edge. At this place it is quite pleasant, there is a small clearing sloping to the river, and the ground is firm. One can see the mangrove on the opposite bank, with its many roots like thick, water-swollen fingers grasping the water, and all around the snake-thick roots are the many thousands of small spiky mangrove shoots, sharp as needles, piercing the smooth river for many hundred paces. I said jokingly: 'I must congratulate you,

Comrade Small Cloud.' She did not answer me, but blushed crimson and walked away.

October 17 Ten of us in ambush liquidated three oppressors near the main water pipe, about seven miles from here. One red-haired devil and two Chinese traitors were executed. We tied up the four Malay special constables, removed their rifles and equipment and lectured them. Others of our Unit lectured workers at public meetings on the estate, distributed pamphlets, planted flags, slashed trees and so on.

October 30 Today in the rubber met a Tamil tapper who ran away when he saw me. I shot him, as I was afraid that he might report to the Police. He fell on his face and kicked his legs several times. I wondered that the soles of his feet should be so pale, when the rest of his skin was so dark. On returning I reported the matter and was severely reprimanded for killing without sufficient reason. I argued, however, that it was necessary as the man was surely an enemy; why did he run away when he saw me?

November 1 Ah Mao is in trouble. When he was in another part of the jungle, he started a love affair with a female comrade. The Party did not approve as Ah Mao is married and his old wife is in detention camp with his three children. But the woman and he have been corresponding secretly, hoping the Party would reverse its decision. Today Ah Mao heard that his friend has been transferred up North, and has decided to break her relationship with him. So he is sad, and for once his tongue does not wag in his head.

December 10 Terrible things have happened; I have been unable to write my diary, but now it is possible for me to tell what happened in the past few weeks.

On Nov. 2 our camp was suddenly attacked by troops newly come to the area. Luckily half of us had moved away two days before, but the other half were not to move for a week. We rushed for our weapons when the alarm was given, but already the troops were upon us, firing. Luckily they were not the Gurkhas, but red-haired devil troops; many of us were able to run away. I was lucky for I was dressed and preparing to go to work, and saved all my equipment and my diary. But it was not so for others. With Ah Mao and Ah Kei I crept through the spear-grass and escaped, but then I heard the sound of weeping and crying. I could not see but I knew it was Small Cloud that they had caught.

For two days and two nights we walked, resting only a few hours at a time, crossing the jungle and the swamps. The soldiers did not follow us. We came to a resting place where we had some workers. There we found some more of our people. We rested and after a few days we received a message to come to this place. So here we are.

I heard through our workers and the tappers and our friends, how Small Cloud was captured, and four comrades were killed, how she was twisting her arms and weeping as the pig-faces dragged her away.

December 15 We have been reorganized. In twos and threes we are to proceed to another area. Our main task will be to look after our communications with Singapore. We shall be based near Todak. Todak has nearly 8000 people, many of them Hakkas, whose men are with us, the People Inside.

It is important for us, Comrade Sen said, to keep supplies coming to our camps in the jungle. Food and equipment. Food we would get from the women of Todak, for it is only natural that the women outside should pass food to the friends of their husbands, their husbands, brothers and sons. Thus we shall always have enough to eat.

Finally Sen said: 'Remember that in the Organization there is no such thing as defeat. There is only change of tactics.' I watched his face; it was the same as usual. As if Small Cloud were still with us . . .

I am to protect one of our courier lines to Singapore from here. Perhaps I shall see my mother again. She has been an Aunt, a courier worker in the Movement for nearly ten years.

Up the gravel drive of Quovilla went the car, between the clipped green lawns of grass conjured by our headlights out of
smooth darkness. Bright hard stars protruded from the ebony
sky. The car climbed between the odorous frangipani to the
lighted porch, with its clusters of mock-marble columns, strung
with red, white and blue electric bulbs in honour of the guests.
On the front steps stood a small man wearing a pair of enormous glasses, and a sharkskin white coat and a black tie, both
loose on him. It was Quo Boon's number two confidential secretary, Mr. Chiap, who now bore down upon us beaming, raising
his hands above his head to indicate that we had reached the
right place.

'Welcome, welcome,' he cried, peering in front of him to discover the whereabouts of our hands, then shaking them deter-
minedly. 'Mr. Quo Boon will be delighted you have come at
last. We are all waiting for you ... oh, no, you're not late, not
late, it's quite early yet.'

As we went up the steps, a Malay syce with a black velvet
songkok upon his head, and a white buttoned uniform, with a
purple and silver-threaded sarong round his waist, got into our
car and smartly drove it away. Another car roared up the drive,
and Luke Davis came out of it with Maxine Gerrard, his
fiancée. Mr. Chiap repeated his welcome.

'Welcome, welcome, Mr. Davis, and Madame, we are all waiting for you.'

'That means we're damn late,' said Luke Davis.

'No, not late, not *very* late ... still some more to come,'
beamed Mr. Chiap.

Government House with its graded aides-de-camp, arrayed in
formal stiffness, could not outdo Quovilla in the fine pomp of
entertaining guests. Another of Quo Boon's henchmen waited
for us in the hall. It was Lam Teck, who often called Quo Boon
'Third Uncle', because their ancestors came from the same
village in China. I had already met him with Luke Davis; he
seemed to turn up everywhere.

Escorted by Lam, we walked into the reception room. Quovilla, built twenty years ago, was, as much of Singapore, grimly
1924 in everything but its bathrooms. Often Quo Boon spoke of
tearing it down and building it anew. He had many houses,

new, modern, streamlined, in the Federation and in Singapore. But he had grown fond of Quovilla, and contented himself with improving the sanitary arrangements; like all Asians, he knew the bathroom as a hallmark of progress.

There were so many people under the plaster cherubs grasping garlands of roses on the ceiling, the straight and blue blazing neon rods running round the walls dispensing acrid gusts of light, so many sitting or standing against the heavy carved furniture (Victorian Chinese), that it was only when looking for a chair to sit on that the hundred guests divided neatly, strictly as if they had never met, into their various racial professions.

In a cluster on the heavy settee and on other chairs covered with sanitarily white slips sat English women, police wives or wives to be, in flowery dresses, speaking intently and in an accumulation of high-pitched voices, with that emphasis which in tropical lands clings to details of housing, the servants' duplicities, and personal digestive troubles. On ornate upright chairs drawn against the wall, sat three Chinese women in long Chinese dresses with high collars, and three more dressed in the fashion of the *babas*,[1] with filmy *kebayas* and flowery sarongs. These smiled into infinity, not bothering to talk or to move. Two Malay women with the long flowing tunics of Johore hiding their slim bodies sat together, nervously holding hands; next to them stood their husband, a wizened little man, who occasionally emitted a loud squeal of laughter, then sucked at an empty pipe to check himself. The rest of the room was occupied by standing groups of men; British police officers in mess kit talking shop to other police officers in mess kit; or talking of the Emergency with government officials in lounge suits; Chinese towkays, belonging to the various companies, clans, guilds and associations of Quo Boon, who all, through their various trades and concerns, had to do with the police: timber merchants, who could not fell timber without police licences; contractors, who built houses for the government; rice merchants; rubber merchants; lorry company owners, who ran their trucks in food convoys up and down the roads, under police protection, in danger of ambush; sellers of barbed wire to a government which needed hundreds and hundreds of miles of barbed wire; they were all there, in tight little knots, with a uniformly fixed smile upon their faces, trying hard and always boisterously to appear at ease.

[1] *Babas* and *nonas*: names given to Chinese men and women born in Malaya whose families have been resident for a century or more.

Occasionally one would detach himself from the orbit of his own group: tiptoe perilously across the foot or two which separated him from a circle of white police officials, and, raising his glass, holding it with both hands, gesture that he wished to drink with one or the other Englishman. Upon which the white man, turning half round, would raise his eyebrows to manifest his delight, convulsively clutch his own glass and drink slowly, with every gesture of delectation and exquisite enjoyment. After which ceremony, with a sigh of relief and mutual bows and smiles of extreme good will, each would return to his own kind.

Among them circulated Cantonese amahs in black silk trousers and white tops, with smooth, oiled hair glossy as lacquer, carrying round trays of metal, advertising Tiger beer, upon which were placed glasses of whisky and brandy neat, while other girls in flowered tops and trousers reluctantly distributed soda water and ginger ale and ice cubes. And among them, like a lone ship purposeful among the vague and meandering waves of the ocean, preceded by the rumble of his own laughter, followed by two bodyguards with crew cuts and the shoulders of gorillas, exuding benevolence, friendliness and power, his greying hair strongly pushing upwards from his cranium, his round face with the massive rugged features, so deceptively cherubic in the photographs, his eyes black and young and alive, amused like a baby's, talking, shaking hands, holding a glass of brandy and knocking it against everyone else's, giving the impression of drinking by the tumblerful and scarcely moistening his lips, Quo Boon the banker, the rubber king, the millionaire, the company director, one of the men whose life, dedicated to create wealth, had created Malaya, Quo Boon went up and down, greeting his hundred guests.

'What a dear, sweet, nice little chap,' said Maxine Gerrard.

'We must learn to crawl,' said Sir Moksa, 'before we can walk.'

The banquet unwound itself through its set and multitudinous courses: sautéed prawns, walnut chicken, cold duck's liver, Chinese ham and abalone, shark's fins soup, and then the main dishes, one after another. There were ten round tables, and at each ten guests: two women, and eight men.

Sir Moksa sat on my right. In the middle of our table lay on a silver dish the brandy-coloured roast suckling pig indispensable to a proper feast, its snout turned towards us, its tail stuck out at the other end. Maxine exclaimed: 'Isn't it SWEET ... poor little thing!' The Malay gentleman politely sipped orange juice. He did not eat, all the food was contaminated with pork; but he was Quo Boon's friend, and came to lend his presence, and had eaten at home before coming.

Perhaps it was the sight of the piglet which interrupted Sir Moksa's profound cogitation within himself and made him turn his dark good looks upon me. Upon him sat true oriental dignity in its most mythical tradition. He showed none of the awkward and raucous haste to please which repels the rulers. On the contrary, his was the colonial phenomenon: in contact with alien rulers types emerge which in their faithful imitativeness are unconscious caricatures of their masters. His easy manner, courteous tone, made him trusted, if not trustworthy. Surely since he was so urbane, he must be sound, straightforward, loyal ... surely since he played such superb cricket, he must be a man of profound reasonableness. How else could the rulers judge their creatures but by their mastery of the conspicuous outward manifestations of their own habits? Sir Moksa was coming into prominence as a leading light in Malayan politics. His formula was simple and commended itself to those in authority: 'Go slow. No independence until we're quite, quite ready. We must learn to crawl before we can walk.'

'You must come to the inauguration of my new party. I have named it the "Progressively Independent Party". "Progressive", because we are really-go-ahead and enlightened. Our aims are to give everybody his due. Reform, not revolution. We must train ourselves for what lies ahead. Any undue haste will only upset everything. We must listen to those with long experience of ruling, not to the young and the foolish. Our party is supported by all the prominent people in the country, including the Colonial Government,' he added, looking at me with fiery eyes, as if he had just made a world-shaking discovery.

'I don't doubt it for a moment, with that slogan,' I replied.

'PIP's aim,' said Sir Moksa, '(that's the name of the party, for short) is to please EVERYBODY. We are truly representative of every interest in Malaya. We have therefore the backing of all the right people. Planters, tin miners, merchants, the rulers, of course' (he said it reverently) 'and ... erh ... the masses. The interest of the masses lies very close to the heart of PIP,' concluded Sir Moksa.

The laughter of Quo Boon floated to us from the next table. His Malay friend at our table giggled, sucked at his pipe, which gurgled emptily. This seemed to amuse him more, and he laughed softly to himself.

'Wonderful chap, Quo Boon, grand character, one of the best,' said Clerkwell, of the Malayan Civil Service, at our table.

'Where are your wives, *Enche*?'[1] I asked the Malay. This threw him into another merry fit.

'They've gone home. The older one is very shy of men. But the younger, ah ... she is wonderful. You must come and hear her speak. She is speaking next month in Malacca. Politically she is ferocious,' said Enche Ismail, and purred with laughter.

'Che Azamah your honoured wife would be invaluable to us in PIP,' said Sir Moksa. 'Too bad she's wasting her time with PUMO (that means the Practically Universal Malayan Organization : I used to belong to it, but left them, they wanted to walk before they could crawl).' This aside was to me.

'She's busy at the moment organizing the young Merdeka Girl Gudes,' answered her husband cheerfully. The word *Merdeka*, which is Malay for freedom, seemed to freeze Clerkwell, who muttered something about the loss of the good old virtues, 'even among the Malays ... freedom hallucinates them'.

'We can't let the Chinese have any say in this country,' Bob Stewart, Assistant Superintendent of Police, was saying to Maxine Gerrard in loud tones between bites of the crackling piglet's skin. 'What I say is, any Chinese who won't be loyal, must be deported ... ship the whole lot of them back to China.' Again he set to crunching the delicious crackled skin. 'Been moved myself fourteen times in the last two years,' he pursued between bouts of champing. 'Just get round to knowing the name of my deputy, and one or two inspectors, plough half through the files on my predecessors' desk, and bang, get transferred again ... the next chap carries on the war against the bandits.'

'It sounds like musical chairs to me,' said Maxine, tossing back her hair, and glancing proprietorially at Luke Davis, sitting at the next table : 'Hope Luke gets transferred to Singapore. At least he'll stay put.'

'Can't avoid being moved around in Malaya,' explained Bob. 'So many of the chaps away on their six months' furlough, or just coming back from it ... but I think fourteen transfers in two years is the record, so far,' he added, very pleased with this distinction.

At the next table Luke sat by one of Quo Boon's daughters, of whom no fewer than five were present. Three of them were in

[1] *Enche* or *Che* : a Malay honorific for both men and women.

kebayas, blouses with open collars and long sleeves, with scalloped embroidered edges, pinned, instead of buttoned, with gold pins encrusted with artificial diamonds, and wore sarongs. It was Malay and yet not Malay, being the dress of an older generation of Malay women. Thus did the nonas dress, Chinese women whose ancestors had lived here for over a century, and who had adopted many things from the Malays round them: the serenity, and some of the indolence; the old dress, and much of the language. 'Baba Chinese,' the new generation of Chinese called them. In Quo Boon's family, the older daughters wore baba dress; the younger, fiercely conscious of their Chineseness, would never do so. The Asian Revolution, Nationalism and the War, had come between.

The daughters of Quo Boon were numerous as were his sons; in police files their numbers, their multiple names (ungraciously labelled aliases by a Force complacently ignorant of Chinese name-customs) were often preceded or followed by question marks. Two informers had been planted in the household to follow its tangle of relationships. But the more information crept between the tan covers of the personal files, the more bewildering it all became. Quo Boon's children were not always his children; some were adopted children of impecunious friends; others had been given to him by members of his clan who knew the future of their sons and daughters brighter in his hands than in theirs. During the Japanese occupation, one of his energetic wives had rescued from starvation and adopted eighteen waifs and strays, among whom were four Tamils. All had been given Chinese names. It was a tribe, and not a family, which went under the name of 'offspring of subject Quo Boon', and no one had as yet been able to number them all.

An American journalist, on one of those hasty tours of South East Asia, once asked Quo Boon what was the secret of his success: Quo Boon looked pensive, smiled charmingly, and replied: 'Investment. The best investment of mankind is man.' Quo Boon never went outside his own kin and clan for managers, secretaries and book-keepers of his many concerns; even his bodyguards were, in emotion if not in blood, related to him: their grandfathers had been servants of his grandfather, back in the ancestors' country, a century ago.

The women next to whom Luke sat was a blood daughter of Quo Boon. In her face, the massive yet cherubic features of the father had shrunk, like those heads manipulated to a diminutive replica of themselves by some wild tribe of the Amazon basin.

Her nickname was The Abacus, her Chinese name Intellectual Orchid, and her English name Betty. The Abacus, renowned for her mathematical ability, was honoured as a financial genius by the men of her clan. Two of her teeth were edged with gold, which gave her a deceptively outmoded look. Gold teeth had been the fashion for wealthy débutantes in her youth. She had just returned from a fleeting trip round the world, which she discussed with sharp humour with Luke, and her latest venture was a company of taxis to run between Singapore and Kuala Lumpur. 'The train is derailed every night, and the planes are crowded. My taxis can do it in a day, easy.'

'But will anyone dare to board these taxis of yours? Suppose they get ambushed and burnt down, like the buses?'

Her long eyelids like willow leaves fluttered. 'There will always be business men in a hurry, who will want a taxi ... too bad not any red-hairs,' she added, demure and malicious.

'Wouldn't you just love a red-haired devil like me to be shot up in a taxi of yours?'

The Abacus laughed heartily, and deftly ladled the pigeons' eggs soup in silver bowls with a silver ladle. Mollified, she toasted him; he drank stengahs, and she orange juice. Obligingly, she proceeded to the business which lay behind the dinner.

'My father wants to discuss getting some special constables for his rubber estates near Todak Resettlement Camp.'

'I did not think it was love of us red-hairs which prompted him to give us such a banquet,' replied Luke, grinning.

'What you say, lah? On the contrary, he loves the Police Force. He calls you his friends.' The Abacus reverted to Malayan English, bantering, teasing Luke. 'We know how we depend on you ... we are very grateful,' she said.

'Rot,' said Luke. 'Don't rub it in.'

'Anyway,' said The Abacus, 'we are your real friends, although you don't know it, and you don't trust us, the Chinese. But my father wants special constables for his estates, and you don't give them to him. You give them to his neighbours on the right and on the left ... and why? Because they are white skins, like you. You don't give them to my father ... and then you blame him if his poor estate manager pays subscriptions to the jungle, because otherwise he gets hacked to pieces.'

'Special constables are not my department. You must ask the Chief.'

'My father is going to. Your new Chief. What is he like? I

hear he does not like us Chinese. He likes the Malays too much. A 'good-old-days' man.'

Luke glanced at his Chief, freshly down from Kuala Lumpur, armoured with a higher rank than the previous one, and with the obvious advantage of having been 'in the bag', a prisoner of the Japanese at the fall of Singapore. People who had been 'in the bag' together now stuck together, and formed the higher ranks of the official hierarchy up and down Malaya, in the Police and elsewhere.

Due to the Emergency, the Police Force was now vastly swollen in power and in numbers. Inflation of ranks and salaries was going on at a risk pace. One could not turn round without bumping into Senior Assistant Commissioners, Assistant Commissioners and Superintendents, promoted in the course of months. 'It is like a Police State,' thought Luke, 'and necessarily so, I suppose ... The Force is promoting itself now, in view of the pensions to come. Look at India. All the high ranks got pensions as soon as India became independent. We'll all get pensions when this country goes.'

And looking round him, suddenly, Luke saw this banquet in a different manner: no longer the ordinary tribute required from the local Chinese community to feast the advent of a new Police Chief, as of any other newly arrived official of the British Government; no longer the recognized pattern of the British levy, so much more easy-going than the Janpanese one; but the marshalled forces of law and order, and wealth and property, exhibiting their compact and their dependence upon each other, the owners of business and their bodyguards paying, in their own way, the uniformed white Force which was here to protect them.

And between the large array of white-sheeted tables, under the neon lights harshly dispensing vision so crude as to be hostile, there was friendliness but not friendship, laughter but not joy, for beside each man stood a watchful other one, knowing only the law of self-interest, the law of the jungle.

The jungle was never far. Not for Luke Davis. Others might lose it, forget it in a room like this one, looking through the black square of windows into a sky now gorgeously studded with gem-like stars, feeling only the marble floor underfoot. But the jungle was here, at the back of the minds of every one present.

'I'm sorry, I did not hear,' said Luke to The Abacus.

'I said,' replied The Abacus, 'that you have the reputation of being pro-Asian now, but of course you'll change when you marry.' Her glance, malicious, searched and found Maxine Gerrard, gesticulating as women do in the tropics, talking and laughing loud to prove she was having a good time.

'The Police are my best friends.' Quo Boon bent over the Police Chief he had thoughtfully placed at his left, the seat of honour, and filled his small plate with a tender morsel of sea slug. The Chief shivered as he looked at the grey, sponge-like and expensive blob upon his plate, and smiled politely at it from under his impeccable moustache.

'Ask me anything. I always do my best. But I expect in return a little understanding of my position ... appreciation of my difficulties ...' Quo Boon was genial. 'We the Chinese who co-operate with you in this country risk our lives all the time. I am afraid you forget it very often, Mr. Stallart.'

'I am sure,' said the Chief stiffly, 'that we all appreciate the loyal co-operation with government which you have exhibited in the past, Mr. Quo Boon.'

'And what do I get out of it?' Quo Boon's laughter rang out, cheerful, carefree, but his words were incisive. 'I could do so much more, my personal influence being not inconsiderable ... I might even persuade some of those poor young men who go to the jungle rather than take up a *glorious* career in your Force, to come out ... but you won't give me the chance.'

At Quo Boon's table sat his bodyguards and members of his own family, the new Chief and himself, so that no spies would tell the jungle what was said under the drowning noise of the banquet. But Quo Boon was too politic to pursue business other than by hints at the dinner table. He knew Englishmen considered it bad form. So waving his hand amiably, he added: 'But we'll discuss it later,' and rapped the table for silence, got up, and made the usual speech of welcome to a new government official ... 'How pleasant it was to have Mr. Stallart, with his long experience of Malaya ... he fully understood the local situation, hope he will not be transferred away too quickly ...' (At this dig even the government officials present permitted themselves a bleak smile.) ...

The new Police Chief also got up and made a speech praising the loyal co-operation of Quo Boon with the government. And then the party broke up. But The Abacus said to Luke: 'My father's secretary will come to your office tomorrow about the special constables,' and Luke knew he was to brief the Chief for the coming interview. And Lam Teck shook Luke by the hand, as a signal that he might come that night, with some information. The gentle small Malay whispered something in The Abacus's ear, and she went on picking her teeth with a wooden toothpick from the pink plastic holder on the table.

'I've arranged,' said Sir Moksa, 'for PIP to hold an inaugural ceremony to open a Branch in Johore Bahru next year. I talked about it to the Police Chief. Two hundred policemen will be on guard duty that day ... we'll get good protection.'

Lady Moksa's Chinese name was Fragrant Orchid, her nickname Moonface, and her English name Alice. Her sister, Musical Orchid, Sir Moksa's other wife, had been permanently retired to Switzerland upon Sir Moksa's elevation to the knighthood, and spent her time in a flat with windows shut, gambling incessantly. Alice – Moonface – Fragrant Orchid shrugged. 'Politics,' she said. 'No use to anyone. Why don't you stick to business and make money?'

'It is my duty,' replied Sir Moksa.

'And what if the communists come? You'll be shot ... It's all because the whites were stingy,' said Fragrant Orchid. 'If they'd offered the Anti-Japanese Army some land and a thousand dollars each for their guns in 1945, there would have been no Emergency. And now it's bandits, bandits, bandits, but we all know they're not bandits. They're soldiers, too. The more of them they kill, the more they are ... I don't think this will ever end.'

'Do you think,' asked Sir Moksa, who never listened to his wife, 'they'll make me a Legislative Councillor soon?'

'More trouble and expense,' replied Lady Moksa tartly. 'Good thing we've got some money from business, and my father, otherwise I don't know how I and your children would live ... I think you and father are mad, collaborating so openly with the red-hairs ... it's their fight, not ours. Pay and ask no questions,' said Fragrant Orchid sleepily.

'Darling,' said Maxine, 'what on earth could you find to talk about with this frightful little woman with the gold teeth?'

'She isn't frightful,' said Luke, 'she's quite intelligent really. And amusing.'

'You never looked at me at all,' said Maxine, pouting and tossing back her hair. It had been a very pretty, fetching gesture, tossing back a slight mane of sleek gold hair, two years ago, when Maxine had come to Singapore to work as a confidential secretary in the Colonial Government.

'I was working,' said Luke shortly.

'Darling, don't tell fibs.'

'Honestly.' Whatever he said, or did, Maxine could always put him in the wrong. His mind went back to the bachelorhood now ebbing from him of his first years in Malaya, during the British Military Administration, and before the white women, the mems, had returned to the land; ... to the pliable, docile Malays, to the pert, amusing Chinese, so thoroughly practical about love; but he put the memory away. Social intercourse had been easier then. Young Englishmen in Malaya went out freely with Asian friends. They still did, and chiefly when they were bachelors. But when the white woman came in, often – though not always – it no longer became easy, nor even at times possible. Luke wondered why, and found no answer. With the wife of his own kind, his social life, like a yoyo, would go back and forth between the club and the bungalow, consorting mainly with one's likes. With Maxine, he would no longer be able to see much of Lam Teck, only in secret, perhaps, feeling half guilty, telling Maxine that he was out working.

He wanted to marry Maxine. He wanted a European wife, not an Asian. Too well he knew what would happen otherwise. The half-formulated disaffection with his world would crystallize; the shaky certainties would become vague, obliterated; he would never be sure that he was doing the right thing, here and now. Maxine would save him from all this. She was so sure. Her voice said so.

'After all,' Maxine thought ... Fifty men to a woman in Singapore, they'd said. What rot. It had taken her two years to grab one and she was getting tired. She put one hand on his, looked in his eyes, and he smiled briefly, but the soreness remained.

'Pa,' said The Abacus to Quo Boon, 'I think the Police may be on the lookout for Pearl. She has been foolish again.'

'What is it this time?' Quo Boon sat, his guests gone, sipping his milk drink. He always had a glass of milk at night. He hated milk, but was told by his expensive doctor that it was good for him. Hence he drank it.

'Passing messages, posting newspapers ... the usual. Enche Ismail told me. His wife's cousin works in the Police Registry in Singapore. She saw the informer's report being translated, they know her name now as Pearl.'

66

Quo Boon sighed very softly. 'These young ones. These foolish young ones ... I will talk to her.'

'You know why she does it...' said The Abacus, 'she always loved her brother, all these years, she has written to him.'

'I'll see her tomorrow,' said Quo Boon. 'I'll tell her to stop. Find out if there's anything definite against her. If there is, I'll send her off to England, she could study there. Otherwise she'll run away one day, to the jungle, and no one will bring my daughter back to me ... not from the jungle....'

There was a picnic-with-charabancs air about the procession, but the charabancs were large, sleek cars, flanked by machine-gun turreted vehicles, front and back, and a jeep of mata-matas bristling with guns, thrown in for good measure. This was the official inspection committee on its once-a-year tour round the detention camp.

In the first car came Sir Moksa Bakrar, holding a striped blue Pyramid handkerchief in front of the lower half of his face. Next to him sat Mr. Poh Cho-yee, a hilarious and benevolent gentleman whose sparkling eyes refuged behind thick Rayban sun-glasses. Mr. Poh, owner of a string of pawnbroker shops and houses of dubious fame in the chief cities of Malaya, had been labelled 'traitor' by the guerrillas in the jungle for colla-boration with the Japanese during the last war. This in turn had made him an earnest supporter of the British Military Ad-ministration when the British came back. The 200,000 dollars recently donated by Mr. Poh towards charity placed him in the customary honours' list, and on the Council of Inspection of Detention Camps, Malaya.

In the next car sat Mr. Clerkwell, whose eager face looked younger than his years, possessed of charm, a candid glance and a ruthless way of reporting everything he heard, and he heard a lot. Quo Boon, in a palm-beach suit; a Malay gentleman, dis-tantly related to the Prime Minister of a State; the Chief Police Officer, Mr. Stallart, filled the car.

'We're getting there,' said Clerkwell, who believed in chatty conversation. 'Just round that corner. Hope the driver knows the way. Hey! Stop! Stop! Stop!'

The eucalyptus trees had come to an end and beyond the unkempt tangle of gnarled rubber from an abandoned small-holding rose the *attap*[1] roofs, close pressed, and the four towers of the detention camp. Three high barbed-wire fences sur-rounded it. Four khaki-clad and smiling mata-matas struggled open the ponderous outer gates, and the mechanized procession wormed its way into the perimeter of the camp.

The men got out of the cars, shaking their trousers, which stuck damply to their thighs. Clerkwell paced up and down, breathed largely, and remarked on the excellent quality of the

[1] *Attap*: palm leaf roof.

air provided for the detainees.

'A healthy spot!' he said impetuously. 'Beautiful site! *I'd* like to live here. Wouldn't you, sir?' This remark he addressed to Mr. Poh, who opened his mouth wide and said: 'Yes, yes, yes,' happily chuckling at Clerkwell's wit, while his glasses gleamed in sudden terror ... ('Was Mr. Clerkwell joking, in the subtle manner of the British rulers, or did he really intend to relegate Mr. Poh to this salubrious spot one day?')

Sir Moksa Bakrar, to whom Clerkwell next communicated his delight with the atmosphere, took his handkerchief off his mouth for a moment, then put it in his pocket.

'Good morning, sir!' The Chinese interpreter now came up to Clerkwell: 'I am sorry the Commandant is not here yet. You are a little early. Please to follow me. Ah! Here is Commandant Hinchcliffe!'

Commander Hinchcliffe had changed his shirt after an early morning hurried tour round the camp, but already was damp right through. Six foot tall, and a great beer drinker, he was one of the kindest men alive. Although doing his job ably, he never forgot that detainees were human beings, and would aver that fully one-quarter of the people in detention camp had done no harm at all and were there by mistake. Of all the commandants, detention camps, Malaya, he was one of the best.

With a clang and drawl of wood the gates of the second enclosure were now drawn open and the party, on foot, walked around the offices, the police barracks and the huts where 'white' detainees, on their way to rehabilitation, were allowed to work during the day, twining rattan baskets, sewing slippers, cutting barbed wire for fences, and machining police uniforms. Hinchcliffe explained about the three grades of prisoners. The 'black' grade were the hardened ones, that had never shown the slightest willingness to co-operate; the surly ones; the really bad lot. His burred voice dropped to the whisper of official secrecy. Only a week ago the 'blacks' had again formed a communist cell within their enclosure, and some of the ring-leaders had been extracted and removed to solitary confinement ...

The 'greys' were the undecided ones, more or less good, more or less happy in their environment. But the 'whites', ah, the 'whites' ... Hinchcliffe straightened. His eyes sparkled with happiness. 'Those fellows,' he said, 'are the real nice chaps. They'll soon leave here and go to Taiping Camp to be rehabilitated.' In order to keep tabs on the prisoners, police informers were planted among them. 'But on the whole this is a good camp, gentlemen. Detainees, as you know, are not criminals. Many are in preventive detention ... erh ...' He caught Clerkwell's furious eye and desisted. 'We really do try to help them.' Suddenly enthusiastic, his blue eyes moistened, as he launched into his favourite story, the story of the detainee who came back:

'Poor old chap, we used to call him Grandpa ... he was brought in a swoop last year ... I don't think he'd hurt a fly ... in rags too, just picked up. I was pretty sure, when his case came up to the Committee of Review after his two years, that he'd get off. We used to let him knock about the garden, doing a spot of weeding ... the *mem*[1] was so sorry for him. Well, he got ill one day, awfully bad he was, groaning and moaning, carrying on with a bellyache. So we packed him off to the Hospital; and they took out his appendix, in no time. Well, Grandpa wasn't able to move for a week or so after that. The mata-mata sent to watch him got recalled here, and as we were short of staff, we never got round to sending another one. The Hospital forgot he was a prisoner and discharged Grandpa one fine morning, without first phoning us up. So there was Grandpa, a free man, on the road. We didn't know he was out, and it might have been weeks before we'd get round to asking the Hospital what they were doing to him.'

Hinchcliffe looked round, enjoying the suspense he had managed.

'Next thing we knew was at breakfast, when the mata-mata at the outer gate asked to speak to me. Said there was a chap outside wanting to come in. He'd been there since the previous afternoon, he said, and they'd already driven him off once or twice, but he kept on returning. Said he lived here, said he wanted to be let in ... can you imagine: wanting to be put in a detention camp ...? So I went down with the mata-mata, to the gate, and who did I see on the other side of the wire, sobbing with joy and kneeling in the road? Old Grandpa. He'd walked all the way up from the Hospital, and when he saw me, he was that happy? ... Kept on saying: "It's my home. I've nowhere else to go. I live here," he kept on telling the boys at the gate. My, was that man happy when I took him back!' Again he looked round, nodded: 'I believe,' he said solemnly, 'some of them have found more comfort and security inside the camp than out.'

The inspection committee stood between the tables where the

---

[1] *Mem* and *Tuan*: honorifics for female and male Europeans.

detainees sat at work. Smiling, as if for a camera, Sir Moksa leaned over a sewing machine, but found nothing to say. Quo Boon stood at the back and wiped his glasses and looked at the ceiling of the attap roof. Mr. Poh nodded vigorously, murmuring 'Home, yes, home, sweet home...', for he was having a good time, and so he should. Was he not holding power of attorney for several detainees who were still among the 'greys' or the 'blacks'? It was indeed a merry day for Mr. Poh, controlling the wealth of his friends behind barbed wire, friends once wealthy owners of rubber estates or timber felling areas, guilty of paying their subscription to the jungle. It was in vain they protested that they couldn't do otherwise, that had they refused they'd have been ambushed and shot or hacked to pieces. Mr. Poh was immensely relieved to find that not one of his friends had been promoted to the 'whites'.

The kitchens, the barracks of the 'greys'; the hut where across ten feet and a double hedge of barbed wire the detainees once a month were allowed to see their wives. They shouted cheerfully at each other. And then the 'blacks', with triple guards; and the cells, the huts, confined from each other by barbed wire. No tree, and no shade, and silence.

'Do they get anything to read?' asked Quo Boon.

'No,' said Hinchcliffe. 'It is difficult. What can they read? Lots of them can't read,' he added hastily.

The inspection body went by and from inside the barbed-wire fences the prisoners stared. They were all men in this section. They wore khaki shorts and no shirts.

'They're healthy, awfully healthy,' said Hinchcliffe. 'The doctor comes round once a month to inspect the camp.'

The Censorship department; where smiling Chinese girls opened the letters of the detainees and translated their contents. The Accounting department; where scrupulously the detainees' pocket money was recorded, their small daily pay, and any money sent to them by their families. And then going swiftly through the remaining 'grey' section of the men, and through triple wire fences they were at last in front of the women's and children's section. Mr. Poh and Sir Moksa were getting tired, but Hinchcliffe did not perceive it. Jovial he turned on the group, and suddenly motioned in front of him, through the last fence: 'I think our detainees have got up a small welcome party for you,' and pointed at the children of the camp, carefully graded in size in three rows, who on a shouted order raised their hands to their foreheads, screaming 'Tabek, tabek!' with great glee. Hinchcliffe looked happy, proud: 'We've got one hundred and fifty-four of them, with the babies, and a healthier lot of kids you couldn't find anywhere.'

Hinchcliffe's own small unpretentious bungalow, to which he now brought back the party, was within the outer wire, surrounded by its own fence and a fairly large-sized garden, where geese, hens and a turkey roamed. The inevitable red and yellow canna lilies stood at the door and two young detainees, good, hand-picked boys, cut the grass. A third one helped Cookie with the drinks, padding in with the trays on soft naked feet. Clerkwell was not sure that he liked this comparative freedom and made a mental note that Hinchcliffe was again becoming too kind. Mr. Poh also thought that it was dangerous.

'They may shoot you,' he said, and laughed the high-pitched, cackling laugh which reminded Hinchcliffe of his prize turkey.

'Are there any questions, gentlemen, before we leave?' asked Clerkwell. The iced beer and the fruit squash had been distributed and sipped, and he leaned back, benevolent, implying: 'I defy you to find anything wrong with our system. We are doing our best for these people.'

Sir Moksa wanted to know the exact numbers of men detainees, women and children, and wrote them down in a tan leather note-book. Mr. Poh wanted the police guard to be tripled. He thought there were not enough. He also thought that the detainees should be kept more busy.

Quo Boon asked: 'Tell me, Mr. Hinchcliffe, who and what decides whether a detainee will be white, grey or black? Is it their files, or the police reports while they are in the camp?'

Clerkwell jumped into the breach which the question had riven into the smooth landscape of the committee's approval.

'I don't think this concerns Mr. Hinchcliffe,' he said. 'It concerns the Revision Board. Every two years the detainees have a perfect right to appeal to the Revision Board for revision of their cases.'

Quo Boon withstood him.

'I know, but that is not what I am asking. When their appeal goes up to the Board they are not allowed to call witnesses. Everything is based on the reports made by the police and their previous files. Many of them, to my knowledge, are detained, because it is presumed that *if* free, they *might* give trouble. Under Emergency Regulations nothing more than suspicion is necessary for detention. So, I want to know whether Commandant Hinchcliffe or anybody else can help to clear them, with any information gathered during their ... ah, stay in this camp. What makes him grade them into white, grey and black?'

Hinchcliffe looked appealingly at Clerkwell, and then, with the courage of a good man much troubled, he said:

'I will tell you, Mr. Quo Boon. You have put me in a spot and this is confidential.' He looked round at the others. 'When they are sent here from other places I am not given the files. The files stay in Police Headquarters. I don't know anything about them except I'm told whether they are very bad or just bad. I've got nothing to do with their past. One day they're here, and that's where I start. Got to make up my mind and I make it up the only way I can ...'

'And that is ...?' prompted Quo Boon.

Hinchcliffe threw another agonized look at Clerkwell, but received no help. Clerkwell was smoking furiously; and so Hinchcliffe said:

'It all depends. If they're polite, if they salute and smile, and call me Tuan, call me Sir, when I go round; if the interpreter wallah tells me that they say how *happy* they are, then I put them among the whites. But if they're surly and bad-tempered, and won't answer my questions, and won't laugh, they stay among the blacks. Now, is that fair or isn't it?' And he looked at each in turn, for approval. His sad blue eyes betrayed the turmoil of his mind, the frustrated kindness of a man caught and trapped in his ignorance, knowing the system inadequate, but standing his ground. What else would you do in my place? his eyes seemed to ask. What else *could* you do? I do not speak the language. I do not understand these people. I am not told what else to do. What other measure have I got but the measure of their good behaviour, their servility when I walk among them through the camp? And isn't good behaviour the standard in every prison?

There were no further questions, and the party returned in the sleek black cars in the same order in which they had come.

Big Dog Tsou straightened the shantung silk along the paper pattern which Mrs. Stallart had left with him. Mem Stallart had rushed in the night before with the silk. 'I want my dress day after tomorrow, tailor. Mind, you had better start right away. Leave everything else.' Big Dog Tsou grinned and said: 'Can do, Mem, can do.' And then Mrs. Stallart had gone upstairs to see the Commandant's Mem, and the Commandant's Mem, later, had come down to Big Dog Tou's workroom.

'Be sure to finish that dress in time,' said Mem, wagging her finger at Big Dog Tsou. 'Otherwise, you get no more goodies from me, and back to camp you go,' and she tried to look severe. Big Dog Tsou showed that he knew it was a joke by hunching his shoulders, looking humble and frightened, but grinning too.

'O.K., Mem, O.K., Mem. I do, I do.' Big Dog Tsou had picked up quite a lot of English working as a tailor for the officers' wives of the town. All the mems needed dresses, but it was such a bore going to Singapore to order or to buy new dresses and, besides, passing the customs from Singapore to Malaya one had to pay tax on new clothes. Of course, the customs clerks were often frightened to search cars, and sitting at the wheel of the car with the boot full of liquor and clothes, one could nearly always get through by saying loud and clear: 'Nothing to declare!' But still there was a risk. Mrs. Clerkwell, for instance, had been caught the other day with a case of six bottles of whisky which she had not declared. The Malay customs official had insisted on looking through the boot, although Mrs. Clerkwell had lost her temper. After that all the ladies of the town became more cautious. They wore their new dresses on their bodies and brought them in only one at a time. They wore their new shoes and dirtied the soles. All very boring and tiresome.

Big Dog Tsou proved a godsend. It was the Commandant's wife who had discovered him when he had been promoted from 'black', through 'grey' to 'white'. 'A find, my dear!' she had screamed down the telephone at her friends. 'He will make up dresses in no time. He can make shirts, too! So convenient for our husbands. So cheap. I am fixing him up with a machine in my bungalow, downstairs, so that I can keep an eye on him while he works.' Big Dog Tsou had come out of camp into semi-freedom. Of course, for the clothes he made he could not expect to charge more than half of what an ordinary tailor would ask. 'Such a find!' said the Commandant's wife. Big Dog Tsou even had time to make little things for her on the side for which he charged not at all. 'Oh dear!' said the Commandant's wife, 'I don't know what I'll do when he's released!' For released Big Dog Tsou would be, for having proved himself decommunized by giving much sartorial satisfaction to the police and army wives of the town.

Big Dog Tsou grinned over the silk, pinning it to the pattern, cutting carefully with pinking scissors closely following the edge, and thought of the future and how, now that he was well in with the Police, he could get on with his real work, the

Organization. It would be easy; easier than before he had been in detention camp. He had learnt so much. From here he would go to Taiping Rehabilitation Camp. Big Dog Tsou liked the idea of Taiping. He no longer had to fend for his food ... three times a day the government fed him. Food, good and plentiful, far better than he could manage for himself when free. And in Taiping there was everything else : games to play, books to read ... After Taiping he would come back here, and with the help of the police mems, he would rent a small shop, if possible, next to an army camp. There he would work for the mems. Soon, reluctant to go out in the heat, they would ask him to come to their houses, to try on their dresses at home. This he would do willingly, he would walk inside the wire fences ringing these forbidden places, army camps, and the eyes and ears of his heart would be open. Big Dog Tsou was an intelligent man.

He thought again of the 'black' section where he had spent some months after the murder of Meng had been discovered. The police, called in by the estate manager, had surrounded the wired village and searched all the houses and questioned the tappers. Finally they'd taken half of them away. Some information must have leaked out, for Big Dog Tsou had been taken along with the innocent others. Then a few had been released, and again Big Dog Tsou wondered how the selection had been made; it seemed so random. For instance, the girl who collected subscriptions and had whipped the tarpaulin off the body of Meng, had been released, and now she had gone Inside. But Neo and his family had been taken, and Big Dog Tsou laughed to himself, well pleased that Neo the surly and the silent, so grudging in his subscriptions to the Organization, should have been put with the 'blacks', and be still among the 'blacks', and probably never come out from the 'black' section. 'His brain,' thought Big Dog Tsou, 'does not turn on itself quickly enough.' Big Dog Tsou's brain turned very quickly. It had taken him little time to find that all his jailers wanted was his servility. That was the key to freedom, there was no other. Big Dog Tsou knew himself to be a valuable member of the Movement. There was no gain in defiance. Wheedling, gentle, meek, submissive, Big Dog Tsou worked his way from 'black' to 'grey', and 'grey' to 'white'. He rediscovered his craft as a tailor for he had been a tailor's apprentice in his youth and for a time had made uniforms for the People Inside.

Invaluable now this art, for here he was outside the third wire fence, within the bungalow of the Commandant himself, the great white tuan, the eyes and ears of his heart well open, and making clothes for the mems of the rulers.

He could not help laughing, as he cut along the silk, laughter curling out of him in little hiccups.

'Tailor! Where are you, tailor?' It was Mem Hinchcliffe calling.

'Coming, Mem, coming!' Big Dog Tsou called back.

Bowing, smiling, cheerful, Big Dog Tsou sped out of the workroom to greet yet another white Mem, her arms carrying lengths of cottons and silks for frocks.

Hunger was painless desire, impotent need mounting as the heat steam mounted and danced in the endless vistas of the rubber jungle. It was thirst, however, which had terrorized Neo and his children. Thirst was not of the mouth, but of the whole body, a twisting of the entrails and a burning upwards into the mouth. Thirst made images dance like fountains spraying clear and delicate drops. Above the eyes a clamp, and giddy gold-black spots running softly round and round. Thirst was a terrible treacherous enemy, for ever waiting behind one to turn the undrinkable white milk of latex which rained into the pails into delicious water.

From six in the morning when the family went tapping until two in the afternoon when they returned, there was no food and drink but one small bottle of water between them, and often the mata-mata would taste the water to be sure that no sugar had been added, for that was forbidden. But still some tappers occasionally put a little sugar in, for the children, and were caught.

Neo had never done anything wrong about his hunger and his thirst and that of his wife and children. Never had he taken sugar out, nor rice. And yet he was in a detention camp. 'It is not fair,' he thought, 'it is not fair.' But further his thought, benumbed would not go. He had even stopped worrying about Neo Saw and the children, knowing that they too were behind wire, together.

Outside the attap huts of the 'black' section fell the rain, swirling sinous rivulets of yellow-red mud round the stilts of the huts. Here among the 'blacks' the prisoners did not speak one to the other, as among the 'greys' or the 'whites'. In unrainy weather they broke stones and carried sand. When it rained, they were confined, each to his cell, and the mata-matas walked along the sheltered wood verandas, peering in through the small barred window in the doors; and yet the 'black' section was full of news and silent talk.

Even Neo had picked up some of the secret passes and gestures, the drumming of fingers on wood, the talk of the secret societies. There was a way of lifting a stone which meant one thing, and there was a way of hammering it and how many blows of the hammer which meant another. All the time they talked thus to each other. And many of the things which happened outside were also known to the brotherhood within.

Neo did not know that he knew these things, incapable of describing his knowledge in words. With him the knowledge was like hunger and thirst, which bound all men to each other. And now imprisonment had become one of those wordless states through which one existed and felt and knew other's thoughts, not spoken of in words of man.

Outside the rain swept back and forth like the palms of a drummer on a skin drum; its relentless, high music changed pitch and tone whether it drummed upon the roofs or the pathways. Endless, wordless world of tones and sounds and messages conveyed by fingers drumming, rain beating down, slapping as dark-smooth fingers of hands upon the tight drum-skin of the earth. Even the rain carried messages.

When Neo and his companions, hunger and thirst, toiled in the rubber forests, where liquid white gold to be neither eaten nor drunk fell into his pails, rain had been an enemy, stoppage from work, gap in his daily wage. It had meant more hunger, more cramps in the belly, more dancing shadows in front of his eyes, more stifled sighing from Neo Saw, and weeping from the children. Sometimes if the rain came briefly while tapping they would not stop but wait for it to go, look heavenwards from under the leaves, and opening their mouths, drink the water that came trickling between the rubber trees.

The sallow young man with a tiger tattooed upon his left shoulder, the secret spring of messages that went through the 'black' sections held the men together in brotherhood; this sallow young man had suddenly gone, between six armed policemen, last week. It was his tattooed tiger which had both betrayed and saved him; and when he had gone, the drums of silence, hammering softly on plywood wall and stone, told how he had been bought out by the brotherhood, and now deported, sent to the ancestors' country.

Among those caged within the triple barbed-wire fence, and a forbidding wordlessness, a new leader would be selected from the inner ring of the 'black' section. There would be no meeting of men coming together as is done outside the wire fences, and yet each man would cast his vote. The predestined leader Neo had not seen but knew. He was so feared by the white-skins that he had not been allowed outside in the fresh air, for two months, in that other camp called the Camp of the Specials, one hundred miles from this one. Neo would vote for him like the others after the rain had stopped, for the drum song of the rain, loud and imperative, allowed no other talk.

'A sullen dog, a real bad one.' Thus the Commandant with the inspection tour trailing behind him like a pi-dog's tail, pointed at Neo breaking stones that morning before the rain, and playfully lifted his swagger stick, pretending to bring it down smartly on Neo's shoulders. But of course it was well known that the Camp Commandant had never beaten a prisoner, and the committee of inspection tittered as one man. Neo did not look up, his face was shut as usual. He would not smile. 'It is unfair,' he thought, 'it is unfair.' And the knowledge of this unfairness kept him from making the gestures, from giving the smile and the glance that would make this unfairness lighter. Neo might learn the secret passes that would make him communicate with others of the 'black' section, but he could never learn the language, the language that everybody outside the wire fence spoke to smoothen life, as stealthy murderers rub oil on their bodies to make the grasp of would-be pursuers futile: the language of smiles and servility.

And thus, although Big Dog Tsou who had murdered was now among the 'whites'; and Fong Kiap who had carried so much meat to the People Inside was in rehabilitation camp; Neo, who had done no wrong, but was unable to smile, sat in the 'black' section, listening to the rain.

7: Vipers, Little and Horned

Barbed wire surrounds the Nissen huts erected among the dusty pink buildings of Police Headquarters. In these huts were lodged surrendered terrorists, in police jargon, S.E.P.S (surrendered enemy personnel).

S.E.P.S were sent here from all parts of the State, after being used 'on the ground', which meant their immediate interrogation by a detective, and often leading Security troops straight back into the jungle, to their previous camps, to ambush their former comrades.

When their practical use in the jungle was over, they came here. It was better living than the jungle, and also better than what had come before the jungle. Here was shelter, food and seventy dollars a month. And very little work. Just talk. Tell everything. And a new sense of importance. A perception of their power, obtained from what they told.

Police Headquarters kept on tap Chinese and Malay inspectors and interrogators and translators. Hours, days, the interrogation of S.E.P.S proceeded. It was a thing which always astonished the English police officers: the readiness with which S.E.P.S poured out their life story, their passion for minute descriptive detail, their phenomenal memory of events, places, names and physical appearance of their contacts and comrades. One, a woman of fifty, who had been a communist courier, remembered thus over six hundred people.

After the statements in Chinese, translators took over and turned them into English. The welter of information would then be typed, and often ran to a document close to a hundred foolscap pages. The British Assistant Superintendent in charge would sift this material, check points, countercheck this confession with others already in the files, and classify the information. Some of it would go back to the 'ground', to be used by the army units; some would go to higher levels; to Kuala Lumpur for general information and overall planning. Thus, from all over Malaya, information slowly accumulated about the people inside the jungle.

S.E.P.S. were of great interest to the higher departments of Psychological Warfare, and to the American scholars who wanted to write theses on Asian communism for their doctorates. Few more exciting themes, or more appropriate, than those

79

gleaned in this tumultuous and tangled battlefield of hazy notions, misunderstood movement, revolution gone awry and colonialism preparing its subject country for independence. Few more immediate and burning questions than those that perhaps the S.E.P.S could answer: What makes a communist surrender? What makes a young man or girl go to the jungle in the first place?

In these psychological appraisals and studies of the motives and impulses which led the young to the armies of the People Inside, and then led them out again, Ah Mei found herself often the subject, the heroine, the chief commentator. Chiefly because, of course, she was not a S.E.P. She was that rarer bird, a C.E.P. (captured enemy personnel), and alive. C.E.P.S were hanged, or went to prison for life, for many years. Ah Mei was exceptional. Her crime, punishable by death, was deemed worth ten years rigorous imprisonment, but she was spared now, to dwell among the S.E.P.S.

'She is thoroughly decommunized. She has been, from the beginning, a most able and loyal helper of the Security Forces.' Thus the Police Chief committing himself in a minute on Ah Mei's personal file.

'A Red is a Red,' said Bob Stewart to me. He was the police expert on communism. Numerical inflation forced those officers who were making their number with their elders, keeping a watchful eye on promotion, to hack out for themselves niches as experts. There were experts on the art of writing pamphlets, experts on interrogation procedures, experts on Chinese methods of gambling, experts on opium smuggling, there was even a horse-betting expert in the Force. Among these experts Bob Stewart had been quite lost until placed in charge of the S.E.P.S. and transformed in a week into an expert on communism.

Bob pontificated: 'I've never read Marx, but I know a Red when I see one. That girl is fine. She's thoroughly decommunized.' (Bob looked exceptionally profound whenever he thus echoed the Chief.) 'When we plant her with some former comrades, trust Ah Mei to come out the next morning with the goods ... information? She's worth ten interrogators.'

'Does that make her utterly trustworthy, that she comes out with the goods on her former comrades?' I asked.

'She's turned right round, she's doing all she can to redeem herself. That girl is going to be our biggest asset, if we handle her right.'

Indeed Ah Mei was redeeming herself. I don't know how many pages her confessions ran to, but she was for ever adding to them. Her usefulness, the way in which she fulfilled every task assigned to her, had made the police lenient to her case. Instead of being in a prison cell, Ah Mei was here, among the S.E.P.S.

And here, too, Ah Mei proved herself. For in a matter of days she split on a scheme to blow up some of the police officers in Headquarters. Four disgruntled S.E.P.S, on one of their permitted journeys to see a film in a Singapore cinema, had contacted a comrade who was a lorry driver employed in the British Far East Land Forces, whose brother was the cook of one of the Colonels in charge of a British Army unit in Singapore. Through the lorry driver they obtained British Army grenades, smuggled them past the customs office at Johore Bahru (they were riding in a police car, and therefore not searched). Their intention was to pretend to have some valuable information, demand to see the Chief in his office, throw their grenades, and escape in the confusion. Unfortunately, they told Ah Mei.

In the Nissen huts there were about twenty to thirty S.E.P.S, all men except for Ah Mei, another girl, and for a brief while a fourteen-year-old called Mui Set.

Mui Set's father was Inside. Her mother and her aunt had supplied him and his comrades with food when they were rubber tapping on one of the European estates in Johore. It was easy, for the special constables were rather slack on that estate, and Ah Kei, her father, went in and out almost daily, and sometimes stayed the night with them. One day a worker in the Movement, one of the food suppliers, was caught and on questioning informed on them. The Army then raided the tappers. Mui Set's mother escaped, shouting to Mui Set to follow. But Mui Set had always been a slow child, and half-deaf, both her ear drums had perforated when she was a baby. The soldiers caught her easily, as well as Mui Set's aunt, and four children. Old grandmother stumbled after them, screaming: 'Take me also, take me or I shall starve if you leave me behind!' They took her, for it was a cardinal principle that families should, if possible, not be separated, but detained or deported together.

Mui Set was held in prison for a week. Ah Mei was planted on her, and Ah Mei asked her questions, many questions. Mui Set, dull and slow, answered as best she could.

Mui Set was up for trial, for consorting with bandits, which meant death by hanging. But it was then discovered that she was fourteen years old. The judge ordered her sent to a probation school for three years. She was too young for prison; too young to be with adults.

There were no probation schools for girls in Malaya when the judge delivered himself of this judgment. Mui Set could have gone to the local detention camp (over one hundred children under twelve were in it), but she was ordered to probation school, and nothing could be done till the case was reconsidered.

Clive Macaulay, the police officer in charge of Mui Set's case, did not know what to do with her. He was young, earnest, well-meaning, had been a travelling salesman for Shell Oil in the Midlands before coming to try his luck in the Police Force in Malaya.

He did his best and kept Mui Set alone in a room in Police Headquarters pending her ultimate disposal. To prevent accidents, such as a Malay mata-mata interfering with her, Macaulay locked the door.

Mui Set screamed and screamed. In the shack, among the rubber trees, she had never been alone. Now she was alone day and night.

Macaulay then tried keeping her at Police Headquarters, with the S.E.P.S. For a few days it seemed all right. Then regulations interfered. Mui Set was not technically of any value to Headquarters. No one could supervise her, she was slow-witted, fourteen, and there were many young ex-bandits about. Macaulay had to take her back and keep her in the locked room, meanwhile pressing for 'disposal of Mui Set, female, age fourteen'.

After a week of confinement, Mui Set was no longer a dull normal. She was mad. She understood nothing of what had happened, except that she was in the hands of these frightening red-haired devils who were hunting her father. At first she had called, sobbing, hour upon hour, for her mother. But now only screamed without stop: 'I want to die, I want to die!'

Macaulay took her to the Hospital. In the ward, Mui Set twisted and writhed on the bed. A wardress, a nurse and a doctor held her down. The wardress spoke to her, kindly, soothingly, but Mui Set was beyond human contact. She could only fill the ward with screams. The one hundred other patients in the ward became uneasy and disordered. Some were surgical cases, awaiting operation. Others were just recovering from operation. There were several heart failures, asthmatics, an old woman dying of cancer of the liver, two or three typhoids, the usual jumble in the single woman's ward. Along the corridors

Mui Set's screaming echoed and reverberated.

The houseman on duty decided to give her a sedative injection. He approached Mui Set with a syringe, and called two orderlies to hold her down. The injection had no effect. Finally they strapped her to a stretcher and took her by ambulance to the Mental Hospital. It was night; the doctor at the Mental Hospital, overworked and ill, gave orders to put her in a room by herself, since she was violent. Mui Set was left alone, and somehow the straitjacket was forgotten. The next morning, when they came for her, Mui Set was dead. She had strangled herself with the sleeve of her hospital gown.

Miss Lee alias Lee Mui (sister Lee) alias Lee Yok Ching (Moon Quietness) was found sprawled on a jungle path, in uniform, unarmed and starving, by the Security troops in Perak. She said she was on her way out of the jungle to surrender, and immediately proved her worth by giving information, leading to the discovery of two abandoned terrorist camps, the capture of a food supplier, the collective detention of a village, and the shooting of a Branch committee member. Miss Lee gained several hundred dollars in reward for the latter, who, as a high-ranking terrorist, had a price on his head. She bought herself new clothes, and ate well; she was particularly fond of drinking Guinness, which she found nourishing. As she began to fill out, a susceptible young Englishman in the Force bought her a radio and a bicycle. She was thereupon hurriedly removed from Perak and sent to the State furthest from it.

Miss Lee and Ah Mei, living in the S.E.P. quarters, grew restless. The male S.E.P.S who lived there had little to do between adding to their confessions, remembering more details about their lives in the jungle and the people they knew, appearing at trials to give evidence against former comrades, or being planted in prisons and detention camps to break up the cells which were forming; or going to the films in police cars. They drew seventy dollars a month steady from government; they were eating much better than they had ever done. With hands in their pockets, they loitered about a great deal of the time. Not surprisingly, they wooed Ah Mei, and Miss Lee, fairly often.

Ah Mei complained of this to the Chief, and suggested being employed in the household of a police officer. Everyone thought this an excellent idea. Servants were scarce, and fairly inefficient. They were mostly Hainanese, cookies and amahs whose profession was catering for the white families stationed in

Malaya. All immigration of cheap labour from China had stopped, and since the rubber boom the young Chinese girls went tapping rubber for higher wages than domestic service could ever give them. At least three police wives competed, with well dissimulated frenzy for Ah Mei's services. Later on, when the rehabilitation camp started turning out young girls decommunized but jobless, the Chinese bourgeois families of the town also started grabbing cheap servants.

It took Ah Mei three moves to come to me. In the first house, she complained, the mem changed the bed sheets every other day, made her wash them, and paid her only ten dollars a month. In the next, there were three small children, innumerable nappies, the mem had a foul temper, the tuan drank and then they had fights. I was her third move. I think she had planned to come to me from the start. 'I wanted to stay with you ever since I saw you in the Hospital,' she told me. I felt flattered then. Ah Mei was always and still is plausible, and I was, and remain, gulled by her beauty, disarmed by her charm.

Working for us she was always available to the Police. Confined within the limits of the little town, without an identity card, there was no need of a watch over her. With a police salary of seventy dollars, and nearly as much from me, her emoluments were equal to that of the highest paid servant in the town, the British Adviser's cook.

My own cook, a charming swindler, his seven ravenous and wolflike children, and his enormous and surly wife whom her husband loved desperately and who never did anything except drink coffee and belch, seemed to get on well with Ah Mei.

The first premonition of Miss Lee's extended visit to us was a magnificent bicycle parked in the hall when I returned from the Hospital one lunch time. A while later Ah Mei ascended the stairs to the living-room to tell me that Miss Lee had come to pay her a visit ... could she be allowed to stay a few days? The Police Chief allowed it. I said yes.

Miss Lee came up later to thank me for my hospitality. She too spoke Mandarin, learnt at a Chinese school and later practised in the jungle. She looked at our radio on its small table in a corner of the living-room. 'I have a much bigger one than that,' she said with charming candour.

'We are not wealthy,' I replied.

But Miss Lee was immune to sarcasm.

In the weeks that followed, the population of the s.e.p. quarters became addicted to our bungalow.

In twos and threes, they strolled up the drive. Some pulled their new felt hats (purchased in Singapore) at a smart angle on their sleek hair. They grinned when they saw me at the upstairs window, and waved, or called: 'Doctor!' politely. Some were tall and handsome, and others had brutish faces, and quite a few had the faint marks of cruelty round their smiling mouths; and nearly all had murdered, and all had betrayed; and though they stepped indolently, and looked sleek now, they had been in the jungle, and there was another life behind their smiling eyes.

They strolled to the servants' quarters, where Ah Mei and Miss Lee were indolently doing the washing (not too many sheets; for Ah Mei's sake, we changed only once a fortnight), and the cook's vociferous and restless children were playing with empty tins, or stuffing themselves with our bread, butter and jam. There would be sounds of gay laughter and bantering talk. The radio (Miss Lee's) would be turned on full blast, for half an hour or so.

In the evening, occasionally, they would come again, and sit round the servants' table, in the cool drop of night, while the fiery stars glowed overhead. Decorously they left, at half-past ten. We could hear Ah Mei and Miss Lee's giggles as they retired to their sleeping mats.

From time to time Ah Mei left us. A police car, slightly battered, driven by the Tamil police chauffeur (who wept such large tears upon my husband's shoulder the night his wife was bewitched by a Malay night-spirit), would stop in front of the house. A Chinese inspector, occasionally a British officer, would step out of it, asking for Ah Mei. He would say: 'We'll do our best to send her back soon ... as soon as she's got the info we want ... depends how quick she gets her work done.'

Ah Mei would be locked up in the prison cell with the suspect, always a young girl or a woman, a rubber tapper caught in a raid, or suspected of collecting subscriptions, or found with food outside the wire fences of the resettlement area, or informed upon, or perhaps just brought in on one of those swoops which, like a net catching fish, brought them in, to be sorted out later into the innocent and the probably guilty to be detained.

Usually the girl would be terrified. Sometimes, to soften her, if there was 'something' on her, she had been kept in solitary confinement for a few days or a week.

Names, names, what had really happened, who the girl was, her family – Ah Mei herself with her years in the People's Movement often supplied in her mind the background and the connecting links of which the suspect was ignorant, piecing the information she obtained with her own knowledge. Ah Mei always got the goods.

In the cell together they would sit and talk, united by common misfortune, Ah Mei a half smile on her face as she listened, rapt as a child listening to a story, never impatient, never obviously questioning, extracting from the unsuspecting suspect everything she could tell. When it was over, she would come back to write her report. She could not write it downstairs because Miss Lee was there, and the cook and his family. She wrote it upstairs, in our living-room.

I can still see her, bent under the reading-lamp at my desk, in her flowery top and trousers, her half-long hair sweeping forward, the intent, studious look upon her face, her pen scraping the paper. Sometimes she would pause, think, a child writing a composition, groping for the next sentence.

After an hour or so she would get up, smile at me.

'Doctor, would you like to read it?'

'No, Ah Mei, this is nothing to do with me.'

'I would not like to have made mistakes in words. I am not very educated.' I do not think that she really worried about mistakes; she seldom made any. She wanted me to read what she had written. Why?

I read, handed it back. 'There are no mistakes.'

A day or so later, sweeping my room, Ah Mei would come round to discussing her latest 'case'. Ah Mei had a natural delightful grace of movement which made her sweeping and dusting symbolic gestures rather than efficient ones. I did the housework again after her.

'That girl last week, it was really pitiful. She was not passing food at all. She was praying at the ancestors' grave. It was Ching Ming Festival. She brought food for the ancestors' spirits. They caught her. She cried so much.' 'They,' in our conversations, always meant the Police.

'You should have told them so in your report, Ah Mei. The trouble in this country is that nobody knows anything about anyone else's customs. That's why terrible mistakes are made.'

'I did write down what she said. But I hear she is up for trial all the same. They did not believe her. But of course the matamatas are Malay, the troops are British, and they punish us, the Chinese. There are many injustices today, doctor.'

'You can help a great deal, Ah Mei, you and the others, by telling the Police when they make mistakes.'

'But then they would not think I write good reports, if I cannot find something wrong.'

'But it cannot be right if it is not true. You must not find something wrong every time, Ah Mei.' I became very disturbed.

'There are a lot of private revenges being carried out now, doctor. People with a grudge will accuse their enemies to the Police, and the Police can never check, they never really know ... there are many mistakes, doctor.'

Sudden nausea seized me, as it did so often in these cruel and stupid days in Malaya. 'I know, Ah Mei.' The muddles of ignorance, the suspicions based on race, the heavy hand of Emergency Regulations, condemning without trial, needing not evidence but plausible suspicion. And that was enough to detain anyone for a minimum of two years. I did not want to discuss these things with Ah Mei.

'You must remember, Ah Mei, that the people in the jungle have done terrible things ... that they must be defeated. If no one helped them, they would quickly surrender. Then things would become more normal. The People Inside must be made to surrender.' I hammered the sentence, woodenly, exactly like an official of the Information Department, and to convince myself more than Ah Mei ... for after a few months in Malaya, I could no longer hide from myself my own conviction, that of this cruel and colossal muddle there could be no end with the means that were used.

'Surrender...' slowly Ah Mei blushed, up and up to the roots of her hair. 'Surrender, you say, doctor. Yes, some do surrender. But the good ones, they never surrender ... don't you think so, doctor?' Softly she said it, but in her face was all the passionate violence which I would never see again upon Ah Mei.

Barbed wire is incorporate to the land, another vegetation. It swings its leagues along the roads, unnoticed of motorists whose vision leaps the miles by the speedometer's mutation. It encloses the resettlement areas, where six hundred thousand ex-farmers now live. Thickened to triple depth and height, it bristles with the watchtowers of detention camps, loops around police posts, straggles up and down labour lines and factories, dodges the jungle to enclose the forests of rubber with their managers' bungalows, special constables' quarters, and machinery sheds. Barbed-wire wooden gates, flanked by sentry posts for police searches, open along the metalled roads winding through villages and towns. Unseen from the air barbed wire delimits the jungle, the front line palisades of its retreat. Barbed wire fences the clearings where man survives, and outside it is the grey-green toppling surge, all-engulfing, of the jungle.

Standing upon the small hillock of the church, within the resettlement area of Todak, Father Destier looked furiously around him. From that modest height the perimeter wire of the camp, frail and vulnerable wisp, threaded the air against the orderly grey boles of a rubber plantation, lost itself in the plots of tapioca and the banana clumps further towards the road. Angular as grasshopper legs, the stakes paced up the hill where the brown barracks of the police post of Todak dominated, in martial fashion, two thousand identical squatters' huts in uniform straggling rows of grey-brown attap leaf roofs, plywood walls, and tapioca and the privy at the back. The motor road ran east to west and cut Todak neatly in two; the higher land, with police post, church, huts and the Resettlement Officer's bungalow, and the low land, also covered with huts, slithering down into the mangrove swamp of the river. Against the horizon sky the jungle humped and reared, a shaggy, partly sliced prurient green broccoli.

Father Destier's anger was a priestly passion, the bursting ire of the missionary identified with his flock, forgetful of their sins in the tragedy of their punishment. 'Les imbéciles ...' he was muttering. 'Mais quels idiots. Sainte Vierge ... mais regardez moi doc ça.'

The Church militant, of which the French missionaries in the East are an exuberant expression, abounds in short-statured human dynamos. Father Destier painfully reached five foot one. His large head, Napoleonic profile and darting brown eyes were inadequately supported by short legs, round which a cassock gone russet wrapped itself tumultuously. His fingers were black with nicotine. Behind him, framed by the cloud-inhabited sky, rose a structure like a barn made of nailed planks, with a perilous crooked outer staircase leading to a veranda above, the whole edifice surmounted by a hunched attap roof and a wooden cross. Nailed above the front door a wooden board proclaimed in Chinese characters that this was the Catholic Church of Todak Resettlement Camp.

Father Destier had written to me a few days previously. 'You, as a Catholic and a doctor, would perhaps be interested to come to Todak. Here, and in the resettlement areas around, are more than ten thousand people without a doctor. It would be good if you could come sometimes. I ask not only for the faithful, but also and much more for the others, so many of these unfortunates have relatives in the jungle.'

I drove to Todak, one sultry Sunday morning, only to fall in the middle of a clampdown curfew, with police and army units doing house-to-house searches, armoured cars heavy with men and guns turned outwards patrolling the mud tracks between the rows of huts. Cars and lorries going through Todak were being turned back, except for military or official vehicles. Father Destier was waiting for me at the police searching post of the village gate. 'Don't for heaven's sake think it's as bad as this every day,' said the tired young army officer who checked me and my car (Father Destier in voluble half-French guaranteed I was *une doctoresse*). 'But I'm afraid the R.O. here has just been bumped off. Stinking business.'

'The Resettlement Officer,' explained Father Destier. 'He was found last night hanging on the barbed wire in the swamp over there with three bullet holes in his back.'

As we went up to the church, I could see little family groups, women and children and a few men, coming out of the huts and walking wordlessly down to the centre of the village, where a small level area, like a central village square, had been reserved for some public buildings to be erected later. Grey-green uniformed British soldiers in groups of twos and threes came out or went into the huts, looking for arms, ammunition, pamphlets, anything suspect. They brought bundles of clothing and cooking utensils, and threw them in heaps outside the huts. At a side of the main road was a chain of trucks and a prison lorry into which a few men and women were being led with their hands clasped on their heads.

Up the slope, stepping aside for the soldiers and the cars, Father Destier became more wrathful with every step. At the church door we stopped, looking down, and Father Destier muttering: *'Les idiots, les idiots.* As if they will ever arrest the real murderers. I knew it was coming, of course, and I know why ... Ah,' he turned, half-comical, half-woeful, to me, 'had the good God made me an Englishman, or given me the gift of speaking English correctly, perhaps "they" would have listened and this could have been prevented.'

A posse of two hundred men from a famous British regiment was combing the jungle round Todak. Four hundred more searched the rubber plantations, large and small, European and Asian, on both sides of the resettlement area. All the shops were closed, the region under curfew. 'Probably a twenty-two hour a day curfew. Only two hours a day will the people be allowed out of their shacks to draw water, buy food, throw away the refuse – the business of living.'

'And then "they" will bomb the jungle,' Father Destier was fiercely derisive. '... throw bombs among the trees. Paf, paf, paf. Psychological warfare, it's called. And strafing the area. Then the newspapers will say that Red hideouts have been smashed. Nobody but a few trees will have been smashed ... not even a wild pig. And then I suppose they will again move these people, transport them elsewhere, pull down the huts ... ha, if only I could have spoken *le bon Anglais*!'

'Calmez-vous, mon Père,' I soothed.

This was the beginning of my knowledge of Todak, and of Father Destier, and of Oliver Daley, later to become Resettlement Officer in place of the man who had been killed by the People Inside.

At the back of the church Father Destier lived in a hut of dimensions and beaten-earth floor identical with a squatter's. But the walls were lined half way up with shelves of books, and above the books were photographs of France, and a photograph of the wire fence, dramatic, reared against an orange setting sun. Above a picture of Christ pointing to his heart aureoled with golden rays was a motto painted in bright vermilion on cream paper, embellished with a painted garland of crosses and lilies:

> *Better to die young, worn out*
> *Than to get old, decaying*

Certainly Father Destier was doing his best to thin his span of years. His motor cycle tore along the roads of his parish, in the hot sun. Mass at Todak in the morning, mass at five in the afternoon for the rubber tappers who did not appear in the morning; in between, exhortations, family visits, very occasionally a conversion. ('But I have nothing to give them, and when I see them here, within the wire, I am ashamed to preach to them. The Protestant chapel over there gives five dollars a conversion.') Doctoring, which he had done in China, and continued in Malaya. Catechism, 'trying to turn the young from communism' ... negotiating for the purchase of a hut to be turned into a small nursery to keep the babies in the morning, when the mothers went to tap rubber. ...

With cups of excellent coffee, Father Destier poured out his bitterness and his biography. Earnest or humorous, passionate or soberly reflective, truculent or humbly contrite, his moods of fervent unreason or cold sanity were altogether self-forgetful. It was bitterness which prevailed, that morning at Todak.

'I've been here nearly a year. Yes, I was in China ... *ça se voit, n'est-ce pas? Ah, ça marque, la Chine, la grande et terrible Chine* ... I was priest for four years in a Hakka district in South China. Before that I was prisoner of war for five years in Germany. That was the good God's wisdom, you see, giving me, so long ago, the habit and the taste of the barbed wire. I have come back to it, as a familiar landscape; *"Au tournant de la vie de chacun, il y a un camp qui attend, avec du fil barbelé autour ..."* That is what a deported person once said to me. He had been in seventeen camps.'

His parish in China had been thirty scattered villages among the hills, all Hakka. 'As you know, the Hakka form a sub-group of their own. And when I came to Todak, I found fully seven out of ten people here were Hakkas ... you see, Providence again. It made it so easy for me to get on. In fact, they came, the people, as soon as they heard that I spoke Hakka as well as they, and, miraculously, some of them were relatives of parishioners of mine, back in China ... it gave me such a good start.'

Till 1950, Father Destier had been happy in China except for dysentery. 'The communists came, but they left me alone. The villagers gave a good report of me, and I went on for a few months.' In his voice sounded a naive and wistful pride.

'Then there was the Korean war, and suddenly there was suspicion in every eye. I went on, but after three months, very politely, they asked me to leave, gave me my ticket, put me on the train. My neighbour, the next priest, who lived thirty-four kilometres away (we visited each other once every two months – it was a three-day expedition every time in a sedan chair, up ten hills and fording three rivers), was not so lucky. He was accused of spying and sent to prison and worried himself so much that when he came out they had to send him back to France for good.

'But I was fit, and I came here, to Todak, when they were resettling it, and already at the beginning there was this trouble about the swamp, and the Resettlement Officer ...

'How undramatic, trivial it all was ... and so hot too, and you know what heat does to you ... makes you not notice, makes you forget ... they were still putting up the wire fences, round the high ground. Some lorries had come in filled with people to be resettled, and armoured cars, and everywhere policemen with guns levelled against everyone round them, and soldiers. Then the people came out of the lorries and stood in groups, there on the central square where they are being assembled today, and the Resettlement Officer, now no more among us (God forgive me for not feeling more sorry), shouting at them, waving his arm and his stick: "Come on, get cracking over there..." and the quiet hard hatred seeped out of them thick, thick ... I could smell the hate hitting us full in the face, great waves of it out of the docile people lining up in the square. I said to him (his name was Uxbridge): "Is there anything I can do to help? I speak Hakka as well as French." Of course my English is not good.

'There was an interpreter with him, a Chinese boy that I do not like, servile, servile ... and they were telling him to tell the white man that the land was too low, it was swamp, it would flood, they could not grow anything upon it ... they could not build in the swamp, and there were palm trunks still sticking out ... and the land was wet ... "Tell those bastards to put up their huts, the roofs are there, and if they don't start quick they'll go to detention camp." All he said to me was: "Why don't you carry a gun? You ought to get a gun, these brutes are bad, treacherous bastards. They've been passing food for months."

'And then it became like a refrain, one of those terrible and stupid contagious formulae repeated without ever thinking ... that the people of Todak were a bad lot, and needed a firm hand. Whenever I saw an official in the town, at one of those government meetings; when Mr. Clerkwell asked me to come over and I tried to explain, it was the same thing; "They're a bad lot ... we're satisfied with what the R.O. is doing..."

'*Mon Dieu*,' cried Father Destier, 'it was like a nightmare. I knew it couldn't go on, there was so much hate, like the stench from the swamp, rising in silence ... something would happen, but I did not know what, and I was unable to move....'

Tommy Uxbridge had been a captain in the Indian Army and a major in Palestine, where he had acquired a bad knee and a slight limp. He was forty-three, childless, fond of dogs, and his wife had left him years ago for an American. He had served the Empire in its outposts before the Asian Revolution had become respectable, and his notion of the world, like Mont Blanc, consisted of a white top and a submissive yellow-brown-black base. In Malaya he was not yet an anachronism.

Coloured folk were on the whole loyal, and strove hard to achieve equality (which meant as fair a likeness to an Englishman like himself as striving could achieve). But they were still a long way off it, and meanwhile they were misled by 'bad lots'. The appellation Sahib, Tuan, or Master, uttered with native respect, mingled with an upward gaze of devotion and trust, evoked in Tommy Uxbridge fairness, benevolence, generosity and a paternal protective glow.

Tommy Uxbridge had no vices, but his meagre personal income did not allow in England the reasonable supply of Scotch, nor induce in his neighbours the hospitable friendliness, to which he had grown accustomed; when the Colonial Office advertised for Officers to deal with resettlement camps in Malaya, Uxbridge applied and favourably impressed the Selection Board.

There had been few applicants. The High Commissioner – later himself to die in ambush in Malaya – was anxious to get zealous men with a sense of mission. The task was difficult. Over half a million people, mostly Chinese small farmers, one in five of every Chinese in Malaya, one in ten of the whole population, were to be placed behind wire in over three hundred resettlement camps. In the first years of the Emergency the methods dictated by a frantic urgency had turned many against the British. Entire villages had been burnt down, pigs slaughtered, lorries full of people removed wholesale, unprovided with food or water, and brutality had reaped its dubious rewards. But now a new attitude was necessary. Resettlement, on the scale involved, could, if the temptations to harshness, short-term expediencies, and the inevitable corruption arising from these vast scale displacements of helpless thousands were indulged, make the country more quickly communist than any terrorism could. Already it was said that this was war against the people, and not against the jungle.

But resettlement was always urgent, essential to the success of the military campaign; one made use of the men available. It was therefore a very mixed bag, ranging from ex-China missionaries to retired sergeant-majors, who went resettling in Malaya.

Before sailing from England Tommy Uxbridge was issued with a pamphlet entitled: *Handbook to the Emergency*. He flicked the pages, catching a paragraph or a sentence here and there: 'The Briggs Resettlement Plan,' he read, 'is essentially military, to deny sources of food and supplies to the terrorists ... There is an aura of hero-worship round the terrorists ... during the last war the Chinese guerrillas who fought the Japanese from the jungle, and now form the hard core of the terrorists battling us, obtained their food, equipment and recruits from Chinese farmers scattered on the lands at the edge of the jungle ... land to which they had no title ... no one else had the energy to clear or cultivate it ... hence they are called squatters...' Uxbridge turned the pages, his mind already dividing the new world to rule with near-absolute authority into 'loyal' people and 'bad lots'.

'The plan must resettle this half-million in compact areas, surrounded by barbed-wire fences, where they can be under police protection ... By servering contact between the jungle and its supporters, it is hoped to starve the bandits into the open ... Mines and estates will concentrate their labour forces behind barbed wire ... Night time curfew everywhere ... Anyone found with food beyond the wire fence, will be considered as aiding terrorists and under Emergency Regulations liable to penal servitude, or to death. . . .'

'We should have been as tough in other places,' thought Uxbridge of the shrinking Empire.

'The greatly enlarged Police Force ... guard these areas ... military patrol the roads and jungle edge to catch the terrorists as they come out for food, and to make raids into the jungle ... the first concentration of squatters in the State of Johore...'

'Why, that's where I'm going.' Uxbridge closed the pamphlet, well satisfied with his grasp of the situation.

On the ship were police officers, ex-Palestine, going to Malaya to add their numbers and fighting experience to its ever-swelling

Police Force. Promotion came quickly in an Emergency. At lunch and dinner round the tables the talk was all of pensions, cost of living, and expatriate allowances; of old so-and-so, sergeant in Palestine, now assistant superintendent in Malaya ... Blocking the way to higher rank, the police officers who'd been 'in the bag' together had to be reckoned with, those whose years of Japanese captivity in Singapore's Prison, had cemented a brotherhood of mutual self-help. But the Palestine contingent owned representatives too, and felt strong enough for some of the pickings of senior posts.

Thus the talk went on, the issues of the Emergency of very secondary interest, the war in Malaya an opportunity; duty simplified to a formula approximating that of Tommy Uxbridge: good happy folk longing to be ruled, and the bad boys who made trouble.

Thus it had been in Palestine, with Jew and Arab; thus it would be in Malaya, with Malay and Chinese, the latter interlopers and Reds out for trouble, and to be dealt with. And, dealt with, all would again be fine in the colonial garden, until somewhere else things would be hotting up and the surplus police would be shipping it to another Colony, another Emergency, further promotions, pensions and allowances.

This ship's talk completed the mental preparation with which Tommy Uxbridge would resettle eight thousand Chinese in Todak.

Sitting with Oliver Daley, thin, timid, bespectacled ex-missionary from China governing the next resettlement area, and Police Officer Crufts, in charge of Todak Contingent, on the veranda of his bungalow; in the slack Malayan night, insidious with softness, with the earnest stars craning down from the star-crowded sky, and the insect whispers, shrill or soft voices by the thousand rising from the jungle grass, the lallang; Uxbridge would reminisce: 'Invaluable experience, Palestine' (waving his pipe), 'after a few weeks there one could look a chap in the eye and tell straightaway whether he was loyal or not.'

He expected to achieve the same perspicacity in Todak.

Todak had an original nucleus of a small village on the high land above the road, a cluster of huts, a few shops lining the edge of the road, two hundred inhabitants. Now the hill overtopping them had been cleared and a large Police Post erected, wrapped stoutly in the sturdy defence of barbed wire wound close round tripod stakes. The perimeter fence of Todak itself, for economy's sake, had single stakes.

When the lorries began to roll in, packed with the dreary first few hundreds of the eight thousand, Crufts, the Police Officer in charge of the resettlement area, already looked worried.

The soldiers let down the tailboards of the lorries; the women and children jumped down. Impassive and huddled together, the first impression was of the children; so many of them. Little boys between ten and fourteen in shorts; little girls, large and small, carrying babies as large as themselves astraddle on the left hip. Pregnant women staring, with set brown high cheekbones.

'Look, Uxbridge, we've got thousands coming. Where are we going to put them all? There isn't really room, you know. This has been rather badly planned, I'm afraid. Hadn't we better notify Headquarters?'

'What's wrong with the land on the other side of the road,' said Uxbridge loftily, 'once we've cleaned it up a bit?'

'Why, it's mostly swamp, man, swamp going down to the river. Not really good, you know, I mean, when it rains . . .'

'Won't do them harm to feel a bit damp,' was the reply. 'Cool them a bit. Depends how they behave. Don't think we should coddle them, Crufts.' Decide their fate he would, Tommy Uxbridge. Depend on instinct. Pick out the bad lots.

He strolled to watch them file between armed policemen in the square space reserved for a future school and a communal hall. Ah Kim the contractor was there. Uxbridge nodded briefly at him, Ah Kim bowed and bowed again. Uxbridge trusted Ah Kim. 'He may be a Chink but he's got his heart in the right place.'

Ah Kim was watching the people. His son, interpreter to Uxbridge, a young man with a dark-gold cruel face, sat at one of the two tables placed under a temporary shed in the square and barked orders: 'Line up, line up, you must register for your roof.'

Government put up the roofs of the huts, one to each family. The people built the rest. Ah Kim the contractor bid for the tender put out by the government for the roofs.

The first day Uxbridge appeared in Todak Ah Kim came to pay his visit. He stood at the bottom of the steps of the R.O.'s bungalow (constructed by Ah Kim: it had cost the government twelve thousand dollars and Ah Kim made five thousand four hundred on it), and bowed and scraped his bare and horny feet on the cement, for he had removed his shoes out of respect.

'Tuan, Tuan.' He looked up at Uxbridge, standing above him on the bungalow veranda. He smiled and bowed again. Ah

Kim's son, next to his father, translated: 'My father comes to pay his respects to our honoured Resettlement Officer. Welcome, welcome, Mr. Uxbridge.'

Uxbridge flung himself in a rattan armchair (furnished by Ah Kim, who supplied, on contract, government offices with standard issue furniture). 'You're the contractor, Ah Kim. I've heard about you from Lieutenant Crufts. Mind you behave...' he wagged a finger, '... no nonsense with me, savvy?'

Father and son laughed delightedly, heartily, loud and long and oilily. It turned out the son was named Georgie, had failed the English School Certificate, and rendered many services to the Police as unofficial informer. 'If I may be of any use...'

Ah Kim got the contract for the roofs (two thousand of them), for the rest of the perimeter fence wiring, for the felling of trees, for clearing the lallang; Georgie became interpreter-assistant to the R.O.; life for Uxbridge became easy and comfortable. Crates of Black and White whisky materialized on his veranda. ('My father Ah Kim, Sir, he has a small grocery shop in town ... they want to show their thanks.') Servants were found for him. A good car, very cheap, became his. ('My father has a small garage, Sir.') The coffee shop in Todak supplied meals and drink and unlimited credit. ('The manager is my father's friend.')

'Ask Ah Kim,' and a shout for 'Georgie' solved every difficulty. Uxbridge could drive to Singapore for a week-end's well-earned romp, and leave it all to Georgie. ('My father has many good friends in Singapore, Sir, they will show you the best things ...')

That day when the lorries came Ah Kim, in front of the coffee shop, watched and counted the people. Perhaps he could now bid for the rice monopoly from that red-haired fool; and there must be a contract for building the market; and water wells must be dug, there were far too few of them; and the pigsties...? Meanwhile Georgie would keep tabs on them. Was he not their interpreter, their lives in his gold smooth hands? He could twist their words into meanings he wished, to the red-haired devil who ruled ... Ah Kim stood in the shadow of the coffee shop, and watched the people.

They filed before the tables, in orderly queues. Bundles and babies protruded from them everywhere.

'What is your name?'

The women stared.

'They are Hakkas,' said Georgie. Georgie was Hokkien himself, but spoke four Chinese dialects and Malay as well as English. The second interpreter from the Police, drafted to help Georgie, started again in Hakka:

'Name? How many children? Age? Where is your husband?'

'No husband . . . husband, none.'

'Are you a widow?'

Giggles. 'Yes, a widow.'

After the ninth widow, Uxbridge turned to Crufts. 'You mean to say, all these women have lost their husbands? They say they are widows.'

'Nonsense,' said Crufts, shrugging his shoulders. 'Ask them when and how their husbands died.'

Smirks. Giggles. Choked small laughter. Because Europeans, red-haired devils, were talking, the widows spoke Malay. '*Laki t'ada*' (no man), they announced between spurts of enjoyment. Their hip-riding babies, startled, began howling. Hastily shushing them, the women lifted their jackets, baring their brown swinging breasts, and gave suck.

Uxbridge felt the familiar, quick fury which in India, in Palestine, in all these God-forsaken places, rose and grew and exploded with the heat of the day. Whiteskin fury it is called in Malaya. Here it was again ready to burst in his head. 'What's the meaning of all this?' he shouted. 'Ask them where their husbands are hiding.'

Inane, the laughter rose, jeered, spiralled and spread. The babies sobbed gently, the bundles heaved. The sullen little boys were now smiling, sucking their thumbs or their rubber dummies tied with thread round their necks. The little girls looked up into their mothers' faces and laughed.

'*T'ada laki, t'ada laki.*' The mothers swaying back and forth in the sun, in the heat, sent the singsong derisively down their line. They now varied it, turned it round. '*T'ada laki, laki t'ada.*' (No man, man none.)

Uxbridge, Georgie and Crufts counted them. In this lot there were seventy-eight families, consisting of one hundred and thirty-five women over thirty, including several grandmothers, two hundred and forty girls and women under thirty, and seven hundred and sixty-four children under sixteen. There were twenty-eight men over fifty, nine men over forty, and no man between sixteen and thirty years. Not one.

Crufts again shrugged his shoulder, the lift and fall of resignation, to heat, to circumstance, to these incredible people of stupid courage and crafty cowardice.

'Don't get high blood pressure over this, R.O. It sometimes happens. The whole lot of men have gone underground to the jungle. They were warned.'

'Well, sir,' said the red-faced sergeant in charge of the lorries (he came from Kent and was holding a baby for one of the mothers), 'we thought how they'd been warned, though we cordoned them off at dawn, ever so early before they'd got up. Nobody escaped while we were there. They must have gone before. The women came out so quiet like from the huts. Just stood there, putting things together. As if they knew already. It made one feel ... kind of funny. And they didn't say nothing when we rolled away from the place. Not cry or anything, like a lot of them do. Just looked and kept on looking. We thought they'd been warned.'

'Damn cowards, thugs ...' Uxbridge was furious. His sense of property injured, he strode up and down the line, glaring at the women. He felt like striking them, but he was English. 'Running away, leaving their women and their children behind.'

'They can afford to,' said Crufts, philosophical. 'After all, they know we won't touch the women, rape them ... that's the only thing they can't stand ... and these girls are tough and faithful. They'll be organizing contact, passing food in no time. We'll have to look to our fences, R.O. The worst are the young ones, sixteen to twenty ... the unmarried ones. They're in love with adventure and the guys in the jungle, think they're heroes ... poison they are in any resettlement camp, worse than the men.'

'*T'ada laki, laki t'ada.*' Buoyant, laughing, the little girls carrying their little brothers in premonition of future loads, now took up the mothers' refrain. They sang it loudly. The mothers hushed them, some raised a playful hand pretending a smack, looking at the R.O., laughing in his face. Triumph was upon them, a great gold sun of victory. And Uxbridge then knew that he hated them, hated their high-cheeked faces, their surliness.

They'd pay for this. Not enough land, eh? Well, he'd show them. Down in the swamp they'd go, for he was the R.O. He'd put them in the swamp. All the bad ones would go into the swamp.

It was getting hotter all the time. The inevitable clouds pouted grey under-bellies. Up and down the red-brown roads the jeeps and armoured cars, with grinding brakes and grating gears, trundled in their own heat haze. Their wireless antennae whipped the dusty air like small fists shaking.

'None of these bloody drivers can drive,' said Bob Stewart, who wore a built-in frown as befitted the occasion. 'No army or police driver that isn't a menace on the roads. I caught one who had been driving four years and didn't know how to back. Worse than civilian learners.'

Crufts mumbled listless assent. The sleepless night had smudged dark rings beneath his eyes. And in the pale fumes of dawn all Police Headquarters had converged upon Todak. Bob Stewart and Luke Davis of Special Branch, Che Ahmad of the Malay Section, and a brace of Chinese detectives and inspectors, in and out of uniform.

'You'll have to change that.' Bob came to stop in front of a black signboard pointing the way to Crufts's wooden bungalow. Upon it, in English, Malay and Chinese, painted in white, were the words: 'Police Post, Todak Resettlement Area.' 'It's New Village now, so you'll have to take that off and re-write it.'

'New what?' said Crufts.

'New Village, Todak New Village. Orders from high up. Re-settlement area doesn't sound good. Got to have a new spirit, and all that sort of thing,' said Bob. 'Battle for the hearts and minds of the people, co-operation, psychological warfare, get the people on our side. Don't you read the papers? We've got to win the hearts and minds of the people, or we'll lose this bloody country.'

Crufts did not reply. He thought what a nuisance this is. It wasn't often a Resettlement Officer was bumped off. There had been two or three. One, way out east, done in with an axe because he'd tried to set fire to somebody's hut. 'Wasn't in line,' he said, 'with the barbed wire.' There'd been another one near Malacca, finished with a bullet between his eyes as he sat drinking beer. They had put a Chinese assistant R.O. there now and it was better. Here it was Uxbridge, a bloody nuisance when he was alive, and a confounded nuisance now that he was dead. That was the whole trouble with this hot-oven country, thought Crufts. It all depended on the man, one man in a district, one bloody little so-and-so alone in charge of thousands of lives. Even if you weren't bloody minded and did your best, you were still bound to make mistakes, a hell of a lot of mistakes, and when you were like Uxbridge, well, you had it coming to you.

You had to be pretty tough and humble not to acquire a fuehrer complex. And then there was the heat, a casque of metal pressing on the bones of your head, squeezing on to your brain, on the back of the eyeballs, making you furious, blind furious just with the sight of another human being, like a mad dog. Uxbridge had been like that lately, and Crufts had caught himself too, shouting, his mind out of control. But what else could they do, what else could Crufts do? Even now it was too hot, being ten o'clock and just before the daily storm; too hot for sustained attention even on the scene of Todak raked for a clue to the obvious murder of its R.O. ... as if it wasn't obvious enough.

'Ah,' said Bob, as they turned into the main road, 'they're here. Good.'

The masked vans were being parked. There were three swathed in grey-green canvas, as if hoarding bullion, but they contained surrendered enemy personnel. In each sat two, three or four ex-terrorists now turned informers, who peered through slits in the canvas while the whole village was being filed singly, walking slowly past them. Around each van stood Chinese Special Branch inspectors wearing black pongee trousers, and white shirts, their hair dark, shining, lustrous with oil. Around their slim hips went thick black leather belts, with a revolver on each side, they strutted self-consciously, mincing a little, fingers on their hips. And among them, remarkable for an aura of indomitable purpose, bobbed the curly Italian head of Pang, the star Chinese detective, pillar of the Special Branch, the Chief's right-hand man, who, in his full sweeping strides from van to lorry, marshalling the villagers into meek single file, was yet able to take with him in step, as surely as if his hand had been upon his shoulder, an emaciated bespectacled young man, the representative of the Malayan-Chinese Association, always summoned in case of trouble and to show co-operation with Government. Mortally frightened this young man appeared, especially when Pang turned round and smiled at him brilliantly and threateningly.

'Out of the top drawer, Pang,' said Bob Stewart, watching him. 'Terrific value, he knows everything. Got more facts in that head of his than in all the files in our register.'

Pang knew everything about everybody. Perhaps his years as a member of the Malayan Communist Party before he worked for the British Police helped him in his brilliant swoops and captures. Although there were rumours about his methods of extracting confessions, his blackmail of shopkeepers, and especially of the use Mrs. Pang made of girls who had gone through detention camp, yet these were not pursued because no one came forth to give evidence against him.

Invisible, Ah Mei and other informers peered from the slits in the canvas and picked out, among the trudging people, those they might have seen, known, met or recognized from their previous lives: ex-comrades, ex-contacts, ex-food-suppliers, members of the Movement, the People's Movement, said to be a hundred thousand strong, which kept the five thousand fighters of the jungle supplied with food, medicine, arms, money and recruits.

'How many have you got so far, Pang?' asked Bob as Pang came running past, sweat glistening on his sun-burnt healthy face, and a large triumphant smile on his lips.

'Twenty-seven so far, sir,' carolled Pang.

'Not bad,' Bob Stewart nodded. 'Wonder how many Ah Mei has picked out this time?'

'Only one, sir, this time, an old woman,' said Pang, 'that one crying there, and she's not sure about her.'

'Never mind,' said Bob benevolently. 'What about the others, eh? Doing their stuff?'

'Yes, sir,' said Pang. 'Chang got about ten. He knows this place quite well, used to tap rubber around here.'

'Jolly good bag,' said Bob, 'carry on.'

And Pang's agile fat feminine buttocks in their tight black pants ran down the slope.

The two police officers watched as the parade continued past the vans. At the canvas sides of each van stood other detectives, ears pressed against the folds to hear the whisper from inside. 'That one,' and the Special Branch men would go up to the woman or man now standing in front of the slit and push the suspect out of the line up to the waiting barred police van, parked a little further up the road.

Heat glares, pressing down armour of solid heat, encasing, paralysing. Crufts lost sight, lost touch, refugee from the heat into the half-consciousness of a daydream, a daydream resolved into a merciless, glazed repetition. . . .

Of the terror-stricken mata-mata surging out of the glittering ecstatic full-moon night, the silver world outside his bungalow. Moonlight trickling on the huddled huts, and the mata-mata panting, forgetting to salute.

'Tuan, tuan, apa tuan Uxbridge.'

'What the blazes are you talking about?'

Between hiccups of terror he spoke. He and a comrade on night duty detailed to check the perimeter fence had come to the low-lying swampy part, and seen a bundle lying there. Cautiously they challenged, their weapons cocked, approached, fingers on triggers. The unmoving shape, it was a man, a white man, it was ... The Malay could not and would not go further. 'Tuan must see himself,' he said.

And Crufts had run out in the lovely silver moonlight, with a posse of six mata-matas, and come upon Uxbridge the Resettlement Officer, leaning as if asleep on the barbed-wire fence sagging beneath his weight, dead on the wire fence, shot in the back, and cold. From the thick green mud upon his clothes he must have been half carried, half dragged from some distance away. His revolver was gone, his identity card was gone, but his money, three hundred dollars of it, was in his wallet. That was the supreme insult, and Crufts felt himself flushing with anger in the moonlight. Show off, he thought; want the people here to know they were not after his money but after him. Justice, he thought, and for a moment stood unbelieving, turning his flashlight into the death-drowned face, stiff and blue-jowled, the eyes coagulated like latex, the uncovered teeth coated with a thick yellow creamy substance.

And then he looked round. The silver night pressed her stifling brightness on him, and the huts were shining silver humps, abandoned cocoons, glistening on a swallowed earth, Crufts would never remember how he had reached the body, but all his life he would remember the journey back. The mata-matas not refusing yet standing passive, unwilling to move, to bear the dead unclean body, frightened of the ravenous white ghost; and finally one had been prevailed upon to take one foot and one the other, and Crufts carrying Uxbridge by the armpits, and what a weight the man was!

And the silence, the frightful listening silence, expectant, breath-withheld. Crufts knew as he bore the load, and heard his steps biting into that knowing silence, that all the village knew and had known already before he had, while he was still sitting on his veranda. And in the blossom-bright night the disjoined plywood planks seemed to flower with invisible and peering eyes. There they were, holding their breath, immured by law, by the curfew, within their huts, not allowed on pain of being shot on sight to leave the suffocating smallness within. And so in the moon-filled night he knew the breathing inside, breathing knowingly the whole eight thousand of them, without a word.

'Now let me see,' Bob's voice; 'how soon after discovery did you say it was when you rang me up?'

He is trying to pin something on me, thought Crufts.

It had taken nearly half an hour to get the body back to the police post, and only then had he thought to ring Headquarters.

'As soon as I found the body, sir,' said Crufts.

Ringing up Headquarters, and now Headquarters was here, and not only Police, but also Army, a full battalion with armoured cars on the move, preparing to comb the country round Todak. It had been difficult getting the Army last night, for it was Saturday night and the liaison officer had been away in Singapore, but they'd discovered him at last, at Prince's Restaurant. And then there was the R.A.F., always keen to harass the enemy and drop a few bombs among the trees to smash hideouts. Already a report had come that two miles from Todak along the road an abandoned car had been found, and there were six hip pits, three on each side of the road, covered with leaves. No sign of struggle. They must have marched him into the jungle and finished him off there, and then dragged him across the swamp to hang him on the fence so that the people of Todak would know: the people – those impassive, stony-faced, surly and silent and dumb people of Todak.

'Hell of a lot of women,' said Bob, looking at the crowd, 'very few men. It's one of *those* villages, isn't it?'

'Yes,' said Crufts, 'they came like that.'

'Female of the species, eh?' said Bob. He spoke lower, although no one was there to hear, out of respect for the dead. 'I don't suppose there was any girl mixed up in this, was there?'

'Not in these parts, sir,' said Crufts. 'Uxbridge went to Singapore.'

Father Destier continued, eloquent, nearly garrulous. 'I know that it is wrong of me, and I pray to the good God to give me his forgiveness. But I didn't like this Monsieur Uxbridge, God have mercy on his soul. There was that evening when we had gone up to the Resettlement Officer's bungalow and found Crufts there and Uxbridge, arguing. Mr. Crufts is young and well-meaning. He doesn't know much, but he has the heart, and sometimes he would speak to me. I hope he will not be shot.'

'Bonsoir, bonsoir,' the voice of the little French priest had sounded; charity ordered him these courtesy visits, and, cassock flapping, big head on small body, outlandish among his own, he climbed the steps to talk to the Englishmen in authority. 'Are you ready,' he said, 'for a little festivity, a little joy in this forsaken concentration camp of ours?'

'*Vous comprenez,*' he said to me, 'I was only joking.'

Uxbridge had looked him up and down, and: '*Bongsoir* to you. What's the racket now? You're still not carrying a gun, I see.'

'He was always telling me to carry a gun.'

'You had better watch out,' he said, 'if you don't you will catch it one day.' Obviously Father Destier enjoyed the way Providence had turned the tables on Uxbridge, although he would probably repent, beating his heart in half-willed remorse.

'I bring an invitation,' said Father Destier, 'an invitation from some of my Catholic squatters. You know we have three hundred of them in this village? They are inviting us to a dog feast.'

'A what?'

'A feast to eat dog,' explained Father Destier happily. 'Your police, they have killed a lot of pi-dogs in this village so tonight and tomorrow the people will eat them. They can't cook tonight because of the curfew, but tomorrow,' he rubbed his hands with glee, 'but tomorrow *c'est fête, c'est kermesse.* I bring an invitation to you to eat dog.'

'Monsieur Uxbridge turned livid, for he loved dogs.'

'It's frightful. I've never ... They must be stopped.'

'Oh no,' said Father Destier, 'it is quite the custom you know, besides it saves money. When I was in China I had a dog. Unfortunately one day he died, and my neighbours ate him. At first I hated them for it, but that is a long time ago. I assure you,' he added earnestly, 'it is a detestable dish, I really have to pray before I take a mouthful, but they would be so hurt if I refused.'

'And after that,' said Father Destier miserably, 'Uxbridge would not listen to another word from me. Obviously a man who ate dog was beyond the pale to him.'

They walked in the lower part of Todak, Oliver Daley and Luke Davis and Che Ahmad, between the emptied huts and the piles of refuse and the stubborn rotting trunks of coconut trees felled and left lying. Clumped like banana trees, six mata-matas stood guard round the spot where the body of Uxbridge had bent two stakes in the fence. The barbed wire sagged, a child could have stepped over it safely.

Stumps up to the knee stuck out of the grey-green ooze of the paths. Underfoot squelched the mud floors of the huts they entered, and even there were stumps, decaying, steaming forth that half-sharp stench which is the life-in-death smell of putrescence. The ditches were clogged with human dirt, cabbage stumps, like lopped white bloodless necks of midgets, and scumspread water ran into the paths. Privies, urine and rottenness. And the wire fence so close to the huts, the huts without space between each other, scarcely two feet between the last plywood wall and the stakes of the fence.

'Hell, I didn't know it was that bad,' growled Luke. 'Why wasn't this reported before? Who's been inspecting this village, anyway?'

'There was an inspection, but only of the higher ground, and that was before the last four thousand squatters came.'

'Four ... and how many are down here?'

Daley moistened his lips. 'I don't know, about half, I should think ... The others are up there, on the higher land....'

Luke Davis swore vigorously, abundantly. Oval beads of sweat collected on his brow, ran in single file down into his neck. 'Four or five thousand of these poor blighters stewing in this cesspit, Daley. That's bad.'

'Yes sir,' said Daley, and hated the tone of his own voice. Mustn't think ill of the dead ... must forget you hated him just for this....

They came to the last row of huts, furthest from the road and in view of the smooth thick glassy water which seeped out of the swamp under their feet. Luke pointed further down. 'What are those huts over there?' sharply.

'Those? Oh, those are the huts beyond the wire.'

'I can see that. They're out of the fence ... are they Malay huts? Even if they are they should be brought in ...'

'No sir, they're Chinese too. They just were not wired in. Seems there wasn't enough wire.'

'But that's murder,' shouted Luke, exasperated. 'Why, Daley, the whole point of tearing these b....rs off their own bits of land and carrying them here and putting them within the wire fence is to PROTECT them ... to keep them under police protection ... control if you want to be nasty. It's not fair ... the bandits can get all the food they want from these huts outside the wire....'

'Yes sir. But there isn't much food round about here; the people tried to keep ducks and chickens, but there wasn't room. There isn't room for pigs. They were told to go fishing in the river ... there are about fifty families....'

'But they can still be blackmailed, Daley ... they can be made to buy food from the shops and give it to the bandits ... why, it's ...'

'Excuse me,' said Che Ahmad, interrupting Luke's exasperation. 'I will go up to the police post now and talk to Inspector Abdullah and perhaps find out a little about all this.'

'Do,' said Luke. 'Now Daley,' he added grimly, as soon as Che Ahmad had turned his back, 'I expect there's a lot more dirt. You'd better tell me all. I'd better know the worst.'

'*Tolong*, towkay, help us. The white man put us in the swamp.'

'What can I do about it? You displeased the white man.'

'Please, towkay, is there no way? It takes me four days to put up a hut again, and during this time I will earn no money tapping rubber ... Why is he doing it? Why?'

'To punish you. You displeased him. He who cannot bend is broken.'

It usually cost them fifty or a hundred dollars, depending on their means, for a better hut. They owed the money, paying ten dollars monthly, with thirty per cent interest per month added on ... or thirteen dollars a month – to Ah Kim, the contractor, the 'government' man.

'Ah Kim ran a labour force of Tamils, because they were cheap. But now he found it more convenient to get help from the villagers themselves....

'Old Ah San, you will clear for me this patch.'

'But I have to go tapping.'

'When you come back from tapping. You have plenty of time in the afternoon.'

Ah San owed money, and did not want to go in the swamp.

And now the police post took its cue from Ah Kim. If *he* could get away with it, then it was permissible for a poor Malay mata-mata to get his small share.

The families moved to the swamp were without water. The ditches were of earth, shallow and overflowing with dirt within a week. The wells were across the road. When the village of Todak had been planned, the upground had been wired in, then the swamp.

To get to the road, and then up to the highground wells, to the shops or out to the rubber estates, the people of the swamp crossed two police posts. Soon it was an unwritten rule that the people of the swamp must pay ten cents each time they crossed a post to collect their water from the wells.

Then there were Georgie's collections, presents and gifts. . . .

'The white man will consider your request for a pigsty, I will talk to him for you.'

'Thank you very much, Towkay . . . please accept these two chickens. . . .'

'You need not be so polite . . . send them to my house.'

There was silence at Todak, silence ominous in the plywood huts. Uxbridge was well satisfied because all complaining had stopped. Father Destier tried to tell him about the water money. Daley tried to tell him that he was too hard on the people. 'But they haven't complained,' he said. On his visits to Headquarters he gave a succinct report on the morale of the village. No incidents. People were buckling down to work. Curfew was working.

Still more people came.

The high land was crowded, the perimeter fence could only be readjusted there in one direction, encroaching on the area reserved for the police playing-field; when that was taken, Ah Kim sent word that a certain sum of money was to be raised to be distributed to the police for compensation. . . .

'But Uxbridge wouldn't believe it, and I had no proof. I heard it all in my own village, and could not believe it, knowing how these things get about, until I came here myself once again.' Thus Daley.

Todak, a still afternoon. Sullen, shut faces. Silence. Even the children ran away when Daley walked past them. They did not shout. They hid. Doors slammed, weakly. Uxbridge was in his office. In front of him stood an old woman with a wrinkled face, dressed in rubber-tapper black, hands stiff, gnarled as tree bark, on both sides of her. Georgie was translating, shouting. There was much shouting always, in the R.O.'s office in Todak.

'You've got to move. You're in the way of the wire.'

'Tolong, please, Great Brother, tell the red-haired great man I cannot move my hut. Have compassion. I am an old woman. It cost me eight hundred dollars to put my hut up, then another two hundred to take it down and put it up again. . . .'

'Tell her if the hut isn't down by tomorrow morning I'll shove her in jail,' shouted Uxbridge, wiping his forehead. 'And now throw her out. Oh hello, Daley, didn't see you come in.'

'What is the matter with the hut?'

Uxbridge's face clouded a little. 'Oh well, it looks as if we'd used up more wire than we thought . . . I got a government chit the other day saying no more wire . . . I've got to bring in the fence a bit. I'm satisfied Ah Kim did his work all right, it's just that we must get the huts together, squeezed a bit ... we've overstretched ourselves.'

'Which means,' Daley thought, 'that Ah Kim has pocketed the wire and Uxbridge is too lazy to measure.'

'Don't forget the field of fire,' said Daley.

A regulation laid down that there must always be enough room within the wire to allow the police to deploy at the four corners of the camp. There they built small earth posts covered with an attap roof. On these machine guns could be erected to rake the village in case of riot, or aimed outside in case of assault by the jungle fighters.

But in Todak already the huts were squeezed tight together, with no room for poultry runs, no room for pigsties, no room for vegetable plots. Then an order came from Headquarters that no building could be done on the area reserved for the police playing-field in high Todak. Hastily, the roofs erected there, and for which 'pleasant money' (for the police, it was said) had been collected, were pulled down, and forty more families went down in the swamp.

Luke Davis looked at his watch. 'Nearly eleven,' he said. 'We agreed to meet at the coffee shop round about this time with the others. Let's go.'

Daley followed Luke Davis as they picked their way through the garbage heaps and the stumps of low Todak; they reached the road, for a moment stood to look at the screening van; the people filing, the Chinese inspectors in their black trousers walking among them, trying to get those who had already been screened to talk. Pang was much in evidence. He was interrogating with great courtesy, a smile of encouragement on his beaming face, two rubber tapper girls with crisp waved hair, who stood like stones, in front of him.

'And did you not hear any noise that night?'

'Which night?'

'The night the R.O. was murdered.'

'We heard nothing.'

'Have you ever heard or seen any bandits coming near your village?'

'Which village?'

'This village.'

'This village?'

'Yes, anyone from outside who has come near, whom you

may have seen?'

'We have seen nothing.'

Young Detective Inspector Huang was having a worse time with a cheery-faced buxom woman whom he had collared, together with her fourteen year old son.

'How old are you?'

'I don't know.'

'How old is your son?'

'I don't remember.'

'Don't you know how old he is? Where did you come from?'

'I don't know.'

'Do you know where you are now?'

'No.'

'It is incredible,' said Luke, 'how dumb they can become. A wall of impenetrable stupidity ... their only defence. Not to know, not to see, nor hear, nor speak ... unable to remember their names, nor how many children they have. I had a village like that to screen once. Not one person there knew there was an Emergency on.'

'They are so terrorized, so much more terrified of us and unable to understand what has happened to them, that their only refuge is complete idiocy,' said Daley.

'I don't know what the answer is, do you?'

Daley did not reply. He thought then that he knew what the answer was. The two men walked on, Daley holding on inwardly to his answer ... perhaps he'd still be able to show them, one day ... Love was the answer, he thought, and then, confusedly, but Love is such a nauseating word in this heat. . . .

Che Ahmad walked up to the police post. Fat Inspector Abdullah, massive and smooth, glistening hair and brown eyes, sat at his table, virgin of any paper dossier, the picture of deferent efficiency.

Bob Stewart was trying to grill him. Inspector Abdullah had not risen to this rank for nothing. He was due for a Colonial Police Medal any time now. He was good at his job, knew his men, religious, and had a sense of moderation in his pickings.

Not that Inspector Abdullah was averse to pickings. Everyone made pickings out of the Emergency. In the towns on Saturday nights you could often see him do his round, Sikh or Malay or Chinese detective, moving quietly from hawker to shop, collecting weekly dues; Abdullah's brother-in-law, in the Singapore police, had transferred to the Traffic Branch, where the pickings were even larger. Everybody had pickings, even the white tuans. Abdullah smiled in perfect composure as Bob Stewart blustered and swore. Had not Bob Stewart a few months ago investigated Burly Ricketts? Abdullah, then in C.I.D. Anti-Corruption, had been a great help to Bob.

Burly Ricketts, once officer in charge of Rice Control, had arranged a contract with a Chinese rice firm, to supply with rice, in the usual police escorted convoys of lorries, a number of wired-in resettlement areas. His task was to supervise distribution, check rice weights, and see that they were not short. One day a zealous investigator came down from Headquarters and toured the district, and found that, officially, rice was being supplied to eighteen resettlement areas, but that only eleven existed. Seven areas did not exist, yet Government had paid for rice for them, for twelve thousand people who simply were not there.

The head of the Chinese rice firm abruptly disappeared in Indonesia. The manager of the lorry company (who merely delivered the rice) was detained for corruption; and Ricketts was boarded out for medical reasons and retired to honour and an intact pension in England.

When the rice contract was then given to Quo Boon, it was whispered that it was Quo Boon, through his agents, who had informed Government of the non-existence of these resettlement camps. Since then no relative, friend, or agent of Quo Boon's manifold companies had dared to visit, on pain of assassination, the town where the family of the former rice merchant still lived (professing complete ignorance of their father's whereabouts).

Inspector Abdullah, then, while in Anti-Corruption, had been able to ignore the more damaging information concerning Rickett's knowledge of what had happened, and lose the records of the ample commissions he had received from the rice firm. And thus in turn Bob Stewart, in charge of the investigation, had been able to find Ricketts merely negligent, but not guilty: the honour of the Service, the Force, and everyone who mattered, had been preserved, to the great relief of all except the lorry company manager, who did not matter.

And now Inspector Abdullah was in Todak.

'Awful mess, Abdullah.' Bob Stewart's technique was to browbeat and bully. He employed it in his interrogations. First bully, then cajole, then suddenly look terrifying again. Most effective at three a.m. under strong light on a Chinese merchant deprived of cigarettes and sleep for the past twenty-four hours.

'Tuan,' Abdullah stood, a rock of confidence and efficiency from his shining head to his shining boots, in his spick and span office, his quiet voice and great dignity.

Bob's voice lowered immediately. 'What I mean is, damn it, Abdullah, there'll be no medal or promotion for you, I'm afraid ... bad show, you know....'

'Mr. Uxbridge was killed far away from Todak, Tuan, on his return from Singapore, after the curfew was already down. He was dragged here, Tuan, a distance of three miles across the swamp. My men have already found this out.'

'Really.' Bob was impressed.

'My men have also found the car.' Quiet triumph was in Abdullah's eyes. 'It was driven into the jungle, from the road. May I point out to the Tuan that, from the position on this wall map which I have prepared, the ambush occurred well outside the limits of my district of Todak. Information from the Malay villages was followed up by my men and the car is being guarded by some kampong people, since my men are not allowed outside of my district.'

'Good show,' said Bob, and bit his lip.

Abdullah stood full of dignity, and in injured silence.

Che Ahmad came in quietly. 'Good morning, sir,' he said to Bob Stewart.

'Good morning, Ahmad. How're things?'

'Mr. Davis is still down in the swamp. He is meeting you at the coffee shop later.'

When they were alone Che Ahmad sat peaceably with Inspector Abdullah, proffered cigarettes; Inspector Abdullah refused with his hand on his heart. They exchanged brief news about their kampongs, Malay villages, and Inspector Abdullah's eldest son who had failed the entrance examination to the College. He was a good boy, even-tempered, but rather prone to romancing. Abdullah was marrying him off in a few months' time. 'It is better to marry them *before* they go to England.' Ahmad agreed.

So quietly they came on to talk of Todak ... What can one do? Who is the man who can resist money? The forest rats were paying well for everything and even the kampongs might be giving them plenty of food.

'A great responsibility for you,' said Che Ahmad.

'It is the will of God,' said Abdullah.

'It is difficult, I suppose,' said Che Ahmad. 'Perhaps,' he suggested diffidently, 'a zigzag road had been followed by some people here also, within the fence, as well as outside.'

To which Abdullah replied in substance, but with a great deal of hyperbole, that a policeman's salary did not remove him from temptation.

'Allah sees the heart,' said Che Ahmad. 'No one of us can say, before the majesty of God, that he is without sin.'

'It is the wells,' Abdullah said thoughtfully. 'People all want water. Water should be free, as rain is from Allah. Alas, there are too few wells in Todak ... it was hard on my men, having to guard the posts, all these people coming and going all the time, saying they wanted water ... perhaps something improper then occurred ... it is hard for one man to keep his eyes open upon everyone....'

'And there are the roofs, and the fence, and not enough wire, and the felling of trees,' said Ahmad easily. 'There was short measure in the rice, and a great many other things.'

'These things were done mostly by the Chinese contractor, this Chinese Ah Kim is insatiably fond of money, Enche. And not reasonable in his demands.'

'Many drops of water can make a big storm,' said Ahmad, meaning that eight thousand people, however poor, could still produce a fair amount of cash if squeezed.

Abdullah answered neither yes nor no, which meant yes.

'When the head is blind, the limbs fall into the mud. Tuan Uxbridge trusted Ah Kim and no one else.'

'Did Ah Kim collect pleasant money in your name?'

This was so direct that it disconcerted Abdullah. However his courtesy made him reply: 'If it did happen, I was largely ignorant of it. The money did not come into my pockets.'

He could have added that Ah Kim had appeared one day, a small gift of two hundred dollars in an envelope, smilingly forgotten on Abdullah's desk. But Abdullah had given twenty dollars away in charity, and after all, he had many children. And two hundred dollars was only a fraction of Ah Kim's pickings....

'It is hot, I must go down before it gets hotter,' said Ahmad, courteously taking his leave. 'I expect there will now be changes. It is good. A man must not always be in the same place. He must travel ... I wonder where your next post will be, Inspector Abdullah.'

'It is in the hands of Allah,' replied Abdullah, equally court-eous, seeing Ahmad down the steps to the road.

'Let's go to the coffee shop,' said Luke. He waved his arm at Crufts and Bob across the road, two figures in khaki looking hot even at this distance. 'We might also get the little French priest. After all, the Press will be on to this in no time ... we must get some sort of coherent story for the headlines, eh Daley?'

'Yes, of course.'

'I expect,' said Luke, sitting down gratefully and wiping his sweating hairy arms with a handkerchief, and then opening his shirt and wiping his neck and chest, bright with sweat, 'I expect you'll be asked to cope with Todak now, Daley. We haven't got anybody ... but I guess you might like to have a go at this place, your own way. . . .'

Daley's tongue licked his dry lips, he polished his glasses, put them back. Straightened. Take over Todak. The toughest eight thousand. He remembered their faces. Just above Luke's shoul-der he could see the square, the people from here so placid, moving obediently, in files, the vans. . . .

He felt empty, marrow hollow, but he said: 'I can try.'

And his faith flooded him again. I will try. I will win them over ... God ... Love ... He became confused with his emo-tion and his weariness.

'That's good,' said Luke. 'Try. Try to win them over. That's the slogan now, you know ... we can't win without the co-operation of the people ... so we've got to win the hearts and minds of the people ... the hearts AND the minds,' he repeated, 'not that we haven't done our best at times to lose them, but you have a try, Daley. I'm cheering for you.'

Meanwhile there was so much work to do. A nuisance, as Crufts thought, this murder. First of all the Press, thinking up a lot of nice kind things to say about the late Tommy Uxbridge, R.O., killed by terrorists while courageously doing his duty in the fight for freedom in Malaya. He always was a good sport, reveals ex-China missionary ... Dastardly murder of Resettle-ment Officer ... Achievement of Tommy Uxbridge praised by Government ... we shall all miss him, weep the mothers of Todak ... He was my friend, says French priest ... Thus the headlines would read.

That afternoon the bombing began, of the jungle and the swamp which continued it for miles along the seeping river, swamp held together by mangrove roots tenacious of mud, and now the mud went up in heavy liquid brown clouds as plop, plop, plop, the bombs fell. For three days and nights the strafing continued, until the R.A.F. could claim itself well-satisfied with the result of its battering exercises on the swamp.

Todak, now a New Village, became interesting. First the inhabitants were punished with a curfew of twenty hours a day, lasting ten days. During those days each family in Todak was furnished with a questionnaire printed in Chinese, which asked:

1. Do you know who killed your Resettlement Officer?
2. Do you know who is helping the bandits in Todak?'

Meanwhile propaganda officials came to Todak, to study new measures of psychological warfare; the school and the communal hall began building out of funds provided by the Malayan Chinese Association; Todak was now a priority project: money, experts, social welfare and Red Cross aid came in. There was talk of a cinema hall, and on the square a loudspeaker was installed, to relay music for the relaxation of the people of Todak.

The battle for the hearts and minds of the people of Todak was on.

Meanwhile Luke Davis and Bob Stewart had collected in large sealed boxes the questionnaires, and went over them, one by one, with police interpreters at their elbow, ready to translate. But there was nothing to translate.

'Bloody, bloody nuisance that man was, alive or dead,' said Luke, exhausted, throwing the last of the two thousand blank questionnaires, still blank, on the floor.

And Bob Stewart couldn't agree more.

In a Malaya promised independence Sir Moksa Bakrar was one of the self-asserted leaders, acceptable to Authority, who formed and deformed parties at the bat of an eyelid.

Most parties owned two things in common: nebulousness of economic programme; and assertion that all would be well if the people trusted them and their aim, which was inevitably: INDEPENDENCE AND SELF-GOVERNMENT, or self-government and then independence. Endless discussion as to what these words meant ensued.

There was also, opportunity for violent inter-party quarrel concerning the number of years before independence (or self-government) could be safely achieved.

The boldest of the parties (owning the thickest files in police records) were unwilling to endure more than a year or two, at the umost five, of protection against the fearful evils to which free nations are prone.

The best-beloved of Authority (its leaders wealthy Chinese or Indian businessmen, Malay officials of standing in the aristo-cratic bureaucracy of the Civil Service) asserted that they were incapable of managing their own affairs for the next twenty.

Sir Moksa Bakrar, President of PIP, compromised with fif-teen, and knew himself bold, planted on the narrow and ill-defined ledge of Opposition to Colonialism, which now over-hung precariously the yawning pit of subversion. Subversion was such an elastic word; it was getting more difficult to know where a legitimate demand ended, and subversion began ... but fifteen years stood on the margin of safety, bold, bold, but not too bold.

Sir Moksa's speeches were long, as all political speeches; they were loud, and peppered with stimulative slogans, demanding the abolition of racial discrimination, a rightful place in the sun for everyone, and a good life for everybody. These demands were passé enough to displease no one and to give 'the masses', as Sir Moksa termed them, an impression that Sir Moksa was both brave and an anti-colonialist (the first requisite for any politician in South East Asia). He hoped thus to collect votes, and never to discuss fundamental issues, such as Rubber.

For Rubber, and also Tin, were sacred, and the only man who had dared to talk of nationalization of the country's resources had lost his job, and Sir Moksa's friends all agreed that independence must come only very very slowly; none of them felt 'ready' for it. They never would.

Sir Moksa found Rubber easy to keep out of his speeches. After all, everyone he knew had money in rubber, and no one in rubber (or tin) wanted to be nationalized, income tax increased to that exorbitant rate which the often invoked British taxpayer (a dire example of the expensiveness of freedom) forked out without a squeak.

Having given Government assurance that, whatever might be said in the hot clangour of speech, the Progressively Independent Party would fully respect investments, Sir Moksa was persona grata to form a political party and compete for the elections. Tethered freedom is better than no freedom at all; however unpleasant detention camps may be, one could come back and out of them, but one never came back from the grave. And that slight edge of virtue was worth crawling for, even if the time of walking never came in sight.

Starting in life as plain Thomas Jones, son of Joseph Jones, a Christian Tamil, with a Scots ancestor from the East India Company in the family tree, Sir Moksa had done the best for himself by changing with the times from Thomas Jones to Moksa Bakrar.

In the Asia-conscious Asia of today, where on every sidewalk, here called five-foot way, white or brown or darker Indians, light brown Malays, swarthy Chinese or fair Eurasians, and all the other wonderful mixtures of South East Asia, now aware of the selfsame sky and earth, were speaking pridefully of 'we Asians', a European sounding name might go less far at elections than an Asian one.

In his veins flowed the bloods of half a dozen cultures, and even Sir Moksa at times felt fiercely Asian, burningly anti-white. But he was a rich man, possession-tied to a beneficent colonial status, the law and order which had made wealth possible. And then the First Secretary, at golf on Thursdays, took his arm, and called him 'Timmy', and every time Sir Moksa knew a little catch in his throat, and a surge of love for the British in his breast.

And so, to bridge the uneasy period from a servitude he had never felt to an independence he feared (but now a word to conjure governments with), Sir Moksa sacrificed himself into politics. And Authority agreed that far better Sir Moksa and others like him, safe and reliable and 'one of ours', than hotheads, adventurers and extremists who might do unpredictable things.

And thus PIP grew into headquarters in Singapore, and now sought to extend itself beyond the Straits of Johore, crossing the Causeway into Malaya.

Heavily guarded by four hundred mata-matas, our local Pantheon cinema hall had been taken over by PIP for its inauguration ceremony in Johore State. Besides the four hundred protectors in khaki, there were about two hundred adult spectators and three hundred children, happy milling round fifty hawkers' stalls issued by magic in a ring round the cinema. There was much chewing of cane sugar and spitting of betel juice and tasting of fried crabs and shrimps and great sizzling blue cloudlets of smoke springing out of frying pans. Little groups shrank or ventured from hideous white-hot sun to the cooler urine-scented shade of the cement steps leading into the dark echoing cavern of the hall and winging up on both sides to the balcony stalls. These were occupied at the back by Malay women, their eyes outlined with kohl, startling and liquid and in compact addition, like black prunes floating in coconut milk, their faces round and covered with cooling white powder, and the inevitable row of front-teeth work of the goldsmith. It was a rose-musk wafting, colour-gaudy bevy, full of hushed titter, and tranquil with the long habit of waiting for nothing at all but for life which came and went of its own accord, not to be assaulted with action as it was by the whiteskins and the Chinese.

Their husbands of course sat downstairs, thin phalanxes of men, their heads covered in velvet black songkoks, and dressed indecisively (not knowing whether this was meant to be a rejoicing occasion or not) in a variety of garments, open flowing nylon shirts and tapering corduroy slacks, sarongs and white flowing blouses. Treble-voiced children ran up and down, losing their red and green and blue and yellow rubber slippers on the cement steps.

But in front of the ladies, the first two rows of the balcony stalls seated white police officers and members of the Government, dressed in obvious approval of the oncoming function.

And now on the dusky green-curtained stage came Sir Moksa himself, in white sharkskin, greeted by resolute applause from a corner of the hall, who sat down and then got up again to call for a cloth to wipe the dusty chairs. Mr. Poh Cho-yee and a few other bespectacled and rotund businessmen of the local Chamber of Commerce filed in, also wiped their chairs, and sat, framing Sir Moksa and a table covered with pale blue linoleum on which stood six bottles of Green Spot, a local orangeade, uncorked, with straws emergent ready to be sipped.

The manager of the cinema and his thin son, the local photographer, weighed down with three cameras and trailed by a small boy with lighting apparatus, now adjusted the microphone; two nieces of Sir Moksa, in apple-green organdie, with fresh permanents and rouged cheeks, garlanded him with flowers, a wreath enveloped with glittering translucent paper letting out frangipani perfume through tiny holes.

'All set?' asked Sir Moksa, when the last photograph of Mr. Poh Cho-yee shaking hands with him (Mr. Poh owned the cinema) had been taken. 'Now we can begin, yes?'

But he couldn't, for up and down the middle aisle like a bustling collector at church went Mr. Bee, squat and strenuous and streaming, whose function in life was to belong to committees and to organize inauguration ceremonies. Mr. Bee's energy was tremendous ('I belong to forty-one committees, man, forty-one, lah'), and perhaps what pleased him most about his displays of vitality and public spirit was that none of his efforts ever came to anything. He never prognosticated less than total failure, and was invariably right.

'You know,' he said happily, shaking his head at me as he seated two or three government officials recruited within the last half-hour to fill the seats, 'I don't think PIP will last more than three months, maybe six, if they've got funds.' He rushed down to throw out a hawker edging his food-stall in, came back, signalled to Mr. Poh and pointed at his watch to signify more waiting, and added: 'You know, man, we aren't as foolish or as stupid as Government thinks. We're even getting cleverer, I'm telling you. We *have* got eyes in our heads. We don't want anything that's got too much of Government's hands behind it, pushing ... lah,' and glared away from the overhanging rows of police officials, presenting the square back of his grizzly head at them. And suddenly blew out his cheeks, again seized with agitation, and stalked round shushing more people into chairs and ordering young boys on incomprehensible errands.

'Responsibility,' said Mr. Bee, returning. 'It's a tremendous responsibility, every time, I tell you. And it's all on me, man, all on me. Suppose someone blew up those fellas on the stage there ... I've got to have eyes everywhere ... The moment I see someone doing something suspicious ... ho! ho!' He shook his head. 'It takes a lot out of me, that and my committees ... I couldn't sleep last night thinking of the responsibility. One grenade, just one hand-grenade, would finish that lot, man, I'm telling you.'

We both gazed longingly towards the stage. 'Yes, man, when I was a kid I could have aimed that far, but I tell you now I shall be happy-lah when this is all over. It's sending up my blood pressure.'

And Mr. Bee held out his wrist for me to take his pulse.

I murmured that nothing would happen, but 'That's what people always say,' retorted Mr. Bee. 'But "They" have us on their black list, the *shu tsai* (the forest rats). Anyone who works with the whiteskins. I know I'm on a list. Maybe I'm at the head of one. I hope the police are doing their duty. But these Malay fellows are no good, they sleep standing up...' If anyone had been caught with a grenade, Mr. Bee would have felt that his life had point and meaning. Later he flitted by again. 'I'm taking all precautions. *I* am not caught napping. I have a permit and I have a gun on me.' And he slapped his bulging pocket. 'A gun,' he repeated, looking round, daring anyone to come for him.

And now we were all getting hungry, and Mr. Poh came down the stage and he and Mr. Bee conferred importantly. And then the microphone's prehensile black claw rose from the stage floor and thrust itself up to Sir Moksa's face, and all of us – Chinese shopkeepers, hawkers, a few *trisha* pullers asleep at the back, Malay teachers and Indian clerks, and plain clothes men and informers – re-arranged our hands and feet and prepared for the next four hours of speech making.

Down from the gallery a solid row of khaki and black belts and polished badges loomed upon Sir Moksa, the Chief Police Officer and Clerkwell presiding deities, intimidating as any Olympus gazing upon mere mortals and it really looked as if Sir Moksa was terribly brave, especially when in the first half-hour he raised his hand and banged the blue linoleum cloth and said: 'Colonialism must come to an end,' and from the Malays present both above and below, came quick light handclaps.

After the ceremony Mr. Bee got hold of me again as I stepped out of the now steamy cinema into the more suffocating street.

'Where you putting? Don't you run away, man. You come to lunch. I invite you. We are having a lunch, the Police and Sir Moksa and the other Big Shots. You better come too, give me face, lah.' And added: 'Anyway, the *makan*[1] will be good. My

[1] *Makan*: food.

restaurant make it, man.' He ticked on his fingers. 'Three kinds of curry we cook. One for Malays, one for Indians and one for Europeans. You can have all three,' he added generously. 'You know my motto: Good food for good men ... hahaha.' And on these mysterious words he rushed off again.

And on the long white-draped trestle tables, under the whirring inevitability of fans sending lukewarm sprays of curry-scented air above our heads, the curries lay in white dishes swimming in their own brown-gold, red-gold and yellow-gold juices.

Sir Moksa sat next to Mr. Stallart and thought the crowd had been quite good. 'How did you like it?' he asked me.

'Very much,' I replied, 'everyone had a wonderful time, especially Mr. Bee. He was so worried about a hand-grenade being thrown.'

Sir Moksa shook his head with great seriousness. 'It has happened.' And went on to speak of another prominent leader who, he asserted, showed his guests a blood-stained garment kept under glass in his living-room, on a table of lacquered wood, beneath a portrait of his grandfather and a representation of Queen Victoria surrounded by her family. This garment was the result of a genuine attack upon his life, but Sir Moksa disagreed violently with the gentleman he talked about. 'It's a cheap political trick,' he said, 'showing your shirt.'

And Mr. Stallart, bright red in the face, half-stifled from having accidentally eaten the Indian curry instead of the European destined one, grunted with superhuman effort: 'Of course we'll give you a police escort to go back to Singapore.'

Dear lovable Mr. Bee, when the guests left, remained loquacious. His anxiety relieved, he was looking for more. 'Whew, I'm glad there was no grenade,' he said regretfully. 'It's all due to foresight, of course ... I believe in taking all precautions well in time ... Next time I'll arrange a smaller cinema, the empty seats won't show so much then.'

'People aren't really interested in independence,' said Bob Stewart, who stopped to chat with us and wipe his streaming brow. 'If you ask me, the good honest guy over here doesn't want to be worried with independence and elections, he just wants his rice bowl full and would be quite happy if we stayed on for ever. I think today's show proves it.'

Mr. Bee bent down to adjust his shoe, and when he lifted his head he was furious. Joviality, bustling eagerness had gone from his dull-red face.

'You heard him,' he said. 'That's what they really think of us, those red-haired devils.' He spat. 'Of course, man, I'm not interested in this sham party of yours, nobody is, when they see the front rows all filled up by Police. And then Moksa, Sir Creep-before-you-Walk, takes makan with them. No fooling, man . . .' He shook his finger at me as if I were a child, '. . . no party is going to win that's only a stooge, a running dog, I tell you, and for running dogs there's only one thing.' And mild, helpful Mr. Bee drew his hand across his throat, reinforced it with a sound : 'CRRRRRRRRR' he said.

Damp fingers grasping pen, Luke Davis sat and squirmed in his rattan chair, scratched the prickly heat studding his neck with a few white pustules of nascent heat boils, smelt sweat feral trickle down his armpits. He was working on a report on terrorist supplies smuggled across the Straits from the island of Singapore to Malaya.

Luke was happy; not merely was this a strenuous and intricate piece of detecting, long hours of patient fitting together of fact and counterfact, minute collating of more or less reliable information from agents and spies and counterspies (all to be paid out of special funds for the purpose); his absorption freed him of that disturbing inner malaise which made him question the purpose of his efforts and the validity of his intentions.

For he was of the tribe called tender-minded, to whom compunction clings as native skin; who expect others and themselves to act as they ought instead of behaving as they do. Such people are more likely found among those miscalled Intellectual; hard upon their own failings, no dogma is secure with them. Their minds are unable to leave mental stones unturned. They remain for ever suspect, disadvantaged among the many who stifle dubiety with the clamour of conviction.

In a country and in a job where thinking is nearly out of bounds, and bound to withhold action, awareness of this fault kept Luke a little apart from his fellows and consequently lonely. He had gone into the Police hoping to lose this weakness in action, as men sincere enough to know themselves capable of being afraid live dangerously, for ever to test the edge of their fear.

But in the Force he had found another kind of loneliness, that of the white man cut off from the world around him, clinging to disfigure shreds of his own.

This collective loneliness, a morose mass blight, insecurely forgotten in drink and women, gave rise to the all-night stuporous sessions at Club or Mess, when, gathered round stengahs under the star-thick sky, with the brain-fever bird in the black loom of trees pitching high jabbered soliloquy, the frogs booming and the crickets rending the silken stuff of darkness, white men and women talked and talked and went on talking, progressively thicker-tongued and more tedious, of plays seen back Home on leave last year, films seen last week, dances and mess nights long gone ... so tired of each other yet making no move to wrest their cramped somniferous minds away, dreading the hour of parting, lingering with hand on car door over the last lamentable joke; anything but to be alone, body thrown back upon itself, brain unriveted to the familiar.

Sitting in the charmed circle round their drinks, unwilling to stay, unable to go, Luke wondered whether they were all slightly insane, their tranced logomachy the senseless parody of the fever bird among the trees.

Within the claustrophilic narrowness of people like themselves they placed all their emotions, pitched their success or downfall. Only the opinion of the circle, the Club, the Service, the Force, counted: they knew no other. Only its Lilliputian likes and dislikes, loves and hatreds and gossip for ever renascent. Here was treachery, comfort, laughter, microcosmic tragedy, and above all good fellowship, a back-slapping joviality macabre in its violent exaggeration, its strained emphasis on being 'a good chap', possessing esprit de corps and the impassioned conformity which mitigated their loneliness.

Tropical neurasthenia it was called when the women began to weep all day and stayed up all night talking and drinking, reluctant to regain the conjugal car and depart ... a spell of Home was then indicated. For the men there were of course 'let'ups' inaccessible to women. Such as mess nights.

On mess nights loneliness exploded, council school humour in full smut romped unbuttoned in jocose abundance of lavatory and sex words relentlessly conjoined, roared its inane enormities in songs long past obscenity with age. Pitiful hour by hour went on the stale unsteady bawdiness, and at five in the morning all good fellows together, glued in weary confraternal maundering, nursed their splitting heads, while below the veranda in the steely dawn Luke saw the faces upraised as to manna from heaven, early hawkers and sleepy servants tarrying ashamed and pleased, imitating the tuans, the demigods.

His malaise had increased. Even swamped in work tracking

down men and women for their political beliefs, he often wondered what he was doing; repeating to himself that his duty was to put down terrorism, he would wonder why the means employed to do so should upset him so much.

And thus doubt was with him, as the smell and feel of jungle putrefaction attends the birth of new plant life; the helpless conviction that he was not convinced against all reason; and so he suffered a vision in which what was most right and proper seemed to him grotesque and trivial. He had no words for this but 'soft watches', having once seen a book of Dali reproductions, and with a shock recognized his own mind when warping doubt twisted all shapes and gestures. All Malaya became as this painted dream, confusion systematized, a deliquescence of intentions and of ends discrediting the rigid and geometric system of the Force with its nightmare deformities ... He looked in others for the same hesitations, found them occasionally in newspapermen wearily trudging South East Asia; in young men reared in a liberal tradition and bewildered by injustice compulsory and systematic; at evening, sipping beer under the torrid neon of the Chinese restaurant, with the lights along the Causeway dipping immeasurable elongation into the dark core of the Straits, and the shuffled nostalgic pounding of the night mail, its pilot engine streaming a forward light upon the tracks, expecting derailment; in Oliver Daley, speaking slowly, shy from the depth of his illogical faith in human kind.

But more often he found no answer but the essential rule, the law of survival, the law of the jungle:

'All weapons must be used. It's THEM, or US.'

'The end justifies the means.'

Words, comfortable planks set together to make a specious floor above the chasm of doubt.

And so Luke remained troubled and guilty, ignorant that this very doubt wearying the strong and perfect springs of ruthlessness was perhaps the vital essence, the soul and meaning of the freedom he was defending, even though it was also true that it was rubber which he fought to keep.

Because of this flaw there existed for Luke friendship beyond the magic circle of the stengahs, but he derived little comfort from the unmasked trust of Asians, people not quite like himself, whose opinions did not exist for the Club and the Mess. And there was Maxine Gerrard.

It was better for one's nerves and work to be suited early on in a tour with a nice girl than to run around chopping and changing. Seldom was there trouble, and if so, it did not leak out. The most recent mishap, to be repeated at least twice a week in a burr of manly whispers, its titillation guaranteed to last quite as long as the historical rancour against Somerset Maugham, concerned an officer who had hired his chauffeur's wife for service every Thursday night. His own spouse was returning by P. & O., and three days before her arrival the tuan ordered his syce to tell his wife not to appear the coming Thursday. The message miscarried. The Malay girl had gone to her kampong to visit her mother, and returning late in the evening headed straight for the tuan's bungalow without first visiting her own hut. That night the mem woke with a start to find a woman naked bending over her husband in the twin bed and shaking him softly: 'I'm here, Tuan, it's me, Yalah, it's Thursday.' And then there was the chap caught plying amorously a charming Malay dancer upon a pingpong table; the latter collapsed suddenly, the fracas bringing a small posse of mata-matas guns in hand to the scene.

But apart from incidents like these, enough to keep the conversational ball rolling for the next twenty years, everyone suited themselves in comfort and secrecy. Difficulty in starting acquaintance was slight; there were always people like Lam Teck, and other loose agents of the Force, too willing to help. Lam Teck, with his vast number of contacts of all categories, was always ready to introduce nice healthy girls to 'honest, clean and generous friends of mine in the Imperial Government'.

For several months Lam Teck had living as guests in his flat two buxom eighteen-year-olds, full blown and robustly curved as are the new generations of Asia, both mistresses of white police officials. He spoke of them fondly as his nieces, shielded from blackmail by their presence, tangible symbols of the favour of the Imperial British Government.

'Of course, of course,' with charm and his usual air of hidden compassion he would exclaim to the secret society man collecting half-yearly subscriptions: 'My friend, I am only too happy, too pleased to help your esteemed charitable organization ... but at the moment I have loaned my last two thousand dollars to the dear wife of Mr. Gibson ... you know Mr. Gibson of the anti-corruption bureau, don't you? His dear wife is my relation, staying here at the moment ...'

It was while buying socks in Raffles Place that Luke Davis and Bob Stewart, hunting together, had acquired, Bob the cashier and Luke the salesgirl.

Delightful Alice, round and golden, scarcely to his shoulder, hesitant and proper. Her father was a small, always tired baba Chinese, English-speaking clerk, twenty-five years stooped in fear of losing his job; there was conservative mama and a third grand-auntie much to be feared, now working at night shift as rubber packers, for there were many many children, and life was so expensive now, and Alice was a good girl, turning in all her earnings to help her family. Luke made her an allowance, and Alice was docile and so gentle.

In that perverse twist of mind which attends upon the tenderminded, and had made Luke choose the Force to cure his doubts, he derived satisfaction from the very fact that he was suited when he met Maxine. It conferred a spiritual superiority upon her, which subsequent hasty fumblings on her bed in the perspiring darkness of her room had not dispelled. And Maxine was so jumpy, always worrying that people might know. And now he needed a few strong brandies when he met her to create sufficient urgency ... she gave in with bad grace, but if he did not ask she was plain angry.

Yet still Luke believed that marriage with Maxine would give him peace from himself, and he would summon back the memory of his first meeting with her to help him bolster his faith.

It was when his discontent had become strong enough to spill into words upon paper, in a police report: *Often the measures we are adopting are turning a passively non-co-operating community into deep hostility....*

We have complained of the passiveness of the people, not only the Chinese, but all communities in Malaya ... it can be argued whether any colonial setup can expect people who feel themselves in bondage to co-operate more ... to the rising exasperation of nationalism, local communism may appear preferable to alien rule ... our only hope is to implement definitely our promises of handing over independence....

And again: *The peoples of Malaya, irrespective of race, appear to want colonialism and communism to exhaust each other, while they stand by and wrest what concessions they can from the struggle....*

The report lay on the Chief's table and the frowning Chief's small moustache hovered above it, like a falcon with pinions outspread to pounce. Luke was being put on the mat.

'General policy is not our pigeon, Davis ... these opinions frankly hostile ... in future confine yourself to a straightforward account of the measures we are taking to cope with the problem.'

'That's just the point,' said Luke, 'we are not.'

Exasperation made the lean man with the worried brow confide to Blenkinsop, fat goggle-eyed Blenkinsop, exuding sweat and good fellowship, Blenkinsop whom at all times he disliked for the gossip which dribbled unendingly out of him. Blenkinsop's nickname in the Force was the Crystal Gazer, for his uncanny talent in predicting transfers, promotions, who was 'making his number with the Chief' and who was not. The Crystal Gazer sympathized at once and lengthily, and immediately hurried round to the Mess to tell everyone, and at five p.m. repeated at the Club over the very first stengah pouring its mellowed ice in bodies tired with sweating, that Davis had mucked himself up good and proper this time, served him right too, nearly a socialist he was, with his damn queer theories on freedom for Malaya....

That night Luke saw Maxine in a cluster of other girls fresh from Home, recently arrived from England. The men in short white jackets were subtly excited, looking over the new cargo and striving to wit more than usual under the gaudy bulbs upon the green lawn, with the photographer taking flash pictures of groups with glasses in their hands, and inch deep the high heels sank in the damp sward. Shoulders moved framed by darkness, laughter pealed, a wholesome noise covering cricket and frog, and the toctoc bird was mute when Luke found himself talking, talking his doubts and bitterness to the girl whose hair was a soft gold wave. She placed a hand upon his and said: 'I understand, I do so well, it's because you're gentle and kind...' More than the words, which in memory annoyed him, there was her voice, the sympathy of it, as if she too owned these doubts, hid them from common view....

'You ... we ... maybe we're a little bit ... idealistic...' A little burst of deprecating laughter, for the word is insult in Malaya....

And a few weeks later the Chief again, but how different. 'That report of yours, Davis ... mind you, no one here agrees with your general point of view ... but some of the Psychological Warfare chaps seemed to think there might be something useful in a few of your suggestions for handling people ... it's in line with the new approach, you know, winning the hearts and minds ... go easy on them....'

Luke glowed. At last, he thought, some sense ... and did

not notice that what he wrote as a statement of principle, an end in itself, had become yet another weapon, a means ... to what end?

But after that he bought his socks elsewhere, and Maxine's body was occasionally in his arms, replacing Alice, Maxine to be formally owned when her three-year contract with Government was up (a few more months to go), since marrying now meant he would have to pay back her passage money. Increasingly he put away a growing apprehension that the safe, comforting, desired cage of Maxine of the glowing hair would also safely thrust out other things he liked. The companionship of Asians, not of course on a par with his own people, but so pleasant, brimming with life and laughter. And Oliver Daley ... Luke had developed a deep friendship for Oliver Daley, now struggling to win the hearts and minds of the people of Todak. Lately Maxine had become conventional, cutting off his dubieties with a curt:

'It's THEM or US. . . .'

He felt she would not like Oliver Daley. Only Che Ahmad might pass muster, and then not to be invited to parties, just to see him, Luke, on business, and be offered a cup of tea.

But with Maxine the Magic Circle, the Club, the Mess, once palpably hostile, now welcomed. They, people like themselves, all liked her. Her laughter rang and chimed with theirs. With her he was the prodigal returned, and the strong grip of their joviality (however part of him shivered from it) still held him. Unless he belonged, only the terror of being alone remained. And so he hoped against hope, forging his own chains, that with bright curve of lip and mane of hair Maxine would hold him safe from the unseemly hydra-headed fantasies rising within him, which, as the thick dun curtains of monsoon rain sweeping the land, bleared the harsh landscape in which he functioned, wielder of Power almost absolute, a police officer in Malaya.

'It has been known for some time,' wrote Luke, pen biting deep into the paper, 'that the terrorists operating in the jungles of Johore have been receiving steady supplies of a quantity of material of all kinds from the island of Singapore.

'It is not unknown to us that the Communist Party Executive Committee of Johore controls their branch in the island of Singapore, which in their geography is but an offshoot of Malaya.

'A look at the map' (Luke frowned at the map of Johore State which adorned his office, spread like a large green lobster claw holding between its two pincers the island of Singapore) 'will show that there are thousands of small inlets along the coast, up any of which smuggling has been going on for many years already, chiefly from Indonesia. These accessible inlets can be utilized by the communist organization, and, furthermore, there are the *kelongs*, those fishing stakes studding the sea from three hundred yards up to a mile or two off the coast. There provide convenient storage space and halting points for any number of small boats plying the Straits in their hundreds.

'We have not manpower enough to cover the beaches and search every small craft. The operation would take up the whole of the Force now in existence upon this side of the Straits. On the Singapore side there has been so far little successful attempt to control the flow of goods which, in a thousand ways, are smuggled aboard the small boats and taken across to Johore.

'It is not so much a question of negligence as a question of attitude. To us, bound by our own legal assumptions, Singapore and Malaya are two countries, each with its own Police Force. Singapore is a Colony and a great city, and therefore its communist organization wears a different face and uses different weapons from the militant terrorism which is possible in the rubber estates and from the jungle.

'To put it crudely, we have established our own mental Iron Curtain, a "you look after your house and I'll look after mine" outlook, which is a danger and a fatal inefficiency at the moment.

'This, as it negates all our efforts to end the Emergency, is perhaps one of the reasons why terrorism in Johore is more intense than in any other of the nine States of Malaya. Half of the incidents of the Emergency take place in Johore State.

'The Japanese have already proved to us that half a mile of water was no barrier when they took Singapore, crossing the Straits and not even utilizing the Causeway, which we blew up. The communists, too, are not mentally impeded by this myth of the island's separateness.

'Through our intelligence work,' wrote Luke, 'we have been able to plot, more or less accurately, five probable courier routes. Information shows that in the links utilized, passing goods in small quantities from person to person, women are used, some well-trained in underground activity during the Japanese occupation. We expect these women to be the inoffensive-looking, nondescript and respectable old lady type, travelling slowly by bus, carrying nothing more guilty than a cloth-bound parcel, which she will unwrap slowly to show the road block searchers some innocent purchases. Such a person can be very useful especially for carrying messages written on cigarette paper and rolled very thin in the hem of a garment.'

Luke paused. Should he make it stronger? Might as well be hanged ... He thought, and went on blithely:

'A terrorist document captured last week gives the following items as received within a week from Singapore:

20 rubber groundsheets
650 pairs of tennis shoes, man-size, green and tan
200 school exercise books, lined
25 diaries
384 white face towels inscribed "Good Morning"
2000 Aspro pills, 200 Santonin and 1700 Paludrine tablets
10 fountain pens
4 cartons of Lucky Strike cigarettes
1200 grenade cases (these may be part of the haul from the thefts discovered from British ammunition depots in Singapore).'

There, thought Luke, that last sentence will be a bitter pill to swallow. Half a million dollars' worth of military equipment had 'disappeared' in Singapore over the past two years, including fifty-nine large shells which had been sawn and passed piece by piece over the barbed wire....

'It is suggested that the following preliminary measures may not come amiss to ensure greater co-operation. Some of these have already been put forward by other officers whose advice has been sought. Time presses, and we must cut these courier routes and the smuggling immediately. As it is now, Singapore is proving in some respects a base of supplies for the communists of Malaya....'

'No,' he thought, 'that's really going to make them livid. I'll cut it out.'

There was a knock, and the head of detective Pang swivelled round the door, a flash of gleaming teeth and eyes. A handsome young fellow Pang, and so damned clever.

'Come in, come in!' cried Luke. 'Take a pew, Pang, old chap.' There was always much heartiness in their mutual greetings.

Pang remained standing, prancing a little on his toes, hands in his pockets. Luke knew the stance.

'I can see you've got something for me, Pang.'

Pang laughed. 'Something good, very good, sir, you'll like it, you'll like very much, it's even better than a good Chinese makan...' He laughed again, then sat down a little familiarly, knowing his value. 'You remember this morning?'

'Of course I do.' Luke and Pang and Blenkinsop had spent the morning photographing surrendered personnel. There were five, all under twenty-three, come out of the jungle together, decidedly a triumph for the force and the Psychological Warfare guys. Luke and Blenkinsop made sure that they stood well up, face straight to the camera, not bent on chest or turned sideways in a shift to avoid complete exposure; with their shirts white and clean laundered and their long dark pants, similar to that of the detectives, they looked like an incipient basketball team, grinning widely.

Below this group photograph would be printed the appeal to surrender, and then, in tens of thousands, the resulting sheets would be dropped by aircraft flying over the region of jungle they had come from. Perhaps a few of them would filter through the vault of the jungle and be picked up by their comrades. 'See,' said the words, 'these are your erstwhile comrades, now fat and happy here. They have food, they have money ... come out and you will have food, food and money, and a job, and freedom, only just come, walk out of the jungle where you are starving now ... and don't forget to bring your gun with you.'

Out of his pocket Pang now drew one of these snapshots and pointed to the third face on the second row. 'This chap,' he said, 'I've been working on him, in a nice way, of course, in my spare time ... his uncle I used to know a little.' (Pang did not add that it was while he had been a Party member himself.) 'He has a young brother, a waiter in a coffee shop here...'

He paused, a consummate artist of suspense, his bright eyes upon the perspiring white man.

'And he tells me his brother is one of the links for the couriers to Singapore...'

Luke beamed. 'That's good, that's wonderful, Pang, we must get on to him quick.'

'We have already. I've detained the whole coffee shop, the towkay, his wife, everybody, even some people who sat there drinking coffee ... one of them might be another link ... but we'll sort them out gradually within the next few weeks. I thought you'd be pleased,' he added, modestly.

'Am I pleased? Why, that's great Pang, that's wonderful...'

'I've put the waiter in special. He looks like his brother, thinner, and wears a large aluminium clip in his hair. He doesn't look very tough. He'll probably give quite soon. I'll work on him tonight.'

'Go right ahead.' There wasn't much more any white officer could do about this questioning business, except be present and watch that the man wasn't bashed about too much. Only very occasionally did a white man go in for a spot of bashing, and it was officially discouraged.

He was in luck. The joy of the hunt was upon Luke, and he strode out with Pang to inspect the new batch of detainees, and especially the thin young waiter with the large clip in his hair.

Silent and dark is the undisturbed, the rainforest, the jungle, with its large mute lords the trees upsoaring like cathedral pillars to burst two hundred feet above into many-layered ceilings of foliage and tangled vine and creeper, orchids and monkeys and birds.

Through this sieve of roofs the sun seeps, rain filters finely to mingle with the perpetual steaming from the boggy ground. Heaven-warded by the thick shield of leaf, the inflexible white sky of noon beats down upon the flowers of the forest which swing their faces upwards to the light.

Within the sombre jungle Chan Ah Pak the jungle fighter, member of the Malayan Races Liberation Army, felt at ease, enclosed in the womblike perpetuity of its warmth, treading familiarly the hushed temple whose vaulting pillars were spaced with almost mathematical exactness. Such regularity existed also in the other, the man-made forest of rubber, two million acres of similar trees equidistant from each other, dripping with fantastic monotony the white rain of latex from the herringbone pattern of cuts on their boles. Within that jungle, too, Chan Ah Pak walked with a roof overhead, easefully cautious for the sound of pursuit or the stillness of ambush, the manhunt that would catch and kill him one day.

From the small platform erected up a convenient tree in the rainforest he watched the other, delimited by a high barbed-wire fence. There was a special constables' post, erected to patrol this area of the rubber estate. The post was a small wood structure housing seven young men from the Malay kampongs. There were a hundred and fifty thousand of these specials now, patrolling the rubber forests with guns.

It was true, what the specials had told him last night across the fence, their pensive smile trigger-conscious, wary still in a truce which could break at any moment; but after three months in the post they had come to terms, not wishing to be shot at. There would be an inspection of the estate today, they said, with the Tuan Manager, and the Big Tuan who looked after all the company estates, and maybe the Tuan Police Officer.

The seven were stirring more than usual. Two sat under the papaya trees in front of the barracks and furbished their rifles, laughing softly, their movements and voices restrained by the early lethargy which they carried with them from their sleepy kampongs. One was standing at the fence, a wonderful target, peering at the jungle, practising a stance he thought might impress the Tuans. The others, inside the hut, were trying to make the telephone ring. Its black wire left their hut to spring from tree to tree along the estate road to the central office.

It was early yet. The estate manager did not come to this part of the estate until about ten o'clock, and with guests he might be later. Ah Pak felt comfortable in his rubber tapper clothes (standard issue kit for the Liberation Army pack), his rubber shoes, and only a revolver. His orders were to watch, to report on the group. Then his camp commandant would decide and plan the ambush tomorrow.

Ah Pak was pleased with his success in making neutrals of the post specials. It was in line with the New Policy. The New Policy had started over a year ago, but it took time for all the units to be told, and more for them to obey. Sen saw that they did obey. 'We must win the Malays to our cause. They will become more and more useful ... the enemy is trying to starve us out. They are cutting us off from our people. We must get food from the Malays too.'

Ah Pak, with a Malay comrade from the Malay regiment of Mustapha Kling, a Malay communist leader, had been able to talk and to win over the seven naive and slow-witted men. It was a precarious success, for however dull in some ways, they were treacherous, with a mindless treachery, a soft and casual will to murder, especially if money, or religion, or women, was the issue. But at the moment, with money, cigarettes, promises to spare their life, and the name of Mustapha Kling, the specials' post gave the jungle fighters no trouble.

Had Chan Ah Pak suffered from a sense of humour and a

detached mind, he might have laughed wryly, thinking suddenly of the similarity in the tactics evolved on both sides. The British Police were out to woo the people from communism, with soft words, and courtesy lessons for their own constables, with medical aid and money rewards for information. And the People Inside, too, were forbidden now to destroy trees and frighten people, and only allowed to kill planters, policemen and informers.

But comparison, however acridly stimulating to those cursed with a perverted sense of humour, would have been unpopular in the circles in which Chan Ah Pak lived and worked, as it would have been in the circles in which Luke Davis lived and worked. The difference in their punishment, however, would have been important: Davis would have been ostracized, failed to 'make his number', mucked up his career and possibly ruined his prospects; Chan Ah Pak, quite simply, would have died.

Winning the hearts of the Malays, then, the 10th Regiment of the jungle was now engaged in dealings with Mustapha Kling, the Malay communist leader, whose name all the kampong Malays seemed to know. They wagged their heads when they heard it, and smiled acknowledging, not because he was a comrade and a communist, one of the few Malays up in arms against the British, but because he was invulnerable.

Chan Ah Pak, whose frame of mind, being Chinese, was to look down upon the Malays as unreliable and inefficient, believed in this invulnerability of Mustapha Kling. The Malays did have potent charms, and they sold invulnerability spells in tiny amulets containing a cut from the root of a male virgin bamboo with cabbalistic signs and the name of Allah engraved upon it. In the ancestors' country, too, there had been bands in the forests, men like himself, Chan Ah Pak, fleeing to the green shade from a corrupt and tyrannous government and thence dealing true justice, who had been invulnerable. And the Righteous Fists, who had killed the imperialists up and down China fifty years ago, had claimed that silver bullets alone could hit them. Such was Mustapha Kling's boast today.

Ah Pak hitched himself a little further forward, on his concealed platform, noticed that the special constables had relapsed into immobility, and let his mind wander softly, half dreaming.

Unlike Luke Davis, Chan Ah Pak did not know doubt. Bulwarked, felted from hesitation by violence since he was twelve, his only unease was dreams. He had dreams of the most vivid variety, and ascribed it to hunger, which of course he accepted as he did violence, common as breathing, nearly as ubiquitous and casual as death. The most usual dream he had was a bank of gorgeous butterflies skimming the thick green water of a pool, their self-illumined wings gathering all the strained twilight in a blaze of swift splendid colour; then unfelt, soft walking as violence itself and as noiseless, came a gust of wind and the butterflies would suddenly be gone.

'In the floating dream of life, we are but leaves blown from a tree, butterflies playing for a day in the sun...' Despite the slogany creed which made his diary (where he never wrote down his dreams) such dreary reading, Ah Pak was of a race whose poetry was an explanation of existence, of living. Whenever any comrade brought into the jungle a Chinese newspaper, Ah Pak would turn to page eight, which carried from top to bottom the blank verse, the sonnets, the short stories written by the Chinese school children of Malaya, the best of the lot every day.

Oh Pak's memory retained no dates, months or years, but was sensitive as a photographic plate to the time of the day and the people, their gestures, their words, and the words unuttered behind the masks of their faces. In the enduring twilight of the jungle he would think back easily, solacing himself with the stories of himself and the comrades and the world that he knew. This past, always fresh and clear, unexhausted and nourishing, reeled off before his eyes, unrolling like an endless panoramic photograph.

Small Cloud was there washing clothes on the river bank at the small flat place, while further on the mangrove shoots in their myriads pierced the glassy water. Ah Pak saw and felt the slow blush spread upwards upon her face to the roots of her hair, and the blow in the middle of his chest struck again as she turned and left, and then he heard her cry, a rising wail, as she was caught.

Now and always whenever he came, silent on quiet feet and sudden, walking in and out of the camps of the jungle, there was the face of Sen and the body of Sen to be watched, to be seen without looking. And never was anything to be seen on Sen, nor fear nor resentment, nor suspicion nor anger. Nothing.

As wisps of the wind flicking, high up in the forest roof among the flowers, an endless soft rain of leaf and petal eddying slowly downwards to the leafmould ground, so seeped rumours and gossip among the circles of the jungle, those open mat-shed camps where the comrades rested, ate and moved to and from.

In this world, too, rumours led an undying parasitic life of their own; here was Ah Mao, another Crystal Gazer, muttering news confused and unproven, and yet as likely as seed to grow, rank fantastic, indestructible.

These rumours said that Sen was the son of a wealthy man, a millionaire, a traitor, son of Poh Cho-yee, the rubber magnate, the owner of brothels and cinemas and pawnshops and tin mines, secretly secret society man, and that Sen had sworn to do justice and kill his father.

But it was very difficult to kill Poh Cho-yee. Not only did he have a triple wire fence round his house, thick bars at all the windows, the usual Sikh *jagas*[1] armed with guns sleeping on rope pallets front and back, army-trained Alsatian dogs scurrying round the grounds at night, and a crew of bodyguards and a bullet-proof American car, but he very seldom moved without changing his plans at the last moment to put off intended attacks, and never crossed the Causeway except under heavy guard. It was even impossible to kidnap his sons or grandsons, for the children went to school and returned in a closed car with armed guards and amahs on both sides, human shields should someone shoot through the windows.

Others said no, Sen was the son of Quo Boon, had learnt his English at English school and even gone to England, but all the time had been a member of the Organization, so quiet that the British did not know anything much about him. Quo Boon was a traitor too, collaborating with the British, although not such a traitor as Poh Cho-yee, who had also collaborated with the Japanese.

But now rumour said that Small Cloud was also a traitor, helping the pig-faces, giving information against her own people.

Traitors ... Ah Pak knew a hard time was coming, a time of questing for traitors, and sudden execution. It was always thus when Policy changed, the weak ones lost heart, the recruits became disgruntled; the unsteady ones skulked out, to surrender....

Ah Low, who could never count the subscription money correctly, had surrendered in a fit of temper and hunger, angry to be called stupid and laughed at; angry and bewildered because food was less than ever before. Shouldering his rifle one morning he had gone, through the jungle, through the dense abandoned clearings with their devious hidden footpaths, crossing a

[1] *Jaga*: door-keeper.

derelict rubber plantation and tracts of pineapple fields, to stand at last on the edge of the tarmac road where the motor cars whizzed past like frightened rabbits. He stopped a passenger bus by levelling his gun at the driver.

The driver screeched the bus to a stop, and stayed paralysed, blue with terror, while Ah Low clambered on, glared round him and found suddenly the front bench empty, all the passengers sitting at the back, their eyes not upon him but looking above his head, or gazing with intense interest through the windows, or at their hands ... Afterwards, when questioned, not one of the passengers could remember seeing Ah Low get into the bus, not one but looked deeply astonished to hear that such a thing had occurred. The driver was told by Ah Low to drive to the next police station, and there Ah Low climbed down.

But things miscarried for Ah Low. The Malay mata-matas at the station seized him, and claimed that they had caught him hiding, and, there being insufficient evidence of his will to surrender, Ah Low was hanged. Meanwhile his comrades abandoned camp when his depature was noticed, for fear he might bring the Security troops, to buy his life with theirs. And after Ah Low's hanging there were no more surrenders from the 10th Regiment.

There was the day Chan Ah Pak picked up a piece of paper at the edge of a clearing overgrown with dense bush, and found it a propaganda leaflet, with a photograph of two comrades who had surrendered, and the call to come out, bringing his gun....

Bringing his gun ... Ah Pak tore the pamphlet savagely, carefully buried the fragments in leafmould. He would never surrender. Yet the mere fact that he had found the pamphlet troubled him and made him suspicious of himself for a day or so. That afternoon he was more conscious than ever of Sen, his quiet eyes which seemed to see everything. He shovelled his tapioca mixed with coarse rice into his mouth, then belched loyally, heartily. Comrade Chan Ah Pak was not afraid of traitors.

Had he been dressed in an open nylon shirt and long trousers Sen, walking on the streets of Singapore, would have looked exactly like a university student, only perhaps more refined, slimmer than the hefty, boisterous yet timid extroverts which English schools seemed to produce out of Chinese youngsters. He walked in and out of the camps, appearing and disappearing, heralded half an hour before arrival by a bodyguard who would squat waiting for him. Quiet, unconcerned, apparently unarmed, he strolled in to stay a day, or two, at the most a week, and off he would go. None asked his destination, nor questioned the orders he brought, the Policy he would explain, and after he left the camp commandant would once more repeat the orders and the Policy, so that everyone would know that he had understood.

Ah Pak did not know whether Sen would be gone when he returned from his watch. But tomorrow he was sure to be gone. Old Mother would also be gone. Ah Pak's mother had come last night, by the devious ways she alone seemed to find, turning and twisting and always eluding capture, carrying messages. She had given them to Sen, small, identically tiny pellets of tightly folded cigarette paper concealed everywhere upon her, monotonously reciting where each one came from. Ah Pak had been on guard duty near Sen, and had nearly cried out *Aiyah* in astonishment when Old Mother had extracted a message from her belt and said: 'And this is from Small Cloud, given me at the market fruit stall.'

Ah Pak's eyes went up, piercing the swift darkness, looked upon Sen's face. Certainly he would see something ... some shadow of feeling upon that thin and careful face.

But there was nothing to see, absolutely nothing at all. And in this nothingness, this huge calm which Ah Pak would never fathom, he found his strong sure faith perfected against all weapons, hunger, and defeat, and failure, and, of course, death.

Soft is violence, a silken-handed compulsion as of breath moving with secure grace to the idiot slackness of its end.

Rosie Yip, now Chief Wardress in charge of female detainees, sniffed the sleek resistless air, honeyed with the pink-gold surge of sundown, looked at the indigo hills framing the horizon of the Straits, and heard the near and docile voices, the tittered obedient laughter from the class-rooms of the camp. Within the mask of her wrinkleless round face, devoid of those rippled emotions which betray the European, she appraised the intangible with unnamed sense, a spiritual bloodhound on the trail of impending violence. Violence was sediment of long immobility, compact spark of fire from the smouldering placation of endless caging. There had not been trouble in the camp for a long time, and trouble was due.

Such hours of expected eruption marred and marked the police calendar with prophetic cancelled leaves and doubled sentry posts. May and October were months of zealous ambushed moments, when communist-inspired rioting was awaited from the camps. When nothing happened there was a feeling of slight tedium, nearly disappointment.

Rosie remembered (and treasured, though she would not have known this hoarded memory precious) a windless opaque uncounted night when the screaming had started among the 'black' females, gathered into a swelling clamour which pealed from hut to hut until like the fanfare of a forest fire it surged its fantastic shrill roaring through the camp.

Tear gas and seventy-six mata-matas with Stens, two armoured cars spitting machine-gun bellets, and a baton charge, had finally thudded flesh alive with screams into dull moans and sobs, reduced to an uneasy deadened whisper echoed in the grey dawn, when Rosie, suddenly exhausted, felt her strong calves quiver uncontrollably, the cold sweat trickle on the inside of her thighs, as she stood with her revolver painful to grip, and watched the police formation boot up the gravel of the paths in the quick trot of a last mop-up.

And all much ado for that fifteen-year-old, Ah Nia, condemned to death for consorting with terrorists but found too young to hang with her nineteen-year-old sister. She had been kept among the 'blacks' pending disposal, for the prisons were overflowing with the pick of over thirty thousand suspects, and she had begun the idiot frenzy, the ululating infection immortalized in official reports as 'communist-inspired'.

Fong Kiap, with baby proof of her consorting with terrorists, but pregnant at trial and therefore unkillable, had been more lucky than Ah Nia. She had worked her way from 'black' to 'white', and was booked for rehabilitation, owning a vastly contented face and a gum-baring smile. Only capricious madness, thought Rosie, could account for some of the punishments or releases meted out. Whiteskin folly, or turn of fate? Rosie, believing in both, never attempted to intercede or to explain, for it was wrong to meddle in anyone's destiny.

'We can't go on shoving people into camps, Wardress. All right the first few years, but it's not good enough now. Quite dislocated the economy of the State ... do you know that out of ninety thousand pigs three years ago only six thousand are left in this area? That's why we've got to process these people, get them through the machine, and either try and deport them or get them back to production, quick.'

Thus Clerkwell to Rosie, nodding wisely, knowing the Korean war over, the boom in rubber replaced by a slump, and the cost of the Emergency a staggering burden of half a million dollars a day.

These practicalities (and not the ethical scruples which also existed) convinced Rosie Yip that Authority wished to get rid of the camps as soon as possible, and that her duty was to help by making the processing smooth. Expediency is the chief ingredient of a successful administration, and Rosie prayed that until the camp closed no incident would mar the peace and inspire yet another police clampdown with its endless trail of complicated interrogations and investigations and probes ordered from On High.

Where once Commandant Hinchcliffe had struggled alone, infallible as any Infernal Magistrate, determining iniquity or redemption, there were now Interrogation Units, heavily padded with detectives, informers and interpreters, unrolling the complicated tape of histories of the detainees, questioning and reclassifying suspects. To judge by the results (thought Rosie) Hinchcliffe achieved exactly the same with his simple, single-handed 'they're good if they smile and call me Sir' standard, as the Unit with its offers of remission of sentences for help to the police as spies and informers on their fellow-detainees.

And now was the lunar seventh month, the Devil's Jubilee,

and the women's camp was fearful and fear-making with word and gesture and thought of ghosts and demons and blood-drinking spirits, both Malay and Chinese; with apparitions in shadow and the mutterings and the waving of incense sticks and the warding of Evil Eyes and the chanting of Mother Wu, the witch, versed in the crafts of both races, consulted by both, and mixing Allah with Kuanyin; claiming herself the medium of the Third Grand Beldam of Heaven, handmaid of the Gods; compounder of love philters for the lascivious; midwife and abortionist; now detained as a communist suspect for possessing two unopened tins of fruit in a restricted area, and her power in no whit lessened by detention.

Mother Wu was peaceable enough, yet round her spread a hollowness of apprehension in this the seventh month. She was consulted for amulets and safe-keeping charms, not only by the prisoners but also the policewomen. Even the woman interpreter, a hard-faced informer dismissed from another camp for corruption, now re-employed, obtained a straw-plaited male doll, complete with phallus, cinctured with a khaki strip of shirt from her ex-lover, a young British police lieutenant, and kept it under her pillow, reciting conjurations to regain his yearnings.

And the guards watched at night with a strong light, afraid.

With a great show of careless good temper Rosie watched, sprinkling her loud and agile talk with jovial salacity, knowing laughter an undoer of evil.

'Still breast-feeding your Babee, Fong Kiap, and he like a pig suckling and two years old.'

'Three years by our people's reckoning,' replied Fong Kiap, resolute and tranquil now that baby was a lusty bawling infant of enormous size.

'How long will you give him your paps to suck? He'll still be at them when he becomes a papa himself.'

Gales of joy shook the camp. Mother Wu, always supple-spined to Rosie, showed her heavy gold teeth soldered together in a thick yellow bar in her upper jaw, the gumflesh green at its junction with the metal. Fong Kiap rocked so hard she fell off her stool.

Each morning on her way to camp Rosie Yip stopped the driver of her police car at the red shrine of Kuanyin the Mother of Mercy, the All-Compassionate.

She sat, the goddess whom none entreats in vain, her small black face sedate with crust of years of dirt and incense; the altar table in front of her heavied with pewter burners, candlesticks, oranges and pomeloes and cakes in pyramids, the stone three-legged oven with its bronze pagoda roof always smoking, sheaves of paper money rising in smoke redolent with prayer to the Heavenly Mother Never implored in Vain.

The nun in charge, with polished shaven head, lay stuporous upon her mat, savouring a cigarette and smiling at Rosie, while the Tamil nurse Doremy, already in starched white uniform on her way to the hospital, sank the syringe of a liver injection into the barely uncovered buttock. The wireless blasted swing music from Radio Malaya to entertain the Deity as Rosie made obeisance, planted some incense sticks in the sifted ash of the burners, and then saluted smartly, entreating the All-Compassionate in somewhat peremptory manner: 'Keep the devils away from the wire, keep the devils away from my camp.'

Each evening Rosie asked her large eldest daughter:

'Fat one, have you done your praying today?'

Daughter was a Catholic, a convert, student at the girls' convent school, and recited the rosary daily to ease her mother in whose tolerant and ubiquitous mind Kuanyin and the Holy Virgin had much in common except a quibble of names; both incarnations of the same principle of mercy and all-compassion, both efficient housewives and mothers, and sharing with Rosie the quality of a good policewoman, keeping watch and ward over their devotees.

And to reinforce the polymorphic safeguards Mother Wu went round with two respectful policewomen, sprinkling with wisps of feather magic on to the wires whose barbs, like rigid birds' feet, clawed the metal strings encompassing Rosie's domain.

But peace was not to be, for the whispered precursors of dread had seeped and sunk like water in a swamp, whose surface may dry but will one day crack hugely revealing the sogginess below.

It began – like the thunderless lightning lacing, above the palms, a backcloth of grey pachydermatous cloud – when Neo Saw's Child, Son, now aged fourteen, sexually assaulted the bought child of Mother Wu, a girl of eight.

Neo Saw, wife of Neo the rubber tapper, had taken ill to detention. It had warped and destroyed her unsturdy spirit into a constant catastrophe of lamentation. Unlike Fong Kiap, who bided her time and possessed herself of an interminable patience on the long dole of days back to her husband in the jungle, Neo Saw fretted herself, the moments, the hours and the sun-haunted days until their intolerable load of self-torment crushed her.

Lying with thirty other women on the wooden planks forming a single bed along the sleeping hut, round each their own particular litter of babies and small ones, Neo Saw rifled the spent and unconsidered hours with grieving.

Some women sighed and groaned at night, muttered softly in half dream of their males, woke and tossed back to fretful sleep. Some bold and strong with surge of desire in the hot hut, infinitely preoccupied with their self-made dreams, called back sentient memories of flesh close within their flesh, until they sweated and cried Ha with exasperation, or suddenly hugged their babies with soft purring ferocity, or pushed their nipples in the mouths of their three- and four-year-old sons, to appease their own hunger.

And others would whisper to one another of robust coming-togethers, with them lust a clean need like hunger and thirst, and not ashamed obscenities. Their hands soothed their thighs and breasts and their restless heaving bellies.

But most were shy and endured in wordless and actionless waiting, blank as deserts without a mirage.

None, however, wept and sobbed for her man as did Neo Saw, until it became Fonk Kiap's habit to rise sleepily from her place and crawl over the bodies of other women to Neo Saw, and slap slap slap her until she woke and stopped, lest in an excess of sorrow she rend her forlorn soul away from her sad body.

Neo Saw cried at night, wept at meals, stained her sewing with tears, and wore two trails like snail tracks down her cheeks in the classroom where she sat next to Grandmother The Rebel. 'Your face,' said the teacher, 'makes me feel like committing suicide.'

Sitting at rough tables heaving bulging haunches precariously on narrow stools, the women detainees fit for rehabilitation faced the small-boned and highstrung spinster from the Chinese Y.W.C.A. who pointed to the blackboard and said: 'A'.

'AAAAAAIH' chanted the women in stolid square obedience, their distant unseeing gaze wondering what their sons and daughters were doing outside.

'B. C.' screamed teacher, the thin-skinned veins of her neck standing their flurry of quick pulse above the collar of her gown.

When they reached the letter F Grandmother rebelled.

'ABC, ABC,' she shouted, akimbo on her tiny feet (upon which she had hobbled behind the soldiers, asking to be taken, when they scooped her village in a raid), 'ABC, ABC. I am an old woman, come sixty years from the ancestors' country, a whole life behind me, clean and hard with sons and grandsons, and a thin death in front of me, and all you do is to tell me ABC, ABC. Of what use is ABC to me?'

Rosie went to see Commandant Hinchcliffe. 'Sir ... about these classes in English, I think some of the women are too old for learning, they are quite dumb too. . . .'

'But it's regulations, Wardress, look: here's the booklet on rehabilitation: classes in English, domestic crafts. . . .'

Rosie thought: Domestic crafts! These women have sewn and washed and cooked all their lives. 'Perhaps we could have a small holiday from English, lah, and do more embroidery,' she suggested.

And let it be known among the detainees that embroidery was much prized by the whiteskins, and suitable presents for them.

Now presents and gifts though forbidden by the law were commodious and indispensable, and the whites always somehow accepted what was given, so long as it was done in a roundabout way with liquor, banquets and embroidered tablecloths hot favourites. The policewomen under Rosie often brought some dishes for her, for they were all housewives with children; cooked chicken sprinkled with chopped ginger and sesame oil; duck's feet simmered and steeped in thick black soy sauce, smoked ham, stuffed mushrooms, crinkly pork with red sauce, and sweet confections of lotus roots.

These slight easements to Rosie, symbolic wielder of power, made everyone believe that they bettered their lot, smoothed the wheels of fate, and cast the spell of a mutual relationship upon the Wardress, and through her upon the whites who made the sun and the rain for their days and their years.

In many departments, Asian secretaries and clerks, interpreters and translators, saved dollars out of their pay at Christmas and Easter, at birthdays, at the arrivals and departures of their often changed white bosses, to buy gifts for the tuan, the mem and the children of the mem. A previous officer had been given a rousing send-off with two crates of whisky and a gold cigarette case. It was their profound conviction that they obligated the receiver, bound him in honour to some slight leniency should occasion arise; a conviction always defeated by the superb belief of the just white master that these presents were manifestoes of well-deserved love and gratitude for their rule, involving no personal obligation at all.

But Rosie ruled with wariness and wisdom, custom matriarchal and shrewd, careful and lenient yet unmoved by injustice not her business, and sniffed the air in the seventh month, when the great voice of Heat unleashed ten thousand devils from Hell's mouth to roam the earth. And though Mother Wu let it be known that she was witch strong enough to repel the infernal assaults, Rosie knew better.

Besides the English teacher, a Chinese teacher was now appointed to teach the rehabilitees:

> *Little dog, big dog,*
> *Little dog jumps, big dog jumps*
> *Little dog barks, big dog barks.*

chanted the women, yawning between the dogs. Neo Saw wept quietly, opening her mouth, and Grandmother interrupted everybody from time to time loudly demanding to be sent to the death house, to await her dissolution.

It was during the mothers' class that the children in a huddled bevy gathered behind the hut, a pinched crowd staring; and nothing was known of it in the stifling afternoon until the shouting and screaming began, and Fong Kiap's voice loud above the others: 'Save life, save life.'

Rosie seized her gun and rushed to the hut, shouting to the policewomen to follow. She pounded sweat-stained backs, hit and flung arms aside to maul a way to the heart of the pack where Neo Saw lay on the earth, torn coat unbaring bosom, while Mother Wu stamped on her with bare feet, and clawed her face with all her nails.

Rosie hit Mother Wu's nape, tripped her, caught her hair and dragged her away from Neo Saw's body. Mother Wu then threw a fit, foaming at the mouth and twitching her body and jerking; the women cried with terror and prostrated themselves, and a Malay policewoman ran out to avoid being possessed by the devils out of Mother Wu. Neo Saw lay as dead with Fong Kiap rubbing Tiger Balm on her forehead and stuffing her nostrils thick with the green salve, while another detainee ran to the kitchen for ashes and crushed garlic to rub upon her head, and Grandmother sat unperturbed, belching and calling for the death house.

The ambulance removed Neo Saw and Mother Wu to hospital.

At the interrogation later no one knew anything until the hospital doctor rang up to ask Rosie where was the child who had been raped?

'*Amitofo*,' groaned Rosie, fingering her jade pendant, body protector and cooler of the humours, and went to tell Commandant Hinchcliffe.

'Sir, two children were fighting, and . . .'

'Oh,' said Hinchcliffe, who had not understood Rosie's twisted innuendoes, 'so long as it isn't a communist-inspired riot, wardress, we don't have to write a report.'

Rosie smothered her knowledge and held her peace, aware that trouble had begun.

And now the women of the camp truly were constrained by devils out of hell.

A restless languor informed their tasks; sharp scrimmage of abuse; the puncture petulance of muttered curses and chopsticks thrown to fall from table to floor; a foreshortened, cropped insolence in replies; fingers cut while chopping cabbage; privies fouled; a hen running loose and headless, spouting blood; a girl fainting at the well drawing water, and others swearing that they had seen a weed-clammy frog-faced demon with long webbed claws snatch at her, and refusing to draw water until Rosie herself bent over the eye of the well, and peered at the sparkle swinging its lacy net of light in mockery of her. 'There is no face, only the reflection of the sky,' said Rosie.

Then a child strayed to the privy in the iridescent heavy moonlight and the next day was ill, and the mother distraught complained that the moon devils had drained him of blood. And Mother Wu killed a chicken and muttered spells, and rubbed her magic bezoar stone (a vitreous marble with red flecks) upon his body to draw the devils out.

And then the women dreamed, and told their dreams aloud, stacked on the planks as bundles, visited by ghosts and dead ancestors and knives dripping blood, until the policewomen grew thin and nervous and huddled by twos peering in the dark, seeing devil shapes behind the canna lilies, and lurking in the blue shadows of the elongated coconut palm trees; hearing ghosts laugh among the hens.

Only two were immune, stolid and unconcerned in the mounting hysteria, Rosie Yip and Fong Kiap, jailer and jailed, each serving her destiny, both of fertile flanks and the long patience of breeders. Fong Kiap's embroidery was adamant to disorder, and she crooned to her child 'Oh, *sayang sayang*', until Mother Wu, now come out of hospital, warned her not to call out loud her love in that soft Malay word become a Chinese word, sayang, which means beloved, lest the devils hear and take the child away. No, let her beat him and call him ugly names, that the devils may despise his flesh.

And then suddenly it was round Fong Kiap that they clustered, the crapulous with terror, the whining, the tremulous, and Mother Wu now sat by Fong Kiap hour after hour, mumbling softly. From the still core of their unconsented accord eddied billow-spreading confusion, a whirlpool of smothered chaos which sucked in all the females of the camp. Among these were:

Boh Heng, six years detained for possession of a small communist paper flag forbidden, found in a drawer. It was a flag not forbidden in 1945, when her son bought it and forgot it in the drawer, where it was found in 1949 by an informer. And now whenever her case came up for revision it was turned down, until she had accepted voluntary repatriation, a device whereby Chinese born in Malaya could choose to go to a China they had never seen.

Boh Heng did not want China, she wanted her family in Kelantan, north Malaya. But it was China or stay behind wire, and so she had signed, agreeing to voluntary deportation, hoping that her children would filially flee the green hell of Malaya and come to China, the only way for them to be together.

There was Toh Kim, nineteen, still saving for a wedding dress she should have worn three years ago. She did not know why she was detained. She had fainted at the well and Old Mother Wu treated her daily with purgings till she was gaunt and bright with drought.

There was Se Chin, arrested for failing to inform on a terrorist in the next house, whose old mother was blind in the death house, waiting for her and for death;

There was Ah Kiew the idiot, deaf and epileptic;

There was Cha Boh, arrested while worshipping at her mother's grave with a small bowl of rice and a tiny cup of wine, convicted of passing food to the terrorists because of her worship at the grave;

There was Lim Nee the hunchback, who did not know why she was arrested;

There was Neo Saw, wife of Neo, slowly destroyed by grief;

There was Old Grandmother, and two seventeen-year-olds, and many others, the innocent, the guilty, the foolish, the astute, they and their children and their longings for husbands, sons, lovers in the camp or outside, in the jungle or not, each a world of dispossession, revolving now within a heat haze of terror which wrested from them their last property, the solidness of earth, invested the final security of their prison with the unreal vacillation of an old film, a chimerical land sinking the eye to a blur, a fantastic landscape deposit of hearts unpeopled and bereft, corrupt with caging.

All things amass to an end, so these, in entanglement of dread and strenuous longing, came to the rapt hours of another self, the ecstasy delivered from the wire, when they issued forth unsubstantial gods, their destiny strongly in their hands, and not the whim of others.

Besides the intercessions of Rosie to Kuanyin and the Virgin, the feathers, the strong lights, the incense, were other buffers against Evil, mirrors above the head to reflect back man-eaters; small paper altars to Kuanyin; multiplied amulets round the babies. And now Mother Wu the witch in a crescendo of power prayed aloud every night, rocking herself back and forth upon her crossed legs, with burners on both sides and incense sticks aureoling their blue haze about her heavy features. Her eyes gleamed in her sweating face as endlessly she chanted, calling by name the goddesses of heaven, the wardresses of Paradise who with horsehair whip and magic flower-basket guard the fruit of Immortality, the keys of palaces dangling at their belts; and more and more women in the camp began to call her:

San Ku, Third Beldam, Handmaid of Heaven, Immortal Soothsayer of Mankind.

Mother Wu filled the huts with the low monotone of her chant till all the women were song-haunted; at night endlessly she repeated, while the moon in round softness soared above the feathered palms and cut an unwithered swathe of golden light across the Straits:

> *All-Compassionate, deliver us from evil.*
> *Immortal Goddess, hear us.*
> *Mirror to turn away affliction, protect us.*

As ineffectual wooden demiurges standing diminished and

badly in need of paint at the doors of temples shielding vast
Deity, stood the policewomen, their lips mumbling the litany:

Immortal maid of Heaven defend us.
Kuanyin never implored in vain, come down, come down
and deliver us from evil.

Then one night Ah Kiew the epileptic went into a fit.

Her voice went crashing into the cataleptic chanting, an
agony of strangled, sheep-like bleats.

Stiff with hypnosis, Rosie Yip (who stayed on guard those
devil nights) moved, saying with lips of wood, 'Get your guns
ready.'

Insubstantial automatons, fingering guns strangely unreal to
themselves, in their cast shadows the policewomen flashed their
torches upon the women on the planks.

And saw Fong Kiap standing rigid in a trance, eyeballs white
turned up, arms outstretched, fingers pointing backwards, heavy
body rocking, while Mother Wu grovelled in front of her, and
the other women in chorus twisted their bodies and their hands,
swaying:

'Kuanyin, Kuanyin, Kuanyin deliver us.'

While the epileptic lay upon the ground stiff with a dead
froth upon her face.

'Fong Kiap, Fong Kiap,' called Rosie, but her voice sounded
small and weak. From Fong Kiap's chest issued a deep soft
rumble, like an immense storm purring distant thunder.

'Be still,' said a policewoman sternly to Rosie, 'she is possessed, in trance, do not call her or she will die.' And fell
promptly in an adoring stance, hands joined, eyes fixed.

'Kuanyin, Kuanyin,' ululated Mother Wu, 'Kuanyin has
come to earth.' And she kowtowed, knocking her forehead on
the ground before Fong Kiap with dull thuds.

Fong Kiap moved her arms and legs, stepped down from the
planks, and came slowly walking towards Rosie, her face marble
serene, her eyes rolled back to show the whites only and the
women followed, hands joined, repeating the Blessed Name.

'Make way, make way,' chanted Mother Wu, waving the
bundle of fuming incense sticks in front of Fong Kiap, wreath-
ing her in smoke. 'Make way for the Goddess who walks among
mortals, the Immortal Mercy.'

'Kuanyin Pusa, Immortal Maiden, Third Great One, deliver

us,' chanted the detainees. 'Amitofo, Kuanyin Pusa,' groaned the policewomen, and all, Malay and Chinese, brought their hands together in prayer and bowed to Fong Kiap.

Fong Kiap continued her ponderous advance, still pouring forth that ceaseless growl from her throat, like an enormous mongoose singing, and stopped two feet from Rosie.

'Bow and pray, great-aunt,' called Mother Wu to Rosie, 'reverence in front of Kuanyin.'

Rosie looked round her, looked at Fong Kiap, and her hands came together slowly, and she stood aside, letting Fong Kiap pass out of the hut and into the moonlight.

'Kuanyin Pusa, All Merciful, All Powerful,' chanted Mother Wu, 'speak, speak, and succour our miserable humanity.'

Words then came out, harmonious verse, stumbling in Fong Kiap's dialect, repeated by Mother Wu in Hokkien for those who did not understand Hakka:

Forgiveness for all, great-aunt, great-aunt, this year peace and harmony for all, and you, Wardress, fruitful and mother of a son, a future ruler of our people.

Thus Rosie Yip received her Annunciation from Fong Kiap. Into the moonlight the women followed Fong Kiap, lips in prayer, hands folded. Up the paths round the perimeter, to the kitchen and the class-rooms, to the well. And now they were back, chanting, the policewomen trailing behind, and Rosie still stood at the entrance of the hut. Fong Kiap crossed the threshold and suddenly stopped rumbling, yawned, looked round her, then with her usual waddle climbed on to her accustomed place near her child, and fell asleep.

'Kuanyin is gone, back to heaven,' said Mother Wu in a natural voice, smiling at Rosie. Stubbing her incense sticks like a cigarette she went to her place and turned her back and slumbered. One by one the women came in and went to their place and their children, who had not cried at all; perhaps they too had been in a trance. The epileptic was left on the ground, breathing heavily, asleep.

But next morning as Rosie, sallow with a wide-awake night, was wondering whether to report the Goddess's riot to the Commandant and draw a lot of trouble upon herself and upon the detainees, a policewoman came running in saying Neo Saw had gone. She could not be found until Rosie came to the well and saw the green mocking water laced with its net of light, from which a face stared up at her like her reflection from the shining hole of a pupil, and it sas Neo Saw.

It was the devils, but that would be small comfort for Big Dog Tsou.

Big Dog Tsou had made an excellent impression upon the Rehabilitation Committee. Not only was he a good basketball player and a magazine reader, but he gave the most convincing reasons why democracy was better than communism. Armed with a glowing report, he was helped to acquire a small shop and to set up in his tailoring business.

'You see,' asserted Hinchcliffe, 'that's all people really want: decent treatment, a living wage. Give it to them, and there won't be any communism.' And went on to say a lot of things about the past, and how badly the Chinese had been treated, until Clerkwell who listened unmoved decided that Hinchcliffe was beginning to talk like a socialist.

'The Resurrection Smart Tailor' Big Dog Tsou named his shop, in foot long Chinese characters and smaller English ones, and hoped the red-hairs would understand the delicate allusion, without his pointing it out, which would spoil the effect.

He was an immediate success. His old clients, the mems, soon came round, glad to know he had been brain-washed satisfactorily, and genuinely wanting to help him. He put up his prices to normal, and they paid without demur. Within a few weeks he had employed two apprentices and one errand girl; the latter was small and round and had the prettiest wrists and feet and eyes, and within a month he had married her. In three she was pregnant.

And now Big Dog Tsou truly became a new man.

Thin he had been, and now waxed fat. Silent and smiling, he grew boisterous with a loud laugh and on his face a permanent bemused happiness. He had walked softly and now stepped with a swagger, as if he owned the street. He worked sixteen hours a day, and still found time to stare often at his pert and pretty wife, with the full bosom and round hips under the flowery coat and trousers, demure and childishly meretricious, stealing side glances quickly at him which made his heart beat and his hands tremble, while the thin clink of her brass bangles as she cut the cloths was like a loud bell ringing his joy to the world.

Happiness made him forgetful. He cut a dress for Mem Clerkwell out of material brought by Mem Hinchcliffe. 'That's not my dress, tailor,' shrieked Mem Clerkwell, as she saw the bright scarlet chiffon instead of the white piqué she had left. Big Dog Tsou tried to look concerned, began to laugh foolishly, and that made Mem Clerkwell very angry. 'Sorry, mem,' said Big Dog Tsou. 'I very busy, nobody help, my wife...' He wanted to say his wife could not help him with sorting the orders, but Mem Clerkwell misunderstood. 'Ah yes,' she said, 'I heard you'd got married very recently. I suppose you don't know whether you're coming or going these days ... well, I hope you'll be very happy...' and she smiled. Absurdly Big Dog Tsou felt an intense desire to cry. Until then Mem Clerkwell, her peremptoriness and her gaunt harsh way of talking, had been one of his pet cold hatreds, but now she was suddenly human, as human as his own woman, and not a pig-face whiteskin, a red-haired she-devil, a woman-with-a-tail, an imperialist whore ... just a nice woman. He wanted to say, 'I hope you are happy too', but did not know how. It might be the wrong words, supposing she was unhappy ... in sudden acute perception, the telepathic instinct which comes with the recognition of another's humanity, he knew she was not very happy ... at least not as much as he, Big Dog Tsou, and something like compassion came over him. 'I buy new material, make you fine new dress, mem,' he promised.

Only one thing bothered Big Dog Tsou in these days of happiness, and that was the Organization.

Until he came out of rehabilitation camp he had been faithful to the Movement, eager to be useful again.

Then had come the Resurrection Smart Tailor shop, and his wife, and the child-to-be, and now he was strangely unwilling to meet his former comrades.

So far nothing much had happened, yet ... a member of the Movement had dropped in casually one day, with his fiancée, to have a dress made. Tailor shops, like coffee shops, are very useful meeting-places, for exchange of messages, for collecting money and subscriptions (who can tell, when one pays for a dress, whether there is not an extra dollar for the People Inside?). Tailors, like waiters, hear everything because no one sees them. Big Dog Tsou was to contact another tailor's shop, for the purpose of obtaining cloth, in Singapore, and thus establish a courier line....

The other shop was one of many near the Naval Base. The apprentice in that shop was a comrade in the Movement; he had a brother who was the 'Cookie' of a white officer at the Naval Base ... so it went on....

Big Dog Tsou showed eagerness to help. But at the moment, he said, he was still being watched ... two informers constantly dropped in, as well as policemen, to see what he was doing ... wait a few months, and he would be able to render service.

Thus he bought time, and now fought against the knowledge, dragging him down, slowing his step, lacquering his face into a fixed but joyless grin, that he had betrayed himself into another way of living and into a happiness which he did not want to give up.

So beguiled himself into believing that he was still loyal, of unsmirched devotion, but merely cautious, for the sake of his friends.

Chinese New Year was coming, his first New Year, in a hot February devoid of crackers because the Emergency forbade their firing, and Mem Hinchcliffe appeared at the shop, her usual energetic self, earrings dangling, bangles bangling, and all her curls tremulous upon her head:

'My dear boy,' she beamed at Big Dog Tsou, 'my dear, dear boy, and how are we? And how's your wife? That little girl, why she's a child, a child, you naughty cradle-snatcher, hahaha....'

Big Dog Tsou was happy and miserable at once. Happy because he could no longer face Mem Hinchcliffe with that polished amiability undented by emotion, and so he showed his shop, the Singer sewing machines, the apprentices.

'Baby?' asked Mem Hinchcliffe, pushing an inquisitive finger in the direction of the wife's navel. 'Yes, thought so, well don't be in too much hurry with the next one, dear boy ... here,' she dug into the huge carry-all she trundled and extracted some Family Planning leaflet. 'I've only got them in Tamil and Malay, I've given all the English ones away and the Chinese ones aren't printed yet.' Amiably she gave some to the two girl apprentices, who examined them with astonishment mingled with fear. 'And now,' said Mrs. Hinchcliffe, 'I want all of you to come to the tea party at my bungalow. I'm giving a tea party for those from our detention camp who've made good. You must come, tailor, you're a winner.'

With panic in his heart Big Dog Tsou said he would come of course, but on that day sent word that he was dangerously ill with a high fever, and kept a handkerchief knotted round his head for a day or two after, lest Mem Hinchcliffe should suddenly descend upon him and doubt his word.

Came the devil month, crawling torrid day by day to the

Devil's Jubilee when all hungry and sad spirits are solemnly sent back to Hell. His little wife was heavy upon her feet, but went on cutting cloth; Big Dog Tsou had booked a bed for her at the hospital, wishing all to be done in a modern manner. He bought tins of Brand's chicken essence, and followed the doctor's advice religiously, but also let his wife paste charms and invocations in yellow paper above doors and windows, and mirrors at the entrance. He went into Singapore and bought soft *gamgee* cloth for nappies as he had seen upon the white babies of his clients. But he bought nothing else, lest the devils be aware of the new life sleeping; and he put the cloth away, saying loudly it was for shirts.

And so he revolved his little world of happiness and absorption with the woman carrying the child that was coming, absurdly reassured against the fear of that other world, the world of the Movement, once so full of power and triumph and now empty of meaning. And made all preparations within his power to the limit of tempting fate; but was never prepared for what he had prepared to happen:

Not expecting the smiling face of Pang, the detective, so friendly but for the too-white flash of too many teeth in too bared a grin; not expecting Pang, and the three other men, two detectives and the informer, a thin sallow-faced youth walking negligently whose hair thick with oil was held in place with a large aluminium clip.

Big Dog Tsou was standing behind his table, heaped with cottons and silks and nylons. The young coffee-shop waiter looked at him indifferently and looked away again, a little over his shoulder, at the wall. This look, like the kiss of Judas, betrayed Big Dog Tsou, but might buy his own freedom. 'Okay,' said Pang, grinning.

So the time had come, the end that was waiting since the beginning in the rubber trees when Meng, the latex weigher, had put up his hands begging mercy and obtained none. Only it was another Big Dog Tsou who had lifted the changkol till the screaming had stopped, indissoluble in body from the man now smiling for the last time, horribly, smiling with his world ebbing and dissolving as the detectives closed upon him, and who could not, did not believe that he was the same man until he heard his little child-wife scream and scream.

It held spirits of earth, the stolid ship lurching through flaccid green-oil sea, its black and orange prow sprouting phosphorescent arches on the night waters of the southern ocean.

Police Officer Crufts was in charge. From Todak transferred to the Cameron Highlands, he had undergone a six-months' intensive course in the Hokkien dialect. The Force now recognized the importance of Chinese as well as Malay to run Malaya, and to be gazetted for permanent establishment, officers could offer either language instead of Malay only, as pre-Emergency.

After six months in the cool pine and mist-scented Highlands of Malaya, Crufts came down to earth and to taking a shipload of detainees (now called banishees), sentenced to deportation, to China.

There were three kinds of deportees on this ship, which sailed under a South American flag; whose skipper was Swedish; whose crew was mainly from the Celebes; and which belonged to a British firm. Political banishees, coming from the detention camps under Emergency Regulations. Two contraband and opium smugglers from Singapore, and one from Kuala Lumpur. A few voluntary repatriates.

The smugglers were wealthy. One of them, it was whispered, was the genuine king of the opium dens of Kuala Lumpur. He was, of course, a secret society man as well, at least a Tiger General. He was being deported to Manila, having appealed successfully against being deported to China.

The other two were going to China, and seemed no whit concerned about the anti-corruption drive now in process on the mainland.

Since these three were free to buy whatever passage they could afford they travelled first class in luxurious suites. Strolling with bodyguards on deck after dinner, they puffed the smoke of three large cigars into Crufts's face.

The voluntary repatriates were also allowed to buy their passages. Detained under Emergency Regulations, born in Malaya and British subjects, they could not legally be deported. But they could ask for 'repatriation', and obtain it. Some did willingly, others as a way out of detention. Among the latter was the woeful, tear-smeared Boh Heng, whose hair had gone iron-grey, a strange event in a Chinese woman under fifty. Carried away on the stark sea (whose red-eyed demons lurking behind crested waves she dreaded with the horror of belief), it was too late to alter her fate. At the port of embarkation her children had stood behind the wire fence, holding out useless baskets of fruit and food and crying and her daughters rending their clothes.

Perhaps, thought Crufts, if she had stuck it another year or so ... someone on the Advisory Committee, on the Revision Board, might have got interested; but the Police always had the right to reverse the decisions taken by any Board or any Committee, in the interests of Security; perhaps Boh Heng had done best for herself after all, and one day her children might follow her to China. . . .

The largest group, the political detainees, were housed according to sex: the men in the hold, the women and children in a large low room separated from the hold by a space for the storing of goods and luggage.

Into the hold Crufts went daily, unarmed, through the battened hatch into the darkness with the usual suffocating heat of any hold of a ship, with the thump of engines, and the smell of human sweat and garlicky urine; and, though queasy with compassion, told himself there was nothing he could do, for Security came first, and he could not allow them on deck. There were, after all, quite a few normal, law-abiding citizens on the ship, and a mutiny would be some picnic.

Up the ladder through the hatch and on to the third class deck he went back towards the sun, the light, the free air. On the third class deck passengers ate and slept, there were no cabins. On a mat lay an opium smoker in a coma, his ribs, covered with yellow parchment skin, scarcely moved. His grown and handsome son cooked the pellets and handed him the pipe in both hands, with love and devotion. Stalls, raucous as hawkers' stalls in any street of Singapore, sold all the delicacies that Cantonese delight in to while away the week of sailing in eating and munching. A heavy smell of Tiger Balm pervaded the air, and the deck runnels were dirty with spit-sour olive kernels, potent against seasickness.

On the second sailing day, there was much agitation among the banishees in the hold, for some were communist leaders of cells, and they started a clamour and a turbulence. The interpreter reported to Crufts how they urged the others to strike against the food and the conditions. 'Well, it's not for long,' thought Crufts, and refused to put them in irons, contenting himself with going down into the hold at meal times and supervising the food they ate.

Crufts had seen the Hinchcliffes before departure, to collect the detainees from their camp, as he had from other camps in

156

Malaya.

He found Hinchcliffe philosophically sipping beer on his bungalow veranda, and Mrs. Hinchcliffe in tears.

'Our dear, dear, detainees,' she exclaimed, looking round her a trifle wildly, 'our poor darlings ... oh we did get so fond of them ... especially my own poor dear boy ... look how he hand-painted this whole set of bowls for me. Isn't it pretty? Did it all as a surprise for my birthday. So handy about the house, he was, fixing up anything I wanted ... so quiet, used to sit on his knees in a corner, waiting for orders ... I'm sure *he* never did anything wrong. I'm willing to bet anything he never was a Red. Told me he didn't know why he'd been put in camp. Every New Year he said to me: "A very happy New Year to you, mem." And I used to say to him: "And to you, dear boy, and I hope you'll soon be free, though goodness knows I'll miss you a lot." Then he'd just smile and say nothing at all ... and now you're taking him to China.'

Her face was swollen with weeping.

'He doesn't *want* to go. My boy isn't a bad boy or anything of the sort. He's begged me to stay ... "I'll work all my life, mem, for no money, if you let me stay..." "What for I go to China, mem, I don't know China, I come here as a small baby, don't know anything about China...."'

'Cheer up, dear,' said her husband, 'you've tried your utmost to help him, you have ... she even wrote to H.Q.,' he turned to Crufts, 'but we were told the decision was final, these were all hardened cases....'

'In a big thing like this, the innocent suffer with the guilty,' said Crufts, knowing he was being platitudinous, but finding comfort in the alignment of these words. 'It's war. These people have no one but their countrymen in the jungle to blame for the fix they're in....'

'But they don't see it that way,' replied Mrs. Hinchcliffe. 'They think it's us ... and my boy was such a gentle boy, so wonderful with my puppies....'

Again her eyelids brimmed.

'You should have seen our girls last week,' Hinchcliffe hastily started another story to stop his wife's recurrent grief. 'About a dozen of them had done their time, and I put them on the train. They were going up north. They're not allowed to return to their old villages, you know, in case their pals the comrades get in touch with them again. You should have seen them when the time came to say goodbye. Tears rolling down their cheeks. Had to wipe their faces one by one with my own handkerchief.

'They were really sorry to go. They'd all been rehabilitated. They were afraid to get out of the wire again to fend for themselves; life isn't easy these days. Here it was some kind of security for them, in camp. . . .'

'And it's perfectly horrid,' cut in Mrs. Hinchcliffe indignantly, 'the way some people will take advantage of them. Their own people, mind you. One poor dear left us six months ago, and landed in Social Welfare last week, just skin and bones. She'd been taken by a family as their servant. It sounded a good job, wealthy family and all that, but they worked her like a slave. Clean and cook and wash and iron and everything for nine people. Never any time off. They didn't give her a bed, she slept on the ground under her mistress's bed . . . and they took her identity card away from her so that she couldn't run away.'

'There, there, dear,' said Mr. Hinchcliffe, and looked as if at any moment he might pull out his handkerchief again. 'You mustn't always believe what these girls tell. They're mighty good at grouses.'

'I've asked my boy to write,' Mrs. Hinchcliffe reverted obstinately to her subject. 'If they'll let him. Just a word, my boy, I said, just: "I'm okay, mem," and I'll understand, I told him. I'll always know it's from you. And I want to know. I want him to be happy, even if it is in Red China. . . .'

Crufts also would have liked to know, as he sat watching the deck upon which people scurried like ants, busy with the business of living, and knew under their feet the others waiting as in a dark tunnel, waiting their emergence in the new land, the land of their ancestors.

Neo sat on his heels, a face and bent body of sullen stone, not raising his eyes as the light from the opened hatch streamed on him when Crufts came down the ladder on his daily visit.

His son was with him, small of frame, but a full man in spirit and knowledge of pain. Left behind in Malaya were the other three children. Although it was a principle not to separate families, but to deport or detain them together to lessen hardship, the death of Neo Saw had dislocated these arrangements, and the other children had become inmates of a Welfare Home.

Crufts's attention was drawn to Neo because of his resemblance to the man in perpetual opium coma lying on deck above his head. Of the quieter detainees he was the quietest, quiet as a stone, never shifting nor moving, nor raising his eyes to Crufts.

'He's a real bad one,' said Mr. Tay the interpreter, pointing to Neo.

'How do you know?' asked Crufts, short-tempered.

Tay's eyes rounded with surprise and the fear which abruptness in his masters roused in him. Tay's spirit was as a fountain for ever spouting upwards, spurting anxiety to please in an unending stream. It gave him high blood pressure, this unceasing agony of love towards his overlords, and for this condition he administered unto himself both Chinese and Western drugs, invariably together.

Mr. Tay came from Penang, the inviolate green little island whose inhabitants, Chinese Hokkiens, settled for a century, are, many of them, devotees of British rule. He was a Queen's Chinese.

He was so loyal, he spoke about it all day, and dreamed of it at night. He was so fervent in his love for the Sovereigns of the British crown that he wept when 'God Save the Queen' was played, and carried everywhere a scrap book where he had pasted cuttings from the local newspapers, going back for thirty years, concerning the Royal Family.

Loyalty was the core, the essence, the reason of Mr. Tay's being upon earth, and his ambition a modest order ('let us say, if I am not aspiring too much, the M.B.E.') which, he declared, he would transmit 'with reverend hands to my posterity, so that they may never do anything which would shame me in my grave against the British Crown.'

And so when Crufts said 'How do you know?' angrily Mr. Tay was pained, but too loyal to resent it. He blamed himself for Crufts's tone. 'Everybody knows he's a bad lot, sir. I think myself, with all due respect to you, that the British are too kind and too generous. You should shoot all these bandits, sir, shoot the whole lot, like the Japs used to do. Ah, the Japanese! They didn't stand any nonsense! They just cleaned up the place. . . .'

'Sometimes,' thought Crufts, 'I don't know why, I feel like kicking Mr. Tay. But his loyalty would not permit him to resent it. He would probably blame himself for being kicked, and apologize to me for kicking him . . . I wonder what streak it is in us that always prefers a good rebel to a cringing, loyal servant?'

'I don't always like the word "bad", Mr. Tay. I've heard it so often. A bad spot. A bad lot. There is a village called Todak where pretty bad things happened. We learnt a lesson there. You can't lump a lot of people together under the name "bad" and then expect them to behave themselves . . . Todak had to go

159

very bad indeed before something was done about it, and now I hear it's better. . . .'

'Oh, sir,' said Mr. Tay enthusiastically, 'I think with all respect that democracy is wonderful!'

'It's only wonderful,' answered Crufts, 'if it keeps on finding fault with itself, and keeping itself up to scratch. And as for shooting, well, it's true perhaps that we're not brutal or cruel, though we're sometimes bloody stupid and unimaginative. Our mistakes are sins of omission and negligence, mental sloth and lack of foresight. They are not deliberate viciousness. And perhaps that's what is going to save us, this edge of mercy and fairness . . . and long may we keep it.'

To himself he added: 'And that is also the excuse our colonialism invokes for staying here. We have seen the writing on the wall, and we are ready to let go, even if only slowly . . . but our credentials before God for hanging on are only this excuse, that if we go, something worse may happen, another tyranny, worse than ours. Whether it's a good excuse or not I don't know. But I do know that if I were Mr. Tay I'd resent *any* master, whether good or bad. I'd rather be free and make my own mistakes; but then I was born free, and he was born protected, and that's the difference.'

'I'd like to know why this man is "bad" as you say, Mr. Tay.'

'I'll find out for you, sir,' said Mr. Tay eagerly, happy to be given a job to do. 'Though with all due respect it's too kind of you to bother yourself with these people; but I'll find out for you.'

Neo had had his chance. No one, not even Neo himself could aver that he had not been given opportunity to redeem himself.

It was at the trial of Big Dog Tsou that Neo failed to grasp his life into his own hands once again.

Big Dog Tsou was tried, as usual, by a judge and two assessors. The commandant of the rehabilitation camp himself testified to his excellent conduct while an inmate. But against him were brought detainees and surrendered enemy personnel, among them the waiter with the clip, and Fong Kiap, and others who had been with Neo tapping in the rubber.

Neo, too, was brought to testify and stood looking across the cool and dusty room with its sombre panelling at Big Dog Tsou, gaunt in the dock.

And could not say what he had to say:

Yes, Big Dog Tsou was known to him, and had collected money for the People Inside. Yes, it was Big Dog Tsou who had shown them the corpse of Meng in the rubber, with the head hacked off, and yes, Meng had weighed the latex on the estate and it was known that he had wanted to go to the police and inform ... and he, Neo, was but a poor rubber tapper, and knew that he had done wrong not to report the matter to the police, but he had been too frightened by Big Dog Tsou, and really, in his heart, he had always hated the People Inside. ...

Neo could not say one of these things.

Instead he persisted in ignorance. He did not know. He could not say. He hesitated, or remained silent. He angered the judge, the prosecutor, the interpreter and the police; even the assessors became impatient. Everyone in court was angry with Neo except Big Dog Tsou, whose eyes stared at him like clenched fists raised in utmost fear and begging, not hoping for mercy. And Neo, confronted with the wordless begging of these eyes, could not bring himself to betray a neighbour, and thus betrayed himself.

Pointedly, then, the judge referred to Neo's 'lack of co-operation with Justice'. Big Dog Tsou was found guilty of murder and sentenced to death by hanging, and knowing the end, with no return to the Resurrection Tailor shop and to the child-wife with the small baby son in her arms, suddenly became a comrade again, a member of the Organization, and spat at the judge, and was taken away struggling and shouting slogans.

But Neo had merely added a deeper blackness to his black record. Non-co-operative, no extenuating circumstances, a hopeless case, incapable of reform, to be deported, with another two hundred and fifty-eight hardened cases from the camp.

The death of Neo Saw roused no grief in Neo. For grief was a word, an emotion worn-out and erased in his long passive waiting in camp. He went on board ship as a stone dreaming, and Son who was there knew him despite the years apart.

He stood by his side, saying politely: 'Tolong, please, this is my father,' when the police officer told him to keep in line. And never left Neo again.

Son knew that his father was a child fast in a fixed dream without word or shape. He looked after Neo, made him wash his face and hands, comb his hair, fed him, both hands holding out the bowl of rice to him, with devotion and love doing all things as he had seen Neo Saw do when he was a child among her children.

Son did not see the stinging bright sea on which their ship rode. There was only darkness and faces to stare at in the hold. Long ago he had ceased to look at the sky and to find shapes in the clouds. He was now geared to survival only, all else withered save the strong inflexible will to go on living. Yet he did not know why he lived.

Often in the darkness of the hold a question carefully unworded, kept secret, came to him:

'When we get to the ancestors' country, shall we be again behind wire?'

Round him he heard the hot exclamations of men promising Paradise on landing, freedom and happiness and revenge one day for all the wrongs they had endured.

Round him he heard, in whispers, the small fears of the older men at night, fearful that they were going to another bondage.

Son armed himself with fortitude, and with no speculation, knowing all preconception futile, expecting and demanding nothing, but waiting for what would have to be endured, never believing, never any more believing in anyone or anything at all.

Son knew himself strong with his empty heart, his careful mind, his ruthless will to live, with no dreams to eat away the solid boundaries of the ship carrying him and his father from the known and tasted terrors to the unknown land, the land of his ancestors, China.

11 : The Cloven Kind

When Todak New Village went under clampdown for the murder of its Resettlement Officer, Ah Mei and other S.E.P.S were taken there in closed vans and through the canvas slits peered and pointed out the people they thought they recognized as having to do with the Organization of the People Inside.

Then Ah Mei went to prison for a day and a half with one of the suspects to interrogate, and when she returned she had a bath as usual, and washed her hair, and changed her clothes, before writing her report. Always, lifting her smiling pink face as she settled down with her fountain pen poised above the school copy book she used, she said to me:

'Aiyah, doctor, it is so dirty in the cells.'

The weeks ambled unperceived, forgotten because unchanging heat blurs, enduring greenness stupefies the alert counting of days. Only clouds, growing and then overswollen bursting; only night and day, for ever. And I had ceased to wonder that at the hospital the Malay women and a good few of the Chinese (usually so calendar conscious) did not know how old they were, nor how old their children. How difficult to remember, when January is as July will ever be. British expatriates, the name given now to British officials, found their memory slipping from them, a tropical disease which they mentioned easily, in that half-pleased manner of people who suffer in a good cause. They told time by another apparatus than the usual feast days on calendars, another precise measure: the tours and the furlough. 'This is our third tour' meant twice a spell of two and a half years in Malaya, with two six months' home leave between. Time for them was set by its recession from the last furlough and the approach towards the next home leave, counted first in months, then in weeks, and finally in days.

The S.E.P.S, like other people in Malaya, had lost the sensation of accurate time, or perhaps never had it. Their length of stay, in or out of the jungle, varied according to the story they were in the process of telling. For Ah Mei, her ten-year sentence divided time into measured portions, and though she knew herself not in the cells so dirty, but in the tethered freedom of any S.E.P., and though she knew her case so favourably influenced by her services that it would be reviewed, yet she moaned and sighed, gently wistful of the years of her non-freedom, until my heart was torn with compassion, counting with her (as white mems count the weeks till the next P. & O. boat), counting the years and months till she be free again.

And repetitious as the leaves of the rubber trees endless along the roads of Malaya, the days shed, carrying me with my doctoring, Ah Mei with her cleaning and washing, and Cookie with his cooking.

My daughter grew and grew, my husband worked and studied, and every evening the male S.E.P.S walked up the garden gravel in the pink clearness precursor of swift night. They sat in the wide space at the back of the house with the jacaranda trees sifting luminous blue petals upon them, and a quivering tall albizzia occupying what was still undark of the sky. In the kitchen yard, helping Cookie hose the drains with water, or feed his hens and ducks, they laughed, gay and childish. Later at night they did downstairs what we did upstairs, lay back in canvas chairs or on the ground and looked at the stars, hugely bright. Hour by hour the stars increased in dazzle until in the fixed trance of gazing even the S.E.P.S, who took so much for granted, would wonder and exclaim whether it was real gold in the sky, and how to reach the uncounted millions poised glowing above them.

And when the moon, out in her brusque full way, peremptory rode the sky and all the world went silver, and from the Malay kampongs behind their banana clumps rose moon-agitated soft drumming, and the wailing for love, throaty songs supplicated unbearably in the swooning soft night; when the whole town huddled spellbound with desirous softness and the insistent drumming, and the Chinese and Indian shopkeepers in their close-shuttered rooms above the shops turned fiercely upon their wives in sudden urge; the S.E.P.S would wander up and down the gravel path, restless silver statues come to life treading a silver world. Then Cookie would turn on the radio full blast, and to drown the soft insistent stream of song and the drum beating steady as a living pulse, they all sang together 'Rose, Rose, I love you'.

And laughed and jeered at each other, little boys who want to be tough.

At eleven the radio was turned off, a concession to our rest. The guests would depart, lingering, throwing black velvet shadows from silver trunks and arms and heads, and the great glittering pale night belong once again to the Malay drums and their zigzag melody rising and falling in tune with the blood in urgent bodies.

Besides the S.E.P.S visits, it became a friendly habit for other people to drop upon us inoffensive proteges.

Our bills for electricity, water, and Cookie's bills for food and especially butter, began to soar. I seemed to be eating more beef, pork and cabbage, than a small hotel, and the three of us, congenitally abstemious of fat, consumed two pounds of butter a week. I protested, but Cookie insisted that we ate more than we thought. Meanwhile his large wife swelled and rounded again, and it became evident that an eighth boisterous youngster would soon be acclaimed with red eggs.

On the telephone voices nasillant, throaty, laughing, or shy asked for Miss Lee, Ah Mei, and unknown others. Ah Mei would always know, even if it was I who took the garbled messages when she was strolling in the Sultan's flower gardens, open to the public. Occasionally I supplied remedies for toothache, ringworm, diarrhoea and esoteric diseases such as tingling over the right eye and a pain in the left side starting at nine in the morning but ending just before supper was due.

One afternoon Evangeline was dropped. Evangeline was twelve and had been a bandit for two years in the jungle. Captured by the Gurkhas in a raid on the terrorist camp where she lived, wounded by bullets in the assault, she was treated at the hospital for seven weeks and became rather spoilt. Everyone in the hospital, from the friendly and vigorous English matron to the sleepy, coconut oil-smelling Malay sweepers, brought her toys and sweets and petted her and sat on her bed, admiring her.

Evangeline came up our stairs dressed in a gingham cotton gown with red, green and yellow checks, made by a Scots nursing sister at night and fitted on Evangeline with the whole of the nursing staff brimful of advice standing round. Her two hands clutched the first toy she had been given, a duck fluffy with white downy feather, on wheels, and with a yellow papier-mâché beak. Evangeline's hair was cut crew style, parted and brilliantined like a boy's, and to cultivate a wave she wore a large curler on a spring. But her hair was too thick and alive and the curler snapped off and fell to the ground when she moved. Then she clipped it on again, firmly.

Gravely she bowed. Her eyes lingered upon the polished wooden floor and remained scanning it, measuring its extent, noting its surface.

'Go ahead,' I said, 'try it.' Immediately she produced a large key from her pocket, wound up the spring and put down her duck. It went round and round in wide ecstatic circles, rolling its wheels with tremendous whirrs and whooshes, beating its wings in time together, veering upon the slight bumps on the floor and saying quack, quack, quack.

The duck having adopted our floor, Evangeline signified she would stay, and remained eleven weeks.

Softly Ah Mei came upstairs, happiness upon her face, and took Evangeline's hand, and called her Little Sister, and seemed to cling to her with love, and said that she would look after her and arrange a space on her sleeping mat for Evangeline.

And then Miss Lee and I went to Singapore, and bought two lengths of cotton for frocks and a pair of red Bata sandals for Evangeline.

Days later two detectives and an official from the Ministry of Information came to see Evangeline. The Information official was an amiable and gay ex-officer of the Chinese Nationalist Army, Jimmy Lo. 'What a pretty little girl, and so intelligent,' he said, 'how I wish she were my daughter.'

When Mrs. Pang, the older wife of our young and most brilliant detective, came strolling by on a courtesy visit bringing pomeloes and cigarettes, her weasel small eyes wary and appraising in her slightly pock-marked face; searching Evangeline's body up and down, obviously clicking figures in her mind as to how she might sell, a virgin; a strange feeling rose among us. In the rapid darkness one could see the s.e.p.s, Ah Mei and Miss Lee, standing mutely about Evangeline, not leaving her alone with Mrs. Pang, their wordless presence hostile, a convergent, tangibly solid wall defending Evangeline. Mrs. Pang sensed the swift unpleasant feeling ready to turn upon her, and after drinking half a small orange squash and commenting on the price of rubber (which was going down), she left.

Jimmy Lo returned with a camera man, a wire recorder, two aides and a box of chocolates slightly mouldy with heat. His pretty wife was with him. She sat in a corner, gazing at Evangeline. The Information Department had decided to broadcast Evangeline's story as good propaganda. There were quite a few child bandits about, but not many as intelligent as this little girl.

They sat on the large pink and white Malay mat on the floor and placed the wire recorder on a stool in front of Evangeline and Jimmy held the microphone and began.

'Now how long were you in the jungle, little girl?'

Already trained by police interrogation, having answered this question many times, Evangeline replied: 'Two years and four months.'

'Now tell us,' said Jimmy, 'how you came to the jungle.'

'I went with my mother,' said Evangeline.

'What happened to your father?' asked Jimmy's sympathetic voice.

And his silent lips framed the answer for lip-reading Evangeline.

'My father died,' said Evangeline, 'so my mother and I went to the jungle.'

'Who killed your father?' asked Jimmy.

'Bad people,' replied Evangeline, rolling her eyes at the machine squatting attentive in its maroon shagreen skin, its slow wheels turning, 'very bad people.'

'Aha,' said Jimmy happily, 'communist bandits, wasn't it, little girl? Say yes,' he mouthed to Evangeline.

'Yes,' said Evangeline.

Jimmy looked pleased. 'We're getting on, she's really quite wonderful,' he whispered aside, and produced a memorandum sheet out of his pocket, upon which he had jotted the main points of the interview. He now ticked off point 1. 'Parents', and continued:

'Now when you were in the jungle camp with the wicked bandits, did they beat you?'

'No,' said Evangeline.

'Not even once?'

'No ... but once or twice my mother beat me. And the men they shouted at me.' Warming up she added, 'Especially when the food was not ready they cursed me, and tried to leave me behind when they moved.'

'Point 2. Ill treatment,' checked Jimmy and continued:

'Now what did you do in the jungle, little girl?'

'I cooked, I washed clothes, I sang songs, and we walked and walked and sometimes we ran. And I helped to chop wood. And I threw stones to kill birds and lizards. And one day,' her voice rose vibrant out of its artificial submission, 'I saw a tiger. A real one.'

'Weren't you afraid?' asked Jimmy, forgetting the recorder.

'Oh no,' said Evangeline. 'But we were afraid of the Gurkhas, because they are terrible people. They chop heads and hands.

They are Kling devils,' she said.

'Cut,' said Jimmy. 'I think we'll have to prepare her a bit more, to give some shape to the broadcast. Now,' he resumed, 'what happened to your mother?'

'She was killed,' said Evangeline. 'She was killed when I was taken.'

But no tears fell, she said it stolidly and wriggled her red sandals on the floor, and looked at her duck and patted it.

'Now we'll take a photograph,' said Jimmy. We walked downstairs and stood in the garden in front of the bungalow, Evangeline with her duck, and the camera man snapped her alone; then with Ah Mei; then with all of us round her, a gay company smiling strenuously and blinking our eyes in the harsh sun.

Three more times did Jimmy come to the house, until Evangeline was ready and then they recorded her. Each time Mrs. Lo came with him, to watch Evangeline with a rapt tenderness, with love to stroke her hair, and to offer her little drives in the car, and to bring her handkerchiefs and oranges and a bright red plastic belt to match her sandals.

One day Jimmy asked Evangeline what songs she sang in the jungle, and she started:

> *Arise, ye who do not want to be slaves,*
> *With flesh and blood*
> *We shall build our new Great Wall.*

'Ha,' said Jimmy, 'that's a communist song, little girl.'

But I remembered the song, many times heard during the war against Japan; in Chungking hummed by servants as they swept the courtyards.

'Surely, Mr. Lo, you remember this, our war song, yours too. It was not only a communist song.'

'Yes, I know,' replied Jimmy. 'But many things which were not communist have become communist now ... in fact it is so difficult sometimes ... but not for you,' he added, his brow clearing. 'Not for you or me ... we are positively not communists.' He meant to make me feel secure, above suspicion, in these suspicious days when all liberalism is suspect which is not tainted with servile acquiescence, but instead I felt suddenly a traitor, and nothing else.

'I know another song,' said Evangeline. 'Our teacher in the jungle sang it, after lessons, playing it on the flute. He said it was old, from the ancestors' country. But we could not march to it. He sang it alone, after food was eaten, and I listened.'

She sang in a harsh, unmelodic voice pitched higher than normal, off-key and haunted with the old longing and grievance, old as the world of man:

> I will go to the forest for justice,
> For justice and righteousness,
> And become a green-clad man.
> The rulers pursue me with soldiers,
> With riders, chariots and spears.
>
> I will go to the forest for justice,
> The people will flock to me.
> I right their wrongs from the green shade,
> And kill the rulers with arrows.
> The horsemen stumble with fear.
>
> I will go to the forest for justice.
> The wind for my garment I wear.
> Together with my many companions,
> The wind for my garment and the rain my drink,
> We build a new heaven and earth.

'Ah, how typical, isn't it?' mused Jimmy. 'Justice ... the justice of the forest. It's old and steeped in tradition ... A corrupt, incompetent government, and the just and good men going to the green forest and becoming bandits, but Right is on their side...' Suddenly he became nostalgic, uneasy and fretful. 'Of course we call them bandits, I don't think the English understand their idea....'

'Of course they do, they've got Robin Hood, you know,' I said.

But there is nothing more futile than to discuss the rights and wrongs of the Emergency. Evangeline stopped singing, and I dressed her wound, which still oozed a little serum and needed occasional care. With the good life and the food she healed well and gained weight. We now ate three pounds of butter a week and Cookie had a new reason: 'Evangeline eats such a lot of butter.'

Cookie's children and Evangeline raced about the house, in the front and back gardens, climbed the butterfruit trees to shake down the round yellow woolly fruit, built fences for the ducks and chickens, fished in the ditches round the prison, bringing back iridescent fishlets flashing like thunderless lightning in the clear water and all terror-weaponed with red and gold streaked flanks. A monkey appeared, and stayed until he too waxed inordinately fond of butter. Two tortoises, a pi-dog with a hyena sandy coat, six Siamese cats added their wealth of life to ours, until the house was uproarious with shouting, laughing, quarrelling, living, and every day Cookie brought some crockery or article broken by one or another, human or animal. 'Broken,' he would point laconic, carrying the fragments with care on a teakwood tray, and depositing them in front of me at the breakfast able.

The families and friends of our guests came and went in tranquil fishing-craft fashion, in and out of the harbour of our kitchen. They arrived from the *ulu*, the wilderness of secondary jungle, tangled and abandoned rubber estates and fenced-in resettlement areas now called New Villages. They came without food, because Emergency Regulations forbade food outside the wire on pain of five years' imprisonment. Operation Starvation against the jungle went on and on, and there were road blocks and police searches on every road.

Most steady of our visitors were Ah Mei's mother and her brother. They came from near Labis, another 'bad spot' on the police map. Years past, they had owned a few acres of rubber and a hut, but all had gone when the Emergency began, and they had been resettled behind wire and gone tapping rubber for a big British estate. And then Ah Mei's mother was caught in a swoop and detained in a camp, while Ah Mei herself went to the jungle. The mother was later released and now she came with her son to visit her daughter.

The resemblance was great above the nose, but the mouth was different. Unsmiling between the stubborn long upper lip and the small round chin, her mother's was the surliest mouth I encountered among these tight-lipped, harsh and harried farmers dragged by the tens of thousands in and out of the nets of the Police, whose refuge was silence and stubborn negativeness. Little Brother had large intelligent eyes and his head swung freely round on his graceful neck, inspecting everything. Though the manner of his body and the position of his hands and feet was respectful enough, it was a skin-shallow obeisance. 'You know,' said Pang, handsome and genial as ever, on one of his cheerful visits to the S.E.P.S in the kitchen (they always greeted him with the enthusiasm of Henry VIIIth's frightened courtiers), 'that little boy was a member of a cell, leader of a children's communist organization.' And he patted the child's head with benign and clever fingers, and called him fondly Little Mosquito, a term of endearment for all male children.

Ah Mei's case was now being taken up in good earnest by the Law, for relief of her sentence. At that moment justice in Malaya was slightly ruffled by the famous case of Lee Meng, and though what was done was always done fairly, by Emergency Regulation standards, yet never had judgment over enemy personnel, hanged for their offences, been questioned or criticized as it was in the case of the girl, Lee Meng.

Lee Meng, or Lee Teng Tai, known as The Grenade Girl, was not the first woman to hang in the Emergency. But the other cases (a hundred and eighty-two men, two women) had been conducted in secrecy in closed courts.

Lee Meng was tried twice. The first time witnesses against her were all S.E.P.S. She spat in the face of one, calling them all running dogs buying their freedom by selling the lives of innocent people. A British police inspector declared he recognized her, having seen her once through field glasses outside a cave three years before.

There is no trial by jury in these cases, but assessors are appointed to render a verdict. The Indian and Chinese appointed found her not guilty. But the judge, who was British, disagreed and ordered a retrial, for under the assessor system a person can be tried again and again for the same crime. The second time, a European assessor was picked by the judge. The European found her guilty, the Asian found her not guilty. The judge agreed with the European assessor and Lee Meng was condemned to death. In this second trial, three surrendered enemy personnel testified against Lee Meng, and one of them frankly declared that the more information he gave, the greater would be his pardon.

Lee Meng's undaunted and courageous counsel, an Indian lawyer defending her without fee, had the case appealed. And suddenly from the steamy air of the Emergency in Malaya the case of The Grenade Girl was carried to the cold, indifferent and impeccably scrupulous atmosphere of London, and there it was felt that England's rule in Malaya could only compete successfully with communism by applying the highest standards of British justice, even to a 'bandit'; finally, Lee Meng's death sentence became life imprisonment.

Whatever Lee Meng's political convictions, her courage aroused respect in police circles. 'She's quite different,' confided Bob Stewart to me at a cocktail party. 'She won't say a word. "Do what you like," she says, "I won't speak." And we can't get one word out of her.' In contrast to the verbosity of the S.E.P.S, Lee Meng's silence and her utter conviction impressed her captors.

In Ah Mei's case, the verdict depended on the evidence that she had a grenade in her hand when caught. Technically, she too should have been sentenced to death, but she was under twenty, whereas Lee Meng was twenty-six, and immediately turned round offering to help the police. Her defence said she had been bathing, and was partly clothed, when the alarm sounded and someone told her to run. She stooped to pick up some clothes, and there was the grenade. Another Grenade Girl was up for retrial.

Meanwhile Ah Mei came and went in a police car to Police Headquarters, and one day stood in front of me with a request:

'May I go to Singapore?'

'You haven't got an identity card. No one is allowed to go about without an identity card.'

Two days later she returned. 'I have official permission to go to Singapore.'

'Oh well, if you've got a pass...' She showed it to me. 'But I couldn't give you permission, you see, I have nothing to do with the Police.'

'I'll take my mother and little brother.'

I gave them a lift that sunny morning fresh and noisy with golden orioles nesting in the tembusu and the tulip trees, to the Green Express bus parked near the market, and watched it heave itself over the small bridge which spanned the fetid stream, the main sewer of the town, rolling into the waters of the Straits. On that bridge, Ah Mei had told me, the Japanese had lined heads on piles, until each was a hive of maggots and flies, for all to see and smell. Ah Mei waved until the bus turned the corner, and I saw it advancing purposefully along the Causeway towards Singapore.

It was mid-afternoon next day before they came back. Ah Mei's face appeared above the banisters, and I was as relieved and happy to see her as if she had been my daughter.

'I was worried, I thought you would be back last night.'

'Oh please do not worry about us, doctor, spending your heart upon us ... we stayed because we discovered some relatives in Singapore and they entreated us to linger the night.'

'Oh well . . .'

'They may be coming here for a visit. So much trouble for you doctor, all these people, but then you are so kind, it is like a big family here. . . .'

Vanity pampered, weakly I replied: 'Of course your relatives are welcome.'

Then I went to the kitchen and told Cookie quite firmly that from now on we would eat no more butter, not even with toast.

A little girl, shy and quiet, fifteen to look at, though Ah Mei said she was nearly eighteen, with sweet oval face and stubborn eyes and hair waving softly to the shoulder, padded on naked feet upstairs, following Ah Mei, and was introduced to me as Ah Mei's sister-by-affection, Golden Orchid.

Golden Orchid was the daughter of Ah Mei's mother's sister. Not her real sister, but her bond sister, sister by love. Ah Mei's mother, when young, worked as rubber packer in a Singapore factory, sewing the smoked sheets of rubber into square packages bound by jute cloth. There she became a member of a sisterhood. Many such exist in Malaya, women banded for protection and self-help in societies, as men are. There is the sisterhood of amahs, those of the long black braids of hair pulling their bony heads back, always dressed in white tops and black silk trousers, neutral as worker-bees; there is the confederacy of women carriers, those who build roads and carry bricks and lumber, in their uniforms of black cotton with the red bandannas upon their heads. There are many others, bound by vows as nuns, vows taken in the temples before the goddess All-Compassionate or other deities; or lovers of each other, living as husband and wife, adopting children to their coupling; but all binding by affection, which is as strong as ties of blood, and often stronger.

The bond between Ah Mei's mother and Golden Orchid's mother had been strong enough for them to drink wine together, vowing that Heaven might fall to pieces, and the earth consume itself, before their affection for each other should perish. And then Golden Orchid's mother married one man, and Ah Mei's mother married another; came the war, and they parted. Ah Mei's mother hid in the jungle with her children during the war, existing in a clearing on yams and tapioca, and looking for protection to the jungle guerrillas, the People Inside. And now, in Singapore (said Ah Mei), they had found Golden Orchid. And so, of course, Golden Orchid was really her (Ah

Mei's) sister, and could she stay here for a few days? I said Yes.

Golden Orchid came and went quietly, so shy, so well-mannered, she was not a presence, but a fragrance in the house. Unnoticed physically, one was conscious of her as a sweetness within. After her coming a softness descended upon us all. From the kitchen, raucous heart of the house, I often heard Ah Mei's voice, soothed, lulled, talking to Golden Orchid, of the wash drying in the sun, of her arms, from which the leech bites were fading, telling stories of the latest *wayang*[1] opera. The children romping after the pompous mynah birds, too fat to fly, or coming back in triumph loaded with stolen mangosteens, clung to Golden Orchid, holding her fingers, peering up into her face. Even Cookie's wife did not belch so loud, it seemed.

Golden Orchid helped Ah Mei with the housework, and I always knew when she had done it, because where Ah Mei was inclined to slapdash, Golden Orchid did everything perfectly. But I never heard her voice. To this day I cannot say that I heard her speak more than a whispered Yes, or Thank You, so low that it was not a voice speaking. It was a disembodied presence, a fragrance and a sweetness, when Golden Orchid made her stay with us.

I remember precisely the first occasion when I became uneasy concerning Ah Mei. There is no name for this tremulous imperfection of doubt, which one refuses at inception, nor can I define in words that quality in Ah Mei's voice, the precise gesture, which gave birth to this unease in myself.

Let me try to say that it was a sudden awareness, that with some people there is such a thing as the habit of betrayal; that this habit is more widespread than one likes to think; that it would not matter, were it not for the fact that in our days political suspicion has the fervour and confident condemnation of religious fanaticism.

For we no longer need proof, to punish; we are condemned by idle speech, by the gay words in the mouths of our friends. In Malaya, where the informer system is the only way to some kind of control of the suspect population, I became suddenly, nauseatingly aware of betrayal – its power, and its corruption.

With some S.E.P.S, and perhaps with Ah Mei, the necessity of providing material for the police, once dictated by survival, had now become addiction. Like professional witnesses in some

[1] *Wayang*: Chinese open-air theatre.

other countries, like blackmailers, she and they and so many others stored minute fragments of information in their agile and retentive minds, to be used, later, in case of need. . . .

It started, then, my doubt, when the tall and earnest psychologist from Australia, one of those going about Malaya studying the Emergency and its effects, the means of psychological warfare employed to render its measures palatable, came to interrogate Ah Mei. It was extremely hot that day, but the psychologist was wide-awake. He had pored over Ah Mei's files; now she stood in front of him, naked-footed, smiling, answering his questions without seeming to pause.

We were talking of Fong Kiap, moved from detention to rehabilitation camp, and who had developed such talent for embroidery that her linen tablecloths were on sale in the best shops of Singapore.

'Certainly she used to pass food,' said Ah Mei. 'And the baby is her husband's. He and her uncle and her brother are Inside.'

And then the psychologist asked her a question in the precise Mandarin Chinese he had studied at London University. 'In your confession, Ah Mei, that long long one, you speak somewhere of a girl called Small Cloud, who was for a while in the jungle in the camp when you were there. Who is Small Cloud? Have you had any news of her? Do you know more about her?'

'I do not,' said Ah Mei. 'I do not know what has happened to her. I never knew her very well. She must still be Inside. But she is not important.'

'I thought,' said the psychologist, 'that if you had been friendly with her it would have been a good idea to contact her. You know, the usual thing the police do, dropping leaflets appealing to her to surrender. In your confession you hinted that she went to the jungle because she was attracted by a high ranking communist officer in that camp?'

'I know nothing more than what I said at the time,' answered Ah Mei, 'and perhaps it was only rumour, after all.'

And that was the first time, like a hand clapped in warning, inside me, I thought (and refused to know) that Ah Mei was lying.

'A most interesting and intelligent girl,' said the psychologist to me. 'One thing puzzled me when I spoke to her this morning. That sometimes she talks of herself in the third person. Very old-fashioned Chinese, don't you agree? But then they are all such odd mixtures of old superstition and traditional custom jumbled with the grievance which pushes them to the jungle....'

'But I can't fathom why Ah Mei switches herself from the third to the first person so often. I get the impression that she thinks of herself as two people ... one in the jungle, when she says "she", and one now, an "I" ... I wonder whether she has really split herself into two, so that she can now betray where she once believed?'

But it was far too hot (it usually is) to think long and meticulously about psychological problems, and so we disputed heatedly and futilely, as usual, about the beginnings of the Emergency, and the rights and wrongs of the jungle guerrillas, and the whole appalling obtuseness of treating half the population of Malaya as dangerous aliens and the other half as pampered puppets; and finally there was no answer, for we were all caught in this green hell, each treading our own circle of misunderstanding and good intentions.

Ah Mei next day was cleaning the mirror embedded in the wall upon which ten thousand red ant cadavers had been left from their migration, carrying the white specks, the seed alive and growing, of future generations. I found the ants tracking across the glass, erupting from the cracked wall behind it, going to some refuge in the wardrobe, and I poured Shelltox and D.D.T. vigorously from the can always standing in a corner. Now Ah Mei cleaned the shrivelled carcases off with a rag, and as usual we spoke of this and that.

'You had quite a party last night,' I said. They had sung and laughed till eleven, and the laughter had been particularly full-throated.

'Miss Lee was celebrating,' she replied. Miss Lee had recently completed a tour of the new villages with the cast, made up of ex-terrorists, of an anti-communist play called *The Bloody Traitor*. 'And her name is not Lee,' she added softly. 'That was her name Inside. Her real name is Chang.'

'Well, it doesn't matter, does it?'

'She is going to get married,' said Ah Mei. 'Wu is going to marry her.'

'But he already has a wife,' I objected, rather stupidly, thinking that an ex-communist must perforce be a monogamist. 'Isn't that why he came out of the jungle, to see his wife again, and was accused of putting personal feelings and longing for a woman above Party, and so before he could be punished by the Party he surrendered, and led the British troops back into the jungle, captured two of his ex-comrades, and they hanged on his evidence?'

'Wu has not got one wife, he has three. Miss Chang ... Miss Lee wants him to divorce the others and marry her. Wife No. 2 came yesterday to the kitchen but Miss Lee hid from her coming. She may come again today.'

And then suddenly repulsion, nausea; I sat on the bed, not understanding what was happening to me. I could not look at Ah Mei. What had she said? Nothing, and there was a candid smile upon her face.

Wu's wife came again the next afternoon, and I saw her, a small-boned and pretty woman with three children and a loud flat voice which talked and talked. She wanted me to ask Wu to give her an allowance; she wanted me to tell the police red-hair Top Man to put Wu in prison for letting her starve, and her children. And then she threatened to hang herself under the honeysuckle over the front door, if Wu abandoned her and married Miss Lee. Finally she lost breath and I said: 'You may hang yourself if you wish, but please not in my house. I shall not look after your ghost. Why don't you hang yourself in the S.E.P. quarters where your husband lives?'

Miss Shen, my friend, the Chinese teacher at the rehabilitation camp (now staying with us for a few days or weeks or months), sat on the rattan sofa, listening to Mrs. Wu, and rocked with laughter.

'Aiyah,' she said softly, putting her hand in front of her mouth, 'I am glad you have given up talking noble principles to these people, and expounding the morals of the ancestors' country, China.'

But she also whispered that the girl was arrogant to threaten suicide, and that someone must have put her up to it.

'It is Ah Mei,' said Miss Shen, who loathed Ah Mei for no reason at all. 'Ah Mei loves to fish in troubled waters, and when the water is clear, she muddies it.'

But I did not believe her because of her loathing, and because for ever the touching innocence of Ah Mei's face – that lovely mask of which she was not guilty, a physical structure condemning her to be believed and loved – would blur my judgment of her.

I called Ah Mei and said: 'Tell Miss Lee to come upstairs,' watching through the window Mrs. Wu carrying her smallest child astraddle on her hip, small and defiant and forlorn, walking away.

Ah Mei replied gently: 'Miss Lee is drunk, doctor.'

'When she is a little less drunk, tell her to come up. How did she get drunk, anyway?'

'Knowing Wu's No. 2 would come, she bought two bottles of stout this morning. She got the habit of drinking this black beer from the red-hair police officer she lived with up north,' added Ah Mei chattily, 'the one who gave the bicycle and the radio. You know he was sent away ...'

'Yes, I know, I know ...' I was annoyed.

'What did I tell you?' said Miss Shen cruelly, 'she does this to everybody now. What else can you expect? First to save her skin she betrays the People Inside, then the more she betrays the better paid she is ... and Ah Mei is so clever, the game is easy for her ... she can betray back and forth, and keep her head on her shoulders. I wonder what she really says about you ...' added Miss Shen pointedly.

There was a shuffling up the stairs as of my Siamese mother cat herding the kittens step by step in panic lest they should err from her milk-rich nipples. It was Miss Lee coming up swaying from side to side, black frizzed hair over her forehead, hands in front of her, groping blindly.

'Drunk,' said Miss Shen gaily, 'and acting too.'

'Miss Lee,' I said, as loudly as I could, 'please make yourself behave more tidily.'

'I cannot,' replied Miss Lee. 'I am drunk. I have drunk two bottles of strong stout.'

'Well, you will make your body sick, and that is all. You are giving a lot of trouble, and I'll have to complain to the police, and then you'll have to go behind the wire again.'

Miss Lee hiccuped and beat her breast, but she was not very worried. She started lamenting her sad fate, and the injustice of heaven. I could not help smiling, and anger faded.

'I cannot prevent you marrying Mr. Wu, who already has four wives.'

'Three,' amended Miss Lee.

'That's what he says,' I replied. 'Three, four, five ... he will be adding to the number, I know.'

'The others do not understand him,' said Miss Lee, in the manner of the modern films she saw regularly.

'Understand or not, you can do what you like, and throw yourself away on Mr. Wu and his wives and his dozen of children. But I don't want any unpleasantness in my house, I won't have anyone hanging themselves at my door and leaving their ghosts about.'

And I sat down, feeling unpleasant and ineffective. But Miss Lee took the matter ill, and left me, removing her radio, her bicycle and many trunks of luggage.

'Pang's wife,' reported Ah Mei, 'has found her a little room, near the prison.' Ah Mei chatted away, sweeping a negligent feather duster, cunningly avoiding a spider's web spanning the lampshade. 'Pang's wife and her sister run a small brothel in Singapore, you know, but she keeps it secret from Pang – anyway Pang is not a very good man either, always running after women, and sometimes he is very rough with people ... especially people in the new villages, but no ones dares to report him, everyone is afraid, he is so mighty, and the red-hair officers in the Police trust him. It is as Fong Kiap always says, we walk between two terrors, the jungle, and the Police, between fire and water. ...'

On she chatted, smiling, deftly moving small objects and putting them back. Miss Shen's delicate nose wrinkled slightly, she pretended not to listen. And then Ah Mei went downstairs, and we could see her with Golden Orchid, both in their gay flowered cotton trousers and jackets, saunter towards the flower gardens round the corner where the dove-orchids had burst overnight into a spray of luminous white flowers, after a spell of coolness. Ah Mei's voice was full of laughter, and her arm was about Golden Orchid's shoulders, and they did not turn their heads.

7–9 a.m. Zodiacal Sign: The Scales.
    Mystic Significance: Seed Time.

A China pheasant morning of sharp brilliance, a garden of
emerald lawns, sprayed with the vermilion petals of the flame-of-
the-forest; jacaranda and angsana, luminous in blossom of
malachite and chrome; buttercup trees flinging a golden wave
against pink walls; frangipani, oleander and bougainvillaea rose
and white in a mosaic of light.

The Abacus, Intellectual Orchid, otherwise known as Betty,
daughter of Quo Boon the millionaire, Chinese female aged
thirty-eight, born in the British Colony of Singapore, rose from
her bed, leaving her husband, Johnny Tam, asleep in the other
twin bed of their large bedroom, which The Abacus loathed
mutely.

She disliked the bedroom for its air-conditioning, which
made her bones ache and abrogated her sense of time. The
machine's persistent drone, the unchanging artificial cold within
the sealed room, cut off those small variations of the glittering
night outside, the rise and fall in the scent of flowers, the lift
and paling of the darkness, the ellipse of tree shadows absorbing
the lawns, all infallible timekeepers of her body. Her instincts
were the only mechanism that she trusted.

Within the bedroom, time denuded and therefore incomplete,
she waited awake for the trill of the expensive Swiss alarm clock
upon the rosewood carved side-table. At its purr she rose and
opened the French doors to the veranda, and the Honolulu
creepers bowered her, a crimson avalanche swung from the
lattice roofing.

Dawn glittered into morning, morning was quickly swollen
with gold heat, heat would soon bleach the sky to a dull tin,
thicken the soft air as milk curdles, people the horizon with
sluggish back-to-back clouds. Heat-ravished, the sky would
stoop ominous about the city, wearing its noon-load as a menace
poised; thunder crackle, rain in great slinging swathes slash at
the houses and the sea, the harbour and the ships. And then
light, a little space of coolness, and bougainvillaea rain-studded
lifting their eager leaves-in-flower; all afternoon the slow sleazy
steaming, the suffocating stew of glossy streets, the bright

puddles of the roads exploding water jets under car wheels, and the open sewers of the city running their narrow torrents in peaceful hurry. The first hint of evening on the pink and grey roofs, the silver tarmac drying in a topaz lapse of sun, the fabulous set madness in the west, orange, vermilion and purple, to which no one paid attention. Then curt, abrupt, night.

The Abacus knew it all, with pleasure watched it, and never said a word. How her family would have laughed, her husband, relatives and friends, laughed with that shrieking boisterousness which practical, sensible people reserve for dreamers. 'You a business woman,' they would have exclaimed, this being the highest compliment in any society in Singapore, 'talking of the sunset and the rain like a poet, there must be something wrong with you.'

'Mabel!' she called. Mabel, her adopted daughter, a nurse at the tuberculosis hospital, appeared in a white sharkskin dress girt with a wide black nylon elastic belt, the latest Hollywood fashion in Singapore. Her Chinese name was Thoughtful Jonquil, and her pet name at the Chinese Athletic Association, where she won all the prizes as amateur weight lifter, was Marilyn Monroe, for she was all over honey-gold and of wondrous architecture. Half a dozen young men (among them a lawyer, a doctor and a detective) could not sleep at night for thinking of her, and pestered their mothers to arrange for them a marriage with Mabel. But Catholic Mabel of the superb curves wore a small gold cross between her breasts, and desired to be a nun in the happy convent of her school days.

The Abacus lay on a rattan long chair, on a Dunlopillo foam-rubber mattress covered in orange cretonne, and deft Mabel pounded her back, small hands rounded to soft dimpled fists, padding evenly and quickly up and down the spine, up and down firmly, beat, beat, beat, until the muscles tingled, the blood ran stronger, the ache went and The Abacus lay limp and happy. 'It's that damn air-conditioner,' she said in English.

Johnny, her husband, insisted that air-conditioning was essential to his efficiency. He always felt too warm. He was that type of Chinese current in South East Asia, exuberant of flesh and spirit, boisterous, exuding an aggressive, apprehensive jollity, the unconcealed expression of a perpetual fear. Sons of the toil in all the rich fair lands which would be neither rich nor anything but backward kampongs without them, the Overseas Chinese wield wealth but not power, remain at the mercy of officialdom and political change, which for generations they have placated with bribery. Thus Johnny's father had paid hierarchies of British and Malay officials regular sums of money to carry on his business, and Johnny knew in his bones, bred in Singapore, that without money a man was nothing, nothing but labour, contract labour to toil, to be deported or brought in, as occasion pleased and the refusal to work of the native peoples demanded. Only wealth achieved human dignity. His banks were air-conditioned, and his company offices, and the block of flats (ultra-modern) he was building to overlook the Singapore river. The Abacus protested, but over their bedroom Johnny won.

When the Tams threw their enormous All-Singapore parties (their guests the Commissioner, the Governor, the Colonial Secretary, the Air Marshal, the General, the Admiral, bankers and businessmen of the larger variety, and the wealthiest racehorse owners, many of them doctors in private practice); when expensive motor cars chauffeured by haughty Malay syces lined up for a mile or so, and the City Traffic Police diverted ordinary motorists from the road; how nice it was – said Johnny – for The Abacus to take the ladies upstairs after dinner to the large, air-conditioned master bedroom with its four bathrooms, two by two, heliotrope, turquoise, cinnabar and amethyst their sanitary fittings; with the two beds enthroned, spread with black brocade embroidered in gold and silver thread; with the niello silver-backed combs and brushes, and the solid gold ones; with the Chinese thumb paintings of chrysanthemum and cassia, traditional Cathay loveliness maintained at the equator by the last of the thumb painters; and the lampstands of ivory and yellow crystal with pale cream lace shades, and the curtains of French imported silk, zebra black lines spiralling on a white background, and the white velvet carpet, and the black marble floor! And the air-conditioning! What great face, concluded Johnny, this gave to The Abacus, Betty, his wife!

The bedroom was the design of Fanette Archway, Johnny's present mistress. Mrs. Archway had come to the city after the war, and with a French accent, a good carriage, and interior decorating, had made her way into society. Fanette Archway only did the houses of the Chinese; Europeans meant credit and little cash. Chinese gave her the freedom of their bank accounts, with results startling and financially depletory, but with a great acquisition of standing.

In Singapore, where money alone makes the grade, Mrs. Archway's income from art assured her of invitations to Government House, to the races, to the select gatherings open to all those convicted of wealth, or of a position in the Administration entitling them to the overt bribery of feeding and figuring in social events.

At the Tam parties, Fanette, in scarlet slashed with lime-green and high-piled coils of shining hair, appeared with Sir Thomas and Lady Weatherbore, her dear friends, and smacked her painted magenta lips an inch from The Abascus's thin cheeks, 'Darling, how *charmante* you look, more exquisite every day,' to which The Abacus replied with a gold-toothed smile.

But she was secretly gratified that Johnny's present mistress was so presentable, a sound woman of business, quite unlike that young Hongkong singer at the Happy World cabaret who had made away with thirty thousand in cash, and nothing to show for it but a heavy medical bill. Fanette seemed fond of Johnny and being a red-haired she-devil would not take him away from his family. Putting up with an air-conditioner was a trifle, and as for being hurt The Abacus was too sensible. 'After all, men are like that,' she told her sister, 'I have better things to do than waste my time with Johnny.'

But she slept in the bedroom when Johnny was home, for she knew him afraid of being alone at night.

After the pounding, she put on a pair of navy slacks and a shirt, her working clothes. Her Cantonese amah laid breakfast on a small table on the veranda, a fried egg, a piece of toast, and some Kellogg's cornflakes; listening to the bulbuls and orioles asserting, in loud melody, their claims to tenancy of the tembusu trees round the water lily-pond – where a few frightened goldfish, remains of the swift pouncing kingfisher, sank in the dark glass of the water – she sipped hot Nescafé, looked over her business mail and the bills, invitations and company reports Johnny had left on his desk. At eight, seated in the black Chevrolet, the syce with the modelled Javanese face and the curly hair under his black velvet songkok, at the wheel, she sped across her garden, past the gardeners bending over the flowering hydrangeas of the lawns, past the orchids, the bougainvillaea, the oleander, the wrought iron gates, and into the road with broad-leafed mahogany and pink cassia trees still wearing faint scarves of blue mist about their crown. The ochre winding track of Holland Avenue led on to Bukit Timah Road, lined with new housing estates, satellite rows of shops and grey dusty factories, amoebic elongations from the body of Singapore city, growing and pushing its sprawl into the island, every day reaching out its pseudopodiae of factory sites further towards the Causeway, towards Malaya on the other shore of the waters of the Straits.

7 a.m.

Luke Davis woke as Ah Hong the mess boy knocked at his door, pushed it open and walked in with the morning orange juice. Ah Hong never put anything down without spilling it, and this morning again as the saucer clattered on to the bedside table it was swimming round the full glass with tepid yellow liquid.

The room was untidy. Through the windows barred with vertical iron rods the sun drifted in a broad pale wave upon Luke's bed. The uncouth black furniture (government issue) was littered with ash trays full of cigarette butts, and odd clothes: a sock lay upon the bookcase, a tie looped round the chair back. On the table were piled tan-covered files bound with pink tape, their voluminous foolscap contents half out. The room smelt of stale cigarette, sweat and the whiff of male which pervades service messes anywhere.

Eight o'clock. Luke gulped breakfast, lukewarm coffee and some wilted toast which Ah Hong seemed to have prepared the night before, crossed the hall and was on the lawn with the sunlight glazing the glossy round leaves of the mangosteen trees massed in a stooped bulk at the end of the garden. The knobbed dark fruit was ripening, and soon it would appear among the imported Sunkist oranges, Australian apples and local bananas on the Mess tables. An albizzia, with nude smooth trunk and boughs like an elongated Bali carving lifting her wooden hair with her fingers, spread a tracery of leaf against the sky.

The Mess stood unimaginatively four square, each window iron barred. A solid house, built in no style at all, it belonged to a Chinese rubber millionaire, a relative of Lam Teck's, and was rented to the Police for a large monthly sum. The towkay and his family now lived in two attap huts on some waste land at the back. It was odd, thought Luke, how the Chinese could disregard all comfort and beauty, and live crowded in a small house in perfect happiness. It was this mental and physical agility, this instantaneous adaptation to noise and discomfort, which always awed him. Owners of this hundred thousand dollar property, they were content to live in a plywood shack, not much better than those of the rubber tappers in the new villages, and did not feel put out or lowered in their own esteem, nor in anyone else's. The towkay's two grown sons were studying law and medicine in Australian universities, but their father, strolling in striped cotton pyjamas, was occasionally mistaken for the Mess boy's old father, a cured leper from the Leper Settlement three miles out of town, who often ambled in and out of the servants' quarters on rubber slippers, smiling horribly from a face gnarled with burnt-out disease.

Luke's car turned into the road, at this hour full of little girls in white shirts and blue school uniforms, going to the convent school. There were Indians with dark skin and flashing eyes and teeth, tossing their plaits and giggling ... 'Janiki, Vijaya, come on, hurry faster...' Little Chinese girls with serious round faces and glossy black hair crimped in the rigid locks of identical permanents, going from various dialects into English and back again into dialect : 'I didn't do my homework, let me see yours, tolong lah...' Eurasians with green eyes and black hair, looking Chinese, or looking European with golden hair and brown eyes ... 'We've got another baby, my mummy brought it home last night from the Hospital after makan...' Some on foot, most in cars, quite a few in very large cars with chauffeurs, the daughters of wealthy Chinese businessmen, the daughters of Malay officials, all went to convent school. A limousine drove by, out of which the Princess, daughter of the Sultan's eldest son, stepped and immediately merged, indistinguishable among dozens of other little girls. Heads bobbing, a blue and white stream of little girls and their soft laughter flowed towards the buildings of the Convent, in front of which a white stone statue of the Virgin, donated by the Moslem Sultan, showed stark and new.

The Convent was constantly growing in size, adding wings of extra classrooms; acquiring more land, as more and more little girls from Catholic or pagan Indian, Catholic or pagan Chinese, Catholic Eurasian and Islamic Malay families, docile, blue clad and happy little girls rippling with talk and laughter, poured into the Convent, their goal the Cambridge Overseas School certificate, their English new and fresh and flavourful, lilting Malayan singsong English lovely to hear.

'Come, I will show you.'

'Die for you, lah.'

'I say no, Mai.'

Luke Davis thought : 'This is the first time I really see this little town in Malaya.' After months of going to the office and back to the Mess in his car without noticing anything on the way, this morning, his work completed, driving into Singapore to unfold the project upon which he had toiled, his mind had become observant of things other than the Emergency. Perception gave him a pleasurable feel of enchanting newness, fresh as the sudden perfume of a rose. He looked and listened and saw and heard for the first time in months, sprightly of spirit, excited by the lavishness of sound and colour. Malaya was wonderful. Look at them, the little girls of the future Malaya, filing into school, so many races, so many golden shades to melt and fuse together into one nation ... he felt as if his heart would burst in fragrant tenderness, a moonflower's abrupt blossoming. These little girls must have been babies during the Japanese occupation ... one war should be enough for any little girl....

In this state of intense mindfulness, he passed the Sultan's flower gardens and the Zoo with the peacocks flying across the road to perch on the walls of the Judge's house, the small flame-coloured pony eating the morning grass; left the mosque on his right with the smooth lawns sloping away from its white walls and domed and cupolaed towers; and had the straits of Johore in front of him, the water silver-sapphire and rose-opal, smooth-shining softly under the sky, fringed by the hoary rain trees and the filmy casuarinae along the road. Here and there in the water rose the kelongs, fishing stakes looking like long-tailed crabs perched on high legs strutting the water. They were made of wooden piles driven into the sea, hundreds of yards away from shore. A small house was erected at one end of a platform, nets spread from the piles. Two to six men lived on them for a week or more, catching fish, salting and curing it. Luke, slowing, gazed at them, thinking of the communist courier routes – convenient for smuggling, these kelongs. At night the sampans and motor boats could anchor there, goods could be unloaded, hidden under piles of nets, fish heaped to hide them ... There were hundreds of such stakes along the long and complicated coast, standing out to sea like moored ships. Three were definitely known to him as stopping points in a communist route, smuggling ammunition from Singapore to Johore.

Past the Johore State Customs, with polite smiling inspectors waving him on; on to the Causeway, three-quarters of a mile long, bridging the Straits. The Causeway, an umbilical cord of stone linking Singapore to Malaya. On his right lay the large round pipe carrying water to the city of Singapore from the mountains of Johore. The railway ran alongside the pipe, and the road next to it. How vulnerable it all looked. Perhaps it was the knowledge of this tenuous link crossing the unsolid sea which kept Malaya and Singapore far apart instead of uniting them ... as if the Straits were a new English Channel, unspanned by road or rail or needed water. In the war, the Causeway had been blown up to prevent the Japanese crossing; they had crossed anyway, undaunted.

And now Luke was driving on Singapore Island, and it was another country, another government. Singapore was a Crown Colony, and Malaya was nine Moslem Sultanates grouped in a Federation, nine medieval Chairs of State propped up by British power. Independence had been promised to both as soon as the people were 'ready' for it. But what being 'ready' meant, Luke, for one, could not explain. Would Singapore be independent first, or Malaya first? Obviously they must form one country one day, for this absurd separation was like making London one country, distinct from the rest of England. But there was feeling against union at the moment. The three million Malays of Malaya did not want Chinese Singapore, with its near-million Chinese and its handful of Malays, to swamp them; and the million Chinese of Singapore were not keen to put up with the kind of racial discrimination and the special privileges accorded to the Malay race, which kept the three million Chinese of Malaya in a state of perpetual grievance ... And in this dilemma the British ran everything of importance, though promising independence, and even, if goaded enough, making gestures towards it, which were not insincere, even if liberal tendencies were always denounced with overwhelming emphasis by the vested interested, the big companies, as hasty, premature and ill-timed. All over South East Asia there were white men pointing out, loud and long, how bad freedom was for anyone but themselves.

But the people of Malaya were getting impatient. Some were saying quite loudly that the longer independence was denied, the more chance for communism, for only a truly free country would fight. 'Set a thief to catch a thief', said the Malays, currently talking of the Police and the People Inside the jungle. And they said that they preferred a bad government of their own, rather than to be run by others.

Of course, thought Luke, the end was inevitable. One day people like himself would have to leave on a pension for life, and people like Che Ahmad and Abdullah would take over. Meanwhile the Chinese were fobbed off with those extraordinarily complicated citizenship laws which very few understood. Citizenship was so difficult to get, it was openly admitted that the law had been devised to keep the Chinese *out* rather than to bring them into the fold of the country ... and now it had succeeded in making one million stateless people in Malaya, one in six of the people of the country.

'And after that,' said Luke aloud to himself, 'how *can* we have the bloody cheek to ask for their loyalty?' It was such a mess, he thought, all this balancing and weighing and hedging, this rule by expediency in which people were but pawns, in the local game of power or in the larger scale game of the cold war in South East Asia. And in this war Malaya was RUBBER, and not people; a FACTOR, not a country.

Rubber was a boon, it had made Malaya the wealthiest possession in the world. Rubber was a curse, for Malaya was a pawn in the hands of others. Malaya would never be thought of as a land with a mind of its own; always, here the divided mind, the divided peoples, the divided purposes, and though it was true enough that in spite of the differences and the divisions there was a new, a growing will to freedom and to nationhood, too many people were still intent on division.

He passed the Singapore customs shed, the police in blue-grey shirts, and on his left the Naval Base, famous of infamous memory. From Johore Bahru the Base could be seen, its grey ships moored, its white buildings spotless in the sun, its bungalows on the undulating land within its heavily guarded gates.

Would it be any use in another war, or would it fall without a blow again, as it had done in the last war?

The Bukit Timah road stretched in front of him. Already lorries rumbled along it, loaded with pigs in cylindrical wide-meshed rattan baskets, the pigs stacked snout to tail, in three superimposed layers, squealy noisy lorries rolling into Singapore from Johore. Those were squatter pigs from the Chinese farmers. They were breeding pigs again. In the first years of the Emergency so many pigs had been killed, resettling the farmers. Now they were starting again. Looking at the backs of the lorries with their medieval pattern of snouts and tails, Luke felt like singing. Hell, he thought of the farmers, they've got guts, they deserve better than what we've given them so far.

Timber lorries, each one loading three sawn trunks of chengai, meranti or seraya wood from the timber concessions in the jungles of Malaya, rolling forward to the building boom of the city. Lorries of sheet rubber, packed in square blocks sewn in jute bags white with lime dust; lorries of liquid latex, painted silver or painted red, lumbering at twenty miles an hour. Lorries filled with Chinese factory girls, standing in the packed vehicles, dressed in vests and trousers of flowered cotton, all with permanents stiffly fringing curls round their faces, all with gold-edged teeth ... Gold teeth, so fashionable now at factory level. Twenty years ago they had been the fashion among the wealthy Asian bourgeoisie (only at that time they had been called Asiatics, not Asians, and made to keep their place, while now Raffles Hotel was full of them every night, and even the Tanglin Club had its one night a week for Asians). Asians now spoke of themselves as *we-Asians*, as if Asia were an entity, when really it was a huge agglomeration of continents and cultures and races and religions and governments further apart from each other than any European country could be from any other European country. And yet *we-Asians* gripped the imagination ... it meant something. There was a feeling of akinness, from Egypt to Japan ... and all these countries were changing, changing, running the centuries into days, hurrying and scrambling forward, at a breathless speed which left European prejudices and platitudes about them as far behind as the buggy horse was left panting after a jet plane. Somehow Europe appeared so staid, stay-behind and unimaginative beside this surging exaltation of Asia....

Gold teeth, thought Luke, as his car flashed by and the factory girls cheering his speeding, bent over the lorry sides to smile at him in exuberant early morning happiness, jeering also, to observe once again that it was a police officer breaking the traffic law (but then military and police vehicles were always in a hurry), and he waved at them out of his car window. Who was it had gold teeth like that? It was at that party at Quo Boon's ... his daughter, she of the small thin face, and the neat wit; strange with what pleasure he remembered her ugliness.

As a miracle, flowering in this lovely morning of acute perception, he saw a car draw up ahead of him, slow and stop in front of a rubber-packing factory on one side of the road. Out of it came a woman, small, thin, in slacks. She bent towards the Malay chauffeur, giving directions, as Luke came up to her level. He recognized her, slowed, honked twice. She looked, but it was already too late, he was past and she had not seen him, but he caught sight of her face in the rear mirror, looking towards his car. He felt absurdly light-hearted. 'Funny little woman,' he said aloud. He liked her. He liked everybody and everything that day ... the factories, belching and smoking, the pigs in their lorries, the factory girls, the sun already a steady glare beating upon everything, the road stretching in front of his car, the Bukit Timah road going southward to the city, Singapore.

7 a.m.

Quo Boon paced the red-tiled veranda while round him Quovilla woke, stretched and yawned in that soft cacophony of a big family, where every man, woman and child goes about his own way of waking up. His fourth daughter-in-law, the pretty and astute Silver Bangle, also named Milly, a daughter of the wealthy Mr. Poh Cho-yee ('and much too nice a girl for such a father' was Quo Boon's comment whenever he saw her), tripped gaily and importantly up and down, serving everyone else. She was the youngest daughter-in-law to be married into the family, and wanted to make a favourable impression. Behind her two little girl servants, adopted by Quo Boon as daughters-by-affection because they were the offspring of his cook (and he did not want his able cook to leave for a big restaurant, which had offered a larger salary), tripped in pert jackets and trousers of printed nylon, and all three carried steaming coffee cups in both hands.

Quo Boon paced, breathed deeply the scented morning air and looked over the garden where mynah birds strutted belly forward on the lawn like Legislative Councillors in converse. Across the grass came Quo Boon's youngest son ... (*Was* it his son? Quo Boon was suddenly perturbed to discover, when the boy turned his head, that it was his grandson and not his son, and his heart smote him. The generations grew in his house until he, an old man full of life and vigour in his sixty-fifth year, reigning over this vast clan, no longer distinguished the parent from the child.) Quo Boon saw his grandson in white shirt and shorts and tennis shoes, and a school-satchel on his back, shooing the mynah birds before him.

He called: 'Little one!' and the child stopped, smiled at his grandfather, looking more like Quo Boon's son than ever, clambered over the low stone parapet of the veranda and threw himself at the old man. 'Grandpa!' he called. 'I'm late for school, Grandpa. Will you lend me your big car so I don't have to catch the bus?'

'No,' said Quo Boon, patting the sleek black head. 'Only spoilt sons of rich men go by car. You have to learn to walk, little one, to the bus. I don't want my family to become spoilt.' For Quo Boon had learnt this in his years in Malaya:

That the Chinese who came from China, hardened and trained to hunger and labour until human endurance could do no more, prospered and founded great wealth and vast houses and clans; then were born their sons, in this tropical lush land, where heat sapped their vigour. Reared in soft luxury, most of them squandered their fathers' wealth, became lazy, vacuous-minded, careless. Quo Boon had seen great enterprises founded by men like himself, come to Malaya sold as contract slaves, wearing but a pair of blue trousers round their loins and a pair of wooden slippers on their feet. They had toiled as he had toiled, in the rubber estates, in the tin mines, in the timber concessions; and, after having repaid the contractor for selling them, had a few coins left. With that and nothing but their hands and the will to survive he had seen them, in little dark shops, selling anything that could be bought or sold; and then buying slightly larger shops and a piece of land, and selling that. When bicycles came in, they invested in bicycles. They built the roads, and they felled the jungle and they sold the timber. They grew peppers and pineapple, they mined tin, they ran lorries, they planted rubber. When the first cinema came to Malaya, it was the Chinese who opened it. Take away the Chinese of Malaya, and there would not be any Malaya: only a collection of kampongs, nine Sultans, a lot of Malay and British officials sitting in government offices. Proudly Quo Boon knew this, tasted every day the full scope of Chinese enterprise and the full bitterness of the Chinese grievance. Quo Boon, still of that generation of builders, had been careful with his sons, and was now careful with his grandsons, that what had been so difficult to hoard should not be easily lost.

But there was always this vexed question of the cars for school. Quo Boon sighed. So often he had to say: 'No. No cars for you. No cars. I didn't go to school, yet here I am today. Your fathers went to school on foot because at that time I had no money for cars. And now I have twelve cars, three Jaguars, two Cadillacs, a Buick, a Rolls-Royce, which I never use myself, but which I bought anyway (and once I lent it to the Commissioner when his broke down), and a few others, small and big. My daughters-in-law use them for shopping, for driving to mahjong parties and bridge parties, all these things which women do to waste their time, which keep them restless, shrewish, avid for jewellery and money, buying what they will never need, and of not much use except to breed children.' But that is Singapore, thought Quo Boon, where wealth is everything. His thoughts rambled to a past clearer than the present. Women ... He had had many wives. Some had died and some were alive. He could not remember them all. None but the first had meant much to him, but he had always given them plenty of money to spend, unlike mean Mr. Poh, who made an allowance only of a hundred and twenty-five dollars a month to his first wife. Clear alone stood Quo Boon's first love, the little girl sent out to him from China, unseen the bride until a wife, silent and hard-working in that small dank shop in Kuala Lumpur, where he had started to be rich. She had died so frightfully of cancer, some years ago. But her children were the best of the lot: Intellectual Orchid, and the son in the jungle, her last, the lean and silent son whose name Quo Boon never uttered now.

Impatiently the little boy tugged at his sleeve, tugging Quo Boon's mind back to the present, the morning in Singapore: 'Grandpa, Grandpa, let me have the car, just this once.'

They all said that, 'Just once. Just once let me have the car.'

'No,' said Quo Boon. 'Not for school. For picnics and when you go out with the family, to the cinema and the circus, and to the Happy World, but not for school. I won't have my children going in big cars like the degenerate sons of others.'

The little boy pouted, stamped his feet: 'It isn't fair!' he cried, 'we're the wealthiest of them all, and they all laugh at us, for here I go to school on the bus as if I were a poor man's son.'

'You'll be poor yourself if you go now in a car,' said Quo Boon. 'I'll buy you a bicycle just like the others. You can go on a bicycle when you are a little bigger, but no car for you.' And suddenly irritable, he pushed away the little boy, who disappeared howling for his mother. Immediately, with a sound like doves flurrying their feathers, the women of the house were round him, soothing and fondling him, holding out sweets and promising ice-cream; anything to stop his crying, to stop him hurting himself in sorrow.

Quo Boon resumed his pacing, and looked at his platinum Rolex watch. Soon his secretaries would be here. He shouted for the servants to be sure to call the Malay syce with the sapphire Buick, for after the session with his secretaries he would drive to the airport and catch the Malayan Airways plane to Kuala Lumpur. He was going there to see a general.

There would be time to go to Johnny's bank, before lunch at her sister's, and the meetings this afternoon, at the Chamber of Commerce, at the latex storage factory....

Intellectual Orchid remembered it was March, and it would be cold in Hongkong. The amah must pack her warm clothes ... She hoped Pearl hadn't forgotten some warm wear, it was cold in China. Then she remembered that Pearl was not going to get to China, since she, Intellectual Orchid, was flying to Hongkong to stop her.

The voice of Lam Teck sheathed in customary dulcet innuendo, syrupy with caution on the telephone, had preceded by half an hour Lam Teck in person gliding into the office courtyard ensconced in a sea-green Cadillac (borrowed from a friend), with Ismail by his side, reticent and smaller without his black songkok. Out of the Federation the Sultan's edict, ordering Malays to wear their velvet hats, lost sway; Ismail abandoned his headgear but not his pipe.

Both the men, one Malay, one Chinese, both devoted friends of the House of Quo, sat on the foam rubber chairs in front of Intellectual Orchid's desk, while behind her through the open slits of the louvered glass panes, the traffic of Bukit Timah Road was seen sliding unruffled as on a screen. Lam Teck made certain no one listened behind the door. 'It is about your Sixth, Old Eldest One,' he addressed Intellectual Orchid familiarly, as clansman and quasi-relative: 'Ismail tells me she left Singapore on the *Thibania* for China with twenty others from her school.'

He spoke Hokkien, which Ismail knew. Many Malays of Johore speak Hokkien dialect, infused with pleasant emotional Malay words: thou, like, love, darling, my heart, and please.

'How did you find out?' Intellectual Orchid asked Ismail.

'The Police have the list of students who sailed at ten a.m. yesterday. They typed it last night, I saw the carbon copy this morning ... I rang up Teck, told him I was coming to *makan angin*[1] in his friend's new car....'

So Pearl, the little one, sixth daughter of the House of Quo, had escaped. Not to the jungle, but to China. It had to be China.

By the hundreds, from Malaya's Chinese schools, boys and

[1] *Makan angin*: eat the wind, equivalent of the French: *prendre l'air*.

girls went to China. From the countries of South East Asia ten thousand had gone back the year before. They felt no hope of career or enterprise in the Southern lands which their fathers' toil had built. Deprived by the accident of their birth and their schooling from equal opportunity, they could not become lawyers, doctors, engineers, architects, or anything but at best a business merchant and at worst a waiter in a coffee shop or a manual labourer. And so they left the lush fair lands once full of promise and accomplishment for their fathers, and sailed for the China which their fathers had fled in the extreme of poverty.

For this – time's somersault, the jocund turn of fate, the wheel gone round – was the present, in this tremendous bestriding Asia, where the countries ran away with the centuries, devouring time and space in chunks and not pausing to chew. And now the young of the Chinese in Malaya – those who had not received their education in English schools – hemmed in without hope in Malaya where they were born, were turning back to the newest America, the earth's old country, the ancestors' land, China. In the enhanced exaltation of their bitterness and frustration it appeared marvellously holy, of mighty achievement and fearless enterprise, of wondrous hardship and labour sanctified in mystic communion and soaring singleness of purpose. Here were the anvils that would forge a world of the future. They went to give their strength, their enthusiasm. They went to study and to work.

Winged was the desire that drove them, and no accumulated store of wealth, no cupidinous sapience of their fathers would hold them back from possession of that promise which is Youth's prize, the Future.

Intellectual Orchid sat, forgetting the two men who tried to look concerned for her sake, and she too heard the songs of the singing tomorrows, before which the torpid and the avaricious, the selfish and the cynical, were undone in their half-hearted measures and their quiet expediencies and their loud brandishments of moral principles which they had never practised and how could their children believe them? They had nothing, nothing but stones to give to hungry Youth.

But in the undoing of hypocrisy and meanness were also undone other things: sober intent and selfless building; patience and tolerance which puts up with small injustices rather than drown mankind in blood.

In these, too, the young had lost faith and belief. These, too, they derided as weakness ... would they believe again one day?

Intellectual Orchid saw the faces, all as the face of her sister, stubborn and hidden, in nothing startling but with ardour of bone and delicate glow beneath the tense skin; with eyes merciless with truth, twin judges without passion or pity for the foolish old ones who claimed wisdom, and preached patience, but had forgotten to provide for the dreams of the young. The faces were wrapped in a dream of a world, their world, their youth together, unattainable.

They *were* unattainable now, and it was frightening as it was fascinating. They never spoke to their elders now, the young, but went their own way in unswerving self-possession. Puritans and pure, saints or knights on the new great adventure, the children of the Chinese schools had no small defects, no puny weaknesses, they were neither servile nor placid with the contented souls of the content to serve; but they were dangerous, for the exaltation of saintliness is always dangerous. They had courage and brilliance, they had idealism and honesty: they were the stuff that heroes and pioneers are made of: and what happened to them?'

They could not find jobs, except in business. They could not go to university, because the only university in Malaya catered nearly exclusively for English-speaking Asian youths, who knew neither Malay nor Chinese, but only English. They were condemned all their lives; to bitterness and frustration, to smallness and mediocrity. Intellectual Orchid thought: 'Yet surely they are the best of the lot. They've got rebellious courage – they've got ardour, and somehow I like them better than the others, the docile sheepish ones.' But her spirit sagged, as she saw courage running its audacious course amok, to murder and to bloodshed – courage and idealism soured and harshened to brutal carnage and the law of the jungle, for want of an outlet worthy enough.

Sen, best beloved son of her father, wealthy, unbitter, unfrustrated, had become such a rebel. He had chosen the forest for justice, the darkness beneath the trees, the horror and the blood spilling ... Intellectual Orchid's forehead wrinkled with pain thinking of Sen and the absorbed, dedicated look on his face, the inner concentration on something so vast, that it was worth hell upon earth ... Was it worth it, all this violence, the nightmare endured for a dream to come?

He sang: 'The wind for my garment, the rain for my drink.' What had the long years in the jungle done to his soul? But then what did that other jungle, the ravenous, stupid, loud, brash jungle of money-making, what did *that* do to one's soul? 'Perhaps I have no soul,' thought Intellectual Orchid. 'In this jungle of money I am a machine, counting money, The Abacus clicking as the wheels roll and the rubber goes forth from the factories and estates of the House of Quo.'

Fate spun one as at blind man's buff, round and round, left one wandering, arms outstretched, in blind groping ... Hermetic in fatalism, Intellectual Orchid accepted to be neutral to herself and to what might happen through her own living and the actions she performed. Hers was an intimate detachment, knowing life an inevitable burden better upon her patient shoulders than upon others. A practical mystic imprisoned in business concerns, she was of those Asians who dream of cherished solitude, yet are plunged by the turmoil of Asia into hectic action and paltry concern. 'Perhaps I have no soul, since I do not suffer,' she repeated to herself.

But Pearl was of another century in this raging acceleration of crescendo, Asia; where events shaped the future before the present was yet wholly perceived. Skywriting jet prophesying while its engine roar lagged futile behind it as a cloud.

What would be Pearl's future staying here? Frustration, rancour, bitterness, revolt, police surveillance, at last surrender, marriage to a fat-souled businessman, a hectic busy-bright money machine shaped as a man, intent on success, someone like Johnny, her husband, or Sir Moksa Bakrar, her brother-in-law?

Let her go. Let her go, as Mabel would go to a nunnery, let her go to China.

And then Intellectual Orchid thought of her father, and saw the old man (for he was old, Pa, though vigorous his laughter, shrewd his eyes and hearty his speech in business conferences), sipping milk, slippers on his feet, and talking of Pearl his little one, and her mind was made up.

'Lam Teck, get me a ticket on tonight's airplane to Hongkong. I shall arrive tomorrow morning, the *Thibania* won't get there until afternoon. I'll meet the ship before the children can land, and I'll bring our Sixth back to Singapore.'

She picked up her telephone, put it down. Wires were tapped. Better to go to Johnny's bank, to the icy air-conditioned office where he functioned, dictating and eyeing importantly his demure slim secretary with the Audrey Hepburn coiffure. She would still have time to get dressed for lunch at her sister's house, Fragrant Orchid, Lady Bakrar, whose husband, Sir

Moksa, was earmarked by Colonial Government to become a great and sound leader in Malaya, when Malaya became self-governing and later on independent, both events devoutly to be wished as late as possible, their consummation perhaps years from now....

9–11 a.m. Singapore.

Luke parked his Wyvern in front of the grey stone massive Special Branch building, Singapore, and with a spurt of pleasure saw that Symonds's Jaguar reposed two Citroens away. He'd poke his head into John Symonds's office later, after the conference. He liked the sacrilegious ramble of Symonds's voice, which miraculously never affected his standing in the Force. If only he, Luke, had had that gift....

He strode the smooth iron-grey corridors with their distilled sternness, passed two informers, recognized an S.E.P. giving evidence at a trial, stood back to wall to let police constables go by with two manacled tattooed young men who might be secret society small fry – locally known as 'grass slippers' – and knocked at the door of the conference room.

Here five officers were assembled, to greet with grim, granite jowls their colleague from that other land over the Causeway, Malaya.

Elation extinguished in recurrent knowledge of an unpopularity inescapable as a smell, Luke Davis sat down, ungeared by the chilly reception. Eager to be liked, he was unduly sensitive to real or fancied hostility. Although the five amiably composed to listen and to stare with the good-natured frown of men well on the job, their bulging attentive eyes glazed with the new preoccupation which the shaping of future tactics demanded, he felt on the defensive and consequently ill at ease.

In Kuala Lumpur, a general uncertain of temper and blunt of speech was shouting: 'I'll declare war on those b ... rs of Singapore if they keep on aiding the b ... rs in the jungle.' And now here was Luke, weighed with a bulky tan file bound with the ominous pale pink tape of Security, enfolding evidence of communist smuggling over the Straits of Johore. But soon the absorption of the work he had done, dovetailing into the work of many others, overwhelmed them all, and it was two hours later, with charts and maps on the table, courier routes plotted in red and blue pencil, lists of names and aliases dotted with the usual question marks opposite suspects, accommodation addresses involving coffee shops, garages, fishing huts and innocuous seeming fishing boats, that with identical sighs of relief the men sank back into their chairs while the Chief's hand stretched out to the papers and the Chief's voice asked him to leave the file behind.

'We'll have all this checked up by our own Intelligence, Davis.'

Luke felt dismayed. The attitude of the Force towards upcountry colleagues sometimes annoyed the latter. With their smartness, their spick and span uniforms, their living quarters, their immovable jobs confined to the island, and especially their higher cost of living allowances (known as COLA), the Singapore Force had some edge of superiority in its manner. It openly declared that it had thoroughly smashed the communist organizations of Singapore many years ago; whereas in Malaya upcountry, police officers trundled from one State to the other, one posting to the next, in an endeavour to catch up with the never-ending work of the Emergency. Some stayed no more than a few weeks before shifting again. Apart from the few towns, they lived in more or less primitive bungalows in small villages or amid kampongs. Since they went jungle-bashing they got killed fairly often, or shot down on the roads. Above all, their COLA was less than in the city, though the cost of living in Malaya was higher than in the free port of Singapore.

'Don't think I can leave the stuff behind, sir, we've got only one copy for security reasons.'

The Chief frowned at the implication of leakage. 'You ignore, perhaps, Davis, that here in Singapore we have an *efficient* system of confidential secretaries,' he replied coldly.

Of course. Maxine Gerrard was a C.S. In Singapore and Kuala Lumpur, wives or wives-to-be of Police and Army officers were employed in typing out confidential documents, their work and their confidential salaries the cause of much resentment among Asian and Eurasian typists who felt as loyal and capable, but were not so considered.

And now the Chief's outstretched hand grasped the file and Luke stood bereft, swinging empty arms, feeling absurdly deprived of merit; his creation, the passionate toil of many months, a bundle of much thumbed foolscap in someone else's grip.

The Chief now delivered cordiality in a lucent stream, the papers securely clutched to his heart:

'It was good to see you, Davis, do appreciate all you've done

on this ... must come over more often ... brother officers ...
exchange ideas, freshen up one's point of view...'

11 a.m. to 1 p.m. Zodiacal Sign: The Lion.
> *Mystic Significance: Ascendancy of Female*
> *Element.*

Luke walked out of the room into the corridor feeling inadequate and young, an unexplained small boy loneliness, and
thought himself architect of his own disfavour, his brusque un-
tactful honesty leaving him no measure of unctuous fulsome-
ness. At the moment, the Chief was saying to his Assistant:
'Jolly good worker, Luke Davis,' Luke felt most out of place in
the Force he served.

He thought of ringing Maxine, but his mind's eye saw her
typing a confidential document, and the vision was disagreeable
... meanwhile here was the way to John Symonds's office.

Symonds was Luke's counterpart in the Singapore Force.
Pushing the door of Symonds's office from within came a young
man of dark angelic face, a long-necked and slim Byzantine
angel with features delicate and pensive, smile-wreathed and
sadly radiant, walking with light wavy footfall as though dancing to an evasive tune. Casually, one of the two plain clothes
men who sat in the corridor waiting for him to pass, got up and
followed him.

Luke recognized Mahudin, ex-student of the University of
Malaya, detained for nearly two years when Police had swooped
and raided the University dormitories for seditious literature,
and arrested a few young men. Some were free, in England,
and others still under surveillance in Singapore.

Apart from keeping a diary of his actions, having to be indoors by seven p.m., reporting once a week to the Police, and
being tailed by a detective, Mahudin was told he was quite free.
Under such conditions he had not been able to get a job.

Mahudin could not bear not to visit the police once a week,
for in that relationship of love and hate, hostility and attraction
which develops between master and slave, jailer and prisoner,
police and detainee, his senses hummed like a homing pigeon
when he saw the grey stern building which he mightily detested
as the emblem of tyranny and oppression.

He entered it defiantly, with a strange sense of underground
power thrilling his sensitive elongated body as he fronted his
foes, the officials committed to professional suspicion.

Never was he more vibrantly alive, his cause the cause of freedom noble, true and clear as when he looked with cold scorn, in this bastion of the Old Order, upon the mercenary army which stayed the foundations of a system in which Mahudin was not equal to John Symonds whom he spoke to across the table, and perhaps would never be.

Talking to John Symonds, he, Mahudin, knew that he loved Symonds and wanted to call him his friend, and yet hated him at the same time because he had to remember that Symonds was also his master, his jailer, his tormentor ... in power over him, for ever.

'Hullo, hullo, haven't seen you for ages, come in, take a chair, put up your feet, had this desk specially designed for putting up feet, note the oval inset for the ankles.'

John Symonds, tall and fair and lanky, with luminous eyes and a warm lovely smile, had a trick of wiping his mouth with a white handkerchief, as if to keep his lips clean enough for truth. He stood, smiling at Luke, who entered as Mahudin went out.

'Cigarette, have a cuppa? Got a secretary who makes most excellent tea, good looking too, fine bust ... got some Indonesian blood she tells me, lovely skin ... What brings you from your healthy jungle haunts to the corrupt licentious city? Not work, I hope....'

'What else?' Foolishly relaxed, nearly happy again, Luke put up his feet, inhaled deeply. Here the air was good, not the stultifying rarefaction proceeding from some of his colleagues, exuding uncertainty in bluster. Here was a mild and seafree breeze of swift nonchalant cynicism blowing clearness into his mind....

'My life work is now in the hands of your Chief. Communist links between Singapore city and Malaya. Your city stands practically accused of aiding and abetting our terrorists, and I'm afraid I've had to write a report on our side of it....'

Symonds pursed his beautiful mouth: 'Treading on susceptible toes again, Davis? Trust *you* to trample where angels hover, to excoriate us with your efficiency at this time, when we've not yet recovered from the theft of half a million dollars' worth of armoury from Army Headquarters and other dumps...'

He laughed: 'Don't look so hurt, you've just handed in a packet and they're a bit sore with you of course, but they'll get over it ... and get to work on it. And when something is done, it'll be thorough. The System does work, you know ... but the whole thing will have to be kept dark for a bit, just as these thefts ... By the way, that reporter, Ronnie Closeup, was up here this morning ferreting ... I advised him to transfer himself to the sports section of his newspaper pretty soon. ...'

'Why, John, it's not like you, "the most liberal police officer in Malaya"', quoted Luke. 'Closeup is a good reporter, though we also had to head him off at Todak when the R.O., Uxbridge, got bumped off. ...'

'That's just the point. He's too, too keen. Goes on finding out all these lovely juicy bits of corruption and slackness and he'll get himself fired. It's not only the communists we're fighting, it's just as much the old-type morons on our side, and you and I know they abound and prosper. They think any Asian who doesn't grovel and whine and thank his stars he's got such good masters as we are is a Red. I've advised Ronnie to take a temporary holiday in sports. He can't go wrong reporting badminton, can he ... or can he?'

He lolled back, luminous eyes fixed upon his guest.

'Young Mahudin was here just now ... he's still under my care. His visits stimulate me. I look forward to them. He's intelligent and imaginative, and I find myself talking to him more freely than to most of my colleagues, whose conversation plunges me into a stupor.

'Perhaps it is because Mahudin and I are technically enemies ... beloved opponents, that sort of thing ... but when he comes, I find myself twice as alive, I become the eager beaver type, back in my young days as a would-be socialist ... I, Symonds, tracker of Political Subversion, in charge of our brand of thought-control, become as ardent and impatient a believer in freedom as Mahudin, and my voice shakes much as his over the indignity of political subjection under the guise of tutelage. The rubbery hypocrisies became clear to me, and I wax nearly as bitter as he does over the Tanglin Club, the senior officers, and the expatriate problem, the white official who comes here on a fat salary and goes away on a pension for life.'

'And works jolly hard for it,' interposed Luke Davies, an indignant expatriate.

'Luckily it doesn't last.' Again Symonds gave his bewilderingly lovely smile. 'That side of me evanesces ... it's a temporary schizophrenia. I recover my other, my efficient, my career self, and become again strictly dishonest or honest (I don't know the difference any longer) to earn my living.'

He wiped his mouth daintily.

'Mahudin and I were discussing an interesting subject ... one that you too have touched upon, in your hesitating fashion. The role of a colonial police force in a colony promised independence and nominally being groomed for it.

'Mahudin claims it's all eyewash, Malaya is a Police State and the Force an instument of oppression pure and simple, only infinitely astute, our claws sheathed in velvet, as he put it. He says: "You've really perfected thought-control to an unequalled finish, Symonds." (He loves to call me Symonds, it gives him a feeling of equality.) "Symonds," he says, "the Gestapo, the Kempeitai, the Ogpu, why, they're medieval, crude, torturers hitting butterflies with sledge hammers compared to you."'

'Now how the hell does he explain that?' asked Luke, dumbfounded, and angry.

'I'll tell you in a moment. Mahudin says British colonialism has got two great assets. The first is the comparison with Japanese rule. All over Malaya you still hear people say: "But the Japanese were much worse." Although a lot of Asians call our return after the war the Reoccupation, and Liberation only when there's a white man around, all will admit that we are infinitely less willing to spill blood than others.

'The memory of Japanese harshness, and the off-hand casual murderings of the jungle guerrillas, remind them that however proud of being Asians, they're not convinced that any Asian rule would be less bloody than ours.

'You may come out of detention and prison; you never come back from the grave.' That's an important difference, and perhaps an essential one.

'Secondly, Mahudin says, we've learnt an infinite flexibility. There's no limit to the disguises, the cloaks of virtue and principle, in which we will clothe the expediencies by which we rule. Not only do we have on hand a whole array of stooges ready to do our bidding, but we are for ever ready to manoeuvre even a staunch nationalist like himself into some kind of co-operation.

'"You cajole and threaten, you smile and frown, but most of all you use gamesmanship." That's Mahudin's way of putting it. He's read Potter. "You sap our self-confidence until we exist merely to court your approval. You've made 'That's not fair' tantamount to 'That's not British'. You keep us perpetually off balance, unpleasantly aware of our inferiority, and that's the whole secret of your skill and power."'

'Is he talking about himself?'

Symonds lowered his eyelids. He had long, blond lashes,

darker at the tip. 'Underneath it all he sees a merciless resolve to keep rubber and tin. Meanwhile, whatever Government may come in as a step towards independence, we'll do our best to sap its self-confidence, says Mahudin, and to give it a nervous breakdown. We'll be perpetually hovering in the foreground, loudly criticizing and pointing out how wrong and inadequate and inefficient things are; we'll for ever threaten to cut off the liberties we've granted on the plea that their conduct shows that the people are "not ready" for it. With true Victorian hypocrisy we'll go on our knees to pray for our unworthy offspring, and like any ageing woman jealous of her young daughter, we'll always be telling them how they really can't expect to be as good as we are ... oh yes, I must say,' continued Symonds, laughing, 'that I don't see our old die-hards refraining from gleeful prophecies of disaster at any opportunity. And that's what Mahudin calls our thought-control ... an induced hypnosis of inferiority, destroying confidence and initiative, prolonging the period of tutelage which we would like to go on for ever. . . .

'And I think that in saying this he has also pointed out his own weakness, for he is British-trained in our English schools, and he cannot escape us. And so he hates and loves us all at once.'

1 p.m. Singapore.

They went to Raffles Hotel for lunch. The tailored traveller's palms in the courtyard waved their hieratic fans in a stately breeze above the American cars of a large Chinese wedding party at that moment munching its way through the menu in the ballroom.

It was nearly fifteen years now since an Asian diplomat had been refused a room at Raffles Hotel. There was no longer such a thing as racial discrimination, it had gone the way of history. In fact, the wheel had nearly come full circle. Discrimination against 'white ants' or 'whiteskins' in Asian businesses, offices and circles, was as audible now, as was at one time, talk of the colour bar.

Luke and John had no feeling but mild curiosity as they glanced, on their way through the lobby, at the Chinese bride enthroned among orchids in a creamy slipper satin dress and veil, the groom in a cut-away making a speech in Cantonese and translating it to himself in English, to the applause of immense crowds of relatives, friends and photographers whose overlapping edges eddied in the corridors. A Chinese songstress, exquisitely curved, made the two men slow their pace for a stealthy inspection, and in the middle of her lilting rendition of *Carmen* she smiled at Luke, who blushed and quickened pace behind John Symonds, but felt elated none the less.

They ate in the air-conditioned Elizabeth Room, where it was so cold that they shivered, and ordered hot oyster soup and steaks. John Symonds was still talking about Mahudin.

'Of course Mahudin is not a communist ... He's that rare bird, a rebel from the English schools. There are few of them. I prefer to call them the non-castrates, though to my beetle-browed colleagues he's just a Red.

'Have you ever thought about the emasculating effect of our education upon thousands of Asian youngsters? I suppose I could talk at length about the liberalizing influence of English in general, but it's not altogether education now. It was all right twenty years ago, when we wanted docile and happy clerks and super-clerks, efficient and courteous, honest and willing, aspiring to nothing but to give satisfaction. But it's not good enough now.

'These people are Asians living in Asia, and in Singapore they're nearly all Chinese. Round them Asia is seething, heaving with impatience and change, wanting to devour time and space. The Chinese Revolution in Asia is a change as momentous as the French Revolution in Europe. Things are moving so fast that we never keep up with them at all.

'And what do we do to fit our English-speaking Chinese, our docile and happy, our truly loyal servants, for the Asia of the future? What do we teach them?

'We teach them English history: Henry the VIIIth, Elizabeth and Victoria. English geography, three-quarters of the book the British Isles, one-quarter the rest of the world. Literature, *Lamb's Tales from Shakespeare* and *The Mill on the Floss*, all in Basic, as they aren't to know the complexities of our tongue.

'We cut them off by the accolade called the Overseas School Certificate, from their own learning, their traditions; if that were cutting them off merely from the past, it wouldn't matter; but also and more dangerously, it cuts them from the present, and perhaps the future of Asia.

'With these happy eunuchs who are bound to us by their knowledge of English we have run this country well as our colonial preserve. But we cannot pretend to think we can leave it to them to run it for themselves. All the revolutionaries in

India were people who went back to their own literature and language. We'll see the same phenomenon here.

'We've given Malaya a lot, I don't deny it. Somehow along the lines of a gigantic RSPCA, we've always been kind. Peace, security, contentment, safety. And they're grateful. They are convinced that the law and order we gave them is something they could never achieve for themselves. They have no faith or belief in themselves since they only exist as second-class replicas of us. They're afraid, mortally afraid of freedom and of independence. With independence their livelihoods, which depend upon their being cogs of our system, will be swept away ... They're not equipped for Asia, they're only equipped for a British colony, and freedom is terrible travail.

'But Mahudin isn't like that. The knife slipped somewhere, and he's a rebel. There are a few of them around. Of course they're handicapped. They haven't got the real ruthlessness of communism. They're cut off from Asian Asia. They know it's wrong, and they get lost in the no man's land of violence between us and the jungle ... And that is why Mahudin is at twenty-five learning Chinese and Malay, because if he does not, he'll be a stooge like the others, and he does not want to be a pallid reflection of an Englishman, and nothing else.'

Symonds wiped his mouth clean and attacked his lobster cocktail:

'Perhaps we've done this country a disservice by not living up to the prototype of tyranny. We've promised independence; we're teaching them fair elections; we *half* give them a measure of freedom ... and they have the feeling that they won't have to fight hard for anything. Not enough prisons, not enough oppression, and therefore, perhaps, no Nehru. no Gandhi. If we'd been ruthless and harsh perhaps we'd have united the whole country – English-speaking or non-English-speaking – Chinese and Malay and Indian, against us in one great surge of patriotic fervour.

'That's what some others have done with their "bad" colonialism. But we haven't. And perhaps that's what Mahudin describes as astuteness. He's hard to please.'

Symonds paused. His eyes were enthusiastic.

'That brings me back to our Force. The philosophical implications of a colonial police force ruling, with Emergency Regulations giving it a nearly colossal power, in a country on its way to independence. A pretty paradox.

'The old days of clapping into prison anyone who talked self-government, and rebellion, are definitely out. Prison as an answer to all problems of colonial rule no longer exists. Instead, as Mahudin points out, we buy and cajole, offer scholarships and distribute honours.

'The Police Force also has to acquire a different viewpoint. We may be the oppressive instrument of colonialism, but we've also got to become the protectors of freedom or independence I don't think we've all understood this metamorphosis. Too many of us are still thinking along the old colonial lines ... go in and get your man ...

'Our historic role is now, in the process of handing over power (however reluctantly and slowly), to change ourselves from a colonial force to a service; not to maintain alien rule, even if it be law and order, but to protect the peace and the sovereignty of the people. And to teach our successors. In order to do so, we ourselves must love freedom, learn to curb our own power, and finally bow ourselves out.'

He raised his water tumbler and the ice cubes tingled merrily:

'Let's drink a toast to ourselves,' he suggested, and recited to Luke, slightly worried that occupants of other tables might overhear:

> *These, in the day when heaven was falling,*
> *The hour when earth's foundations fled,*
> *Followed their mercenary calling*
> *And took their wages and are dead.*
>
> *Their shoulders held the sky suspended;*
> *They stood, and earth's foundations stay;*
> *What God abandoned, these defended,*
> *And saved the sum of things for pay.*

'That's Housman,' he told Luke. 'And that is what we are, we the Police Force. Worse mercenaries than ourselves have defended old cultures and rotting empires from barbarism, and saved what was worth saving, without knowledge, and often without clear intent ... So when you feel your brother officers a little too pompous with suspiciomania and inability to see the present and their own place in history, just spout these lines, and then, my dear chap, get ready to run!'

Kia Peng Road; Yap Quan Seng Road, Chow Kit Road, Loke Yew Road, Yap Ah Loy Street ... driven through Kuala Lumpur by his nephew, the manager of the local branch of Quo's Bank, an eager pointer-out of new flats, hotels, housing estates and government building, lands in which Quo Boon money, enterprise and labour were invested, Quo Boon took pleasure in reading once again the names of his own countrymen, the Chinese founders and builders of Kuala Lumpur, who had been here before the British, had lived and worked and fought for the British, and died full of wealth, British honours and years. Passing in front of Suleiman Building, a cross between St. Pancras Station and an ideal version of a Turkish mosque, hearing through the traffic the shrill cries of thousands of swifts whose nests flattened in the complicated cornices of the edifice, Quo Boon glanced at the war cenotaph planted in Victory Avenue and thought of the pasts, the near one and the far. . . .

They were still current in men's mouths, the chronicles of the Chinese builders, undeified, human, inaccurate; coarse poor men risen to wealth, and in so doing creating the Malaya which today beheld their sons and grandsons with suspicion, and made life hard for them in the land of their toil.

Yap Ah Loy, who had been a leader of men, general of soldiers, head of his clan, friend of the Sultans, advisor of the English Viceroy, ruler of Kuala Lumpur ... Yap Ah Loy had mined for tin, planted pepper and spices, a hundred years ago. At that time the Chinese had prospected for tin everywhere in Malaya, and developed the open-cast system. The Malay Sultans had given up mining and collected revenue off Chinese mining instead. Yap Ah Loy had fought for the Sultan of the State against a usurper, been made a *Dato*, a nobleman, given a silver seal, a drum, two bodyguards and recognized by the Malays as equal to their own Chiefs. The British had come and Yap Ah Loy had fought for the Viceroy and for Kuala Lumpur, and later ruled Kuala Lumpur, rebuilding it three times, much of it with his own money, when the contending Malay Sultans burnt it down. In the end the British had taken over the State, and Yap Ah Loy, their faithful friend, had died and now a small street to his name stood in the city he had helped to grow from a mud village to the capital of Malaya.

There was Loke Yew, Towkay Loke, C.M.G., come as a boy to

Singapore from China, washing dishes in a coffee shop and dreaming of wealth. He had become chief of his people in Kuala Lumpur, issued his own currency, sounder than the British Government's currency at that time. He had endowed Hongkong University, opened tin mines, drained swamps, cleared large tracts of land, built roads and administered justice where the Government could not. The British ruled through him, and had given him the management of their revenues, the gambling, spirit, pawnbroking, chandu and opium farms, from which the Government derived most of its wealth, a practice which it had continued, diminishingly, until 1947. Loke Yew had built and remained honest and incorrupt, loyal and keeping faith though his power was great, and he had been honoured and now was dead, with a road in Kuala Lumpur bearing his name.

There were others, whose labour had transformed the jungle into cities, remembered in Kuala Lumpur the city of tin and now the city of rubber, capital of the Federation of Malaya, but still a Chinese town, as Chinese as Singapore, with a thin sprinkling, as a parsimonious layer of icing sugar upon a cake, of British government offices, on top of its miles of Chinese one-roomed shops and foot-high characters fronting the clamorous streets. 'Yes,' thought Quo Boon as the car drove through the streets, 'without us nothing is left of Kuala Lumpur. Tomorrow it becomes jungle again.' Quo Boon found it hard nowadays to be fair to the British, whom he, along with many another Chinese in Malaya had much loved before and during the war, and still liked with an affection sorrowful and betrayed.

His nephew talked on, garrulously, of the price of rubber and how the British companies were producing more concentrated latex, keeping the rubber liquid, shipping it in tanks direct to England, instead of turning it into pressed smoked sheets, bundled for export ... and the tin mine was going out of tin, and the guards should be doubled, or the people might become restless through unemployment and then they would go to the jungle. ...

He had his family well in hand, Quo Boon, did not allow them to become profligates and wasters, had them educated in both English and Chinese, weathered them to want and to hardship, seasoned them in his companies and his offices ... and yet, as he listened to his nephew's respectful drone, nodding his square and jovial head in approbation, he was sad, for he knew that none of the males of his seed, not one of the many sturdy able sons grown to manhood was quite as powerful or vigorous as he had been. There were still many small ones, and grandsons, and there were adopted ones too. For Quo Boon, in the tradition of Asia, did not deem his family the only recipient of beauty, wisdom or intelligence; as the emperors of old, he would rather adopt as his successor the able son of a beggar than to see the empire go to waste under his own son. In so many countries of Asia this tradition of adoption survives. Who knows what genius, enterprise, saintliness or heroism is concealed by Destiny behind the sad eyes and the pale face of a poor slum waif ... and beauty but too often is plucked out of the gutter to rule, to overthrow kingdoms.

Such is the democracy of Asia. Quo Boon practised it, improving the House of Quo by adoptions many and generous.

Yet none, of his blood or not, had shown that fusion of talent and energy which he sought, except perhaps Intellectual Orchid. Alas, she was a woman, and it was difficult for a woman to be in business. She had no child of her own, though married to great and vigorous looking Johnny Tam, whose father and Quo Boon had broken stones together in a road gang, labourers on contract when they were fifteen years old....

There was Sen, the son in the jungle. Quo Boon's son Sen, had always been so unpredictably ruthless, so quietly violent, so definite and sweeping in his dreams, intense and savage in wilfulness. But the essence of creation was measure, harmony and steadiness, was to let the dream shape the creation, but also the creation modify the dream, that they may keep pace with each other ... and Sen had always dreamt too big, too impatiently.

He dreamt of a great new world, and for this had left home, brooking no delay to his justice. Sen did not know that even the future must have a past ... he wanted the future too clean, and so he had gone. Quo Boon longed for him with a hopeless longing, but would not speak of him, 'nor will I raise a finger to help him', thought the old man, wearily, as he had thought a thousand times, knowing the ache of his love, knowing his best-beloved son gone from him, in the jungle, hunted like a wild beast. Sen had never asked for help, and would never ask. But as a ship lost to sight leaves an uneasy sea-swell behind it, there was, in the House of Quo, an occasional uneasy tremor due to the memory of Sen ...

There was Pearl, child of a concubine, wayward last daughter of his blood, cherishing with the fierceness of youth the memory of the half-brother she had seen but once or twice as a small girl, and now she too was deep in the struggle of the young against the world that hemmed them in, with others, young like herself, full of the indignation and bitterness of justice and rebellion.

Quo Boon sighed, an old man's sigh, and his nephew, thinking he pondered some business scheme, waited respectfully, mouth half open, ready to speak if necessary, while Quo Boon thought bitterly of his old foolish dream of placing Sen – the child with the eager bright face, the thin mouth already closed in too much firmness, the great cold silences that spoke of power – at the head of the clan, above all his brothers, who would obey Sen because he had been chosen by their father, for the sake of the mighty edifice of wealth and commerce, in Manila, in Saigon, in Djakarta, in Singapore, in Bangkok and in Rangoon, which they, a family, held together, as they held the world of South East Asia together; as nerves, children of one brain, transform the body into one living, sentient organism. For the sake of the House of Quo, selfless for its own, ruthless to others....

And Sen would have proved the most unfit of all. Thus blindly rolls the Wheel of Fate, foolishly grinding love into sorrow, bright promise into the noisome decay of the jungle....

And now, thought Quo Boon, Sen would always destroy, he would never build anything at all.

Malaya still needed builders, men of labour. Over the sprawling acres between untouched jungle and unalterable sea lay the forests of rubber, exhausting the soil. But Malaya needed not only rubber. It needed food. And to grow food, only the labour of hands, putting into the soil the seeds of food, with love and with devotion, squatting, toiling over it foot by foot, would make the land fertile, would make food grow.

'But they will not give my people land,' said Quo Boon aloud. 'My people, who are the builders. They have forgotten the past, the British. All they gave was three hundred dollars for a gun when my people came out of the jungle the first time. That is why there is an Emergency. That is why they become destroyers.'

The nephew now burst into a cackle of laughter, for he had not understood Quo Boon's words. 'Oh, there won't be independence for a long time yet,' he reassured Quo Boon, 'not for a long time, we are quite safe ... as long as RUBBER is needed, the British won't let us go.'

1–3 p.m. Zodiacal Sign: The Crab.
   Mystic Significance: Fruit of Folly.

Fragrant Orchid, wife of Sir Moksa Bakrar, sister of Intellectual Orchid and daughter of Quo Boon, lived in Millionaire's Row in Singapore, inhabiting a mansion with a large garden and a long drive, casuarinae, bamboo, Honolulu creeper, bougainvillaea, and orchids in the garden, air-conditioned bedrooms in the house.

Fragrant Orchid was a smart woman, a good mixer in company. It was reported that she drove pitiless bargains and this was unjustly attributed to her husband's Indian mixture. In Singapore where they dwelt, Sikh and Bengali moneylenders and *chettiars* are reckoned a somewhat grasping lot with interest at thirty per cent per month. Several of them can always be seen turbaned and lanky, leaning against the pillars of the five-foot way on the main streets, waiting for the small and harassed Baba clerks, the Malay peons, coming out of the company offices at five p.m., needing, for a new baby or a dead father, money to tide them over until the month's pay came due.

It was Fragrant Orchid's own nature to be slightly vindictive. That is why she had married Sir Moksa after he had already been wedded for two years and no children to Musical Orchid, her garrulous and noisy sister. Musical Orchid, after one of those mahjong sessions which three times a week hallucinate women of all races and superior wealth in Singapore, had taunted Fragrant Orchid on her spinster state. (All the other grown-up sisters had married Chinese, but Musical Orchid had to be content with Moksa because of a rumour that she had scoured the United States in pursuit of an ex-consular attaché who had finally eluded her.) Fragrant Orchid took the slight badly. 'You are mocking me,' she cried imperiously, 'you will be sorry, I tell you. I'll get myself a husband ... *yours*.' And did.

Musical Orchid undivorced but retired (Sir Moksa had confidently discovered enough Moslem tradition in his ancestry to permit himself a shade of bigamy), played mahjong in Switzerland, while Fragrant Orchid, Lady Moksa, dwelt in state in Singapore.

Clad in a long *cheongsum*, a moulded Chinese gown, which fitted each bulge of her figure, she greeted Intellectual Orchid and led her to the terrace where Lady Weatherbore, Fanette Archway, and a few others enjoyed the breeze, the garden scents, and the scrutiny of other millionaires' houses with similar verandas, gardens and drives.

Fanette Archway greeted her Betty darling enthusiastically. Old Mrs. Chang was also there with her blue-rinsed hair, and as usual the O.B.E. embroidered in gold and silver thread and precious stones upon her dress. All were bending with genuine admiration over a small parcel wrapped in a dainty lace handkerchief.

'My stones,' explained the owner proudly once again, having just returned from the States with an expensive operation scar and three stones removed.

How quaint and too thrilling, the ladies declared, and Fanette poked a silver enamelled nail at the brown round pebble and said it felt crumbly ... medical science was too wonderful these days, the things they did, think of dear Tony Eden and His stones ... but Lady Weatherbore asserted that there were still many diseases unknown to science and baffling to physicians which only Divine Agency could heal. She herself had suffered with terrible pains in the back for years until Christian Science had cured her, and now she played bridge and mahjong nearly every day and golf twice a week without the slightest twinge.

It was true, said Fragrant Orchid, doctors didn't know everything. She herself, fallen into deep incurable melancholy a few years ago, had been unable to eat until her mamma had taken her by airplane to a famous wise man of Bangkok, and in a tiny hut among the klongs, the canals, she had been made to kneel, bared to the waist, while the flame-of-the-forest petals on the floor shrivelled with the heat and the hours, the coconut milk dried in the cups, and the banana leaves wrapping saffron rice and tobacco moved with devouring ants. The incense sticks hazed the air with their substance of smoke, and the wise man with the droopy eyes and sleek hair, fat and smooth skinned as any buddha, had chanted over her, until suddenly out of her left shoulder had jumped a long black hair to the mat on which she knelt. 'Now this is your disease, come out of you, placed by an enemy while you were sleeping, poisoning your body.' Since then she had been well.

And then some talked of their sons and their daughters, safely studying in England or America or Australia, having such a good time, only of course becomingly homesick for the food and the comfort and the gardens of Malaya ... but London was a bit unsafe, nowadays, too much freedom, look at poor Mrs. Toh's daughter, for instance, come back a Socialist ... but perhaps there was bad blood in the family, these tendencies could be hereditary. . . .

And Fragrant Orchid talked of her new enthusiasm, Family Planning, and asked her sister to help, for truly Singapore's birth rate was alarming; but Intellectual Orchid, in spite of Fanette and Lady Weatherbore's instances, found herself too busy with Tuberculosis, also alarming in Singapore. Finally the ladies struck a bargain. They would help their dear Betty with her Charity Ball for Tuberculosis, and she would help them with a Charity Bazaar for Family Planning. . . .

It was with a pang of envy that Intellectual Orchid left for her meeting at the Chamber of Commerce (involving a complicated deal with Indonesia). She went feeling their eyes upon her thin back; unprotected, exposed, vulnerable because of Pearl and of Sen. In her the small voice of despair whispered that she could never explain to the ladies, nor to anyone in her circle, why Sen had gone to the jungle, and why Pearl was running away to China.

3 p.m. Singapore.

'By the way,' said John Symonds as he and Luke Davis drove back from lunch at Raffles Hotel, 'speaking of students going to China, another batch of twenty left yesterday. Twelve girls among them. More girls than boys this time. There's bound to be a bit of a rumpus in Hongkong, because one of the girls is going to be hauled back . . . Quo Boon's daughter.'

A picture rose in Luke's mind of the morning's missed encounter, of Intellectual Orchid in slacks at the rubber factory. 'Which daughter?'

'Must be the youngest, though one never knows, he may still be producing them . . . the man has a fantastic family, fully as large as the Sultan of Kelantan's. The old ones are all right, business and no politics except the Progressively Independent Party, old Sir Moksa's what's his name Pipsqueak . . . and that's safely conservative. They're as scared of independence as we are. The young ones are of course what we call "infected with the Red Virus". This girl's English name is Pearl, Chinese name in our files something Orchid. She left yesterday on the *Thibania* for Canton. Her sister is flying over to collect her when she lands in Hongkong. Our informer at Kallang airport rang up this morning to tell me that a ticket had just been booked in the name of Mrs. Johnny Tam . . . that's Betty Quo, the eldest daughter of Quo Boon.'

'Alias Intellectual Orchid,' grinned Luke, but his mouth lingered over the words, as his eye held her picture after she was out of sight.

'I'll show you some snaps in my office ... we had these youngsters' pictures taken, while they were climbing on to the boat, for our records ... they did the usual stuff, trying to hide behind newspapers, but we got Pearl all right.'

'I've seen that face before.' Luke scanned the picture, the stubborn oval face looking straight at the camera without blinking, a hand half up to cover it, a blur in front of her breast. 'Where have I seen her?'

'They all look alike to me still,' John Symonds complained. 'I thought it was because they were much alike, until my friend Mahudin told me that he had the greatest difficulty distinguishing *us* ... we whites all look alike to *him*, he says. I think he's boasting, trying to make himself more Asian that way, pretending not to know one red-haired devil from another, don't you?'

'I've seen that face...' Luke held the snap strongly in his hands, staring at the girl who stared back ... where had he seen her? Why should he remember her? Somehow it wasn't in Singapore ... then it must have been in Malaya, possibly in Johore ... 'May I have this snap?'

'Certainly, we've got the negative.'

'And you say Betty Quo ... Intellectual Orchid will be leaving tonight from the airport?'

'Yes...' John Symonds looked quizzically at Luke Davis. '... would you like to go and wish Mrs. Tam a pleasant trip to Hongkong?'

Luke grinned, still gazing at the snapshot. 'I might,' he replied.

3–5 p.m. Zodiacal Sign: Man and Woman.
Mystic Significance: Female Supremacy.

His nephew's wife, thought Quo Boon, in Kuala Lumpur, became more round and motherly every year, though she remained sterile after a decade of marriage. She had studied for the Bar in Lincolns Inn, and was, in Kuala Lumpur, a favourite of relief and charity committees. But her lack of children had had a strange effect upon her. Intent on proving to the world what a perfect old-style Chinese matriarch she could have made, instead of practising law, she remained at home. Apart from good works and committee meetings, she devoted herself to the most punctilious observance of those minute etiquettes which once held a Chinese family together. She spoke and dressed as if she belonged to the old world of the nonas, the Chinese woman born in Malaya clinging to a world of old customs, where impassively the mother-in-law waits at the foot of the bed for the virginity cloth to be brought to her, in the morning, to prove the purity of her son's wife, bride of the previous night.

With hooded eyes Quo Boon looked at her as she played after lunch with the children of the concubine, whom she had purchased in Penang for her husband. The two little girls were taking ballet lessons, and called her Mother. She explained that a third was on the way, and this time it would have to be a boy ... otherwise she would lose patience with the breeder, and provide another. She bustled with second-hand motherhood importance, almost persuaded of her progenitive power, having but borrowed someone else's womb for her purpose. Quo Boon knew that she sought his approbation (as they all did). It irritated him, this constant deference to himself, though at one time he had required it. And now this habit of subservience was the main reason why he found no one to succeed him ... except perhaps Intellectual Orchid, who was a woman, and childless.

'I'm going to Ipoh next week to see the mines, and how they're getting on there.' Another docile son, smooth and competent was there, in charge of the family's tin mines. His nephew's wife misunderstood: 'Their last child died,' she said quickly, 'died of dysentery, I hear.' For she imagined that Quo Boon visited his family for one purpose only.

All Quo Boon's family thought that it pleased him, the old man, to notice the increase, the swelling generations, fantastic and multiplying as seed of ants from his loins. They visioned him with gigantic account book in hand, keeping check of the numbers of his tribe; frowning when he had to cross off one life, adding up the profit and loss of his human capital. And so child after child, baby after baby, all owning him the primal seed, was born in the houses of Quo, in Burma and in Siam, in Indonesia and in Borneo, in Malaya and the Philippines and Hongkong and Mauritius, in America North and South. Yet Quo Boon did not remember having asked for such affluence of manpower, but if they thought it pleased him well, let them.

The interview with the General whom Quo Boon had come to Kuala Lumpur to see was at four, and Quo Boon's secretary, who drew horoscopes, had reminded him in Singapore the previous night that his first wife's birth-hour was between three and five, when female essences are strongest. Though Quo Boon pooh-poohed such beliefs he felt a pleasurable glow at the Zodiac's aptness, and waited in his nephew's house, at peace.

And now, Mr. Clerkwell (promoted to Headquarters in Kuala Lumpur) arrived at the house to hint at the best way in which conversation with a general might be conducted.

'He's not in a very good mood, not what I'd call absolutely cheerful, don't you know.' (Clerkwell had acquired in the last tour a trick of rubbing his hands together, like a waiter, meanwhile looking extraordinarily frank and candid.) 'He's been slightly upset lately ... I wouldn't upset him further if I were you....'

Quo Boon's round head shifted owlishly on his short neck, quizzical wise.

'He works so hard, none of us can keep up with him ... in fact he hardly keeps up with himself. And he gets ... erh ... ideas about things. Todak New Village for instance. Wouldn't mention the place to him, if I were you. He's already been down there and ... erh ... scolded them all. It does no good bringing up things like that ... let sleeping dogs lie...'

They drove together to the new and furiously pink house in which the General dwelt.

It was true that the General was in no good mood. Sitting on their chair edges in the waiting-room, five trade unionists, three Indian, one Malay and one Chinese, were waiting. As Quo Boon entered they were being called. The panelled doors with polished knobs turned firmly behind them and no sound escaped. After ten minutes they filed out again, and the three Indians looked definitely paler.

'Your turn, sir.'

Quo Boon crossed the threshold and the doors shut with finality behind him.

The General sat at a large glass-topped desk with his feet in an open side drawer.

As Quo Boon entered, he fixed upon him stern and brilliant eyes.

'Sit down, sit down. What's your name, eh?'

Knowing these tactics conceived to shock and to stun, employed to unhinge and detract from fixed resolve, visitors already labelled opponents, Quo Boon glanced at the desk, his face more cherubic than ever.

'Quo, Quo,' muttered the General, restlessly consulting a foolscap sheet (a condensation of Quo Boon's life gleaned from his police file). 'Funny spelling with a Q. Never seen a name like that before. But then, you Chinese have got so many names. Aliases, one for each of your bank accounts, I suppose.'

He laughed loudly and stopped on a chuckle.

Quo Boon polished his glasses and put them on again.

The General was looking down the file: 'Hmm ... I see you've got rubber estates round Todak, bad spot, Todak ... bumped off a good chap there ... wanted to close down all the estates only it wouldn't help, starving the rats would only make them run to the jungle more quickly, eh?

'What I wanted to say is this.' He bent forward, index finger straight at Quo Boon, eyes piercing. 'We're fighting this war to the death, war – to – the – death – with a dangerous enemy ... a dangerous beast skulking in the jungle ... and we want all the co-operation we can get from the people of this country whom we're protecting from this bunch of murderous cowards.

'We're not getting it. I know what you're going to say ... I've heard all the arguments before. That only a free people can fight communism ... that as long as this anti-communist fight is led by a colonial government, it's our fight and not yours. That's why so many of you are just sitting back and letting us get on with the job. Sitting on the fence.'

Quo Boon replied peaceably, 'Perhaps you cannot expect people to show interest when they are only invited to take orders.'

The General gave his short, sharp chuckle, and smote his desk vigorously. 'I see you've also got the answers. But that's where I'm scoring now. We are going to get more of you people in with us. We've asked others, and we're now asking you, to come in with us, openly, and to take your place in the prosecution of the war against communism.'

'How?' said Quo Boon.

'As members of our Councils, to advise the Government on such matters as subversion in schools and trade unions. We've thought of you specially in regard to schools. You are well known for your generous endowments of Chinese schools. When we issued our Manpower Regulations, trying to draft young Chinese into our Forces, hundreds went underground to the jungle instead. We've been thinking of associating more people in this effort aimed at recruiting students out of Chinese schools into some sort of National Service. Mind you, it's just a project, but we can't get on with it unless prominent leaders, like yourself, urge them to join up.

'I'm told it was through your efforts that we got about forty young men to volunteer for our Regiments, last year.'

'Yes,' sighed Quo Boon reminiscently. 'They cost two thousand dollars apiece, my volunteers.'

The General pretended not to hear. 'That was a noble effort, and we're grateful. We know you're not one of those sitters on the fence, waiting to see who's going to win this war ... you've come over on our side, and your son-in-law too ... Sir Moksa's going to be a great Malayan leader one day....'

Quo Boon's glasses gleamed, and the General hurried on.

'We don't want to rush you, but we'd like to have you head our Committee to advise on recruiting in Chinese schools ... Damn it,' burst out the General, 'a worse pack of hooligans and potential communists than those disloyal young people I've never seen.'

Quo Boon thought: 'Loyalty is a word of many meanings. I suppose I am considered loyal, because I have made terms with the setup as it is now, as I have made money out of it. I can read the wind, see the way the leaves blow, and I keep out of the rain. I do not like bloodshed. I build.'

'Tell me, Mr. Quo,' said the General, suddenly human and wistful, 'is there a way out of this beastly muddle? I've had it before, harangues and speeches, from so many of you ... how it was the Chinese who fought when this country was invaded by the Japs; how we the British got away in boats, leaving stay behind parties of your people, and communists hurriedly released from prison, to fight rearguard actions while we got away. And how, when we came back, we were mean and paid only paltry sums to the jungle guerrillas. But you know, as I do, that this is not the reason why the Emergency happened. It happened because there was a straight bid for power through terrorism by a small section of people, many of whom had fought the Japs bravely, and now turned their guns against us.

'I know that your people have got grievances. The Chinese half of Malaya, *your* three millions, half the population of this land, have had a raw deal from us in many ways. But it's no good dragging up the past. We must get together to build the future. And that means, first and foremost, winning this jungle war.'

'It won't be won only with guns. It's also a battle for the souls of men. And mostly for the souls of the young.'

'I know my statistics,' said the General. 'I know that fifty per cent of the population of Malaya is under twenty-five. That means a hell of a lot of school children, and not so childish youngsters. Like those in Chinese schools I was talking about. Sixty per cent of the children of Malaya are in Chinese schools.

'How would you like it, Mr. Quo, if your son or daughter turned Red and went off to China? What would you do?'

'Before the Emergency,' replied Quo Boon, 'it was only natural for our children to go back to China in order to complete their studies. There were no universities in South East Asia, not anywhere. And now that there is a University of Malaya, it does not admit students from Chinese schools ... they go to China to study ... what can they do here? There is no future for them in Malaya. Careers are closed to them. They can only go into trade, or become labourers or rubber tappers.'

'That's not the point,' replied the General. 'These youngsters haven't got any *Loyalty* to this country. We want to teach them loyalty. Look at this hand,' said the General suddenly.

He extended his right hand and Quo Boon peered.

'Do you know what happened the other day?' The General had become impressive. 'We were having a bunch of fifty-five Tamils up here. Fifty-five. On a civics course. To teach them loyalty. I shook hands with each of them. Each one. That had never happened before. They'd never been to a house like this before. You should have seen their faces,' said the General happily, 'as I shook them by the hand, one by one.'

He looked at his hand with great satisfaction, perhaps discovering in his palm some lingering evidence of its prowess in shaking the dark hands of fifty-five Tamils.

'That's what I mean,' he continued. 'Loyalty. Freedom and democracy. All pull together. We want to teach these youngsters that. And the best place is in the regiments. Make them all feel as one. Teach them patriotism.'

'Then,' said Quo Boon, 'to teach them to be loyal, to be free and to be patriotic, you must first of all stop treating them as aliens, unwanted and unworthy to belong to this land.

'At the moment, they have nothing to reach for commensurate with their ability and their ambition. Their school lives are a perpetual agitation, because they have no future except frustration. You must give them opportunities, General.

'Since you cannot abolish Chinese education in Malaya, you must recognize its place, along with Malay and English. And having done that, you will find one day your best patriots (whose absence you deplore) and your ablest leaders (whose scarcity you complain of), where you found them once before, among the Chinese of Malaya.'

The General sat back, eyes intent upon Quo Boon. He said: 'That is impossible. The Malays won't have it.'

Quo Boon sighed at the often encountered excuse. The Malays, the Sultans, were always invoked, an ever-present brake upon action. 'The day may come when the Malays and the Chinese of this country, and the others, will come together, work together, and discover how much they have to learn from each other, and how they cannot do without one another.'

'Nonsense,' said the General. 'It's because we're here, Mr. Quo, that you aren't at each other's throats. If we were to leave, there'd be terrible bloodshed. Malay and Chinese would be massacring each other, just as Moslems and Hindoos in India. As for your scheme of education, it's all very well, but your young people have got their eyes turned to Red China, as many Malays have got theirs fixed on the Arabian desert. But we're not as frightened of the Arabian desert as we are of China. All this talk about giving a stake in the land, an equal place to Chinese culture ... Our only hope is to have one nation, one country, one loyalty....'

He looked fixedly at Quo Boon: 'Will you help us?'

'All I can,' replied Quo Boon, 'but not in recruiting. It's no good.' He shook his head, a businessman full of practicalities. 'Look at what happened when you had your Manpower Regulations. Drove hundreds of young men into the jungle; thousands back to China. You said yourself they were far gone in opposition. How can you hope that an old man like myself, suspect because of my age, my wealth and my friendship with your colonialism, will persuade and convince these suspicious, rebellious young people to become recruits in your regiments? They will become all the more opposed to you, and the communists will exploit their fresh grievances, and more will go away. And as for me,' said Quo Boon, 'I will lose what little influence I still have with them, for they will call me a straw man, a dummy and a running dog of British imperialism. No, General, you'll have to think up another scheme for me.'

5–7 p.m. Zodiacal Sign: The Bull.
    Mystic Significance: Apotheosis.

Kallang airport of Singapore is a sea-plain, metallic with light, harsh with steel wings and neon, glossy as undermoon water.

Once it was pestilential bog, sea-earth margin bound by tenacious mangrove, rampaging cobra-coiled tentacular roots travailing water and soil to indissoluble swamp.

Then came the builders and took a hill and laid it low, and brought basket by basket red earth to bury the yawning skin of the mire.

Over Kallang turn the rubber wheels, swing the metal wings of the world's airplanes. Whinnying in the blue maned wind of their begetting they parade to stillness, steeds of space fretting the sleek resistless tropic air with patches of lucid thunder.

The harsh neon delineates the airport's white tower and veranda, a ship's deck breasting the sea. At space of evening in flakes gleam the windows; busy men as dummies clad walk their precise shadows; the flat horizon is turbaned in gleaming orange upon which, fine drawn in China ink, sway the languid palms of the land. Unseen the indigo sea sidles a small gracious breeze inland, its fragrance drowned in oil and tarmac smell, its whispers lost in purr of engines fracturing the early night. The beginning stars are dimmed in the raucous green and orange and yellow lights twinkling below the sky.

Intellectual Orchid sat, time and space assuaged, waiting with passport checked, ticket ready, suitcase crouched at her feet, and the small blue plastic bag with white lettering, symbol of air travel delivered to docile journeyers of space, limp-empty upon her knees.

On the white table-cloth, breeze ruffled, the small lamp of plastic pink with spray of rufous roses, a bowl of orchids and a bottle of Green Spot stood waiting while she refused the Australian oysters fresh from Sydney, the Danish caviare, the Hong-kong quail. At other tables, couples and families ate and waited, drank and sat; laughed, a mute facial contraction enclosed in noise, hemmed within the jangle of the great harsh noisy bell of light and engine drone. The stertorous wind of airplanes winking red-green lights annihilated their laughter's trilling, left the sky dark as sleep and as enormously empty.

She heard, not listening, within the tongueless clamour the loudspeaker's prayer, intoning, informing, imploring, ordering, beginning with a gargle and ending with a bray. Those whose time had come to go rose with their blue bag clutched, abandoning the breeze-smooth veranda, marching across a polished floor reverberating all the lights, while the tables quivered, the glasses shook as jelly, the lights twinkled and as a bell the air rang and rang.

'Good evening,' Luke shouted into her ear.

She raised a face unsurprised.

'You have seen me before.' He cried his name, lips close to her ear above the sea roar, her ear a sea shell listening to the sea. He stood above her, entire to the surge within him which thrust aside the self he usually was, as one casts cobwebs on an evening walk under the web-wound mangosteen trees; discovering this nameless thing beyond what he saw or heard or desired until then, which is not lust nor longing, but a whole-bodied enchantment, a flagrant miracle happening once for ever, and never more in time or space.

Knew it then, unworded, unacknowledged and sat down.

Round them as a wild beast, trapped and futile, roaring its obstinate belly roar, the snore and rave of the airplanes went on.

Upon them beat the jarring light, beating their faces and the table-cloth under their hands. Livid, with dark lips and eyes of liquescent marble, they saw each other unsighted. Hidden beneath the clamour they were safe from words, from knowledge, since in the din no word could be heard and what is not said is not.

And she – at first detached as at a play at the Happy World – was caught within his dazzled hope distilling hopelessness, an anguished fascination already fossilizing her in his memory. Slowly, as the sly ocean sifts a persistent breeze beneath the crazy noise and the bombastic whinny of the airplanes, while the loudspeaker brayed, and, nearly squalid, with an overlay of neon as powder, passengers obedient trailed past with small blue bags, she discovered that woman is more than head and eyes, ears and hands, body breeding or not, woman is also focus, fulcrum, pivot of need and want of man, in his longing and necessity transfigured, revealed as Venus rising, born from the cold and noisy belly of the sea, Beauty bared in the unfingered wind of dawn.

His smile told her that he was proof against wrecking knowledge, wrapped in his rapacious discovery of herself without reference to what she was; and thus revealed, happily vacant of words, unclothed of sentences, awaiting only the look, the smile, the gesture, the Word from her that would mean enter into life. Her life.

But she would not, could not, to the braying trumpet of the last judgment would she not say the Word which would become a world to the man in him waiting to be born. The woman in her had waited, but not for this. And so the moment passed on the wings of noise, in the braying harsh light of the neon, flat as the sun; never to return.

She remained sitting, absconded from life, self-disinherited prodigal in Singapore the prodigal island, Singapore profusion for all that the pentagonal mansion of the senses encompass: largesse, extravagance tangible, vision not dreams, touch not apotheosis, fragrance not savour; tropical land rich, and wealthy, and abundantly poor in strong dreams. Land where flower and leaf are large and fat with over-arching nothingness of growth, where man and woman grow ample with tangible ripe fruits of the wealthy earth to encompass within their five-fold large limitations.

Although transfigured by his vision swooping upon her in a world of twinkling lights and roaring engines; knowing herself no longer a tasteless formless lump, mechanical body, Abacus counting money, smooth unseen wheels clicking counters for the factories, the companies, the banks, the shops, the cinemas, the rubber estates of the House of Quo; but Woman, created from the effluvia of man's desire, become through the need of a man eternal mystery, mystic lotus, Beatitude, Beauty out of the sea, breasts and belly and sex, desire's blossom which is Beauty, divided flesh needing division, and in her mouth slowly rising the bitter-sweet waters of desire which is knowledge; yet from this she turned away, unsorrowing, looking mutely into the night, dooming herself and him, refusing tragedy and exaltation. The night enfolded her beyond the engines' cacophony, the parleys of the loudspeaker, the body of the man beside her, bright with enchantment not yet discarded.

Silence came suddenly to help her in her betrayal, her denial for them both.

'Are you going to Hongkong?' he spoke in the lapse of silence, knowing himself naked and ashamed, grabbing at words as at leaves to cover his nakedness.

But he still remembered her as the ear his longing assayed, the memory of her face a spell, and tried to reach her with the fact he knew. 'Your sister ... I've been told....'

She looked unmoved.

'I am sorry if I intrude, I don't mean to ... I understand, I think I do, the young, their dreams, the propaganda, there isn't much one can do.'

Nothing in the prodigal land of their fathers for them.

'If I can help in any way ... if it's not gone too far....'

'I don't know what you're talking about. I am going to

Hongkong to do some shopping, I hope to be back in a few days.'

She smiled. Ultimate coquetry, knowing her smile unbeautied her, she turned her profile, the fine cheekbone, jawbone, the best of her, to him. She could not give more.

She had thrown him back to his uncertainty, and he was receding to the distance of the morning when his car had gone on and he saw her diminishing in his back mirror. The loud-speaker brayed and she rose, while the snarling of the engines began again, and the knowledge of her betrayal was to her clear and boundless as the sky. Gone the pretence of being whole, entire as water, serene and complete. Never again would happen this ecstasy withheld, but also never again the other, the active glib death-in-life, the immured quietness within. She held out her fingers to him, and thus returned her image to its husk, to petrifaction safe from circumstance, and both of them to the dark night of the senses. Both as shades unborn to the soft green prodigal hell trod flat where is no space nor time, nor light nor air nor growth for that strange weed called love.

7–9 p.m. Zodiacal Sign: The Ram.
        Mystic Significance: Exhaustion.

Luke Davis turned, as in deep sleep, while another helical roar shook the emptied glasses trailing on the table-cloth. He turned like a body falling in observable space, having remained fixed near the chair where she had sat. He felt diminished by her absence, like the empty plain where her airplane had been, and now another one was coming in. He walked, unable to find himself as before, knowing this longing as a sore arm laid upon him, and followed a trail of men with blue bags filing down-stairs to another departure, and was in the bright blowsy main hall of the airport, where revolving groups of people eddied in cheerful noise under the unblinking lights.

He saw Quo Boon come out of the sliding bars of the Cus-toms Gate, Quo Boon back by airplane from Kuala Lumpur, a tired old man, heavy and alone, walking heavily, an attaché case under his arm. He strode towards him through the crowd swirling its easily rifted sea. 'Good evening, sir.'

'Ha . . .' Quo Boon peered at him from above glasses with divergent half moons, and gave him a quick and definite smile, then deftly encased himself in the laughing, jocund husk of cherubic ease which was Quo Boon to Singapore, to Malaya, neat, powerful and benign modest multi-millionaire Quo Boon.

'Mr. Davis, good evening ... are you coming or going?'

'Neither, Mr. Quo. I was seeing someone off ... I also met your daughter. She was leaving for Hongkong.'

'Which one, I have quite a few daughters you know ...?'

'Intellectual Orchid ... I mean Mrs. Tam.'

The smile coagulated, then again supple, rubbery, spread on the ample face....

'Ah, these women, always going shopping to Hongkong ... they can't resist it ... Hongkong is so cheap, and there's everything there.'

He turned away. Luke saw his back, more weary than his face. The car drove up, the chauffeur opened the door. Then Luke was there too, helping the old man in, his hand gentle with unconcluded motion of tenderness. Quo Boon sat back and closed his eyes as the car drove away, leaving Luke with the remote pang of all partings lingering in his breast.

9 p.m. to midnight. Zodiacal Sign: Fish and the Water.
Mystic Significance: Root and Rebirth.

Possession is not achieved in the first embrace. It is continual surrender to see, to hear, to know. Seeker groping to a renewal fresh as Creation's first instant, return to the hour when Light was new on grass and leaf, water skin and sky. The world is yours to own.

Heat-bloated, the fragments of a heat-dazed day lie untouched till sundown, when earth no longer cowers beneath the demon eye of heat beating its glare in sap and blood. The world explodes its heart of colour before night's dark peace.

Amber, jade and vermilion, saffron melting into rose, apple-green, amethyst and lilac, ripple round the astonished orange globe revolving above indigo coconut palms and hills; boats are ebony arcs etched on water glowing opal; fishermen deep to hips in luminous water hold black nets like ploughs, driving the solid light of the water before them; sibilant swifts whisk orderly evolutions above the domineering rose-grey government buildings; the green China-tile roofs of the Sultan's palace are a technicolour castle on a hill. Cosy Asian family cars wheel along the lavender road, crammed with mothers, multiple babies, assorted children, a score of pointing hands, a parcel of leaning bodies, a bevy of bobbing heads, an exultation of laughing mouths, oscillating in all directions and in happy swallow twitter giving Father enthusiastic suggestions above the head of his instructor, while behind the vehicle rattles the big L plate of the Learner. This is sundown.

Sundown is soft reconciliation, content, sky and earth like spent foes looking upon each other with lovely peace. It is the time of makan angin, eating the wind; the promenade, the swim, the drive, the amble; the game of tennis at the club; sitting on doorsteps in smile and talk and silence piercing friendship; official time for the first stengah; the time of Malay Chinese Tamil young boys plunging similarly gleaming bodies naked along the goldlit shore; a time for cobras to wake, dangle meek heads above their baskets, flick slivered tongues as the flute gathers volume and a few white-shirted good-tempered spectators; a time of smart rap and chop of knives at ambulant food stalls waking to swift lively music of supper; the blue smoke of charcoal grids, where *satay* sellers spit meat chunks on bamboo sticks for roasting; on the green lawns called *padang*, the schoolchildren crowding to play; time for the rebirth of the watcher, dream-spinning day's fragments into woven coherence; reflecting in coolness on the time of the sun; sniffing the chilli-pepper smell of a tree, the undertow of sour-sweet sewers, the frangipani, feeling the bird-sifted breeze swell the chequered sails of the russet junks, the swelling canvas of Malay racing boats, finger the thatched roofs of the boats of the aborigines, who row with crossed paddles their shallops upcurrent to sell deep-sea crabs at the market; watching the Tamil grasscutters swing their scythes, aureate with sundown gold; discovering the loveliness of Ah Mei's face, gold pink in the garden near the hibiscus blooming red stars over its protuberant greenness, Ah Mei fumbling an orange peacock flower, looking at the orange sun whirling above the palms and laughing because she is free.

News had come of her pardon some days ago, and running upstairs twisted in happiness she had laughed in gusts like sobs: 'I am free, free.'

Today she had come walking gently down the gravel path, and told of her wish to visit her old village at the Dragon Boat Festival. Already she had missed the sweeping of the graves, having been busy in the prison that very day.

Together, neither knowing the day nor the month in our tropical forgetfulness, we turned indoors to look at the calendar.

The Ever Handsome and Joyous Sports Co. Ltd., owning a tumbled shop next to the cemented basketball court of the Hokkien Athletic Association (where at night, in the blue flare of arc lamps, the Chinese school boys and girls played strenuous games applauded by enthusiastic polyglottic crowds), issued thoughtful yearly calendars of modest size (twelve foolscap pages) and encyclopaedic aspiration.

Not only the Chinese lunar, European solar, Moslem and Tamil years, months and days were recorded in inch squares, one for each day, but also the Penang, Singapore and Kuala Lumpur racing days, complete with microscopic picture of horse and rider for the illiterates' convenience; the festivals of all five races in four languages, each with a picture; Deepavali, the lights and the roof of a Hindu temple; the fire-walking day, glowing with embers; Chinese New Year; the fasting Malay month of Puasa, when not even one's own spit is swallowed during the long hot days; and Hari Raya, end of the fast, day of gorgeousness and Malay New Year; Christmas and Easter; the public and private holidays; the opening and closing term days of Malay, Chinese, Tamil and English schools; the birthdays of the nine Sultans and of their fathers. Besides this compendium of knowledge the calendar was lavish with fruit and female figures; durian, mangosteen, jackfruit, mango, papaya, chiku, coconut accompanied dark-haired Malay, Chinese and Indian maidens in sarongs, in tops and trousers, in slit and collared dress, in bathing suits. Each page was furthermore decorated with bats, balls, tennis rackets, racing cars and golf clubs. Each month suggested, diffidently, a different sport; badminton or basket-ball, tennis or water skiing, cricket or ping-pong, boat-racing and football, underwater coral gazing, and of course fishing; gear and tackle for which could be had, cheap and good, at the Ever Handsome and Joyous, which was a Chinese enterprise.

Today was the 20th of May, 3rd of April, 16th of December and 8th of March. We counted the days to the Festival.

'Will Golden Orchid come back for the day?' Whispering an inaudible goodbye Golden Orchid had left two weeks before. I felt the loss of her presence still.

'I shall invite her,' said Ah Mei.

Then it was night. Tender at ease the sky revolved its stars on the spinning wheel of time and space. Through the hours of darkness the earth decanted measured beauty, gleaned from moments of light; Fate dispensed her ends and her beginnings. With torches of woven coconut strands flaring bright fists of golden fire the fishermen now scoured the black mirror of the sea. On the ceiling and the walls the pink and green *chikchaks*, familiar lizards, ran their nightly rampage. Their jet Egyptian side eyes gleamed above sleek faces and their necks pulsated pinkly. Sometimes one would issue the startling wooden clapper chuckle which provided their name. Baby chikchaks, insecurely prehensile, dropped to the floor in a clatter of pitying chiks, chiks.

The small things of the night, slight and eternal: the oscillating recitatives of cicadas, the haphazard knocks of the toctoc birds, Malay and Indian melodies, lizards' laughter, were soldered to the other things, important, yet evanescent, looming ponderous in the day's heat, soon to pass into forgetting: the dull thud of bombs on the jungle; the spit and hiss of machine guns, crouching Fijians or Gurkhas waiting for prey at the edge of the rubber; the road blocks; people lining up outside huts being searched, the miles of wire. Keeping time as a metronome apportioning the hours, a drip felt, not heard, the heaving sap in millions of trees dispensed sumptuous latex, the white gold, the rubber, rubber the live gold for which perhaps all this was happening, for which men fought and died, betrayed or kept faith: the harsh tree-wealth, the curse, the boon of Malaya.

Great or small, mean or significant, Malaya-the-last-defence-against-communism and Malaya-the-last-colony slogans, the words and deeds, sickening or superb, trivial and inhuman and brutal or tender and pitiful, the confusion of cruelty, obtuseness, violence, hypocrisy, courage and devotion, all fell or clicked or slid into place, as amber, as pearls; disparate but harmonious, piecemeal and imperfect, fragments of a land created of fragments, kept together, soldered by its one infallible sap, dripping monotonous as prayer: Give us this day our daily-latex.

And this was peace, perfecting the opposed into a circumferential geometry of life, for which chaos is but a word, the name of an order not yet born; where madness, greed and violence sought to lay their hot waste upon all, where greed, madness and violence were counted in the drops of the latex; this was peace, in the clemency of night to blend the confusion of the fissured land into harmony, smooth as horizon circle, gathered as latex in a cup, complete and flat as death.

Brown and black and rufous ants I knew, omnivorous elegant pacers on soil and wood; and the small shrill bright red ones surging up one's leg plunging ravening jaws into flesh, undeterred by tearing their bodies off. White ants had now invaded our bungalow, and were busy eating it up.

They built tunnels protecting them from light their killer, creeping climbing brown shaggy tunnels up the walls. They ate their way to the bathroom and into a box of soapflakes. Their pearly, flaccid bodies, emaciated maggots trailing glabrous extra skin, moved among the flakes, and through the hole in the wall antennae waved and peered. I found them waving and peering at me in my bath and, clothed again, went downstairs to look for their trail coming through the floor from the servants' quarters below the bathroom.

The servants' rooms were nearly empty. A Chinese *wayang*, open air theatre, was performing in town. Cookie had gone with his family to see the actors wheeling and swirling gorgeous robes under the neon lights. In the abandoned servants' room a naked bulb threw yellow light upon Ah Mei's face as she sat at the table, writing on a small sheet of paper. Opposite her sat her mother on crossed legs on the plank bed, hunched as an owl, staring at her daughter, as if dictating. I wore rubber slippers and coughed, for I dislike to surprise people's secrets. Immediately the mother was up and coming straight towards me, her body held squarely, as a shield. Above her shoulder I told Ah Mei, who had risen with her hand upon the paper, about the ants, and she replied that she would search early in the morning, and I left.

I went down to the garden, still refusing the knowledge that was already in me about Ah Mei, sniffed the night air's mellowness, the soothing virtue of its sweet unmoving, and thought again how right were the Malays to do their marketing at night instead of struggling by day. To night belonged work, and wit, play and dance and eating, all enjoyable actions of life in the coolness away from the killing sun. I paced the quiet night garden, unquiet, still not wanting to know.

The lights of a car bent round upon me and stopped. It was Luke Davis, with Che Ahmad. I waved, and suddenly lonely asked them to come in for a drink.

Che Ahmad, refulgent as a planet in velvet songkok, white satin blouse closed at the neck by an artificial diamond button, sapphire, jasper and silver sarong with white satin trousers beneath, and black leather shoes, appeared slightly heavier with lithe smooth fat. Many men of his race fatten when over thirty, but his face of lustrous amber was still beautiful and sensual, his body still supple and serene, as he stood with a quietly happy smile, a glowing Asian Apollo. Luke Davis, in open shirt and long crumpled trousers looked gaunt, tired and disreputable. He smelt of sweat and sadness, and threw himself in the rattan chair to gulp a stengah. Che Ahmad, deeply religious, only took orange juice and removed his shoes. 'When I am in town I wear shoes, when I go back to my kampong I walk *kaki ayam*.' (Literally 'chicken legged', naked footed.) 'How know the earth that God made, otherwise than with one's bare skin upon the ground?' Every gesture of life had meaning beyond meaning, and chaos did not exist, chaos was but a word, for all was rounded in the perfection of Allah's will.

And of course what was there to talk about but the Emergency, the Emergency in the rubber? One never seemed to talk of anything else. Che Ahmad was at the moment planning to capture Mustapha Kling, the Malay Communist leader, whose doctrine was infiltrating the Malay kampongs.

'He uses the Holy Religion. He tells the people it is not contradictory to communism. And many listen to him.

'The New Age has come to our people too, although more slowly than to others. We Malays have always been divided into two classes; the Sultans and the officials above, representing the Will of Allah in their will, and below the *raayat*, the common people, who submit to their will as to God. But it is not so now. Our raayat are no longer hypnotized by authority, they want more opportunities, less poverty, less inequality, not only compared with the Chinese but also with their own upper class. They are no longer satisfied, in spite of the Koran. They see Indonesia, and Egypt, and other countries remain Moslem, and yet have revolutions. And now we Malays want independence, MERDEKA, and the running of our own country.

'It is the wealthy Chinese, and our Sultans and our Malay bureaucrats who on the whole do not want independence, the first because they feel that when the British go they will have a worse time than now, in spite of the discriminations against them, and the others because they fear to lose their power and their sinecures. But the time for subjection has passed, and we Malays want Independence. If we don't get Merdeka then discontent will come, agitators thrive and preach communism, for they exploit all grievances, among the kampongs too. But I will catch Mustapha Kling,' he added irrelevantly, 'with the help of God.'

We both looked at Luke Davis, plunged in a gloomy trance. Che Ahmad said he had found Luke Davis at the Mess and taken him to the Chinese wayang, then to a Malay open-air dance. 'Mr. Davis works too hard,' he said affectionately. 'Nearly like a Chinese. He must learn to relax.'

'I didn't know you liked Chinese wayang,' I said.

'Of course I do. I have a lot of Chinese business friends,' added Che Ahmad proudly. 'In the mosque our priests always tell us that we must be more practical, we must go into business like the Chinese, we must work as hard as they do ... it is true', he added charmingly, 'that we do not work very hard.'

At which Luke could not help laughing, and Che Ahmad joined the laughter, knowing it friendly and not contemptuous, happy that Luke's sadness had been dispelled. Suddenly it seemed ridiculous to struggle, to work hard aggressively, to toil and to suffer, as Luke did, as the English did, as the Chinese did, as I did, instead of looking beautiful like Che Ahmad, but then I remembered the children, blind with malnutrition, because their Malay mothers spent so much more on dress than on food. . . .

'And what about Ah Mei?' asked Che Ahmad affably, feeling the atmosphere thicken again as Luke reached for another drink.

'She is going back to her village for the Dragon Boat Festival. She's very happy.'

'Mr. Davis,' said Che Ahmad, 'show the picture of that girl student to the doctor. The photograph you showed me this evening at the Mess. The girl who is on the ship to China. The doctor may have seen her somewhere in Johore ... a woman doctor always sees many people. . . .'

'Oh I don't think so,' replied Luke, morose. He fumbled in his pocket, brought out his leather wallet, thumbed out a snapshot. 'Here. Looks like any other Chinese girl to me, but I feel I've seen her before.'

'But I do know her,' I said, giving back the snapshot. 'This is Golden Orchid, the friend of Ah Mei, who stayed with us here for two or three weeks.'

Both men sat up, abruptly.

'You know her? Where is she now?'

'Gone back to Singapore a few days ago. . . .'

They looked at each other.

'Where is Ah Mei?'

'Downstairs, with her mother.'

Quietly, Che Ahmad leading the way on naked feet, they went downstairs.

There was no shouting and no scuffle at first, only dead silence, then a murmur of voices, and then suddenly a voice raised in a short sharp cry, and then sobs, heartrending sobs. I ran downstairs, my legs weak with terror and sadness for Ah Mei, and stumbled on black compact shapes slashed with light, rocking and struggling, and Luke panting: 'Hold, hold that brat,' as Little Brother fought him with tooth and claw, screaming '*Ma, Ma!*' in long braying sobs. And then Luke and Che Ahmad were pushing the three into the car, slamming and locking the doors.

'Wait, our chaps will be here in a jiffy to scour the place.'

They were gone in a bursting ear-shattering roar of engine. The naked bulb remained dispensing yellow light upon an empty table. On the floor Che Ahmad's black songkok, upturned, showed its cardboard lining. One of Ah Mei's small rubber slippers was in a corner, and a rolled piece of cigarette paper under the table. I picked it up, smoothed it and read:

Dear Small Cloud,

  I received news of you through our courier. I hope that you will be able to learn useful things for us, since you are now in a doctor's household. We need nursing care, some of our comrades have been quite ill lately. I am glad my sister stayed with you. Of course I shall not believe any rumours until I see you, when you return for the Festival, and we meet. – SEN.

Thus the small vulnerable, perhaps trivial secret, which was all of Ah Mei's life so far, was a secret no longer, and now it seemed, without astonishment, I had always known Ah Mei to be Small Cloud. I had known of Sen, if not his name, since that day many months ago, when Ah Mei had blushed and cried: 'The best ones never surrender, never.' Ah Mei might have confessed, and revealed, and informed, and reported on everyone, but not on Sen, not on Small Cloud, that part of her, that other she, in the jungle with Sen. Not on her love, if that was love. She had kept this one thing safe.

But now to save herself, she would betray that too, write another confession, detail more information. This time it would be final. There would be nothing left.

And so the hidden passion still alive that had come once, and once only, to the surface, would be extinguished at last. Ah Mei herself would put it out.

I waited for the police to come, with the cigarette paper in my hand, and I was dry and desolate, emptied of pity or compassion, knowing at last that there are places on the earth, in time and space, where is no space nor time, nor light nor air, nor any ground to grow for the strange weed called love.

Pang, the young and brilliant detective, brought Ah Mei back one morning. In spite of the rumours about him, I maintained a strange liking for Pang. His good looks, the laughing devilry of his eyes, the sinister gentleness of his voice when he interrogated a suspect fascinated me. Round him eddied the ugliest whispers: of beatings and of blackmail, of extortion and even, in the past, of a raping or two ... but these wraiths vanished, when he appeared, as figures visoned in a mist dispel themselves when one draws nearer their unsubstantialness.

I decided that what I liked about Pang was his candid ruthlessness, as one admires a pacing tiger through bars, so long as there are bars. Tigers here are not the limp and dreary eunuchs of zoos in colder climates. They come fresh from the jungle. About them hangs a loose, bright tremor of passion and restlessness, which long captivity will destroy.

'There you are,' said Pang, tenderly, with voice and look guiding Ah Mei forwards across the floor to stand before me. 'There she is, doctor, safe and sound. I'm sure you're *very* glad to see her back.'

His words, gentle, mocking, contained an impalpable menace. His laughter hung about me; it spiralled in the room, sinuous as the wooden arms of the strangling fig winding up its tree – choking it to death, preying upon its substance until it crumbles to nothingness – as with polite movements of his hands he gestured Ah Mei to sit down.

I had expected a change. Now I did not know what I had expected ... but surely not this. Perhaps haggardness, despair, something lost and broken in her eyes, which surely must betray her suffering, the tearing out of herself, of her real but concealed self, the Ah Mei inside the other Ah Mei's, Small Cloud her inner self ... her love, then, to use this odd, strange word I no longer understood. The true abiding love which was the core of herself.

I had sat in the evenings, unhappily imagining ... imagining a final loyalty finally wrested from her, her loyalty to the man who had been so many many years in the jungle – and what was he like by now? What did the jungle do to one who lived in it, never to come out? – to the man who would never surrender.

Brooding over Ah Mei, I thought that she had done what I

would do, what any woman would do to safeguard herself; she had become someone else to remain the self left between the trees, left washing clothes for the People Inside, on the river bank, in a clearing between the coiled roots of the mangrove trees.

I had suffered, visioning Luke Davis and Che Ahmad and Pang exhuming her files from the locked steel strongboxes where files are kept; checking and re-checking and cross-checking what she had said with what she now revealed. In my imagination's eye I saw them pore over the thin cigarette paper and scrutinize the characters, the handwriting, attempting to identify it ... perhaps finding, in her clothing, other letters, letters not censored through the Police Department, as they were supposed to be, but brought by heaven knows which 'Uncle' or 'Aunt', couriers for the People Inside, delivered in the Sultan's flower gardens, at the turn of the road under the dove-orchids perhaps ... and the relentless interrogation, hour by hour, words squeezed out of her by questioning as she twisted and turned and wept, words pinned down, set out in black ink on the white foolscap pages ... I had endured it all. I had had nightmares.

But it was not so at all. For here sat Ah Mei, smiling, in a flowered top and trousers, with bare baby feet tucked politely under her; her clothes had a pattern of pink roses. Light and graceful, she smiled, a happy child, happy to be home again.

'Good morning, doctor,' she said.

Pang also sat down, benevolence oozing from him. 'You won't mind my sitting down a bit, doctor?' Suddenly he gleamed with insolence, revelling in the knowledge he had, tasting his power. He was laughing at me, knowing me bewildered, knowing I had been hurt, enjoying it. 'All safe and sound, brought back to you, eh doctor? I'm sure you were longing to see her again.'

The strangling fig tree of his insolence reached and twisted round and round me. He would torture me with this for many weeks.

I said: 'Have you eaten your rice, Ah Mei?' Knowing nothing but the ritual phrase to span the time, the space, the hurt, between us, between my vision of her and what she was. I said to Pang: 'You must be very busy at the office these days. There's a lot of fighting going on at the moment.'

'Oh, I'm not busy. Never too busy to come to see you,' said Pang, beaming with insolence. 'But I will go now. I'm sure you have a lot to say to each other.' And then I knew that Ah Mei had also betrayed me to Pang, told what there was to tell.

She sat, smiling, clean as after absolution, her life, her moods, her thoughts, her intentions, her letters, rifled, every corner of her mind explored ... perhaps.

'What a silly misunderstanding it all was, doctor.'

Was it?

'I mean ... those letters. Of course I was only trying to better myself.'

They had finally understood, the Police at Headquarters, piecing the puzzle, writing it all down until it was plausible and reasonable on foolscap paper which would remain, as all files remain, tangible truth, truth written down, a testimonial and an enduring monument to Ah Mei's soul; her thoughts, her emotions, her words and her actions. What she was when she would have become something entirely different. When she was no more, her police file would remain, attesting that she had existed, had said those words, thought these thoughts, and performed these actions.

'Now they understand my meaning,' said Ah Mei.

It was all a misunderstanding. With fine compassion Ah Mei told me how Luke Davis and Che Ahmad had later apologized to her and to her mother for their roughness. Even Pang had joked about it. 'Mr. Davis is so rough at times. Too impatient. Still, better to be suspicious ... grab them, shut them up on suspicion, don't let them get away ... that's the spirit...' All along, said Ah Mei, all the time she had been helping the Police, she had kept in mind the fact that she might be able to induce *someone* to come out of the jungle and surrender.

This matter she had discussed, she maintained, with the Police Chief, Mr. Stallart, once or twice. With the difficulty of having to rely on interpreters, perhaps he had not quite understood her intentions.

'But now Mr. Stallart knows that I was only trying to help, to render service once again.'

And how could she fulfil this purpose, how could she induce *someone* to surrender if she did not keep in touch? If she did not try to see *someone* and persuade him?

'But when they ... misunderstood, then somehow the information leaked through, and *someone* did not turn up. So the whole plan failed.'

Pityingly, Ah Mei put all the blame for the failure to capture the man in the jungle upon Luke Davis and Che Ahmad. If only they had not been so precipitate. . . .

I sat and listened. Inside me something, what was left of dream and trust, shrivelled, died quietly, like the sensitive weed which grows among the grass of our gardens folds at a touch, disappears, leaving behind a bare and thorny red stem.

I watched Small Cloud die and Ah Mei survive. I watched myself, too, become someone else. Someone who, perhaps, would never believe wholeheartedly in anyone again.

'What a misunderstanding . . . and all the time I was trying to help the Police . . .' Ah Mei shook her head, sorrowfully.

Then I noticed that she had a permanent. Her hair was wavy at the back, the curls brushed the edge of her small collar as she turned her head. Vindicated, assured, justified in her betrayal (which was called loyalty), smooth of brow, having deposited in triplicate upon foolscap the whole of herself, she sat and smiled. Nothing was left.

'Wasn't it silly, to suspect me, doctor? Me?'

'Yes, I suppose so.'

'These letters . . . doctor must not think I was trying to cheat.'

'I don't.'

'How could I lie when doctor has been so kind to me?'

And then she broke down, uncontrollably weeping, lost in sorrow, her hands upon her face, rocking her body, abandoned to despair, and her curls tumbled forward and hid her face and hands.

'You don't have to explain, Ah Mei . . . don't . . .'

But she shook her locks back and lifted her face and said: 'It is true.'

'What is true?'

'That I am engaged. I am going to be married. I am marrying Tong. He is a surrendered one. He surrendered two years ago.'

Tong was a dark-skinned and handsome young man with four years of jungle war behind him. His capacity for absolute devotion, a personal loyalty feudal in its wholeness, was his main feature. Once it had centred on his company leader in the Malayan Races Liberation Army. Now it would fasten upon Ah Mei.

Tong surrendered when his company leader was executed by the Party for deviationism. A few hours after surrender he led a patrol of the Fijians who had taken him prisoner back into the

236

jungle to ambush his erstwhile comrades. Two of them had been killed in the encounter, and Tong had collected three hundred dollars for each one.

I had never taken much notice of Tong. He was quiet, and would sit, chewing a blade of grass, his faithful eyes gazing round him, a slightly bovine stare. But he was highly intelligent and remembered everything that he saw, and his confession had run to a great many pages.

A few days after Ah Mei told me about Tong, the latter left a basket of fruit as a present for me in the kitchen. After another gift of fruit, he sent word through the Cook that he would like a few minutes' talk with me.

Taking off his shoes, Tong padded upstairs followed by Cookie's wife bearing two cups of tea. These she put down and stood staring at us, giggling and patting her own fat bosom.

Tong had his best manners with him and ceremoniously held out his tea-cup at me before sipping. We spoke of the price of rubber (which was going down), and the latest film at the Pantheon Cinema.

Having thus formally introduced himself, Tong took his leave.

With dignity and a little haste, we proceeded towards the wedding.

'You cannot waste time,' said Pang laughingly, 'Ah Mei is already pregnant.'

That was humiliating. I had not realized Ah Mei's condition. But Miss Lee confirmed the news when she came, ostensibly to present me with a couple of chickens and thank me (belatedly) for my hospitality. She was pregnant too, and there were rumours that her husband was now interested in someone else, a virgin from the village of Todak whose father was a detainee...

We talked of the weather and the price of rubber and Miss Lee informed me of the latest racket in a detention camp near Kuala Lumpur. It was called the uniform racket. It consisted in requisitioning from the Government Stores five yards of material for each uniform, then only using three yards. 'It's terrible to be dishonest,' said Miss Lee. 'We, the poor, do not like to know these things of our superiors.'

Came the wedding day, and the second largest Chinese restaurant in the town hired its first-floor room to the wedding party. The room was open on three sides, and faced the Straits. Singapore was across the water, and three fans steadily kept the wedding party cool. There were about thirty people in the party; white police officers, Chinese detectives, two Indian inspectors; the rest were all ex-terrorists. Ah Mei looked hideous with frizzy hair, daubs of rouge patted upon her cheeks a tight-fitting white satin dress with long sleeves in which she must have stifled, and red shoes. On her finger was a gold ring with the words: Eternal Love stamped upon it in English.

We sat at long tables and ate rancid cream cakes, curry puffs and limp sandwiches. We drank Green Spot and the whites drank stengahs. The head of the detective unit, a Chinese with a fine head of silver hair, made a speech. One or two others cracked jokes. Then a few of the S.E.P.S got up and toasted the Police in orange juice, and the Chief replied and toasted the S.E.P.S and the 'happy couple' in a stengah. Round about the wedding party ambled three waiters, smiling.

And now it was time for Ah Mei and her husband to leave for their honeymoon, which they would spend in Singapore. We rose and followed them, escorting them down the stairs to the street. In front of the restaurant stood a large and well-polished car. It was the Chief's. Mr. Stallart had generously lent his car to them for two days. Others among the British police officers had also lent their cars to the S.E.P.S in the party, but for the afternoon only.

We stood on the five-foot way and waved as Ah Mei and Tong drove away, and we waved again and again and shouted goodbye as car after car left, roaring down the street, waved and shouted goodbye and good luck to the procession of ex-terrorists going away in our cars.

Malaya, 1952–53